Praise
IMM

"Robert W. Smith understands mayhem, morality, and the complexities of love and evil. He has written a crackling story that twists like a rattler and bites at every turn."

    --Jacquelyn Mitchard, bestselling author of *Deep End of the Ocean* (Oprah Book Club choice)

Five Stars ~ Reviewer's Choice
"A twisted tale of political and police corruption that made me glad it was fiction."

    --Hattie Boyd, ***Scribes World Reviews***

"IMMORAL AUTHORITY has a fast pace, fantastically developed characters, and a maddening storyline. Prepare to get hooked from the first page and stay entranced until the very end. Only a gifted author can entice so many strong emotions from the reader, Mr. Smith writes a splendidly vivid and gripping story! I cannot wait for more work by this author."

    --Tracy Farnsworth, ***TRRC***

"Robert W. Smith writes with compelling detail and realism, infusing his characters with remarkable humanity. Not your run-of-the-mill suspense, IMMORAL AUTHORITY delights and terrifies at the same time."

    --Dana Elian, author of *Music of my Heart*

Robert W. Smith

IMMORAL AUTHORITY

A legal suspense novel by

Robert W. Smith

Echelon Enigma

Echelon Press
PO Box 1084
Crowley, TX 76036

Echelon Enigma
First paperback printing: February 2002

This is a work of fiction. Names, characters, places, and incidents are either the product of the author's imagination or are used fictitiously. Any resemblance to actual events, places, organizations, or persons, living or dead, is entirely coincidental.

Copyright © 2001 by Robert W. Smith
Cover illustration Copyright © 2001 Stacey L. King

Mass Market Paperback ISBN 1-59080-020-6

All rights reserved. No part of this book may be used or reproduced in any form without permission, except as provided by the U.S. Copyright Law. For information, please address Echelon Press™, P.O. Box 1084, Crowley, TX 76036.

Published by arrangement with the author.

The name "Echelon Enigma" and its logo are trademarks of Echelon Press.

Printed and bound in the United States of America

www.echelonpress.com

DEDICATION

For my wife, Pat. People are solitary beings. They come together easily, not fully revealed, and part at the very hint of winter. You taught me that to fight against the natural order is to be truly human. The rewards are boundless. I hope to get it right some day.

For my friends, the Theodores, whose lives could inspire a hundred books.

For the boys of Bellwood, the never-never land of my memory.

Robert W. Smith

Prologue

By the time Mike Lowry died in 1978, the city, hell, the whole damn country was his oyster.

Ironically, old Mike was strictly a meat and potatoes man. They called him a kingmaker because of the enormous influence he wielded over national politics. Anyone who really knew him, however, would tell you that Mike never gave a rat's ass about what happened in Washington D.C., except insofar as it affected his beloved port metropolis.

It wasn't that the old man was naïve or stupid; just parochial in the extreme, you might say. You see, Mike craved only power, not the trappings of power and therein lay the real secret to his phenomenal success.

In his own unsophisticated way, the man seemed to have an uncanny ability to govern. In modern political jargon, he would be described as the most "micro" of micro-managers; and yet, by all accounts, he never felt overwhelmed.

If you had asked him to define his political philosophy, he would have laughed in your face; nevertheless, an out of town journalist once described it as, "The end justifies the means as long as it doesn't make too many waves."

Mike instinctively understood how to exploit human weaknesses for the common good, although it would be naïve to suggest that he invented the various forms of political corruption. He did however, hone, and sharpen them into an organized instrument of his own will.

It only worked because Mike was, by every indication, immune from the most heinous vices afflicting the species, greed in particular. Although he never suffered from it himself, Mike understood that greed is to political power what a raging river is to electricity and he harnessed its enormous force to serve his purpose.

He single-handedly nurtured his little fiefdom for thirty-five years, not so much by presiding over it as by wading through it, jacketless with clenched fists and rolled up sleeves.

There was nothing complicated about his methodology either. Although he might not have known it himself, Mike was simply engaged in a never-ending search for people with influence. Whenever he identified a person of particular influence, he would find out what he or she wanted most. Sometimes it was status, political office, or city contracts, but mostly, they just wanted him to look the other way. Like Santa Claus, Mike would fulfill every wish and all he expected in return was absolute loyalty.

That's not to say that old Mike didn't have his rough spots along the way. On those rare occasions when he had been challenged or confronted, His Honor had sometimes responded with a profound Mayoral proclamation that would have made Idi Amin look like a civil libertarian; like the time in 1969 when he tried to summarily ban public protests of the Vietnam War.

In those more liberal times, Mike's uncompromising views on law and order made him a favorite target of the ACLU and the national press. He made it consistently clear, however, that the only critics who moved him spoke with a distinctly regional accent. Even in the worst of times, the city thrived, at least the most visible part of it.

Mike Lowry died crossing the street on the way back to his office from eight o'clock mass. He was hit by a city garbage truck no less.

There were those who said that old Mike Lowry expected to live forever and never considered the possibility of his own death. As usual, they underestimated him, for Mike had a young son named Jack. When the old man died, Jack was almost completely unknown to the media and nearly everyone else, except that is, to people of particular influence.

Chapter One

"Frank, it'll take you until Tuesday to get to the airport this way. Don't you think the expressway would have been quicker?"

It was a sign to Frank that Denise was feeling some anxiety over the coming visit of her favorite niece from South Dakota, and so he calculated his response to be conciliatory.

"Oh, the difference either way is probably no more than five minutes. We should make it with time to spare, but I'll take the expressway home."

It occurred to Frank that, not too long ago, a simple exchange like that would have spawned an argument. Three serious bouts with counseling in fourteen years of marriage had lengthened both of their fuses considerably.

Their problems were far from solved, but in the past year they had managed to carve out some *de facto* guidelines which allowed them to communicate and spared the kids from closing their eyes at bedtime to the sound of angry outbursts. Arguments, however, had given way to a dangerously accommodating silence.

Each life had become compartmentalized to the exclusion of the other; his compartment containing his business, the household bills, and the children's sports activities; and hers the children's schoolwork and the house.

They communicated only when necessary and nearly

always with perfunctory politeness. The latest counselor had said the arrangement was actually more destructive than the volatile exchanges of anger, and that ignoring each other was no way to live a marriage. They both knew he was right, but neither seemed ready to make the break, in part because the couple had shared much and conquered many obstacles, in both times of prosperity and adversity.

Paradoxically, there were times when they still seemed to understand and respect each other, and they were generally considerate of each other's feelings in non-adversarial situations. For the moment, though, they were sadly content to live as roommates, loving and raising the same children.

Notwithstanding Denise's anxiety, they arrived at the gate about fifteen minutes before Caroline's flight.

Amidst all the hugs, kisses and tears, Frank managed to claim Caroline's three large bags and herd the family back into the waiting minivan. He drove the expressway home.

Denise regretted living so far apart from her two nieces all these years. The younger, Caroline, was more than ten years the senior of Denise's own Maggie. Denise had always felt a special bond with the two girls and that hadn't changed since her sister's family moved out West eight years ago.

In the first four years of their marriage, Denise and Frank had confronted serious infertility problems, which both believed might prevent a family of their own. It had been a painful time, made more bearable to Denise by a close and loving relationship with her sister's girls.

Although the two had never spoken about it, Frank knew that Denise had seen them as the children she might never have with him.

Even after three children of her own, Denise's loving bond with her two nieces remained strong as ever, notwithstanding the fact that, in recent years, she had only seen them one at a time during summer vacation.

Frank never had a chance to speak during the entire seven-mile drive back to the house.

As they drove, Caroline gave Denise a full briefing on seemingly everything; boyfriends, college, work, her sister, even Frank's beloved brother-in-law, Eddie "the Whale" Anderson.

In deference to Denise's wishes, Frank never used the nickname these days when referring to his brother-in-law, although it was an unspoken truth that Denise and Frank held virtually identical opinions of "the Whale."

Whenever Frank heard Ed's name these days, he couldn't help but call to mind the day in 1986, when the newly married Dohertys moved into their first home. Ed had helped Frank carry in the very first item of furniture, Frank's favorite leather armchair, packed last into the rear of the big Ryder truck. No sooner had the chair hit the floor than Ed parked his 230-pound carcass into it to take a short nap. Other than to use the bathroom, he never rose again until the pizza was delivered at about six o'clock that evening. It had been fourteen years, but Frank could see it like it was yesterday.

After a very satisfying dinner of spaghetti and meatballs, Caroline's favorite, the kids disappeared into the basement and Frank, Denise and Caroline retired to the small family room to plan the week's activities. Denise still worked two nights a week at the hospital, mostly for the insurance, but she wanted to spend as much time as possible with Caroline until next Saturday.

"You must be exhausted tonight, dear."

It sounded very much to Frank like Denise was suggesting some kind of outing for that very evening. It pleased him that, after all these years, he appeared to be gaining some limited insight into the female mind.

"It's Saturday night, Auntie D, and it's the only one I have. I can stay in and watch movies in South Dakota. Let's go out and boogie." It was precisely the response Denise had invited and Caroline knew it instinctively.

Frank was truly making progress at last.

Caroline was not a church mouse, but neither was she in any sense irresponsible. Denise knew this, not from personal observation, but from years of early morning phone conversations with her sister, Ellen, in South Dakota.

Caroline had never been the cheerleader type. As a young girl, her sometimes serious and pensive nature had caused her to be passed over for most birthday party invitations, but she never seemed offended or even interested. There was a sensibility about the girl that her peers were only capable of identifying at around age fourteen.

It was the boys who had noticed it first. Her deeply set and slightly oversized blue eyes were framed by thick locks, the very color of coal, waiving back and forth until they settled just before touching her perfectly rounded shoulders. The face was inviting, but access was not guaranteed. What they had taken for boorishness they discovered had been confident maturity all along.

For the past year, Caroline had been living with another girl in Rapid City, where she was pursuing a course in pre-veterinary medicine at a local university. Her parents' home was a mere twenty minute drive from the campus, and living at home had worked well enough her freshman year.

During her sophomore year, however, tensions between Caroline and "the Whale" convinced her it was time for the calf to leave the pod. Denise had been secretly consulted on the decision and had expressed her wholehearted approval. "Auntie D" was of the opinion that twenty-year-old burgeoning adults should not be subject to an eleven o'clock curfew. Had "the Whale" known of the interference, he surely would have spouted boiling oil.

Although not a country bumpkin, Caroline was clearly enamored with the glitz and sheer scale of the city's entertainment district. It seemed every popular athlete or former athlete had lent his name, if not his money, to a bar or nightclub of some kind. Caroline wanted to see them all from the inside.

By twelve-thirty in the morning, Denise had contributed to the welfare of no fewer than four already wealthy athletes and one particularly well-known group of contemporary movie stars. She was dog-tired and had switched to coke two hours earlier, mindful of the drunk-driving laws. Caroline, on the other hand, was just getting warmed up.

"Okay, Caroline, one more stop and that's it, or my feet are going home on their own." It was called *transitioning*. Denise had found it to be a particularly useful tool in raising preschoolers. She couldn't remember where she had learned it, probably at McDonalds from one of the mothers watching her try in vain to grab up the twins from inside the maze of plastic tunnels and balls that sell hamburgers. She was ready to try anything just to get home to her own bed.

"Okay, Auntie D, we'll have one drink at the El Dorado and then go." Caroline seemed to surrender.

"Okay then, but how do you know about the El Dorado, young lady?" Denise was not pleased, but then a deal was a deal. She had, of course, never been to the El Dorado, but knew that it was the trendiest club in town and, from all accounts, attracted an eclectic mix of weirdoes from all age groups. Instead of answering, Caroline was hailing a cab.

Once inside, Denise wished she were somewhere else, anywhere else.

Although Frank's junior by seven full years at thirty-eight, she had years ago shed her appetite for such self indulgent and physically demanding entertainment. She had fully expected loud music and flashing lights. They seemed to have been the evening's key ingredients. Auntie D was unprepared, however, for the sheer force of the vibrations inside The El Dorado.

Once past the bouncer and down the seven or eight steps into the bowels of the cavernous oval-shaped dome, her senses were assaulted by wave after wave of sonic attack. A legion of black and white strobe lights, striking in tandem, made escape from the alien weapon impossible.

Seemingly hundreds of human forms packed the dance floor like sardines in a can. Denise was certain that, during those momentary flashes when the light was white, she could see the sweat soaked skin on the faces and arms of the dancing forms rippling in time with the so-called music. Between beats, she wondered how quickly she and Caroline could empty a glass?

They made their way to the bar and, after fighting through a line seven deep and eight or nine across, paid for and received one coke and a vodka and tonic.

Caroline was smiling and, after a few minutes, seemed to have been engaged in conversation with a rather good-looking young man, well dressed by any standard.

They turned towards the dance floor and Denise, still holding on, tugged on Caroline's left arm. "Its time to go, Caroline." Her words were exaggerated and loud, delivered six inches from Caroline's ear.

"Auntie D, this is John. He's so nice. We're just going to have one dance." It wasn't a question.

Denise still held Caroline's arm and managed to communicate to her that Auntie D was going to find the bathroom and hope that it wasn't equipped with speakers. She thought Caroline laughed and they agreed to meet at the far corner of the bar in ten minutes.

Denise had never so completely welcomed a visit to the ladies' room. It could only be described as *shelter*, relative to the scene in the club itself and only slightly less crowded. Nevertheless, it did offer temporary respite to the eardrums. After several minutes spent freshening her appearance, Denise emerged from the ladies' room, intent on scooping up her young niece for the trip home.

As Denise began to bump and weave her way to the far end of the bar, her eyes searched in vain for the familiar jet-black wavy hair and tall slender figure of Caroline. She continued her struggle, not fully trusting her own eyesight in the chaotic scene.

Standing at what she calculated to be the spot where she and Caroline had last spoken, she surveyed the length of the bar as best she could and found no trace of either Caroline or her newfound friend.

Now, growing extremely impatient, Denise could not suppress a feeling of irritation at the fact that Caroline had apparently violated their agreement to leave and was frolicking somewhere on the dark and ridiculously overcrowded dance floor. It would be hours now before Denise could retreat into the safety and comfort of her own home and, beyond any doubt, she would awaken tomorrow with a world-class headache.

After another thirty minutes, Denise was satisfied that Caroline was not on the dance floor. She began to move more quickly now, nearly oblivious to the sensual distractions around her, focused only on the nameless faces of the revelers.

Minutes began to pass quickly, too quickly, she thought, as the full force of artificial daylight sounded last call. An hour and a half had passed since Denise had emerged from the bathroom. Caroline was gone.

Denise covered the full city block to the parking lot in less than a minute, holding her black pumps as she ran.

Hope turned to outright panic as she reached the van and found no trace of Caroline. She grabbed for the cell phone in the glove compartment and pushed the "1" on the speed dial menu. The ringer had nearly transferred to voice-mail when Frank finally lifted the receiver.

"Hello," came the obviously sleepy voice of her husband.

"Frank, Caroline's gone. I left her at The El Dorado just to go to the bathroom. She was talking to some guy. When I got back she was gone. Frank, I've looked everywhere. It's three thirty in the morning and she's gone. She wouldn't do this, Frank."

"Okay. Are you still downtown somewhere?"

"Yes."

"Drive over to police headquarters downtown at 16th and Fortis. Go up to the second floor, Detective Division, Missing Persons Section. Start making the report. I'll be there in thirty minutes."

In light of the early hour and seemingly grave circumstances, Frank covered the fifteen-mile drive in less than twenty minutes. As he drove, Frank tried to focus on the more optimistic possibilities, but the criminal lawyer in him knew better. The best thing they could do for Caroline, Frank thought, was to get the mechanics right. He'd have to call her parents right away and let them talk to the police. The police themselves would be another problem. He hoped that Denise was prepared to handle the skepticism she would soon encounter.

A young girl disappearing from a nightclub, while in the company of a handsome young man, would likely not spell kidnapping to an experienced detective. Frank was satisfied that Caroline would never willingly torment her aunt in that way, but convincing the police to act quickly would not be easy. As he drove, he forced himself not to speculate. It was all about information now, and the more the police had, the better Caroline's chances.

Upon reaching the stairs inside the station, Frank ascended in threes and emerged directly into a large, undivided open office space. Denise looked a wreck. She seemed oblivious to the fact that her dress pumps were still in her hands. Tears had cut symmetrical tracks through her makeup, from the bridge of her nose on both sides, down to the corners of her mouth. She was seated in a Spartan gray chair beside one of fifteen or so depressingly gray metal desks. A strong odor of tobacco permeated the room. The young detective seated beside her was conducting an interview and simultaneously entering the data into his computer.

Larry Califf and Frank had met several times before, when Califf was still in uniform. Each of the meetings had been in a courtroom with the officer under cross-examination by Frank, the defense lawyer. He would likely never receive a Christmas card from Califf, but Frank thought him to be both honest and professional.

Frank pulled up a chair from the next desk and sat directly on Denise's right.

Califf pretended not to notice and continued his series of questions, followed closely by data entry.

It was apparent that Califf had seen him, but Frank understood that this was a message about authority and control. Califf had them and Frank didn't. It was okay by him.

Finally, perceiving that his point had been made, Califf spoke to Frank. "We're going to treat this as foul play as of now, Counselor."

He was obviously making an attempt to respect Denise's conclusion, but couldn't resist use of the word *Counselor*. The title itself carried a connotation of respect, but when the police used it, they kind of exaggerated the accent on the first syllable, transforming the word into a sarcastic greeting. It was a compromise Frank could live with, for Califf had obviously shown no inclination to patronize Denise or ridicule her opinions about Caroline.

"Thank you," said Frank.

"You know we can't bring in the FBI for twenty four hours, but there's no shortage of work between now and then. I'll be right back. I'm going to go downstairs and try to get another detective and some uniforms assigned."

In less than ten minutes the young man returned with his requested allotment; one rather old and tired looking detective and two uniformed officers.

"Frank, if you want to help, there's no law that says you can't. The club is closed and everybody is long gone by now, but there are plenty of twenty-four hour businesses around there. I remember lots of small hotels scattered around the side streets as well. We'll talk to everyone we can and hope they saw something."

"Denise, we had better call your sister right away." Frank reviewed his mental checklist.

"I just called her, Frank. She e-mailed a recent photo over here for the police. She and Ed are on their way to the airport now."

"Look, it's really against the rules, but if you want to ride with us tonight, you can. Mrs. Doherty, I know you'd like to go, but someone other than a neighbor should be home in case she calls. I don't mean to insult you, but it's still possible that she could have left the club willingly. I could drop you off and we'll store your car."

Frank suddenly realized that he had never been on this end of the equation before and knew that he would one day re-think some harsh judgments.

"I suppose that would be best," Denise conceded.

"Okay then, I'll grab these prints and get my coat. Then we'll hit the road." As he spoke, Califf was in the process of printing hard copies of the digital photo stored in the general section e-mail.

After grabbing his coat, Califf went to the color printer across the room and stood watching as the image of Caroline Anderson emerged from the state-of-the-art printer. For just a moment, he appeared nearly paralyzed, his eyes transfixed upon the upside down, half-smiling portrait of the missing girl. He had never seen such a telling photo.

The face was not the most beautiful he had encountered, to be sure, but the green eyes spoke to him in a way that would not have seemed possible a minute ago.

It was unnerving the way they entrapped him. They were curious, yet knowing; mischievous, yet sad. In that moment, Larry Califf felt a deep but inexplicable sorrow. It left as quickly as it had come upon him.

On the drive, Denise spoke of Caroline and Larry Califf listened. It was fairly clear that her disappearance was unrelated to her activities and associations in South Dakota, but you could never have too much information, he thought.

Sitting in the passenger seat of the marked squad, he took sporadic notes as Denise spoke from the rear seat. If there were a dark side to Caroline Anderson, he would not hear it from Denise Doherty, Califf thought. Nevertheless, he learned much, from her taste in men to her favorite foods. One of the things that most interested Califf was the fact that Caroline herself apparently believed that she had few real friends.

"She had a very clear, if unusual concept of friendship," explained Denise. "Caroline was considerate of everyone. She had a way of making people feel important. People sought her out and wanted to be close to her, but generally, she kept them at a distance. It wasn't a character flaw at all, but more a product of Caroline's concept of friendship."

"And what was that?" Califf inquired, although he knew that the information was well beyond the threshold of relevance.

"She had an idea that friendship was rare and that real friendship took years to develop. Among her small circle of 'friends,' she included her sister, Beth, and three girls she had met in the sixth grade, during the family's first year in South Dakota. For their eighth grade graduation, the five girls treated themselves to matching gold lockets with identical inscriptions: *The best way to have a friend is to be a friend.* She was wearing it last night."

Even from the bits and pieces, he could see the impact Caroline had made on the lives of those who loved her, and probably on many who only knew her. It seemed somehow comforting to Califf, young and single as he was, to know that one might still meet a young woman like Caroline out there, only just beginning to find her place in the world. On the other hand, it was disquieting to contemplate the tragic effects of her loss.

Califf was still a novice in this world where photographs had families and corpses had grieving survivors; where loved ones grieved openly or maintained a desperate hope well beyond reason.

On the beat, it had been good guys and bad guys, live bodies and dead bodies. In a beat car, if you were called to the scene of a shooting or a missing person, you would interview eyewitnesses and preserve the scene. It was plastic and by the numbers, nothing to provoke the soul.

In the Detective Division, however, tragedy transcended good and evil and became a force unto itself. In Missing Persons, for example, tragedies without bad guys were common and no less tragic; suicides, runaways, abandoned families. Nearly every case had a personal and heart-wrenching story, regardless of its ending.

There would come a time, he knew, when he would no longer feel the pain of the family or lament the unfulfilled promise of the hapless victim. The armor of callousness came to every detective, eventually. True enough that a few were born with it, but everyone succumbed to it in the end.

Sometimes Califf longed for it and other times he

prayed he would have the courage to leave the department before earning it. This time it was a little of both.

Chapter Two

Sean Lowry, or John Williams, if you believed the hotel registry, had never seemed to learn the hard lessons. Lord knows he had been given enough opportunities in his twenty-seven summers. Although raised and educated within the city limits, Sean had lived a life of covert, but undeniable privilege.

There was the family yacht, docked in Lincoln Marina, not nearly the biggest, but sleek, elegant, and most importantly, always available.

There was the vacation home upstate on the waterfront, unobtrusive and shielded from view on the street side by an expansive front lawn, sprouting a neatly seeded pine forest. The house was nearly invisible from the water as well, save a funnel shaped, impeccably trimmed lawn, narrowing up the hillside to a simple white sun deck, hosting rows of glass doors. Those very few fortunate enough to have been invited inside would describe it as understated elegance.

The relatively modest home on the inter-coastal waterway in Miami, however, was Sean's personal favorite from the inventory of the family's covert treasures.

Most people would now balk at the opportunity to vacation in Miami, but to Sean Lowry, Miami had always been heaven on earth, offering all the things he loved most in life. So it was and so it should be, he thought, for the eldest son of the three-term mayor of the nation's seventh largest city.

It wasn't that Sean was unemployed. He was, after all, a highly respected political consultant and partner in one of the city's oldest political consulting firms. It happened that the firm, started sixty-two years ago by one of his grandfather's closest friends, preferred to keep Sean well rested and unencumbered by stress, on the chance that an important assignment should someday require his attention. Sean couldn't even remember the last time he had actually gone into the office, but the checks were always deposited.

At that moment, Sean Lowry was one of two occupants of room 1704 of the luxurious Bridemore Hotel, located in one of downtown's most exclusive waterfront locations. The other, so far as Sean could tell in his cocaine induced, mind-altered state, was a hot young number from the suburbs who had just gotten exactly what she came down here to get, and more!

She would have wanted it like that anyway, Sean reasoned. The small capful of GHB Sean had surreptitiously slipped into her vodka and tonic had merely expedited the process. He had no time these days to wine and dine secretaries.

The odorless and colorless formula was a synthetic *knockout* type drug, first used sporadically in the 1960's as an experimental hallucinogen. Although it did produce a moderately pleasurable "high," cutting edge drug abusers of the period soon discovered that the drug was most useful in dissolving sexual inhibition and, accordingly, GHB gained some modest popularity as perhaps the world's first date rape drug.

A college acquaintance of Sean's had somehow acquired a copy of a book entitled *Better Sex Through*

Chemistry. The book had been published years ago by an underground publisher and was formatted as a kind of cookbook for sexual cocktails.

The kid was a kind of nerd and had experimented with several of the recipes to satisfy his own appetites, but without much success until he succeeded in recreating the GHB formula. Its success rate among the local party animals was nothing short of miraculous and it could be produced easily and cheaply in large quantities from two common chemicals: a powerful solvent used to degrease engines and a caustic chemical similar to drain cleaner.

The formula became so popular among the party crowd at St. Francis University that it spawned a lucrative cash business for the young chemist/entrepreneur.

Sean Lowry had been his best customer through college and, upon graduation, the young drug dealer, as a token of his gratitude, had presented Sean with the secret recipe. Sean had continued to rely heavily on the persuasive power of GHB in the intervening eight years.

The fact that the drug had recently undergone a resurgence in popularity among the local nightclub set was an annoyance to Sean, who considered the drug's renewed popularity as a kind of patent infringement.

Since GHB, even in its heyday, had never before been widely used, Sean, until recently, had not been aware of its many dangerous and even deadly possible side effects, which included seizures, comas, respiratory failure and vomiting. This recent medical research had spawned widespread public health warnings about the drug, at which Sean simply scoffed.

The young brunette was still only semi-conscious, lying on the king size bed, still partially clad in the outfit she had so carefully selected for her night of clubbing in the big city with her Aunt turned tour guide. The only visible cosmetic injury from Sean's sadistic mating ritual was a single drop of dried blood at the corner of her left nostril. She had survived his first frenzied assault in relatively good shape and her surprisingly spirited resistance had provided Sean with an extra measure of sexual pleasure.

After an hour or so, Sean had showered, dressed and was preparing to leave the hotel for a much needed early morning breakfast. Just as he reached the door, however, he glanced back and gazed upon the still groggy, yet incredibly attractive figure, and began to become aroused again.

I think this one really likes it rough, he thought, as he began to remove his Pierre Cardin slacks for the second time that night.

Caroline, still incapable of meaningful resistance, was mercifully rendered unconscious less than a minute into the brutal onslaught, which included a severe beating to the face and ended with a climactic strangulation involving Sean's cowhide designer belt.

Sean, satisfied and feeling purged of all traces of humanity, collapsed on the bed like the wild animal he had become, oblivious to the fact that he had just taken a life.

He hadn't really been sleeping in the literal sense. It had been more like the combination of drugs and alcohol, mixed with the furious explosion of energy, had temporarily robbed him of consciousness. In less than an hour, he was up and on his feet again, naked and wobbling in the lamplight.

Sean had no concept of the time until he parted the heavy draw drapes and stared down into the near empty downtown streets, no longer dark, but still shielded by perfectly spaced rows of glowing street lights. It was as if the light had re-ignited his brain.

He turned quickly back towards the king size bed and was greeted by the gruesome results of his previous night's adventure.

Caroline's lifeless eyes, once so inviting and magnetic, stared coldly upward, almost bursting from their sockets. The blood and shattered bones rendered her face unrecognizable.

Sean looked down at his own naked form and found no reassurance. Were it not for the fact that he was walking without pain, he would have thought his own body had been ravaged and savagely beaten to a pulp. Sean remembered the meeting of his bloody hands and the girl's face and a cold fear began to build in the depths of his stomach.

Instinctively, he reached for the cell phone.

Not quite two miles due north, along the magnificently wealthy shoreline, as the first traces of soft orange sunlight began to vanquish the remaining nightfall, Bradford J. Parkins had already risen and was dressing for work.

As the razor did its usual morning's work with the exact number and pattern of strokes, he thought that he would likely be awake on a morning like this even without the pressing commitments of his schedule.

He was fond of saying that he chose this condominium over several larger ones because the very first rays of sunlight to breach the horizon each day greeted him at his living room picture window.

At age fifty-three, Brad felt he was just coming into

the prime of life. Ever since his first day working for the city as a snowplow driver at age eighteen, his life had been driven by two overriding personal qualities. They were a hungry, naked ambition to succeed and an irrepressible instinct for survival, in no particular order. They had both served him well in his steady, if not meteoric rise to the top perch in the golden nest, but not necessarily in his personal life (He had two ex-wife's, one of whom was still on his personal payroll).

It was rare these days to find anyone in such an exalted municipal position without the benefit of a college education, even in this town. By any standard, he was a successful man.

The Mayor's Commissioner of Aviation adjusted his Armani tie in the bedroom mirror as the nearly risen sun began to reveal the slender and shapely left leg of his newest and currently favorite social companion, Meg Lofton, a 31 year old executive with Trans Global Airlines. He closed the micro-blinds, grabbed his jacket, and was preparing to leave for the airport when his personal cell phone rang at exactly five forty-three.

"Hello."

"Brad, its Sean. She's dead! I killed her! She's not breathing. Oh, my God, Brad!"

"Sean, get hold of yourself. Sit in a chair and take some deep breaths," Brad whispered as he hurried into the guest room, closing the door quietly behind him. "Now explain to me in a calm clear way what is going on."

"There's a girl dead in my hotel room. We had sex. I didn't mean to do it. I woke up and she's just lying there, all gray, and cold with her eyes open. Brad, help me. You've gotta help me or I'll—"

"Shut up, Sean. How do you know she didn't have a heart attack?"

"You know, Brad. You know what happens to me when I take that shit. She was choking a little, but I didn't think I was pulling all that hard. You know I just get carried away, Brad."

"Pulling on what, Sean? Something around her neck?"

"A belt."

Brad was keenly aware that what he said and did in the next hour would define his life from this moment forward. "Okay, Sean, I want you to listen to me very carefully. Don't touch anything and don't make any calls. Sit in a chair until you hear from me. Do you understand me?"

"Yes, Brad."

"Sean, where did you meet the girl?" Parkins needed to know right now if he was dealing with a sitting duck.

"At a club. I was with her maybe five minutes when I slipped her something. We were gone fifteen minutes later."

"Okay, but I have to know right now if you told anybody your real name last night."

"Nobody, I swear. I was going out to play a little bit. I would never use my own name."

Brad seemed satisfied with the answer. "Give me the hotel name and room number."

"The Bridemore. Room 1704."

"Okay, do what I told you and don't touch the phone unless it's to answer it."

"But Brad, what are you gonna do? You won't turn me in, will you?"

"Of course not. You'll know when I figure it out. And Sean, who the hell is the girl?"

"Nobody."

IMMORAL AUTHORITY

* * *

Brad Parkins was not a man given to panic, but as he returned the small flip phone to his pocket, he could clearly see the glistening imprint of sweat from his own right hand.

His personal style had always been to defer risky decisions and wait for circumstances to make the difficult choice. It was part of why he had managed to survive in the sacrificial environment of a Lowry administration. So long as you survived, life was your personal oyster. However, when the day came that a human sacrifice was required to dull the raging political appetite of a hungry news media, your head could be severed and served *la flambé*.

Being a lifetime survivalist of the political variety, Brad's first thought was to go to work like nothing had happened and *fuck that psycho prick*. But it was clearly more complicated than that. The prick had dialed Brad's personal cell phone while the girl was dead and before the cops had been notified.

That meant Brad's choices were narrowed considerably. He could pick up the phone right now, he figured, and *turn the spoiled little bastard in*. Sean deserved whatever he got. He dismissed this possibility, however, almost as quickly as he had considered it. The Mayor would surely love that! In his mind's eye he could see the illustrious and God-fearing Mayor on TV right now.

"And I want to thank my longtime friend and colleague, Brad Parkins, for making the most painful but morally necessary choice. I thank him for his courage. Our stand against crime and drugs must be a line in the sand. And anyone who crosses that line, no matter his name or position, must be punished according to law."

The Mayor was, Brad had come to know, the all-time champion of what insiders quietly called *speaking in the antithesis*. When you say *love* it means *hate*. When you say *person of courage and great moral character* it means a *yellow, sniveling, ungrateful, fucking rat*.

Brad could see it all slipping away; the women, the big cars, the boats, the summer home, all of it.

Some of the perks he couldn't even imagine living without. He hadn't had to make a reservation in a restaurant in ten years. Every *Maitre De* in every fine restaurant in town would fight to have him eat there. Brad loved playing the *rainmaker* for their little bullshit political problems and job requests.

Then there were the lucrative monthly handshakes at the airport from the union bosses, the airlines, the vendors, and the bus and limo companies.

The term *handshake* was really more of a figure of speech these days. It had become much more sophisticated and high stakes, involving things like offshore bank accounts and insider information.

On the rare occasion, however, Brad would still get a cash handshake from an old time player and he wouldn't think of turning it down.

All of it, he thought, he owed to one central and overriding fact about this man named Brad Parkins. He was a man with the power to dispense favors. There it was, he thought; the real secret to Lowry power; no, not even a secret, but bold as brass. He knew that there were perhaps hundreds of Brad Parkins out there. Lots of people made lots of money perpetuating the Lowry Empire and nobody got hurt, at least not often.

The box continued to look smaller as Brad poured over his options there in the elegantly furnished but as yet never slept in guestroom. *Even if I call the cops and somehow keep my name out of it, which is highly unlikely, a scandal like this might be too much for even Jack Lowry to handle. I'll be finished.* The sheer magnitude of such a collapse was almost more that he could comprehend.

Brad could only liken it to the fall of Rome. He remembered from school that the Roman Empire was felled by corruption, but he doubted the Romans could have held a candle to the Lowrys when it came to greasing palms.

No, if Lowry went down, Brad would go right with him. This wouldn't be the first time that Brad had risked prison because of that little prick, but there was too much at stake now to do otherwise.

In a sense, it had been his skill at managing Sean's legal problems over the years that had landed him his plumb position. It had all started some ten years before, when Sean had thrown a weekend party on the family's yacht. The Mayor and his wife were out of town at a conference. Somewhere into the second booze and drug soaked evening, a local high school boy was struck in the head with a baseball bat.

The kid had been taken to the hospital in a coma and all the partygoers, including Sean, had been herded into the police station. Every one of them was still intoxicated or high or both when Brad arrived. Two of the injured boy's friends were pointing the finger at Sean as being the assailant, but with the help of one politically astute police detective and a generous contribution to their respective college educations, Brad managed to quickly convince them that they could not identify the attacker.

Although the matter received significant publicity and proved an embarrassment to the Mayor, it could have been much, much worse. It turned out that the victim, who fully recovered, had been so saturated with drugs himself that he couldn't even remember being at the party. The family sued the Mayor and his homeowner's insurance carrier quickly settled the matter.

His Honor had only addressed the matter once in Brad's presence and it had seemed to Brad at the time nothing less than a declaration of knighthood. "Brad, I owe you," the great man had said.

Brad knew that the ball had fallen squarely in his court once again. As he reached into his coat pocket for the cell phone, he noticed that both it and his right palm were bone dry. He dialed the main number for the city police and asked to be connected to Homicide. He left a message for Detective Lonnie Hartman, identifying himself as Hartman's brother, but leaving his own cell phone number. The return call came five minutes later.

"Hello."

"Hartman?"

"Yes, Brad. Who the fuck else would be carrying my phone?"

"An old problem has reared its ugly head again, if you get my meaning. Can you meet me at the Denny's on 4th in, say, twenty minutes?"

"Make it thirty. I'm just getting off a midnight and I have to drop the car off."

Brad moved swiftly to the kitchen and sat down at the computer workstation as he removed the phone directory from the bottom drawer. He opened to the front section, a directory of local business listings. On the second page of "E" listings his finger moved slowly downward and stopped under the listing *Emerald Isle Salvage*. Brad tore the page from its binding, folded it and placed it securely into his front shirt pocket. *This call is best made from a public phone*.

Brad called from a convenience store phone booth down the street and asked to be connected to the old man himself. Over the years, the two had done enough under the table political deals to keep the U.S. Attorney's entire staff of prosecutors busy for three years.

Paul DeBenedetto was one of those seemingly anonymous figures who had quietly prospered and grown rich during the Lowry incumbency.

Emerald Isle was perhaps his most lucrative enterprise and certainly his favorite because it was, in theory anyway, legitimate. It was operated openly from a recently constructed and ornately decorated office building, miles from the gritty and rust dominated environment of the yards and the docks themselves. Aside from which, the irony of the company's name was an endless source of pleasure and dinner conversation to him.

DeBenedetto was decidedly not some stereotypical *Mafioso*. He was educated at Notre Dame and had received a law degree from the University of Michigan in the mid 1950's. Despite his acquired sophistication, he was not above letting his guard down on rare occasions.

"Let those drunken potato eaters have all the political muscle they can buy," he would say. "They'll never understand that real power comes from having the money in your pocket, not from people kissing your fucking ring. So let them make all the speeches and win all the elections and control all the bullshit jobs. They work for us and the dumb fucks don't even know it. I love 'em."

Such conversations could be heard only in very select company and in the privacy of his own lavish ninety-acre estate and horse farm some thirty miles west of the city. "Without the Irish," he was fond of saying, "we'd still be killing each other over the right to hijack trucks and run hookers."

On paper, Paul was a salaried employee of Emerald Isle like any other. His official title was Assistant CFO. It was clear to even the lowliest mailroom clerk, however, that the company belonged to Paul, although his equity interest had never been established by any government agency.

The old man was perhaps more notable than most private sector friends of the Mayor in that his prosperity had spanned the reign of both Lowry chief executives. Aside from which, it was a commonly known, although seldom-uttered fact, that DeBenedetto was mob connected.

The two men trusted each other implicitly for the best of reasons. Each knew enough dirt to bury the other three times over.

Brad said only that he was calling from a public phone and needed to talk privately. Paul simply took the number and told Brad to wait near the phone for a return call. Brad stood waiting in the freezing cold for nearly fifteen minutes until the phone finally rang.

"Okay, Brad, you've got my attention and you may speak freely," Paul said.

"Mr. D, we have a crisis here. I'm calling you because I was told to call you immediately." Brad thought it best to establish immediately that his authority came directly from the Mayor.

"Within the last three or four hours Sean Lowry killed a girl in a hotel. It looks like she's a tourist from out West. There are no witnesses and nobody even knows the girl's dead, except Sean and us. Our friend has a small team of trusted cops on the way over to clean it all up. They have a hot car with them and they'll just need a way to get rid of it."

"This is not good, Brad. So now that little prick is murdering innocent women. If I help you, can you make this thing go away quietly?" Paul asked.

"Of course I will," answered Brad.

"Please see that you do, Brad. There's more at stake here than even you could imagine."

The old man then went on to explain that Emerald Isle was loading a barge for the Waterfront Reclamation Project. He told Brad when to bring the car and where to leave it.

"What if someone finds the car?" Brad asked.

"Don't worry about it, Brad," the old man assured him. "One of the things we do here is crush cars. By morning, that car will be a three-foot cube. In two days, the cube will be at the bottom of an enormous mountain of old concrete highway pieces under thirty feet of water. I don't think anyone will be digging it up."

It was currently his most lucrative city contract. Only three short years and forty million dollars from now, a beautiful, new nature preserve and park would sprout from the depths of the river itself.

Even in this moment, Brad couldn't help but marvel at his creative ability to manage a difficult situation.

Chapter Three

Hartman arrived five minutes late, but still had to wait ten minutes for Parkins. He thought it best to hide his irritation for the moment.

Their conversation was brief and perfunctory. Neither man had time to touch his coffee cup.

When they were finished speaking, Parkins took a paper sandwich bag from his coat pocket and placed it on the table between them.

Hartman retrieved it, almost in the same motion, and left the restaurant first. Before Parkins had even left the booth a minute later, Hartman, sitting at the wheel of his car in the Denny's lot, was counting out exactly ten thousand dollars from the bag.

Boosting a car had not been difficult. Being the police truly does have its advantages, Hartman thought. He always carried a slim-jim in his vehicle to help the occasional "babe" who might have locked her keys in the car. Although the things were illegal, most cops carried them openly, without any questions asked. Hartman himself had confiscated several this year alone.

The 1995 Buick LaSabre, which he now drove, had been especially selected for its ample trunk space. Hartman had simply driven his own SUV from the meeting with Parkins to a local mall and parked it. He had selected the Buick from a wide variety of choices at the mall in broad daylight. Daylight was the best time to boost a car because nobody expected it.

The front door had opened effortlessly on the first try. Within thirty seconds, he had hot-wired the car and was on his way to pick up some much-needed equipment for the nasty business ahead.

He hadn't felt anything even approaching nervousness during the entire operation because, if anyone had seen him, he would have just flashed his badge and said he had chased away a car thief. There's no other job in the world like it, Hartman thought, as he turned north onto Greenfield Ave.

Hartman was all too familiar with the anomalous proclivities of young Sean Lowry, having in his early years served a two-year hitch as bodyguard to the first Mayor Lowry. Most of his time then had been consumed babysitting the drug-crazed juvenile pervert of a grandson. As he drove towards the Bridemore Hotel, the detective couldn't help but recall his last encounter with the infamous Sean Lowry.

Hartman had been working out of Homicide/Violent Crimes Division. One Sunday morning, mid-way through his day shift, he had been assigned to investigate a complaint of a sexual assault on the campus of St. Francis University, a highly regarded catholic university in the downtown area. He remembered that he had received the assignment out of turn, although he had never been able to determine just how that had occurred.

Before arriving on the scene, Hartman had received a 911 page on his digital pager. The read out said, *Go now to bus barn 18th St.& Clair, Bay14, Bus #25125, rear seat, reach under.*

He did as instructed and never thought about not going. It was a Sunday. All the bays were open, but only a few people were milling about. Bay 14 stored some older buses awaiting repair. He spotted #25125 and quickly slipped inside. What he found under the seat was a thick manila envelope. He opened it instinctively and stared at the neatly packaged and bound stacks of hundred-dollar bills, fifty thousand, he had guessed.

There was a note that appeared to be computer generated. *Don't let me down, Lonnie. Make it go away. Talk only to Brad.* The note, of course, was neither dated nor signed, but Hartman immediately suspected Mayoral intervention on behalf of the chief executive's first-born son. The former bodyguard and babysitter, having once even shared dinner at the Lowry table, never hesitated.

When he finally arrived on the scene, he spoke first with the security supervisor on duty, a fiftyish and slightly overweight Hispanic cop wannabe who, at first, irritated Hartman with his obvious attempts to imitate police behavior.

He then interviewed the alleged victim who told a clear, consistent, and straightforward story of "date rape," going so far as to name the perpetrator as one Sean Lowry. Hartman did his level best to seem surprised.

The supervisor had valued his own silence at five grand, much too cheaply, Hartman had thought at the time. Even the young co-ed herself had come very cheaply, indeed. He kicked himself later for offering her twenty thousand. The thinly veiled threats of violence he had made had probably been enough on their own to insure her silence because she had accepted the offer instantly.

Still, twenty-five grand was pretty fair compensation for something he would have done for free. It was beautiful, really. Nobody would ever know that he had taken money, and the Mayor himself would be indebted to him. There was the real compensation, he had thought. The value was almost incalculable.

His reward, however, had never come. In the intervening eight years, he had learned his lesson and had seen the practical limitations of such concepts as loyalty and fair play when dealing with the Lowrys and their cronies. He had resolved long ago that the next favor he did for the Lowrys would be on a for profit basis only.

Hartman pulled up to the lavishly appointed entrance of the Bridemore and motioned for the young, smartly uniformed bellhop. The young man hurried to the open window. "Good morning sir. How can I help you?"

"Police business," Hartman offered, in his most business-like manner, as he flashed his shield clearly within the man's view. "I need to park this car out of the way for awhile near a back entrance."

"No problem, officer." The young man was genuinely eager to help in any way possible. "Pull into the alley just ahead on the right. Park just before you reach the service doors on the right. Get as close to the building as you can. Anything else I can do?"

The boy apparently wanted to do some police work. "No thanks. Well, on second thought, I'm on an investigation and I don't want certain people to know I'm here. Can I get out of the hotel through that service door?"

"Sure, just turn right as you come off the elevator, before you get to the front desk. At the end of the hall there's a sign on the door that says 'Fire Exit Only,' but don't worry. The alarm's not on."

"Thanks pal." The stolen car was already moving.

Hartman stopped and parked the car as instructed. He popped the trunk lid and moved quickly to the rear. From inside the trunk, he removed a large but fashionable black luggage case. It had rollers on the bottom and could be pulled with a strap. What could be more innocuous, he thought, than a man walking in the front door of a hotel with a suitcase?

The detective knocked on the door of room 1704 and uttered only two short sentences. "Brad sent me, Sean. Open the door."

In a moment, the door swung slowly to the inside, the frightened eyes of Sean Lowry peering past the edge as it moved.

Hartman, partly from impatience and partly to establish the terms of their current relationship, kicked the door violently with his left foot, sending Sean crashing to floor.

"From now on when I tell you to do something, you do it without hesitation. Are we clear, you sick fuck?"

"Yeah, okay, I'm sure glad it's you, Hartman."

Hartman had already dragged the luggage case into the room and was opening it on the floor. He removed a baggy blue jump suit and began stepping into it as Sean had become a silent spectator. After zipping the jump suit to his neck, Hartman stepped out of his loafers and replaced them with plastic baggies, held in place with rubber bands. He then reached back into the bag and removed a large plastic drop cloth of the type used by house painters. Hartman then spread the plastic sheet out over the open section of carpeted floor.

As he forced his large hands into the hospital gloves, it finally dawned on Sean what the suitcase was for.

"Now take all your clothes off and get over there at the foot of the bed, Sean. We'll wrap the bedding around the body and dump the whole mess onto the plastic. That way we won't make tracks."

Sean started to protest, but then thought better of it and did as instructed, helping to carry the body roughly to the center of the plastic sheet. The close-up view of the girl's pummeled corpse, however, was more than Sean could handle in his morning-after state.

When he vomited, it seemed to take Hartman by surprise.

It was perhaps ironic that, amidst all the blood and human carnage, it was the spewing vomit hurled into his unsuspecting face with the force of a garden hose that brought Hartman to a momentary loss of control.

In an instant, Sean was lying on his back with a powerful hand clutching at his throat.

"You psycho piece of shit. You can beat this girl into hamburger, but you haven't got the balls to clean up the mess." He suddenly whirled completely around and was straddling Sean's chest, with a gloved hand pulling mercilessly on the killer's offending member, as though he were attempting to free the sword *Excalibur* from its sheath of stone.

Almost instantaneously, the other hand emerged from the jump suit pocket brandishing a pearl handled switchblade knife. The gleaming four-inch blade barely had time to reveal itself before it swooped down, preparing to sever the evil connection.

Sean's scream, probably one of terror more than pain, seemed to snap Hartman back to reality. Without speaking, he dismounted, wiped his face, and continued with the grizzly packing job. Hartman had come within a single heartbeat of curing what most ailed Sean Lowry. Sean was only too happy to do his part thereafter.

In less than a half hour, the overnight bag, packed with the remains of what had only hours ago been a beautiful life filled with hope and promise, sat near the door of room 1704.

Sean showered and dressed as Hartman sanitized the room as best he could, making particularly certain that none of the girl's personal effects had been left behind. He reached for the breast pocket of his polyester jacket to make sure the girl's wallet was still there. Just before they left, he scoured the room for a final time until he was absolutely satisfied the room was clean. Then, according to a pre-arranged plan, they left the room one at a time.

Hartman went first, pulling the now one-hundred-twenty-odd pound luggage case. As the elevator door opened into the lobby, Hartman turned right and walked directly to the fire door. Once outside the door, he quickly deposited his luggage into the trunk and waited, engine running, for less than a minute until Sean was safely in the car beside him.

Neither man spoke during the twenty-five minute mid-morning drive to Sean's place, one's silence owing to disgust and the other's to fear. As the Buick pulled up in front of Sean's building, Hartman, without even turning his head toward the young killer, conveyed a simple message. "Keep your mouth shut and your head down until you hear from Parkins."

Sean mumbled something in submissive compliance.

Hartman drove the Buick directly to his mother's garage in a near west suburb to await its late night rendezvous with an industrial compactor.

Before Hartman had made his way back to the city, Larry Califf finally suspended the door-to-door canvas operation without any solid leads. It was nearly dinnertime and neither Califf nor Frank had eaten since they started.

IMMORAL AUTHORITY

Califf had now worked a full double shift and not mentioned it once. He accepted Frank's offer to go back to the house for something to eat, but still clearly had business on his mind. He asked Frank to stop at the station first where he had to pick up some more mug shots for Denise to look at.

The mug shot digital photo system was a rare triumph of technology in local law enforcement. The department still kept the big, bulky photo books and most of the detectives still used them, especially the older ones. The computer system, however, was infinitely more advanced and efficient and was favored by some of the bright young up-and-comers in the detective division.

In addition to being easier to update and disseminate, the new system was mobile and allowed the detective to download the specific category of photos to a floppy disk (i.e. known violent sex offenders). He could then simply drop the disk in his pocket for viewing on the personal PC of a potential witness or on the detective's own laptop. It also operated without the disk, of course, when the detective had access to a telephone.

As he left the station with Frank, Califf carried both a disk and his laptop computer.

When the two men reached Frank's home, they found Ellen and Ed in the family room with Denise. Frank's friend and colleague, Ray Paxon, had picked up his in-laws at the airport and was in the basement occupying the kids.

Califf hadn't even considered dinner. Instead of making it an issue, Frank introduced Califf to the in-laws and disappeared into the garage. He returned twenty minutes later with a huge bucket of chicken and a twelve-pack of beer.

Califf, deep at work on the computer with Denise,

never noticed his absence. Not a word was said about the food, but everyone ate his fill.

During the meal, Frank excused himself briefly to return a phone message from the family of a client Sam Walker, who had been arrested earlier that evening.

While he was gone, the only dinner conversation concerned how the two families would cope on a day-to-day basis during the coming investigation. There was general agreement that Ed would go back to South Dakota within a couple of days, barring a break in the case. There was no telling how long this investigation would last and bills had to be paid. Ellen would stay on a little longer to be close to the investigation.

It was just after nine when Califf finally called it a day, satisfied that his database did not contain the answer he sought.

As Califf said goodnight at the front door, he addressed Ellen directly, "The FBI has been notified and will be contacting you here in the morning, Ellen. We'll continue our investigation working with them, but from this point forward they have primary jurisdiction."

"Thank you, Detective," Ellen said.

"Look," Califf began. "This has always been the hardest part of the job for me, but I want you to know that I really feel for you and I won't let this die. Your daughter is an extraordinary and beautiful girl."

Ellen began to cry almost uncontrollably.

It seemed to the young detective that his clumsy attempt to comfort this grieving mother had fallen flat on its face. He kicked himself mentally and was embarrassed at his lack of professionalism.

Then, as quickly as she had started, she stopped. Looking young Califf squarely in the eye, she spoke softly. "Thank you, Larry. I guess I just wasn't expecting someone like you. I think if anyone can find my daughter, you will."

As Califf walked down the front path towards his car, he heard Ellen call his name again. He stopped and turned.

"If you do find her," she said, "I think you would like each other very much."

Saying nothing, he turned back towards his car, feeling that strange sensation that tightens the face and turns the corners of the mouth before the first tear comes.

As Califf had predicted, the FBI appeared at the door unannounced at precisely nine the next morning in the form of Agents Rhonda Everett and James Hubbard. They were very courteous, in a practiced and formal kind of way. The woman was clearly in charge, as Hubbard deferred to her at every opportunity.

Before any questioning began, Everett, a plain but smartly dressed business type of about thirty-five, addressed the family group as a whole. She rattled off lots of numbers and statistics related to the bureau's handling of abduction cases, apparently a standard presentation meant to instill confidence in the family, thus insuring cooperation.

She touched on all of the common motives for abduction; financial gain, revenge, sexual perversion and others.

Frank reasoned that this was a kind of a warning that the questions could sometimes get very personal and painful, but that it was necessary to the investigation.

They set up their temporary interview room in Frank's small office off the foyer on the first floor and began with Denise. The interview lasted nearly an hour.

Denise later disclosed to Frank that a significant part of it had related to Caroline's relationship with her parents, her political views, her personal sexual habits and her friends. The fact that Denise knew virtually nothing about the latter three had not in the least discouraged their inquiry.

Caroline's parents were interviewed next, one at a time, of course. While Ellen was in the room for less than forty-five minutes, her husband's turn consumed twice that time, and it was well past one thirty in the afternoon when the interviews had concluded.

When the agents finally emerged from the room, Denise asked if they would care to join the family for lunch. They politely declined and said they'd like to make some local phone calls while they waited.

After lunch, the agents emerged from the office and appeared in the kitchen, with everyone still sitting at the table. Everett spoke first. "Mrs. Doherty, we've taken the liberty of scheduling you an appointment with a bureau Forensic Identification Specialist at seven o'clock tonight. Is that a good time?"

"Of course, whatever you think," Denise replied, indicating both complete cooperation and lack of understanding, simultaneously.

"They used to be called police artists. It's the same thing, except it's all done by computer now. We're looking for the best picture we can get of the man you saw. It's best if you do it while your memory is still fresh."

"Tonight is fine," concluded Denise matter-of-factly, "but I sincerely doubt that time will dull my memory."

Before midnight, a computer generated illustration, reasonably similar in appearance to Sean Lowry, and possibly two million other men east of the Rocky Mountains, would be disseminated to virtually every state and major metropolitan police agency in the country.

At nearly the same time as the FBI agents first appeared at the Doherty house, Sean Lowry was awakened by the ringing telephone beside his bed. He had been asleep nearly sixteen hours.

"Yeah," answered the nearly inaudible and scratchy voice.

"Get on Interstate 60 and pull off at the twenty-five mile marker rest area north of the city. I'll meet you there in one hour."

"Okay. I'll be there, but if that fucking Hartman thinks—"

"Shut up, you fool. Just get in your car and be there," said the caller, an instant before the line clicked dead.

Parkins thought about arriving an hour late, just to make the little shit stew, but almost immediately thought better of it. If ever there had been a time to be objective and thorough, this was it.

Brad arrived at the appointed time to find Sean sitting in his Porsche, engine running, apparently to keep from freezing. Brad pulled in several cars away, walked over to the waiting Porsche, and got in.

"Okay, Sean, listen to me very carefully, and don't even think about interrupting me. I don't need to tell you that you could go away for the rest of your young life, no matter who your father is. Do you understand that?"

"Yes," Sean muttered.

"Think about that, Sean. It means you would live the rest of your life sucking the black banana and taking it up the ass. I actually think you might grow into the role, but I know the thought doesn't appeal to you right now. So, what you need to do now, Sean, is trust me. If you do everything I tell you when I tell you, I'll make this all go away. Do you understand me, Sean?"

"I understand," Sean answered meekly.

I should have been a fucking psychologist. It was just a natural talent; fear then compassion, threats then understanding. *Guys went to college for ten years to get letters after their names for this shit. Most of them would probably never be this good at it.*

The whole thing was becoming just a mad game to challenge Brad Parkins' wits and cunning. There was no doubt that, despite the grave risks to his future and even his freedom, Brad loved every minute of it.

"Okay, Sean, Where did you meet the girl?"

"At The El Dorado. I just started talking to her at the bar an hour or so before closing."

"Now think about this one very carefully. Was there anybody in the club who actually knew who you were?"

"Not a chance. I knew what I was going out for that night. That's why I got the room. Nobody saw me, and nobody knew me. I used a fake name at the hotel, like I always do and it was nowhere near the club." It was the first time during this affair that Sean had spoken with any semblance of authority.

"All right then, was the girl alone?"

Sean's response to the question was a pensive stare out the front windshield.

Parkins was not optimistic about its meaning. "You didn't answer me, Sean." The objective and business-like framework for the meeting was breaking down quickly. "Sean, I asked you a fucking question." There was no trace left of the self-anointed psychologist.

"No. She wasn't alone. She was with her aunt."

"Tell me her aunt didn't get a good look at you."

"Look, Brad, it was a club. She was standing right next to me at the bar. I couldn't help that. She probably got a good look at me because the bitch was hanging on to the girl's arm while we were talking. I think she tried to introduce me to her aunt, but it was really loud in there."

"You mean you fucking met her? What name did you use?"

"Just John, no last name, just John."

It was instantly clear to Brad that this business was far from finished. Possibilities flooded his mind. Who was the girl? At least he'd have the answer to that question when he talked to Hartman. Her wallet was now safely in the detective's possession. Who was the aunt? If they were people with connections, the disappearance would make the news. If the girl had been some kind of wild-ass party girl tourist, they might just assume that she took off with some guy. If not, then this whole thing could hit the front pages as a kidnapping.

Parkins was getting ahead of himself and decided, then and there, that he would just let the whole scenario play out for a day or two and see how it developed. Details of the media coverage, or the lack of coverage, would determine his next move. One thing was for certain, however; if this thing became a story, there would be trouble.

Jack Lowry's infamous demon-child craved and received more than his share of media attention for his public persona as a handsome and frolicking heir apparent bachelor. His picture appeared regularly in one venue or another, and that could now spell disaster for everyone. For the moment he would wait, Brad thought, and then do whatever was necessary.

The wallet in Hartman's possession provided some cause for optimism. The girl, it seemed, had been a twenty-one year old student from South Dakota. The moment he conveyed this information to Brad in their late afternoon phone conversation, Brad experienced a distinct sense of relief.

"Fucking South Dakota? That's perfect. She's probably some farm girl who's been taking the pipe from her father for the past fifteen years and ran away from home. Christ, that's absolutely perfect. However big the story is in South Dakota, it won't make a ripple in the water here. I'd say we're gonna be okay, Hartman."

Chapter Four

The next morning, some forty-eight hours after Sean's rampage, Brad Parkins picked up the morning paper and saw immediately that his euphoric optimism had been premature. The Post contained a page one story.

> ***Niece of veteran criminal lawyer feared abducted***
> *Sources close to the investigation have reported that the twenty-one year old niece of veteran criminal lawyer Frank Doherty was reported missing by the lawyer and his wife early Thursday morning. The young woman, Caroline Anderson, was visiting from South Dakota and disappeared late Wednesday night while in the company of her aunt at a popular downtown nightclub...*

The story went on to describe how the girl was last seen heading to the dance floor accompanied by a tall, slender, blond haired Caucasian man in his late twenties. It indicated that, according to FBI sources, the investigation was still in its early stages.

The news was everywhere. Local TV news carried the story as a headline. There was no getting around it now, Brad thought. The aunt had to go, and soon.

He stopped at a public phone in a busy Amoco station and called Lonnie Hartman. They agreed to meet right away outside the Holy Trinity Cathedral downtown.

This time Brad arrived first and seemed irritated at having to wait fifteen minutes for Hartman. It was a windy, rain soaked morning, just after the start of the business day. At Brad's suggestion, the two men entered the near empty church and sat in the back row.

"I suppose you saw the papers," Parkins offered, his tone betraying a sense of resignation.

"And the television reports," added Hartman.

"You understand that this will only go away now if we make it go away." Brad decided to call upon his skill in psychology once again.

"Don't screw me around, Parkins. Say exactly what you came here to say." Hartman was considerably less susceptible to this approach.

"Okay, the aunt has to go and you're the one who's gonna do it." Brad thought it would be difficult to be more straightforward than that.

"First of all, Parkins, I don't kill people, not for you, or the Lowrys, or anyone else." Then, Hartman seemed momentarily to qualify his position. "Secondly, if I did kill someone, it wouldn't be the aunt, as much as I would love to see that scum-sucking lawyer suffer. I would kill that psycho pervert, Sean Lowry, and only if the price was right."

"Why in God's name would you do that?" Parkins asked incredulously.

"It's a sure bet that if the Doherty woman ever does identify him, he'll crack the first time the FBI questions him. He'll go right down the fucking drain, and take us with him. If that shithead OD's or gets killed in a car wreck, the whole thing is over and you keep your little piece of the pie."

"Don't you think I thought of that?" Brad countered,

sounding almost paternal now and dangerously close to patronizing. "Think about it Lonnie. If Sean dies, it will be big news. If you think you see his picture a lot now, just wait! If he dies, they'll be cutting into the fucking soap operas to show his picture! That Doherty woman got too good a look at him. There's a good chance she'd recognize him and that would start an avalanche effect that we couldn't stop. Can't you see it?"

Hartman's response was a deadly cold stare, broken only by Brad's next assault.

"Look, if they had any reason at all to connect him to the girl's disappearance, they'd start snooping around high priced hotels and investigating his alias names. Doherty's a criminal lawyer, for Christ sake! Do you think he's gonna lie down if his wife says Sean Lowry kidnapped her niece? Eventually, the whole thing would cave in on us. It's the woman who has to go, Lonnie. She's the only one who got a good look at him. Who else is going to even think to accuse the Mayor's son, based on a computer generated likeness?"

"Don't think for a minute that you calling me by first name is gonna save you a dime, you greedy prick. I'll kill the woman and have a good time doing it, but not for free, not this time. The last time I was young and stupid. I figured Lowry would be so grateful for what I did that I'd end up as Chief of Detectives or something before the year was out. Well, now I know better.

"You can go to Lowry and tell him it'll cost a hundred grand to do the woman, even if she is Frank Doherty's wife. That's just a bonus for me."

"You must be out of your mind, Hartman. I'm not giving you a hundred grand. Do you think I would just waltz in to see Lowry and tell him I need a hundred grand to kill someone?"

"He gave you fifty grand quick enough eight years ago, and that was only for a little witness tampering and bribery." Hartman had been carefully planning this trap since Brad's phone call that morning.

"You haven't changed a bit, Hartman. You're just as stupid and naïve as you were eight years ago. What makes you think Lowry knew anything about our deal eight years ago? You just assumed that he did because the note looked like Lowry had written it. Well, chump, you're no better a detective now than you were then." Brad couldn't resist chuckling audibly as he watched the impact of his words on the face of the detective. It was a mistake that nearly cost Brad Parkins his life.

Right there in the majestic expanse of the old Gothic cathedral, the hand that had nearly choked the life from Sean Lowry struck out at Parkins' neck with the force of a falling brick and wrapped itself around its prey like a slithering python, preparing its feast for consumption.

So big and powerful was the hand that the thumb and forefinger literally touched around the ever-narrowing throat of the Mayor's right hand man. Hartman smiled the wild and rabid smile of a hungry animal, but the prospect of a hundred grand payday was sufficient to terminate his rage short of homicide.

He released his death grip and clutched for a handful of the older man's custom-made dress shirt. Parkins, his face a swirl of red and purple, gasped and struggled to regain his breath.

"You no good motherfucker," Hartman whispered, now appearing more reflective. "All these years I've been waiting for the big payoff that never came, and Lowry never even knew I put my job on the line for his fucking pervert kid. It was you who wrote the note! Well, I'm gonna get paid now, motherfucker. I don't care if you have to mortgage your condo or that fucking yacht to pay me yourself. If I don't get paid, I'll go to jail happily, knowing you'll be in the next cell popping hormone pills to make your tits big for your roommate."

"So now you're bitter because you were taken advantage of. Hartman, listen to me. There's a reason why you slog around in shit for forty grand a year. It's because you just don't get it. See, you never had a chance. Lowry doesn't want to know. That's why he has guys like me. We don't need to talk about it. He just knows that if something goes wrong, we take care of it. We take the risks for a very handsome profit, and we take the fall when it goes bad. Its what makes the whole thing work, Hartman. Just don't take it so personal. There are a thousand guys smarter than you caught up in it too."

"I'll tell you what, Parkins; personally I think you might be a bigger psycho than Sean Lowry. I mean, this is like a fucking Monopoly game to you, but not to me. See, there's one thing I know for sure. You've got nowhere else to go on this one. Oh, sure, you could probably find somebody to do this Doherty woman for you, but you'd be creating another risk factor, just one more thing that could go wrong."

"You think you're the only detective I know?" Parkins managed to say.

"Maybe not, but I'm already involved and my silence is guaranteed. Most important of all, I'm competent. You see, asshole, the truth is that you're no better and no smarter than me. You just need to tell yourself you are. Now, I'll take my money half up front in old small bills and half when the job is done."

Brad was slightly bewildered and off balance, but nevertheless, attempted to make his surrender look more like a conversion. After only a few moments, he made his best effort to look convinced and conceded to Hartman's demand. "What can I say?" For the first time in this whole messy affair, Brad Parkins was truly at a loss for words, at least for the time being.

Brad considered the seemingly impossible situation on the drive back to the airport. He was certain that if he applied his considerable analytical skill and problem solving ability, he could still get a handle on this before it spun hopelessly out of control.

Of one thing he was certain. He simply didn't have a hundred grand to give Hartman, or even fifty right now. Well, he could probably swing fifty, but why should he use his own money?

It was also clear that Hartman wasn't going to reduce his price, and involving someone else to do a killing at this point was out of the question. Brad concluded that he had two choices; gamble that the woman would never recognize Sean, or get the money somewhere else.

This decision was the most difficult he had faced since that little whining pervert had first put him in the middle of all this. The drive back in traffic was just over forty-five minutes, but by the time his car pulled into his privately designated parking space, he had formulated another foolproof plan.

He entered his third floor office at the airport administrative complex to find Meg Lofton sitting at his desk. It was a privilege she had more or less usurped and Brad hadn't really minded until today. There had not been much time lately to indulge his hedonistic appetites and he guessed that Meg was beginning to take it personally.

"Meg, I'm glad to see you, but I really don't think it looks right for you to be walking in and out of my office when I'm not here. I mean you're an airline employee for Christ sake."

"Oh, that's just peachy, Sweetcakes. I don't even hear from you for three days, and now you show up giving me a lecture on business ethics. If that isn't the pot calling the kettle black, what is?" She decided to backtrack a little. "I've been worried sick about you. As far as I knew, you were lying in a ditch somewhere."

They both knew that she had gone about as far as she would. It wasn't love that they shared. In fact, the dynamics of their relationship were the same as in nearly every relationship Brad Parkins had, namely *quid pro quo*. The only thing that distinguished this relationship from the others was that he didn't get his rocks off with people like Hartman and Paul DeBenedetto.

Brad had given more than fair value for the considerable sexual talents of Meg Lofton. The airline had been aware of their relationship since nearly the beginning and had not hesitated to exploit it in an attempt to get a leg up on its competitors.

Meg had delivered things such as choice gate assignments, increased daily flights and, most importantly, a relaxation of city inspections for the massive local operation, including those relating to food preparation, building codes and ground related environmental standards. She had even obtained relief from the strictly enforced parking regulations governing arrivals and pick-ups.

All of these concessions were obtained at the direct expense of competitors. It came as no surprise to Brad that Meg Lofton had been catapulted to vice-presidential status.

Brad knew full well that her anger was as contrived as her expressions of concern. This woman was driven only by ambition, and he would fuck her as long as it pleased him. Brad giveth and Brad might well taketh away.

He glared at her and did not speak.

She knew at once that she had gone too far, and now she could only try her best to keep him from speaking the words that could seal her fate.

"Look, I'm sorry Brad. I really am. I've been so worried that I haven't been sleeping at night. Let's not fight. I've got courtside tickets to the game tonight. How about it?"

This was neither the time nor the place for a confrontation with Meg. It would come soon enough, but not today. "I just can't, Meg. I've just had a lot going on lately. Sorry I didn't call you. In a few more days, I'll be caught up and we'll make up for lost time. In the meantime, I've got some emergency calls to make."

The moment the door closed behind her, he picked up the receiver and dialed Paul DeBenedetto.

"Mr. D? This is Parkins," he said.

"Yes, Brad. What is it?"

"I think it's important that we meet today."

"Fine, Brad. How about we meet down at the Port District? Pier Four. Say about an hour?"

"I'll be there."

Even at the lunch hour, the drive from the airport down to the far South Side was every bit of an hour. Brad grabbed his keys and was out the door.

Although the Port District was outside Brad's area of

authority, he knew something about its operation. It wasn't much different than the airport operation, but had been in place longer and was far more lucrative. The District was the exclusive loading and off-loading point for virtually all international seagoing commerce to and from the area. Control of the District had been a prized political plumb since the end of World War II, and little had changed.

He knew that the Board of Directors of the Port District was to that day staffed largely by designees of organized crime. It was more or less common knowledge, although investigations into its operation had never resulted in criminal action, or even administrative restructuring.

Brad recalled, however, that the Mayor had once told him that there hadn't been a strike at the District since Harry Truman was president. God only knew how much ill-gotten booty had gone onto and come off of those ships in fifty years.

As he waited in the damp wind, Brad tried to imagine the enormity of the undeclared profits that had been taken from the decks of those ships in drugs, merchandise, and cash.

As he stood there watching, a giant pallet, stacked with massive, wooden boxes, lifted skyward from the deck of some nameless foreign ship. The name was there on the bow all right. Brad just couldn't read it because it was written in some damn alphabet he had never seen.

As the giant crane swung the pallet back towards the dock, he heard a single blast from a car horn and turned. There, on the wide expanse of the dock area, he saw a plain, blue Buick parked near one of the many old warehouses lining the dock. White exhaust smoke from the idling car disappeared into the damp air.

As Brad neared the car, the driver's window descended and a thumb pointed his way to the rear door. As the door closed behind Parkins, Paul nodded to the driver and the car headed slowly out of the dock area in the general direction of mid-day traffic.

"Well, Brad, you needed to see me, so here I am."

Brad knew full well that the face across from him would never betray the true thoughts of the mind behind it. Dealing with Paul DeBenedetto had always required great caution and intense focus. Although Brad had never underestimated the old man, he'd always had the feeling that DeBenedetto considered him to be a gopher.

If Brad had perceived that opinion from anyone else, he would have cut him off at the knees, but he had always deferred to DeBenedetto. It certainly wasn't out of respect because Brad had decided that the Italian had long ago lost the grip he once held on the pulse of the city.

If the old man considered him a gopher, Brad would just have to prove him wrong. Both caution and cunning would be required, however, because DeBenedetto was still powerful and continued to benefit from his shadowy reputation as an associate and business partner to some of the most infamous underworld figures of the past fifty years.

"Mr. DeBenedetto, the help you gave us earlier in the week was deeply appreciated. Well, we have another problem related to that same matter, and I've been instructed to ask for your assistance once again." Brad thought the brief summary contained all the elements necessary to pass the ball, although it suddenly occurred to him why DeBenedetto might consider him a gopher.

"Brad, please stop talking in code. Just say what's on your mind."

"Well, as you might have imagined, the Sean Lowry thing was a real mess to clean up and we had to make some financial promises to some cops and—"

It was time for Paul to assert some authority. "So how much for the cops, Brad?"

"Fifty grand total, Mr. D."

"A nice round number, Brad. Are you getting a commission?"

Brad thought it might be a joke, but dared not laugh. "Of course not. It goes to the sergeant. He's made separate deals with the beat guys."

"And since when can our Chief Executive Officer not afford fifty grand in campaign funds to shut up some cops?" Paul knew that there was a political slush fund maintained for just such purposes.

It was a perfectly logical and obvious question, yet Brad hadn't considered it. He decided to play gopher. "On this one Mr. D I'm just doing what I've been told. I'm not really running it, but I'm sure he has his reasons."

"I'm sure he does. I can think of several right now. I don't think there'll be any problem with this request, Brad. It seems young Mr. Sean Lowry is becoming quite an expensive political liability, but it's in the best interest of all concerned to avoid any serious disruption to the stability of the administration."

Paul produced a small cell phone and dialed. After a moment, he calmly issued some very specific orders.

When the Buick pulled back into the port district area thirty minutes later, it parked directly beside an idling black Lincoln Navigator. The driver of the Lincoln exited and walked back to the rear of the Buick. He handed Paul a small package, wrapped in brown paper. Paul turned, handed the package to Brad and spoke, "As always, please convey our warmest regards to our esteemed Mayor."

"Thank you, Mr. D. He will get your message today."

Brad Parkins cranked up the volume on the twenty-four hour jazz music station for the entire ride back, keeping the beat with tapping fingers. He had done it again.

With fifty thousand dollars in his pocket, Lonnie Hartman became considerably easier to deal with.

It killed Brad to actually hand the fifty grand over to him, but in this business, concessions were necessary. He knew that he would extract his pound of flesh when Hartman came looking for the second installment. When that happened, however, Brad would make sure that the near death experience in the church would not be repeated. It was important to Brad that Hartman come to understand and accept his own insignificance in the big picture.

Over the next two days, Parkins carefully reviewed news reports concerning Caroline's disappearance, while Hartman monitored the daily supplemental reports filed by Califf. The reports documented literally every scrap of information collected in the investigation. In less than forty-eight hours, the two had collected a wealth of information on the entire Frank Doherty family, including Denise's part-time work schedule in the emergency room at State University Hospital.

On Saturday afternoon, Hartman stalked Denise all the way from her home into the hospital parking garage. He watched as she crossed Jackson Street at the corner and walked directly into the emergency room main entrance. At eleven o'clock that night, he was parked down the block on Jackson and repeated the entire scenario in reverse.

On the drive back to his apartment, Hartman called Brad and informed him that he had formulated a plan, and told him to have his money ready by this time Monday night.

On Monday afternoon, Hartman didn't risk following Denise to work. There was no need. Instead, he dined alone at Bart's Steakhouse and consumed a 24oz. porterhouse steak with three bottles of Heineken. Dinner, of course, was free to all city detectives.

The plain beige police sedan had disappeared neatly in between the two big trash bins behind the restaurant. It was a habit that had nothing to do with the night's special assignment.

He considered the evening's dinner a kind of pre-game meal and enjoyed it immensely.

It was nearly nine o'clock when he finally began the slow drive through city streets toward The Inner City Shopping Mall, a newly developed and massive complex of upper-end retail stores, sprouting fifty-four floors straight up, instead of out, and occupying less than half a city block. The lowest twelve levels made up the parking garage, and it was from there that Hartman would select his weapon of choice.

He thought it ironic that he should perform the evil deed while on duty. He would be an hour or so late checking out, but that was nothing unusual.

As Hartman made the left turn from Congressional Avenue onto northbound Lakeland, he spotted a late model green BMW traveling in the right lane, just ahead of him. The driver was a short black man with closely cropped hair, in the style *de jour* for fashionable young gang types. Hartman moved into the left lane and started to overtake the BMW, staying slightly outside the driver's line of sight.

When he glanced over, Hartman couldn't believe his luck. The kid couldn't have been more than twenty years old. It had to be a hot car and, most likely, recently stolen. Some of the young drug lords drove even more expensive cars, but nothing so conservative.

Hartman reached into the glove compartment for the portable mars light, pressed it onto the roof until he felt the suction take hold and activated the blue and white flashing signal.

The kid looked over in shock and for a moment considered bolting. It took no more than three or four seconds for the young car thief to make his choice.

Hartman immediately recognized the body language of surrender. The head shook slowly from side to side. The shoulders drooped and the car slowly pulled to the curb.

The detective approached the driver's side from the rear with his service revolver in one hand and his detective shield in the other.

He announced his office and ordered the man to exit the car with his hands in the air. As the young man stood facing him, hands held high, Hartman ordered him to "assume the position" over the hood of the car, returning his identity wallet to his coat pocket.

After patting the car thief down on the hood over the front bumper, the detective turned his glance momentarily to the lower right corner of the windshield, where he could clearly make out the Village of Wittington sticker attached from the inside. It was common knowledge that Wittington was a very upscale, predominantly Jewish community.

Upon noticing the religious object displayed below the driver's inside mirror, Hartman concluded that the car probably belonged to a rabbi or one of those Orthodox Jews with the beards.

What dumb luck. There wasn't even a need to risk using the radio to check the car's status. It was clearly on its way to a nearby chop shop, and most likely had not even been reported stolen yet.

It came as no surprise to him, of course, that the young man could not produce a driver's license and Hartman couldn't resist playing with the unsuspecting driver for a few minutes. Instead of cuffing him immediately, the detective began to ask questions that seemingly offered the thief a glimmer of hope that he might talk his way out of the nearly hopeless situation.

"Okay, so even if I believed that you left your license at home, how do you explain driving a brand new BMW from Wittington? Tell me you're an Ethiopian Jew."

Hartman didn't need to ask the question twice. The young man began talking almost non-stop, explaining how the car belonged to the man his sister worked for…and the wedding Saturday…and he always liked to help the police because his cousin was one…and he knew where there was a stash of guns.

Hartman almost smiled and couldn't help admiring how some of these faceless street punks would never quit trying to get over.

Finally, as the cascade of lies continued to flow from the thief's mouth, the detective pretended to be convinced and told him to run.

The man stopped talking in mid-sentence and stood frozen, his terrified eyes locked on Hartman's. "Now lookie here, Mr. Policeman, it ain't no call to be shootin' a nigger in the back for boostin' a fucking car."

"I'll tell you what, homey; if you really impress me with your speed, I won't shoot you at all. The truth is, I'm hungry and tired, and I'd like to go home."

Before he finished the sentence, the man whirled and bolted up the busy thoroughfare, dodging oncoming headlights with the skill of a pro running back.

As he watched the young car thief, Hartman actually chuckled. It was pure arrogance that prevented him from even thinking to ask the man's name.

He still had over an hour to kill and didn't want to have to explain being stopped driving a stolen car. The gauge showed less than a quarter tank of gas and although he wasn't going far, his plan required as much gas as the car could carry.

After parking his unmarked police squad car on a residential street around the corner, Hartman returned to the waiting BMW with two empty gas cans he had removed from his trunk. He drove slowly down Eastern Avenue, one of the city's main north-south arteries, and noticed the unusually large numbers of local residents milling about on the corners and in front of the dozens of local taverns dotting the thoroughfare.

The neighborhoods changed so quickly in this part of town that sometimes the faces of the pedestrians were the easiest way to keep your bearings at night. It was particularly easy tonight, given this oppressive heat wave, Hartman thought. The faces seemed to change colors almost every mile or so, without warning; first all black, then all brown, finally all white.

In the dead of winter, you could sometimes forget the bitterness that divided these communities because the buildings all looked the same; even the homes along the side streets were common remnants of a less violent and divisive time.

He pulled into the new mini mart/gas station at 16th street, where he filled up the BMW and the two red five-gallon gas cans. By ten forty-five, Hartman was fully prepared and had the BMW positioned on the street just down the block from where Jackson Street separated Denise Doherty from her waiting minivan.

Just after eleven, the first employee from the PM shift, a tall lanky character, emerged from the emergency room in blue scrubs and jogged rhythmically across the street, disappearing into the parking garage. He was followed a minute later by two women, one white and one African-American.

Hartman suddenly realized that he had not allowed for the possibility that Denise could be walking out with someone else. In that case, he would just back off and try again later.

No sooner had he resolved this problem, however, than the familiar scrub-clad figure emerged alone from the large electronically controlled glass doors and briskly approached the crosswalk on Jackson.

Denise was holding some freshly laundered lab coats in her right hand. She held the plastic covered hangars above her head to keep the garments from dragging on the ground.

He eased the BMW from its parking space, keeping the headlights dark. As the blue figure reached the curb, part of a face appeared from behind the hanging lab coats, not unlike the head of a turtle emerging from its shell, looking both left and right.

Satisfied that it was safe, Denise stepped off the curb. She was thinking of Caroline.

The detective hadn't counted on the hospital laundry

as an ally. It occurred to him that, without it, his intended victim might see the speeding car in time to avoid being hit, or at least in time to avoid death.

There were one hundred fifty feet of bone-dry pavement between the BMW and Denise when Hartman's right foot launched the final assault. The speedometer catapulted upwards as the precision BMW engine did its work, almost without strain and Denise Doherty, still thinking only of her beloved Caroline, never did identify the whining sound that was silenced by her death only a split second later.

Chapter Five

Six Months Later

For just another minute, Frank Doherty lay quietly on the plush black leather sofa which had, in recent years, become not only his favorite venue for decision-making, but also the single item of office furniture in which he placed any value.

Although there was contemporary fluorescent lighting throughout the ceiling, he rarely if ever used it, preferring the intimacy and solitude of the old brass reading lamps located both on his desk and credenza. It drove Nora crazy. Nora was his secretary of eighteen years. She had been with him in this same office since the beginning; since before the kids; even before Denise.

Nora had been a friend of his late mother and had come to him originally as a part-time typist after retiring from the phone company at age sixty-five. In recent years, she could barely even see the computer screen or hear the phone, but she drove to work every day. No doubt she would outlive him and be working "part-time" for some other lawyer before his body was cold.

It was rare that he actually fell asleep on the sofa. As a rule, he would lie there alone in the near dark, late in the afternoon, reviewing the day in his head and planning for the next.

This time, however, he found himself thinking of the

three kids. The twins were young enough to eventually overcome even such a tragic loss, but the pre-adolescent Maggie was a different story. She had lost her mother when she needed her most. No matter how hard he tried, Frank could never replace her mother. The unspeakable loss had forced Maggie into maturity before her time. She was a brave girl, he thought.

Over Christmas vacation, he had taken all three kids to a dude ranch in Arizona. It was one of those ranches where the guests actually worked the ranch, performing such tasks as driving cattle to winter or summer grazing, mending fences, even branding yearlings after the spring roundup.

The foreman's first day safety lesson to the kids had included a session on avoiding and detecting rattlesnakes. The lesson also enumerated the rules of behavior in the event of a face-to-face encounter with one of the feared reptiles.

The twins, Adam and Patrick, as would be expected of second grade boys, had paid almost no attention, but eleven year-old Maggie's excursions thereafter were largely limited to the swimming pool and the barn area. While playing in the barn, Maggie had witnessed the birth of a calf, an event she would later recount as the highlight of her trip.

The boys had enjoyed a taste of life on the ranch, learning to saddle and ride their own ponies, climbing hills and running wild for hours without any fear of strangers or speeding traffic.

Every evening, Frank and the kids would join the campfire, where the guests and cowboys would sing songs and tell stories into the night. Everyone had enjoyed the trip immensely, with the exception of Frank's lumbar spine.

The small Motrin bottle in his left front pants pocket had become as indispensable as his pager recently.

It struck him that the week had gone by without any real problems at the office. All the cases were under control. New business had been scarce in recent months, but it wasn't exactly like he'd been focusing on the business lately. He was settling back into the old monotony of routine, which now seemed to offer him a kind of shelter he had not known for so many months.

Oh, the questions were still there. It had nearly driven him crazy when the police ruled out a connection between Caroline's disappearance and Denise's death. He'd never really believed it, but he had begun to concede that they might be right.

His thoughts turned briefly to Montana. Frank had been talking for years about eventually having a small place in Montana with a few horses for vacations and retirement. He couldn't come close to affording it, but in the last couple of years had started looking at small parcels of unimproved acreage advertised on the Internet and in the papers.

Since that started, he had been deluged by information from realtors. The family had enjoyed several memorable vacations out West and Frank always spent a good portion of that time looking at property. He loved the serenity of the rural West and particularly delighted in the panoramic views from atop a well-broken horse.

He thought now of the place he had nearly bought about a year ago. It was a twenty-acre parcel with a creek running through it in the foothills of the Pryor Mountain Range. The parcel backed up to public land, offering endless opportunity for exploring on horseback. On a clear day, one could see three different mountain ranges by simply turning a full circle. He had gone to Montana to see the property not three weeks before his priorities had been altered forever. It was the first time he had thought of Montana since that day.

At five-fifteen, Frank rose from his semi-slumber and walked to his desk to review tomorrow's schedule and forward the phones for the evening. There were no court surprises on the calendar, just the usual assortment of felony cases scheduled for continuances or routine pre-trial motions. Then he noticed the notation in red at the top of the page for January 28; *Sam Walker/County Jail/D32417*.

Frank had made the notation himself after talking to Sam from the prison last week. It was his practice now not to accept unscheduled collect calls from inmates. If you started taking the calls, they would drive you crazy, not to mention the phone bills. Word would get around the jail and you'd have inmates with nothing to do calling all day long for free advice.

Sam's call, however, had been different. He had known Sam a long time. Like Nora, Sam had been there almost from the beginning. It was hard to explain to anyone not intimately familiar with the world of gangbangers, drug dealers and the city police, but Frank liked Sam Walker. He always had, notwithstanding the fact that Sam was a twice-convicted felon who earned his living as the *de facto* CEO of a twenty-odd person drug crew, running a block-long spot on West Sizemore Avenue.

Whatever Sam had done in his life, he was not a murderer. He had never employed violence in his business. It wasn't like he preached about it either. He just didn't engage in it and all of the rival factions seemed to recognize it and respect him for it. As a result, they all left him to his little enterprise.

Sam got along with everyone and that quality of his seemed a more effective and sensible tool for doing business. His "employees" were well paid for their risk and were promptly bailed out of jail following each arrest. It was hardly a lifestyle that Frank endorsed, but within the context of a hopeless and violent subculture, it was certainly something to be admired.

In twenty years of exposure to this culture of crime and hopelessness, Frank had come to learn that in some ways it was no different than the culture of politics, although definitely less tolerated. Nothing was all one thing or all the other. It was a world of gray, of good and bad, even of good and bad at the same time.

It came as no surprise when Frank had learned through a Social Services Pre-Sentence Report that Sam Walker had put at least a significant portion of that drug money to good use.

As it turned out, Sam, up to that time, had fathered no fewer than nine children with five former wives and girlfriends. Each of the women gave a written statement indicating that Sam had been the primary financial provider to the children since the date of birth, and that he visited with each school age child regularly. Two of the women held full-time employment and the other three had never been employed. None of the unemployed women, however, had ever felt the need to apply for public assistance of any kind. The reporting investigator had noted that fact favorably.

What didn't make it into the report, thankfully to Frank, was the fact that Sam still stayed with each of the women periodically, on a rotating basis. Sam Walker was gray, indeed, Frank thought, although it would always be impossible to determine the exact shade. He was, in the final analysis, an unforgettable character.

In a more serious vein, however, it was the unfulfilled promise of Sam Walker, and people like him, that had given Frank pause over the years. He thought that Sam had more personality and raw business savvy than the heads of some big companies. Yet, it had all been squandered in a dead end life of selling drugs and, at forty, Sam's fortunes were not about to change now.

Once, years ago, after Sam had been convicted on a minor drug rap, Frank had ordered school transcripts and medical records to review, in an effort to find mitigating evidence. He was looking for something to keep the judge from sending Sam to jail. What he found sickened him.

Sam had actually graduated from Martin High School, one of the oldest school buildings in the city, built in 1925 and still in use today. The school is located in one of the poorest, most high-density public housing areas in the country. Graduating had been an astonishing achievement, indeed, Frank had noted, for a man who, even to that day, couldn't read and write his own name.

In thumbing through the stack of elementary school medical and health records, Frank's attention had been drawn almost immediately to Sam's second grade hearing test. The standard Board of Education administered test diagnosed Sam as having a sixty percent hearing loss in the right ear and a forty- percent loss in the left. A handwritten notation appeared at the bottom indicating *Mother notified by mail*. There were two subsequent tests administered through the eighth grade indicating no improvement.

IMMORAL AUTHORITY

No attempt was ever made by the school to follow up on Sam's corrective efforts, of which there were none, because Sam's mother and grandmother were illiterate. Sam was not sent to prison on that particular occasion.

No, it's been longer than six months since Sam's arrest. In fact, with a minute to think, he could calculate the number of days and hours almost without effort. It had been during all the turmoil over Caroline's disappearance.

At any other time, Frank would have gone right down to the station himself. With Sam, he had never worried about getting a retainer fee. Sam would always pay eventually and his referrals had helped establish Frank's business in the first place.

That Sunday night, however, Frank had politely declined and advised the family that the next day at bond court Sam could apply for representation from the Public Defender's Office. In the aftermath of his long nightmare, Frank had come to genuinely regret the incident.

The lawyer had been alone in his office last Tuesday near the close of the business day when the call came in. "AT&T has a collect call from County Jail inmate..." came the familiar if emotionless computer-like female voice. Then came the three-second open line, during which the inmate was supposed to say his name.

In reality, Frank knew that they preferred to use the three seconds in the most deceptively creative way possible, in an attempt to get Frank to accept charges for the two dollar and sixty cent call.

FrankitsJoeIknowyouthereMyoldladygotthefivegrandIoweyou. Frank had always found this approach the most difficult to resist. So, even these days, it resulted in lots of wasted time and money.

Sam Walker, however, didn't need to resort to

deception. When the computer lady had finally paused all Frank heard was "Frank, its Sam."

Frank quickly punched "0" to accept the call. "Sam, it's been a long time. What's up?"

"Sorry 'bout your troubles, Frank, but I need to talk to you right away."

Sam clearly sounded agitated; no, not agitated, something else. "Go ahead Sam, I've got time now." That was the lawyer in Frank. He knew that Sam meant *in person*, but he wanted to hear him say it. He wanted to hear how he said it.

"Look Frank, I need you to come down here, most-rickety-tick. This ain't no bullshit, Frank."

Then he said something that had lingered on Frank's mind and provoked his imagination and curiosity to the point that it had dominated his sleep for the past several nights.

"It's not about me, Frank. Its about—" he hesitated, "something else, something important."

Frank arrived at the main entrance to the jail at precisely nine-thirty for his visit with Sam Walker. Early morning was the best time to visit clients. Every lawyer in the Criminal Courts Building was either in court or on his way to court. If you tried to visit after ten, you could end up waiting your turn for hours in the discomfort of the cramped, windowless waiting room. Waiting was an inevitable part of criminal lawyering, but keeping it to a minimum was good for the blood pressure.

The deputy searched Frank and handed him a yellow pass marked *legal visit*. The minor ambiguity of the term was a part of the charm of the place, kind of like the sign in the main waiting area for general visitation, where the hoards of family and friends waited, cash in hand, to bail out their loved ones before the weekend.

It read, RUDENESS AND VULGARITY (SWEARING) WILL BE DEALT WITH IMMEDIATELY-- BY ORDER OF THE SHERIFF.

Frank himself had sat in that smoke filled, overcrowded room more than once and wondered exactly what message the sheriff had been trying to convey.

The county sheriff was a politically astute ass kisser, but not particularly bright or knowledgeable in constitutional law. Frank thought the sign could just as easily have read ANY DISAGREEMENT WITH THE CASHIER OR DEPUTIES WILL RESULT IN SUMMARY EXECUTION OR IMPRISONMENT--BY ORDER OF THE SHERIFF.

After only a minute, a burly deputy escorted Frank to one of four private glass-partitioned interview rooms. The lawyer and inmate spoke through a wire mesh portal in the glass. No contact was allowed. If personal contact were required, arrangements had to be made in advance and the wait could be quite long. Frank figured the glass room would do, since there were no papers to be passed back and forth.

No sooner had the lawyer taken off his coat, than Sam was escorted into his side of the room and took a seat on a plain metal chair, directly across from Frank.

"Sam, its good to see you. Looks like the bologna sandwiches agree with you."

"Frank, my man. It's been awhile."

He appeared to be the same old Sam, if slightly heavier.

"If it's okay, Frank, I'm gonna get right to it. I'm in the middle here and I better just git it out."

"Go ahead, Sam. I've got all morning."

"See, I got this celly named Mookie. He been in here with me 'bout six months now, since a couple of days after I got here, I guess. Well, you know I gets my radio in here cause I minds my own business and gits along. And I'm up here one night listening to the news, talking 'bout your old lady got killed in a hit 'n run. Man was talkin 'bout how some witnesses seen a green BMW speeding out after the hit."

"Okay, Sam, so what does that have do with Mookie?" Frank queried.

"Well, my man Mookie was in here listening too. The dude got real quiet. I aksed him what was up and he just says, mind my own fucking business. He wouldn't talk after that for a long time."

"So then what happened?"

"Then, we kinda got to be homeys, you know. I done him some favors, and I think he looks at me like a father or something. You know, I scored him some shit through the guards, and got him phone calls and library passes and shit."

"Sam, get to the point, please." Frank pleaded.

"I'm getting to it Frank. Anyway, one day last week, he up and tells me he thinks he know some shit he ain't 'sposed to know. I say, I'm not sure I wanna know. But he tells me anyway. See, he got here on a regular old drug rap. But three days before that, he boosted a car from a mall in the suburbs. He did some side work for these chop-shop guys on the West Side. Well, he was driving on Lakeland close to the drop-off spot, when he got pulled over by a detective."

"So what about the detective?"

"Frank, you got a square in your pocket?"

"I haven't smoked in twenty years, Sam, but if you

just finish this story I'll bring you a whole fucking carton. Wait, Sam. How did he know the guy was a detective? I mean, maybe he was an off-duty beat cop or something."

"Frank, you knows better than that. You pretty smart for a white boy. We just knows. It's the package. The dumb motherfuckers just can't hide it. Take it to the bank, my man. If Mookie say it was a detective, it was a detective."

"Okay, go on, Sam. And I will bring you the carton."

"Deal, Frank. So my man starts to tell this detective some shit 'bout he borrowed the car from his sister, but the dude got him dead to rights because the car was registered to some rich suburb, and there was a medal with a Jewish star thing hanging from the mirror."

"So what did the cop do?" Frank asked.

"Motherfucker just starts laughing, crazy like. Mookie gits scared, like he gonna get popped. So he tells the cop where to find some guns. You know, man, it's like them motherfuckers gits points or something for every gun they bring in, even if it don't shoot."

"So what did the cop do?"

"He just keep laughing and tells old Mookie to run for his life."

"So Mookie runs?" Frank prodded.

"Fuckin-A he run, all the way to his grandmother house."

"Did he tell you what time this all happened, Sam?"

"It was a couple hours before your old lady got killed. And I know my man didn't have nothing to do with that. There's something going on here, Frank. I ain't got no idea what it is, but the cops is messed up in it.

"And by the way, Frank, my man ain't talkin' to you or nobody else 'bout this shit. He scared as a motherfucker. And you know better than to aks me to sign a statement or talk to the cops 'bout this. This is between me and you, Frank."

Frank hadn't spoken throughout Sam's running monologue. He sat stunned and motionless, as a blizzard of endless possibilities and questions overwhelmed his suddenly inadequate brain capacity. Finally, as if trying to emerge from slow motion, Frank spoke. "Okay, Sam, okay, I appreciate your telling me this. But if it's true, Sam, do you understand what it could mean?"

"Hell yes, I know. It mean the police runned over your woman!"

Frank could actually see the change in himself reflected in Sam's eyes. He was no longer Sam's friend and lawyer. There was no kindness left in the face. He saw only the face of fear itself.

"No, Sam. It could be worse than that, much, much worse," Frank mumbled.

As Frank reached the door of the small windowless visiting room, he turned back towards Sam and added, "I'll send Ray in to see the judge tomorrow morning about your murder case, to let him know I'm coming in. I'll be back to talk to you about it whenever I can."

"Frank, the squares?"

"Yeah, I'll have somebody bring them over today."

Chapter Six

The drive back to his office was a blur, and by the time he opened the door to suite 216, Frank had no memory whatsoever of how he had gotten from the jail to his office. As he entered, he said hello to Nora and went straight inside to his sofa. The greeting was distant and ritualistic, not at all a product of the genuine affection he felt for her. He had no idea if he had actually seen her.

It had all been over, he thought, but it wasn't over. No matter what came of this new information it wasn't over.

As twilight darkened his inner sanctum, the lawyer's mind wrestled with the husband's flood of emotions and confusion. He was oblivious to Nora's absence, though she had said goodnight some ninety minutes earlier.

It was after nine when the lawyer, victorious for the moment, rose and moved silently in the dark towards his desk. He lit the single desktop reading lamp, picked up the handset and dialed.

"Hello."

"Ray, I need you in here, bro."

"Frank, if it's a night bond hearing, I gotta say no this time."

"No, Ray. It's not a bond hearing, and it's not till tomorrow morning, say seven-thirty."

"You got it, Frank. Later."

Frank disconnected with his finger, then dialed

again. Four rings and a click, then Frank braced himself for the most obnoxious and irritating recorded message he had ever heard.

The answering machine, he knew from personal knowledge, to be perhaps the last surviving Bell Telephone desktop machine, manufactured circa 1978. Bell Telephone had not even existed since the breakup of AT&T in 1984.

The first sound, he knew, was not a voice, but the sound of Mrs. Stavros Panos, age seventy-four, in the background, doing dishes and humming the title song from *Camelot*. Then came the voice of Stavros himself.

"You have reached Stavros Panos, Private Detective. I, er, we are not here at this present moment...."

At this point the static on the 1978 full size cassette tape garbles the remainder of the message, and one listens carefully for a sound resembling a beep. If one is fortunate enough to hear the beep, the message is apparently fully retrievable by Stavros. Frank heard the beep on the first try.

"Steve, it's Frank. I need to see you in my office tomorrow at seven-thirty. Its personal and its important. Thanks Steve."

Stavros Panos was no fool. Along with Ray Paxon, he was one of the half dozen or so men Frank truly respected and trusted. Stavros, or Steve as his friends knew him, didn't work full time at age seventy-five because he craved the excitement. He needed the money to live, pure and simple. He had run a PI agency from the same office down the hall from Frank for the past forty-seven years.

In the late 1960's, he became a polygraphist and, by the close of the 70's, had become one of the most respected and sought after lie detector experts in the country.

He had worked routinely on some of the highest profile criminal cases, administering lie detector exams for both the prosecution and defense on a nearly equal basis. When added to the lucrative low-end market for testing prospective private sector employees and the ongoing PI business, this cushion provided Steve with a comfortable life through his forties. But in the 1980's, a rash of lawsuits and legislation restricting polygraphs as a condition of private employment reduced his income by more than half.

By the time Steve had rebuilt the PI business around 1988, his daughter's husband had booked up to the Bahamas with his personal trainer, leaving her with four small kids and a big mortgage. Steve and his wife never complained. In fact, to talk to them you'd think they were grateful. They paid the mortgage, raised the kids, and sent three of them to college.

Not that Steve was a saint. Frank had come to believe, after some years of casual conversations, that Steve's wisdom was born of experience, that is to say in the words of Oscar Wilde, *life's biggest mistakes*. It was clear that Steve would have done some things differently when his kids were young. Frank figured that raising the grandchildren had been a second chance for Steve, kind of an opportunity for redemption. What was most impressive was that he had not squandered it, but seized it like a winning lottery ticket.

Now here they were, in their mid-seventies and living hand to mouth. Perhaps the most remarkable thing to Frank was how Steve still threw himself into the work with such effort and enthusiasm. Steve had worked with him on some very difficult and even dangerous cases over the years. Although he was obviously a great detective in the old tradition, Steve had a leg up on the competition. His son, George, was a detective sergeant with the city police, and had quietly supervised the Cold Case Unit since 1995.

The old man had been hurt when, following a hitch in the army, young George had legally changed his family name to the anglicized *Payne*. Steve had eventually managed to get past it, however, and the two had grown steadily closer with each passing year.

On balance, Frank had years ago judged Stavros Panos to be a man of common sense and uncommonly sound judgment.

The first one in the office the next morning was Ray Paxon. He was sitting at his desk, door open, in the little cubby hole office on the other side of Nora's work area. Frank had been renting the office to Ray for over two years now, although he couldn't actually remember ever receiving a rent payment.

The truth was it pleased Frank to have Ray around. As a general rule, Ray would go anywhere and do anything Frank asked him. As another rule, Frank only gave him the "garbage" cases or assignments that Frank would rather not do himself. It was a mutually beneficial arrangement. Ray got a free office and some extra money, and Frank, well, he got Ray.

The two first met in 1995 when they happened to represent co-defendants in what is commonly referred to in the criminal courts building as a drive-by murder. Although somewhat self-explanatory, the term usually refers to a garden variety case where members of one drug-dealing street gang, at war with or retaliating against another such gang, load into a car and drive to the territory or street corner of that gang.

Upon approaching the objective, the passengers of the vehicle generally identify any poor unsuspecting souls standing or walking in the area as offending members of the rival gang. Age and gender are generally not factors to be considered in the determination.

Semi-automatic handguns and machine pistols are then quickly distributed among the passengers from under the seats, and hundreds of bullets are sprayed in a multi-directional random pattern. Occasionally, a deserving gangbanger is felled by the onslaught, but more often than not, at least one of the bullets finds an innocent child or senior citizen sleeping in his bed.

Although such cases had become somewhat routine for Frank Doherty, it became clear to him from the beginning of that particular case that young Ray Paxon, although enthusiastic and energetic, was perhaps completely without experience in such matters. His two years as a suburban police officer in the 1990's had never exposed him to urban violence.

The younger lawyer at the time was employed by a considerably less reputable, if more experienced lawyer, named Norman Medelski, who spent most of his time and much of his money making TV commercials. The commercials were sleazy, even by lawyer standards, and usually played in the early morning hours on UHF and local cable channels. Frank had seen them a few times during insomnia-driven encounters with Matt Dillon.

In any event, Medelski had paid Ray next to nothing, and every time any real legal work was required, the kid would find the file on his desk.

It was clear to Frank that Ray Paxon had big balls and knew how to make the best of a bad situation.

With a little help from a friend, he had fumbled his way to an acquittal on the murder case and from there he was on his way. A year later, he finally took Frank's advice and struck out on his own. The kid had become a great lawyer and was an irrepressible optimist. Frank liked him and didn't hide it.

"Good morning, Ray."

"Hey, Frank, what's up?" He was already up and moving on Frank with his coffee cup.

"Let me get some coffee and we'll give Steve a few minutes. He's been pretty slow getting down that hallway lately."

"Don't let him hear you say that."

"Don't let who hear you say what?"

They turned to see the lumbering Greek emerging from behind the open door. Frank noticed the cane and couldn't remember if it was something new or if he just hadn't noticed it before. Best to let it go for now.

"Sit down boys. I've got quite a story to tell you about my trip to the jail yesterday."

They sat and Frank talked. He told them every word of his conversation with Sam. When he was finished, their absolute silence betrayed a clear understanding of the perilous road ahead.

"Well, that's it, so what do you think?" They had to start somewhere.

"Frank, how do we know this guy Mookie didn't just do it himself? I mean, I'm just thinking out loud, Frank, but the whole thing seems crazy." Ray had decided to at least start the speculation.

"Well," Steve said, "we know beyond a doubt that they found the burned out BMW that killed Denise. It seems the first thing we do is figure if there's a way to check this guy's story, I mean, to see if he's telling the truth. If he is, then we find out if we're talking about the same car. I mean, he might be telling the truth, but we're talking about a different green BMW."

"Okay, could be there's a way to do both at the same time." Every long journey started with a first step and it sounded to the two older men like Ray was about to take it. "Frank, did you get a look at the forensics report on the car?"

"A good look. The cops were open about allowing me access to the reports. Why?"

"Well, did it say anything about the Star of David on the mirror?" Ray asked.

"No. I already thought about that. It's not in there, but on second thought, I see where you're going. It's just a report intended to be a summary of the forensic examiner's findings. It's not meant to be a verbatim thing. There have to be notes."

"You would think," Steve mumbled.

"Those stay with the examiner or in his personal computer files," Ray said. "Of course, they might review their notes with the cops by phone or something, but the cops don't get those unless they are subpoenaed by the state."

"As I recall," Frank added, "the report in this case was done by a Laura something or other. She's good. I've crossed her on the stand a few times. But as I recall, the report was completely unremarkable. They found no latent prints suitable for comparison and no fiber evidence. Blood traces matching Denise's were found on the front end. There were traces of accelerant, but no mention of a medal or a star or anything like that."

"Of course not, Frank," Ray interjected. "But if it was in the car, it could be in her notes. And since it wasn't in the report, we know it was never in the news media."

"We gotta get access to the notes, Frank," said the old Greek. "If it's in the notes, then our man Mookie is legit and it's the same car. He couldn't have known about the star unless he saw it."

Ray had gotten the train out of the station and Frank tried to keep it moving. "The question is how do we do that? If the cops don't have the notes in their file, even Steve's kid can't get them for us."

Steve piped in. "Getting background checks on mopes is one thing, but don't think my cop son would be too eager to help his Papa once he found out we were looking at cops. Besides, even if he wanted to help, I'm not too crazy about seeing him lose his job. If we get something concrete, then okay. But I can't go to him on a fishing trip."

"Steve's right. George can't help us here," offered Frank. "So I'll just waltz in and see this Laura and ask her for the notes."

"Excuse me for saying so, Frank, but I think you've been hanging around young Ray too long," Steve observed. "For starters, she's going to want to know why you need to see the notes. What are you gonna tell her? The truth? If you can't charm her into giving you the notes, she'll be on the phone with the cops the second you leave her office. This could get very dangerous very quickly. No offense, Frank, but charming beautiful women is more in the old Greek's area of expertise."

"How do you know she's good looking?" It was a question Ray just couldn't help asking.

"I didn't say good looking. I said beautiful. The very term *good looking*, my young friend, betrays a shallowness, a kind of compulsive need for status and self-indulgence which my psyche does not require.

"*Beauty*, on the other hand, is a word that explores and considers the very depth and individuality of the soul. All women are beautiful, young Raymond, and until you fully comprehend the difference between those terms, your education continues."

"No, I'll do it Steve," Frank intervened. "Despite my lack of charm, the truth is exactly what I'm going to tell her, as much of it as we know anyway."

"If she does make the call, it will work to our advantage, but you're right, Steve. It will be very dangerous for all of us. Whoever is involved will be scared to death and they will have to make a move."

"Look, Frank," Ray offered, recovering from his recent embarrassment. "Nobody has even mentioned it yet, but I can only think of one reason why the cops would have been involved in the death of your wife. It has to somehow be linked to the disappearance of your niece. I mean it has to be some kind of cover-up or something."

"I've thought a lot about that myself," Frank admitted. "They have to be linked. There's no other possibility. She's the only one who saw the guy Caroline left the bar with. It has to be about him."

Steve wasn't finished yet. "There's another way, Frank. We make this guy Mookie talk. There are a dozen ways we could do it, even in jail. The easiest way is just to tell him we're gonna report his story to the cops and ask for an investigation. If the cops are involved, he wouldn't live until morning and he knows it. He'll talk if we promise to keep it quiet. After he puts it all on paper, we turn it over to the FBI and ask for a quiet investigation."

"A quiet investigation? Of what?" Frank replied.

"Even the FBI needs a place to start. Just exactly what can he tell them? That one city cop out of fourteen thousand took a stolen car from him, a car that matches the description of a hit and run vehicle?

"Even if they did investigate, it would require such a high profile, widespread investigation that Mookie would not only die, but the people who killed my wife would cover their tracks and go to ground. No, Steve, we have to make them believe that the threat to their safety is limited and containable. If they believe that, then they will show themselves."

"I'm in, Frank." Ray stood as he spoke, leaning slightly forward with a grimacing look of determination and a clinched fist.

"I know, Ray, Thanks, but you have a wedding scheduled in July, if I recall. Make no mistake, I need your help on this, but I don't want you up front. Do you understand?"

"You got it, Frank, but I've got one more question. If this Mookie is on target, how does he know it was a detective and not just some plainclothes or off duty cop.?"

"That's a key question. He says he can tell the difference. Most of these guys can. He claims he saw the shield, and we just have to make that leap. The chances of him making an ID are almost non-existent unless we find a way to narrow down the suspects for him. There must be over five hundred detectives. We've got to flush this guy out."

Steve nodded. "Agreed."

"Eventually, one of us has to talk to Mookie, but not until I see what happens at the forensics lab. We'll probably get only one shot at gaining his cooperation, and I'd like to have as much information as possible when we take it. Besides, if we start visiting him regularly, it will raise suspicion and put Mookie and Sam in danger, probably us too."

"Okay," Ray added.

"We could be in the shit anyway," Frank pointed out, "the moment this Laura makes the call. If Mookie is right, and the cops are involved, there's nothing they won't do to protect themselves."

"But they don't know about Mookie," Steve offered.

"More to the point, they don't know we have him. They have no idea where he is for the moment. But remember, if she makes the phone call they'll find out pretty quickly. Let's not help them. Everybody just sit tight while we see what develops.

"By the way, you should both know his real name is Melvin Lockett and he's in Division Eleven."

Frank ended the meeting by heading for the coat rack behind the door. "I'm going over to the crime lab and shake the tree. See you later, Ray. Wanna take a ride, Steve?"

"Okay, boss." Steve was already limping towards the door, coat in hand.

Chapter Seven

Laura Stanic was a first generation Serbian-American, and was employed by the state at its Forensics Laboratory. Her official title was Forensics Examiner, a job that most people commonly associated with the terms Criminalist or Forensic Scientist. Although she was not actually a scientist in the traditional sense, she held a Bachelor's of Science in Cell Biology.

As a young girl, Laura had been drawn to science and had shown great promise and inventiveness. Many people who knew her growing up, not the least of whom was her own mother, had assumed that Laura would become a doctor or make her mark in some field of science, real science. She was the first in her extended family to have earned a four-year university degree and had become somewhat of a celebrity in the tightly knit Serbian-American community.

Down at the Serbian church in the Bryantville neighborhood, her proud father, Milan Stanic, did little to discourage the common belief that his youngest daughter was a *scientist* of the first order, hot on the trail of some monumental discovery that would dramatically impact the welfare of the species. Life had dealt her other cards, however, and she had played them admirably.

The term *Forensic Science* really just describes a concept in which all of the known sciences might be applied in some way to serve the law. Her science background made her particularly suited to the job, and many of her peers also held a degree in some related field of science. The job itself, however, spanned a broad spectrum of science and did not touch upon theory or experimentation in any way.

Mostly, she performed analytical testing according to narrowly defined guidelines and conditions. These days, ninety-five percent of the work involved testing for narcotics.

Five of her thirty-three years had been spent on this job, and in that time, she had come to view her work as more akin to that of a produce manager at the supermarket, weighing tomatoes and checking for blemishes.

Laura had decided for herself years ago that the job didn't require any real scientific background. On occasion, however, they actually did receive some interesting and difficult evidentiary problems, and those assignments generally landed on her lab table. She was always grateful for the challenge and the opportunity to exercise her mind.

On that particular Friday morning, Laura was engaged in her customary ritual of analyzing suspected cocaine when she received a page from the administrative office. The numerical symbol "24" in her pager meant *call the main office*. These little police customs had always irritated her, but she had come to accept them and played the game quietly.

This particular call concerned her because it was just the right time for Alex's school to call informing her that he had a headache, or had thrown up and had to be picked up from school. It would be unusual for anyone else to call her at work. It was shaping up to be a bad day. Laura picked up the phone and dialed the receptionist. "Hello, this is Laura Stanic. I believe I have a phone call."

"No ma'am. You have a visitor, a Mr. Frank Doherty. He's a lawyer."

"What kind of lawyer?" It was the first thing she thought of in response to the news. It was rare, but not unheard of, for an Assistant State's Attorney to come over to the lab to discuss a case. Surely, if that were the case, he would have called first, she thought.

"I have his card, Ms. Stanic. I believe he's just a private lawyer. There's no indication he works for any government agency."

Laura thought for a moment and then responded. "Ask him to wait. I'll be right down."

No doubt, it was curiosity that fashioned her decision. An otherwise monotonous day on the cocaine assembly line might offer some small bit of intellectual stimulation. *Who knows? Maybe it isn't about work at all. Maybe somebody died and left me a million dollars.*

She stepped off the elevator directly into the foyer of the seventeen-story building. The receptionist's desk was located in the center of the room, directly in front of her. To her left, facing parallel to the elevator bank, were two rows of connected, plastic bucket-type chairs.

She looked immediately to her left and saw Frank. He was the sole occupant of the small waiting area. She was well behind his field of vision to the right, but could see him clearly. The lawyer was wearing a plain navy blue suit. He carried no briefcase or papers of any kind. Most significantly, his crossed legs revealed the intricately stitched western design on the upper portion of his shiny black cowboy boots. This was no corporate lawyer either.

After studying him for a moment longer, Laura

walked towards him, circling slightly at first to bring herself into his field of vision. By the time she reached him, Frank was already on his feet offering his hand.

"Frank Doherty, Ms. Stanic. Thank you for agreeing to see me."

"It's quite all right, Mr. Doherty. I must confess that unannounced visits from private lawyers are something of an oddity around here. What I'm saying is that whatever the reason for this visit, simple curiosity is the reason I'm here. There's a small cafeteria on the second floor. We could get coffee and talk there if you like."

There was no attempt at conversation between the two until Laura had paid the cashier for the two cups of coffee and they were seated at an empty rectangular table in the corner of the room.

"So, Mr. Doherty, if I had to guess, I would say you are a criminal defense lawyer, and you came to talk about a forensics report I prepared for a case against your client."

"Very astute, Ms. Stanic," he replied.

"Then perhaps I can save you some time. We have a protocol regarding these contacts. I must advise my supervisor of the contact. Since I am a potential witness against your client, you, as the defendant's attorney, have the right to talk to me about my testimony. I, on the other hand, do not have the obligation to talk to you, but may do so if I wish. Well, Mr. Doherty, I do not wish. So, tell me, does that about cover it?"

"Not quite. You're very perceptive and I am a criminal defense lawyer, but I'm not here about a client."

It was in that instant that she realized who he was, and she knew how deeply insensitive her remarks must have seemed.

Frank exploited the opening. "My wife was killed

by a hit and run driver six months ago and you handled the forensic evidence in the case. I'm here to ask you some questions about your report, but it's apparent that you're not comfortable talking to defense lawyers so maybe I'll just go."

"I'm very sorry, Mr. Doherty. I know exactly who you are, and I remember the case well. I'd be happy to help you if I can."

"Let me come right to the point then. It's come to my attention that the BMW you examined might have contained some kind of religious object attached to the driver's mirror. It could have been the Star of David. There's nothing about it in your report, and I wondered if you could confirm or deny that fact."

"It's a very unusual request, Mr. Doherty, and, frankly, it suggests to me that there is some kind of parallel investigation being conducted. I'm afraid you'll need to tell me a lot more about what's going on before I'd be prepared to answer a question like that."

"Look, Ms. Stanic, I don't know you from Adam, but at some point I have to trust somebody, so I'll tell you everything I know. I think there's a good chance that one or more police officers were directly involved in the death of my wife."

Frank then told her everything he knew, withholding only the names and locations of his witnesses. He told her about Caroline's disappearance while in the company of Denise and about the young man in the club. He told her Mookie's whole story about the BMW and the Star of David. Frank even gave her a copy of the computer composite picture of the suspected abductor, which had been created with Denise's help.

"Ms. Stanic, understand that I didn't choose you to

confide in. Circumstances chose you. I just have nowhere else to go right now. When my wife was killed, I suspected a connection right away. I told that to the police and the FBI, but it was too speculative for them. They wouldn't treat the cases as related without evidence of a connection. All the evidence indicated Denise's death was a simple hit and run."

She said nothing.

"Well, now I have evidence, Ms. Stanic, real evidence, only I can't go to the police because they're involved. I can't go to the FBI because my informant won't talk to them. The bottom line is that, for now, I have to do this myself, and I can't do it without the help of a perfect stranger. So will you tell me what the notes say?"

"It's all very interesting, Mr. Doherty, but I could lose my job for doing what you ask. More to the point, if your suspicions about the car were to be confirmed, how do I know this criminal who is accusing the police didn't just do it himself?"

"I guess I'm just asking you to trust me when I say he didn't."

"That's not good enough, Mr. Doherty. I'll have to think about this. I have your card."

"May I at least have your assurance that you won't tell the police about my visit?"

"Good day, Mr. Doherty." She was already standing with her hand extended.

She was already on the phone with Detective Matthew Corliss as Frank pulled out from the parking lot.

Just before three that afternoon, Corliss and another detective appeared at Frank's office.

The lawyer was surprised it had taken Corliss so

long. After only a minute, Frank came out into the waiting area and politely greeted the portly black detective.

"Hello, Frank. This is my sometime partner, Detective Hartman. We'd like very much to speak to you for a minute, if you don't mind."

Hartman did not acknowledge the introduction and made no move to offer his hand in greeting.

Frank escorted the two men into his office.

As he took a seat across from Frank's desk, however, Corliss attempted to seize the initiative from the lawyer immediately. "I need to know what's going on, Frank. I received some startling information today."

Frank's worst fears were confirmed. The cat was surely out of the bag. He had not, however, given sufficient consideration to how he would handle the emboldened Corliss. "I'm not sure I understand, Detective." With those few words, Frank had claimed his ground in this dispute and knew that it would be difficult to hold.

"Don't play with me, Frank. We want to know how you got the information about the Star of David. We want everything you have, Frank, and we want it now."

It was no accident that Corliss had used the word "we" three times. It was a thinly veiled message that all the considerable resources of the state would be employed to power a legal jackhammer over Frank Doherty's head, if necessary.

"I don't know what you're talking about, Corliss. If you're referring to my private conversation with Laura Stanic, it didn't involve anything about a Star of David, or whatever it is you're talking about. I was simply asking her if there were any details her notes could add to the investigation."

Frank would simply deny the conversation ever took place, and it would be his word against Laura's.

"You're playing a very dangerous game, Frank, and there will be many interested spectators."

Frank wondered immediately whether the remark had been intended as standard police intimidation or something a bit more personal.

The two detectives rose abruptly and left Frank's office unescorted, with Corliss convinced that the lawyer was deliberately withholding key evidence, and frustrated by the knowledge that threats and intimidation were pointless in his efforts to obtain it.

Ray Paxon had seen the detectives go into Frank's office and could barely restrain himself until they were gone. The moment they reached the hallway, Ray was out of his little cubbyhole, across the secretarial area and through Frank's open door before the older man had even reached his sofa.

"Was that who I think it was?" Ray asked, clearly suspecting the implications of the visit.

"Yeah, Matt Corliss. He's assigned to investigate Denise's case, and at the moment, he's very unhappy," answered Frank, by then lying prone on the sofa, eyes closed, though never more alert.

"So what's it all mean?" Ray asked, though he had pretty much figured it out.

"The lab tech probably called him before I left the building. Mookie's telling the truth and the car he stole was the same one used by a cop to kill Denise. Otherwise, I couldn't really say."

"What's our next move then?"

As Ray finished the question, Frank rose and moved towards his desk. "Well, first I'm gonna take some

Motrin for this goddamn back pain. Then, I guess we'll just wait and see what happens. If all goes according to our somewhat loosely structured plan, our next move should be a reaction to someone else. For now though, I'm going to call my sister-in-law and tell her everything I know. She has a right to be informed, and may even want to be here when this thing breaks."

It was already ten minutes past shift change when Corliss arrived back at the office. He was scheduled to be off the next two days and decided not to let his report wait until then. He could easily reconstruct the report accurately from his notes, but wanted it on file on the chance it might help someone else shake the information loose from Frank Doherty.

He completed and entered the report in less than thirty minutes and, as required, faxed a copy to the Internal Affairs Division, which would no doubt monitor the case, but defer investigation of police involvement pending the development of solid evidence. He then placed a call to Larry Califf, the young detective whom he knew had been working the missing persons case on the niece.

Corliss pulled a filtered cigarette from the half empty pack on his desk and began patting his pockets in a vain attempt to find a match, when a full book of the things landed dead center on his desk from the left. He nodded to Lonnie Hartman at the next desk over, the phone held between his ear and his shoulder, as he lit the cigarette and flung back the matches with equal accuracy.

Corliss had considered calling the FBI first, but knew from experience that nothing would come of the call without hard evidence. They wouldn't even seriously investigate a possible link based on nothing more than a *he said she said* conversation. Besides, nobody in his right mind wanted the FBI investigating cops.

Califf had begun his afternoon shift only a half-hour before and was still sitting at his desk when the phone rang. "Califf here."

"Califf, this is Corliss over at Homicide/Violent Crimes. How you doin?"

"I'm okay, and what can we underlings in Missing Persons do for the *real* detectives this fine afternoon?"

Corliss took no offense. "I know that you're handling the FBI scraps on that Caroline Anderson case, the niece of the defense lawyer. I'm the primary on the hit and run death of his wife. I wanted to fill you in on a possible connection."

Califf was all ears for the next ten minutes as the older man recalled from his notes the interview with Laura Stanic. He told Califf everything he knew, even Doherty's suspicion of police involvement.

As he listened, Califf took notes and noted questions. "Then there can be virtually no doubt that whoever Doherty's informant is, he was in or near the car that killed Denise before the accident."

"Had to be," said Corliss. "The woman says that, according to Doherty, the guy was laying right on the hood over the front bumper and there was no damage, but like I say, the whole thing's just hearsay that Doherty will deny. Hell, he's already denied it," Corliss added. "There were no witnesses to the conversation. We have no clue who the actual witness is. We can fuck with Doherty a little, but he knows that if he just keeps it one against one, he won't face any serious problems."

"Not unless there really are cops involved," responded Califf. "I know Doherty. He's cocky for an old fart, but very clever. If he really believes there are cops involved, and I think he does, then he's fully aware that he's putting himself in danger. Could be he's just made a calculated decision to stir up the pot and risk being blown away. I mean, it was his wife, for Christ sake. I'd probably do the same thing."

"So what you got in mind?" Corliss asked.

"The bottom line is we know he's onto something or he couldn't possibly have known about that Star of David thing. If you don't mind, I'd like to talk to him about this. I think Doherty and I have established a pretty good working relationship."

"Be my guest, but I'd say you're just pissing up a rope. Fuck, for all I know, the guy killed his own wife and is just trying to deflect suspicion."

It was more an expression of Corliss's frustration than a serious suggestion. Califf did not reply.

Chapter Eight

Brad Parkins' cell phone rang only moments after he left the office en route to an early dinner engagement with Meg at her favorite Italian restaurant downtown.

"Mr. Parkins, I hope I'm not disturbing you," came the sarcastic voice on the other end.

"Frankly, Hartman, speaking to you is always a disturbance. Our business has been pretty much concluded, and I'll contact you as soon as your package arrives, so—"

Hartman interrupted. "Oh, it's not about that package you owe me, you cheap, lying piece of shit."

Although the words were harsh, the voice was still sarcastically pleasant and even jovial. It's no wonder, since he was about to ruin Brad's plan to spend the entire evening enjoying the perks of his vaulted position.

"Seems a mutual problem of ours just won't go away. We have to talk now."

"All right, I'll be at The Little Village on Walker Street. Meg is with me. We're about ten minutes away. See you there."

Brad and Meg were seated at a corner table in the near dark restaurant and still working on their first cocktail when Brad spotted the detective surveying the main dining room from the bar entrance.

Before Brad could leave the chair, Hartman was halfway to the table, taking the most direct route at the expense of several jostled patrons with spilled drinks. He could easily have waited at the bar, Brad thought.

"Mr. Commissioner, I don't believe I've had the pleasure." Hartman hadn't taken his eyes off Meg, even while speaking to Brad.

It was a look that made her skin crawl.

"Meg Lofton, Detective Lonnie Hartman. Now, if you'll excuse us, my dear, I need to talk some business with the detective at the bar. It won't be long. I'll see that the waiter brings you another drink."

Brad had warned her as best he could that the detective he was meeting was somewhat crude and might even be visibly upset. He was supposedly angry over some new administrative policy that would likely result in the loss of his wife's job.

"Sorry to interrupt your dinner, Ms. Lofton. I will do my best to keep the disruption to a minimum."

Brad didn't want to make her privy to his business with Hartman, although she had broken more than a few laws herself in the course of their relationship. Meg would put up with all of it, however, until that next step up the corporate ladder. The big promotion she was expecting at any time would involve a transfer to corporate headquarters in Dallas. Until it came, Meg Lofton wouldn't be a problem.

As promised, the waiter promptly delivered a second vodka martini as the two men conversed in the bar.

"So what's the urgent problem?" Brad queried in a purposefully condescending tone.

"Well, Mr. Commissioner, seems I fucked up, but then what can you expect from a disgruntled employee? You know, they say a happy worker is a productive worker. I think that was the Japanese."

"Get to the point, Hartman." It had taken a while but Brad was losing his patience.

"Doherty has a witness," offered Hartman, in a noticeably more serious tone. "I know his face but not his name. He's some punk who had stolen the car I used to do the Doherty woman. Doherty now knows his wife was murdered and there was at least one cop involved. I guess the worst part is that the mope can probably identify me."

"You are some piece of work, Hartman. You mean you stole the car from a car thief and you left him out there without any idea what his name is?"

"Or where he is," Hartman admitted." Doherty's sitting on him somewhere. I'm pretty sure he won't let the guy surface until he knows who was involved. The last thing he'd do his turn his witness over to the police, so it looks like we've got some time."

"We've got time? Thanks to your stupidity, this whole thing could come apart at any moment, you moron. You find out who that witness is, and you take care of it now! And do it right this time."

Before Brad was even finished speaking, he saw the sarcastic detective begin to morph into the beast that had nearly ended his life in the church. Hartman spoke much too quietly, face flushed and eyes bulging with anger.

"I'll do it, Parkins. I'll do it for myself because it has to be done. I'm gonna survive this thing no matter what it takes. Just remember, when it's over, I'm gonna come looking for my money and you'll give me every penny of it, or I'll take fifty-grand worth of pleasure by ripping every limb and external organ from your living body."

As he drove towards his near north apartment, Hartman tried his level best to be the detective, fully aware that the grave personal risk he faced could easily affect his professional skills and judgment. He would need both to survive this crisis.

He forced himself to examine the facts analytically, hoping for some clue that would help him find the young car thief, now turned informant.

"Okay," he said to himself as loudly as if he were speaking to a back seat passenger. Over the years, he had solved scores of serious crimes using this unorthodox method in which he would simulate a discussion between two detectives by asking himself questions and then answering them.

"What do we know?"

"We know Doherty has the whole story of you stealing the car."

"So what does that mean?"

"It means that he definitely has talked to the mope you shagged off the street that night."

"Then when did he talk to him?"

"That's an interesting question. His wife was killed six months ago. This is the kind of information he would have acted on immediately, so it's safe to say that he only talked to the guy within the last few days."

"Can you learn anything about who the guy is from that time lapse?"

"Well, Doherty meets lots of scumbags in his business. Generally, they are all clients or the family members of clients. It could be this is a guy that Doherty just recently picked up as a client, and in talking to him, the subject just came up somehow. On the other hand, it could be an old client who pieced it together from the newspapers, and is trying to sell the information to Doherty. Either way, a client is the key."

"Good, but what do we do about it? How do we find out which client?"

"That's simple enough. Find out what clients he has talked to lately, new and old. Get inside his office and look at his newest files. He must have some kind of Rolodex or computerized numerical index of clients. Look at his phone message pad to see which clients have called him lately. Look at his daily diary to see who he's been meeting and where."

"I always said you were a fucking genius."

The Monday after his rather abbreviated meeting with Detective Corliss, Frank was completing a witness cross-examination in the bench trial of an alleged carjacker. The woman was a nervous wreck, and the more Frank pushed, the more she buckled. As his relentless questioning began to focus in on the circumstances of the line-up identification, his silent pager began to vibrate.

Nora never worked on Tuesdays and Thursdays, so the calls were forwarded to a digital paging service. As he turned from the witness and walked back towards the podium, he discreetly checked the pager; *Larry Califf Re: need to meet*. Califf's pager number followed the message. It would be an hour before Frank would be able to return the call.

At the same moment Frank was reading the digital message, Lonnie Hartman was seated comfortably at the lawyer's desk in the reclining swivel back leather chair. He had completed his careful search of the secretarial area, including computerized records of appointments, court appearances, and new files for the previous two weeks.

The Rolodex on Frank's desk seemed to correspond

exactly to the computer records of clients. It even included office file numbers and circuit court case numbers, wherever applicable.

Finally, he turned his attention to Frank's personal appointment diary, a leather bound volume, opened to the current date, too big to be carried around in the lawyer's briefcase. His attention was drawn immediately to the notation for January 28, 2000. It read *Sam Walker/county jail/D32417*.

Walker was a client, but had no active file. Hartman thought the appointment could be about an old case. But he thought the notation might be personal, since it appeared to be the only entry that had not been duplicated both in the computer and in the secretary's book. It even told Hartman where to find the guy. He had uncovered several possible leads, but he would no doubt start with Sam Walker. Hartman pocketed the small notebook and checked the office to make sure nothing was disturbed.

Satisfied, he walked confidently into the hallway, careful to lock the door behind him. Unlocking the forty-odd year old door lock with his confiscated lock picks had been nearly as effortless, he thought. Everything would be nice and tidy when Mr. Doherty returned from court.

At about half past four, court was recessed for the day and the two lawyers began packing their files and notes into the large hard-sided briefcase that Frank referred to as *the box*.

As they did so, Larry Califf approached from the gallery and took them by surprise.

"I was about to return your page, Detective. How did you know I was here?"

"It's the detective training, all very secret. You

know, I kinda felt sorry for that woman. I've been where she was, and I can't help but question why you do it. I mean, she was robbed and thrown out of her own car onto the street. Do you think she really deserved that kind of treatment from you?"

"I don't think about that," said Frank. "I'm a professional. I never get emotionally involved in a case. I guess I'm the same as you in that regard, Larry. Personal feelings just aren't a problem."

There was nothing philosophical about the answer. It was personal and intentionally offensive. Even though Califf didn't respond, Frank could see that the younger man had been hurt by it, and decided to backtrack.

"Look, I'm sorry Larry. That was unfair. There was a time not so long ago when I would have relished a question like that. I felt it gave me a chance to defend the Bill of Rights against attack. I'm not sure how I feel now, about anything, but I'll make you a deal. If you stop judging me by the way I earn my living, I'll give you the same consideration."

"Fair enough. Can we go for a cup of coffee?"

"Make it a beer and I'll go, but Ray goes too. You never know when I'll need a witness to what I didn't say."

The bar was a ground level storefront place in the building across the street. It was a kind of after work quickie place that closed at eight every night and was fairly crowded.

Frank managed to get two draft beers and a coke for Califf without much of a wait and the three men made their way to a corner, which looked like the quietest place available. There were two empty bar stools around one of those small round bar-like tables. Frank motioned for the other men to be seated, explaining that the stools tended to aggravate his back pain.

"Frank, I'm sure you already know I had a talk with the detective handling your wife's case, and I was hoping for a chance to change your mind about this."

"I'm listening, Larry." His response was genuine.

"We don't know for certain that Caroline's dead. On the off chance that she's not, how can you justify withholding critical information from the police?"

The older man figured that Califf had decided to simply out-lawyer the lawyer. "Simple, Larry. First off, we both know she's dead. Secondly, if she is alive, telling the cops what I know won't help her. It's the cops we're afraid of here. Let's put it this way. Can you guarantee me right now that no cops are involved in my wife's death? If you can't, then can you guarantee me that the guilty cop or cops won't get access to your report?"

"I guarantee you that nobody can get access to what I don't disclose."

"So, do I understand you're giving me your word that, if I tell you what I know, it will stay between you and me? You're willing to violate policy here?"

"I'm willing to do whatever it takes to get to the bottom of this business. Yes to your first question."

"I believe you, Larry. The trouble is, official or unofficial, you're still a detective, and the first thing you'd do is go and talk to the witness. The problem is he's not ready to talk right now. He'll talk once we get a handle on this thing and find out who's involved. Then we can at least keep him safe, but if you go talk to him now, he'll just clam up forever."

"What if I didn't go as a cop? What if I went with you sort of as your gopher or something? I'd get to talk to him and you can't deny the value of my help. How else would you get access to photos of five hundred detectives and their areas of assignment? We might get lucky and get an ID without all the leg work."

"I like it and I'd like to do it right now, but you can't go dressed like that. This guy Mookie was born on the street and you know what that means."

"Let me guess. No lawyer worth his salt would dress in a detective's uniform of khaki cotton slacks with a short sleeve white shirt and rep tie," answered the young detective, with a disarmingly pleasant smile.

"Exactly, so from here you'd better go home and replace that detective outfit with some jeans and a pullover. That's assuming you don't have a decent suit and some cowboy boots. Either way, lose those clunky black shoes and meet me at the jail around seven tonight," Frank said, as he signaled the bartender for one last round.

"One's enough for me, boss. See you later boys," said Califf as he headed towards the door.

"What do you think of him, Ray?" Frank asked, having just returned from the bar with two fresh beers.

"It's not really my call, Frank, and if you really needed my opinion, you wouldn't have trusted all our lives to him without asking me first."

"Hold on, Ray. I don't know where this is going, but in case you hadn't noticed, I haven't exactly been brimming with self-confidence lately. I've been neglecting my business. The babysitter put the kids to bed twice already this week, and I shouldn't even be in a tavern right now. I need your help, Ray, but if you want out, say so. It won't affect our friendship."

"Bullshit, Frank, bullshit! I don't want out. I want in, *in* Frank. Do you know what that means? Do you have any idea?" Ray shouted above the noise of the jukebox and the after work drinkers.

"I don't know what you're talking about," Frank

said, gesturing with his palms.

"You're just a sentimental slob, Frank. Let's just drink up and go meet Dick Tracy at the jail," Ray said, shaking his head and uttering a sigh of frustration.

It was just before seven when Frank turned into the jail parking lot and spotted Larry Califf getting out of his car. He had opted for the casual look. Frank was satisfied. In all his years in the business, Frank had never seen a detective working in white gym shoes before.

The plan was that Ray would have Sam called down for a lawyer visit in another room at the same time and tip him off about the plan.

Frank understood that Sam would feel betrayed, but he had to be expecting it. Hopefully, Sam would just look at it as paying Frank's fee for the murder case.

They all pretty much knew that Mookie was a thief and con man, with no interest in violence, but he would likely be upset after the visit, and Frank wanted Sam to know it was coming.

The two men were seated in the small room, south of the glass partition, when Mookie entered and settled onto the stool in front of the window.

"Mookie, I'm Frank Doherty, a friend of Sam's and this is my investigator, Larry. We'd like to talk to you a little bit." That was all it took to light a fire under Melvin Lockett.

"Awwwww, maaaan, I don't believe this!" He didn't actually scream. It was more like loud whining, but at the same time, the young man jumped from the stool and struck out at the air with a closed fist. "Man, that motherfuckin Sam put a brother in the jackpot. Man, what the fuck you is, his woman or some shit?"

"No, I'm not his woman," Frank answered matter-of-factly, "and Sam didn't put you in the jackpot either. I want to talk to you about what you know. Whatever you tell us won't leave this room. I need to find out who killed my wife, and you're the only one who can help," Frank said, conveying in his voice an absolute determination to extract the information.

"Look man, do I look stupid to you? How hard you think it gonna be for that fat motherfucker and his homeboys to find me in here? Motherfuckin Stevie Wonder could find me in this fucking place. I ain't saying shit. At least on the street a nigger gets a chance to run before they guns him down." Mookie seemed just as determined to keep his mouth shut.

Califf had been listening and evaluating and decided at that point to intervene with a new approach. "Listen carefully, Mookie. We're not out to hurt you, but we're not playing with you either. Everything possible will be done to protect your identity, but you will cooperate with us one way or the other. We'd like to do it in a friendly way, but we can do it the other way, if you prefer."

"Look , man," Mookie groaned.

"If you force us, then we'll just have to go fishing with you as bait. We'll report your story to the police and, better yet, the papers. We'll give them your name and say you're in the process of trying to identify the officer for the FBI. You'll come to us then, Mookie. I just hope you have the time. So choose your poison right now, dude."

"Man, you motherfuckers is a piece of work! Y'all should be police, man! You just like the motherfuckers!"

Frank and Larry both immediately recognized this as Mookie's concession speech.

After Mookie raved and cursed for a few more minutes, he seemed ready to talk, and talk he did. He recounted details not disclosed in Sam's account, most notably some real clues to the detective's general physical description. "Dude was a big, old, smart-ass, ugly looking motherfucker with one of those country boy, shit kicker haircuts. He had on a big, old black coat, one of them fluffy ones, like the NBA jackets, only long."

A reasonably accurate translation revealed to Frank the picture of a middle aged, overweight, white guy with an attitude and a long black down coat.

The coat might be helpful if they could identify him before spring, Frank thought.

Mookie had seemed certain that the badge the man had flashed on the scene was the rectangular shield of a detective and not the five-pointed traditional silver star of a patrolman. If the man had been an off duty or plain-clothes patrolman, any attempt to identify him through Mookie would be pointless. There were fourteen thousand cops in the city.

Maybe the man hadn't been a cop at all, Frank thought, although these street punks were certainly experts at identifying cops and distinguishing detectives from plain-clothes tactical officers. He was betting on Mookie's expertise.

Besides, the plain beige sedan Mookie described was most likely a police vehicle, and detectives were the only ones who could be found riding alone at night. They did it because they were generally working on some investigation, not out patrolling for crime.

As the three men walked into the jail parking lot, there was no identifiable expression of optimism among them.

"I'll get to work on possibles right away," said Larry. "Even focusing exclusively on detectives, it's a hell of a big job and a long shot at best."

"Are the photos recent?" Frank asked.

"Good question. Bad answer. Some of them are ten years old, but until something else breaks, I'll work that angle. The long black coat could be the key, but I'll have to think of a way to make inquiries without arousing suspicion."

As Larry walked to his car, Frank called to him. "Califf." He waited for the young man to turn. "This could get you in big trouble."

Califf simply waved.

Chapter Nine

On Tuesday afternoon, Lonnie Hartman was in his office, thoroughly occupied with an investigation of his own. From jail records, he was disappointed to learn that Sam Walker had been locked up at the county on the night Denise had been murdered.

Before dismissing Walker outright, however, Hartman thought it prudent to dig just a little deeper and dialed the number to the on-duty records officer at the jail. From the phone call, he learned that, since his incarceration, Walker had been housed in the newest wing of the county jail, wherein each individual cell housed two inmates. Each of the sixty segregated sections contained ten cells situated around a common day room, used for eating and recreation.

Upon inquiry, he learned from the records officer that Sam had been living with the same cellmate since July 27, two days after the death of Doherty's wife. The man's name was Melvin Locket and he was being held in lieu of twenty thousand dollars bail on a charge of Delivery of a Controlled Substance.

He quickly requested and received the man's birth date, and was on his way downstairs to the computer center almost before the connection was severed.

The Computer Center was a relatively new innovation, and had been established to assist officers and detectives learn and navigate the ever-increasing number of cyber-tools available to the law enforcement community.

A specially trained computer operator/police officer staffed each of the six citywide centers round-the-clock. Some of the younger detectives considered it a part of their jobs to be computer literate and fully versed in the utilization of all available law enforcement cyber-tools.

As a consequence, they generally considered it a sign of incompetence to rely on the centers, preferring to perform all of the functions at their own terminals.

To the older detectives like Hartman, however, the centers were extremely popular and heavily relied upon. Even simple and standard functions like obtaining mug photos and criminal backgrounds could be performed in a fraction of the time.

The Computer Center was located in what had previously been a suspect interview room. The transformation did little to increase the perception of space in the small, windowless room. It was so crammed with computer equipment and manuals that there was barely space for the operator to sit.

To Hartman's relief, the operator was occupied only with his tuna salad sandwich and potato chips, both of which were recognizable to Hartman from droppings on a nearby computer keyboard.

"Al, I need a photo and background check on this mope right away. I mean, I would appreciate it if you could do this as quickly as possible," Hartman said, tempering his impulsive and demanding tone in mid-sentence.

Hartman knew that cops were exactly like every other city worker in one respect. Everyone had an inflated opinion of the importance of his own function, and would religiously protect and promote that function to the exclusion of the big picture. It was an endless form of small-minded self-justification that Hartman willingly embraced.

"I think I could do it now," Al said, sounding to Hartman more annoying than important.

Al reached for a large notebook-type manual and handed it to Hartman. "You can follow the ICAM procedures in Chapter Three as I perform them," Al announced, sounding more like teacher to student than cop to cop.

Hartman, trying desperately to keep from being Hartman, handed Al the piece of paper containing the man's name and birth date. "Okay, Al," he forced himself to respond.

Al's mouth continued to flap as he manipulated the mouse and keyboard, but within three minutes a huge grin crossed Hartman's face as he watched the color photo of a smiling Melvin Lockett roll from the printer.

"Bingo," said Hartman. "What kind of a dumb fuck would strike a smiling pose for a mug shot? That's my man, Al. Thanks a lot!"

Hartman was nothing short of ecstatic to find that his young car thief turned informant was safely locked up at the county jail.

Even knowing his identity, Hartman thought, it might have been impossible to find him on the street. Doherty would have made sure of it.

There would be no escape for young Mr. Lockett this time, and Hartman knew immediately that the practical realities of city politics offered him nearly unlimited options.

Thank God for the county jail, Hartman thought.

IMMORAL AUTHORITY

The jail complex was a sprawling web of twelve virtually independent prisons, covering a nearly three-quarter square mile area of the city's West Side. Nine of the units dated to the last ten years, and there had been no concession whatsoever to aesthetics.

The twelve buildings were a quagmire of different styles, colors, sizes and materials. The oldest dated to 1922 and still sported steel bars for security. The only lighting in the post WWI facility was a system of uncovered standard one hundred watt light bulbs, strung throughout the damp hallways, with one single bulb on the ceiling of each cell. But for the Cream of Wheat and bologna sandwiches, it was often difficult for a prisoner to distinguish morning from night.

The building still housed over four hundred prisoners, most awaiting trial in murder and rape cases. It had also once housed the infamous Machine Gun Kelly.

The twelfth and most recent building in the series was a gem of 21st Century penal architecture. From the outside, it resembled an impulsive and mathematically disorganized attempt to recreate an Egyptian pyramid in concrete blocks. The structure housed virtually no windows, making it impossible from the outside to determine how many floors it contained.

There had been no attempt to color or in any way decorate the exterior, or the interior for that matter. Both were natural gray concrete block. The current sheriff liked to brag that not a single ounce of paint had been used to decorate the interior, not even in the administrative offices.

The floors of the six hundred-inmate facility were, of course, bare concrete. There was not a single chair available to inmates anywhere in the facility. They sat on highly durable, low-maintenance, stainless steel stools, fixed in place throughout the inmate dining and recreation areas. Each of the mushroom-type caps was bolted onto a 30" high steel pipe, which in turn was bolted to the floor.

The small sacrifice to the inmates' humanity was more than justified by the impregnable state-of-the-art security systems. There were motion detectors and heat sensors everywhere and cameras covered every inch of space, inside and out.

Mountains of seemingly polished barbed wire flashed in the reflected sunlight, as if reminding the inmates of the futility of escape.

Such was the advanced state of this depressing field of architecture, that the effect was probably by design.

Neither was the trend peculiar to this city. It had become a nationwide phenomenon. The entire place and every other like it in the country had been designed to serve only two goals; keep them in longer and do it as cheaply as possible.

This county jail system was a bonanza of votes and political influence for dozens of city politicians. Even though many in law enforcement secretly acknowledged that the *lock 'em up longer for less* theory of law enforcement was being advanced at a terrible and escalating cost, this political windfall helped perpetuate the trend.

Every new jail development meant hundreds of permanent new jobs for Lowry to disperse through his power brokers, not to mention the construction jobs and their favorable economic impact on the city. There was no denying that jail building and prisoner tending meant real political power.

The prisoners themselves were regarded almost as natural resources, requiring feeding, guarding, medical care and housing. In turn all of those things provided Jack Lowry with hundreds of jobs and no-bid contracts, which he wielded as political currency.

Each of the more than four hundred guards who staffed the county jail complex, officially designated Sheriff's Deputy, knew that the only function for which he or she would truly be held accountable was keeping each and every inmate within the confines of the four walls.

Nearly everything that happened within the walls was controlled by the inmate gang hierarchy. The reason for this paradoxical accommodation was a combination of many factors. They included the fact that the guards were not civil service employees, but worked for the county sheriff as political appointees. The much sought after jobs were low paying, but included health and retirement benefits. Perhaps the most popular feature, however, was the fact that deputies were sworn police officers and could carry concealed weapons round-the-clock.

As a plumb to the Mayor's minority supporters, the jobs were mostly controlled by aldermen in the low-income, minority wards. Obtained in exchange for simple mayoral support, each job increased the alderman's power and helped secure his hold on office.

As a result, the jail was staffed, for the most part, by under-trained and under-qualified minorities from low-income West and South Side wards. That is not to imply that there were not sufficient qualified minority applicants available, but the aldermen from the more affluent black wards and the Mayor's own loyal cronies traditionally did not participate in the arrangement.

Nobody could remember why it had been done that way, but it just wasn't worth the fallout that would occur if Lowry tried to change the deal. It was the one deviation that distinguished Lowry's running of the jail from his operation of things like the airport or the docks.

Since the days of the first Mayor Lowry, there had been an unwritten rule that every effort should be made to fill all political jobs with at least minimally qualified people. Time had proven that a city could run smoothly and prosper under the guidance of marginally qualified, but loyal political lackeys.

The practical effect of this arrangement on the jail system created an abomination that everyone seemed willing to live with.

All of the city's low-income areas were saturated with street gangs. The traditional criminal activities were present in abundance; drug selling, drive-by shootings and intimidation. Some of the gangs had been active in those areas for as much as two full generations and had shown signs of increasing sophistication. Those included the exportation of illegal activities to previously uncorrupted cities and small towns, and the expansion of gang activity to include pseudo-charitable community organizations and local political groups.

To a large extent, these organizations had permeated the very structure of the social and political life of the community. The general population of these communities was as decent and hard working as any other, and probably infected to no greater extent than was the Italian-American community in the heyday of the Mafia, but nonetheless, the influence was present.

This job dispensing arrangement was tailor-made for the street gangs. The *de facto* result of this practice was that they pushed their members, family members and even girlfriends and spouses to apply for these gun-carrying jobs. The real value of the jobs to the gangs, however, was influence inside the jail, pure and simple.

The five thousand plus county inmate population was an incredibly lucrative, captive market for selling drugs. Some of the deputies regularly brought drugs into the jail for delivery to inmate/dealers. Others simply looked the other way. Still others provided special privileges like in-cell TVs and cell phones or conjugal visits.

Even decent hardworking guards with no gang ties quickly faced a decision whether to ignore the goings on in order to keep the job or quit. The system of corruption was so entrenched and pervasive that no one dared complain and then go back to his family in or near the gang-infested neighborhood.

Poor Melvin Lockett and his buddy Sam were dead and didn't even know it, Hartman thought. He chuckled silently as he considered that their last meal would probably be a bologna sandwich on moldy white bread.

Larry Califf had worked on the case halfway through the night and the better part of his much-needed Tuesday off, following the visit with Mookie.

They had names for cops who worked uncompensated on their days off. Most were vulgar and not a single one was flattering. This particular form of ingratiating oneself to the brass was generally frowned upon by the rank-and-file as a despicable form of self-promotion at the expense of comrades.

At around five that afternoon, he received a call from Frank Doherty, asking him to come over to the house for dinner. He accepted the invitation, fully aware that it was really a thinly disguised effort by Frank to expand his access to police resources and information.

As he passed the unmarked city boundary on the westbound Johnson Expressway, Califf marveled that he would let himself be used in this way, and by a criminal defense lawyer no less.

He had, in effect, become Frank Doherty's working spy in the police department. The thought would have sickened him only two weeks ago. Even if he terminated the relationship immediately, he had accomplished more than enough betrayal to be fired, and maybe even prosecuted for official misconduct.

Yet, he felt no animosity towards Doherty. Califf had made the choice freely and did not feel in the least manipulated. The lawyer's motives were completely unselfish. He was reaching out to grab help anywhere he could find it.

"Hell," he muttered to himself audibly, finally admitting that he felt real empathy with the lawyer. Here was a guy with enough problems already to last a lifetime and he finds out of the clear blue sky that cops murdered his wife.

As Califf pulled into Frank's driveway in the early darkness, he was uneasy, but his mind had never second-guessed its absolute determination to ride this case to the very end, whatever the consequences.

Larry rang the doorbell, holding his briefcase in his left hand. Nothing in Larry Califf's twenty-eight years had prepared him for what happened next. The door opened slowly, allowing the light from the porch lamp to rush the otherwise darkened foyer and reveal to the paralyzed young detective the gently smiling face of Caroline Anderson.

In that instant, time stopped for the young detective. Up became down. He searched the sum of his knowledge and experience for some frame of reference and found only emptiness. He felt something akin to weightlessness, more than simple confusion or surprise, maybe even a brush with an out-of-body experience. Although he didn't know it, the young woman spoke to him two or three times before the words began to register.

"Larry? Larry? Are you Larry Califf?"

"Sorry?" The detective hadn't quite returned to earth, but the young man who harbored him was coming around.

"No, I'm sorry," said the simply dressed, yet stunningly attractive young woman. "It was very insensitive of me to just answer the door like that, knowing it was you. It's obvious you didn't know I was here. I'm Elizabeth, Beth, Caroline's sister."

Califf stepped into the foyer and, as he gently took her outstretched hand, stared into the same deep-set green eyes he had seen in the photograph. "I didn't think you were—" His words tailed off, but she picked up the slack without pause.

"Twins?" she said. "No. We're not twins, but you're not the first one to notice the resemblance. I just hope to God you're not the last either." As she spoke the final words, her tone changed, and tears began to pour from those eyes, almost without warning.

She cupped her face with open palms and Califf instinctively took one step towards her. He was close enough to smell the delicate scent of her soft brown hair as he looked down onto the top of her head.

In a purely natural act, accompanied by no discomfort or uneasiness, his right hand reached out slowly and cupped the back of her head in its palm. Her head nestled gently onto his breast, partly from the guidance of his palm and partly of its own voluntary movement.

There they stood, she sobbing and he standing, eyes

closed and cheek resting on her head. Five seconds, or maybe five minutes passed. Time became irrelevant to the moment. It was more than an embrace of strangers, so much more.

Without saying it or even thinking it, Larry knew that he was the one person who understood her grief, the one person who truly grieved in the way she grieved. There was no logic to the connection, but no denying it either.

In that instant, Larry Califf experienced the first moment of true clarity in his life. He had followed his instincts and, in so doing, worried that he had jeopardized his reputation and even his future.

Had it all been a part of some preordained scenario? He saw in that moment that it wasn't jeopardy he had been courting, but his own destiny. He had never experienced such a feeling of absolute peace and confidence.

"I'll find out what happened to your sister. I swear to you," he whispered. Not another word was exchanged between them until after dinner, at least none that could be heard by the naked ear.

As Beth led Larry into the kitchen at the rear of the house, an informal meeting of the dinner guests was underway. It was, as expected, a working dinner, each of the guests being a person intimately connected to the investigation. All three kids had eaten earlier and were playing at a neighbor's. Ellen and Frank were preparing dinner and the rest were gathered around the kitchen table.

Califf greeted them all collectively and then turned his attention to Ellen. "Ellen, I'm glad to see you. I only wish we had better news to greet you with," he said, taking her right hand softly in both of his.

"It's good to see you too, Larry, and I see you met

Beth. You know she graduated last month from the University of South Dakota. She's a journalist now." Before removing her hand, she leaned forward and kissed Califf lightly on the cheek.

"I'm not a journalist until I get a job, mother, but soon, maybe soon."

At Frank's suggestion, Larry helped himself to a beer from the refrigerator and sat at the table, across from Steve and Ray.

"So what's up Larry? Any luck with the photos?"

Poor Frank had a one-track mind, Califf thought, but knew that he was becoming more like Frank in that regard every day.

"It's not going anywhere, Frank. Half of the pictures are too old to be of any use, and a good portion of the recent ones were taken in uniform, including hat. I've been excluding as many as I can, but it will be a long process. It'll take a lot of follow up. I've been calling the detective squads with a story about losing a business card some detective left for me. I only know he was wearing a long black coat. I can't keep doing that without raising eyebrows."

"There are other ways we can narrow it down," said Ray. "We know the guy had a beige police car, so he had to be on duty the night Denise was killed. It'll be a lot of work, but there are records of which detectives were on duty and what cars they had checked out."

"Hold on, Ray." Califf saw a need to stop this train of thought cold. "There are some things I can do, but I have to do them discreetly. I'm not Internal Affairs. I can't just waltz in and seize the Watch Commander's records. It's not my job to investigate cops. I'd find myself standing guard outside the Art Museum all winter. If it would help Caroline I'd do it, but it won't."

"So what happens to you if it gets out that you're helping Frank conduct a private investigation?" Ellen had asked the question that was on everyone's mind.

"Well, let's just hope it doesn't get out. Anyway, I don't look at it as a private investigation. I'm a detective, and it's my opinion that if we disclose what we know now, these questions may never be answered."

"What do you mean?" Larry asked.

"I mean there are cops involved, and they may even be acting to protect more important players. My job, as I see it, is to solve this case and that's what I'm gonna do. At the appropriate time, I'll turn everything over to the FBI, if it's warranted. As to what happens after that, I'm a big boy and I'll deal with it."

The group ate spaghetti, drank red wine and even laughed until nearly nine, when Frank collected the kids and ushered them upstairs to perform their respective bedtime rituals. By the time he came down fifteen minutes later, the revelry had sputtered and the group's collective sense of mission had returned in earnest.

"There seems to be general consensus that we're at a dead end for the moment," said Ray, summarizing the group's discussion for Frank's benefit.

"Given enough time, I still have a shot at coming up with our detective," Larry offered. "But time seems to be the key. The more I work this, the less I work my other cases. Somebody's going to notice soon. Aside from that, I can only make up so many bullshit stories on why I need to know which detectives were working in a brown car on one particular night in July, or who wears a long black coat."

"Do you think someone might be onto you?" Frank inquired.

"I don't know, but these are detectives, for Christ sake. It won't take long for the red flag to go up, and when it does, I'm finished. Just be patient. I'll keep working on the photos and cross-match them with any information I can develop through the records."

"I just don't think we'll have to wait that long," Frank said. "Whoever is involved knows I have a witness now and they have to know I won't quit. I don't think they can just sit around and wait. We'll just keep our guard up and our ears to the ground while you do your thing."

They all sat around for another half-hour and rehashed the facts, trying to make sure nothing had been overlooked.

Finally, Califf rose and thanked his hosts for dinner, indicating he was long overdo for a good night's sleep. As he went to the foyer closet for his coat, Beth was already returning with it. She was wearing hers as well.

"I'll see Larry out to his car," she announced. All said their goodnights and the two headed out and down the driveway.

"Would you mind if we walked for a few minutes?" she asked.

"Of course not," he responded.

As they headed slowly up the dark street she spoke first. "My sister's not coming home. Is she, Larry?"

"No, Beth. She's not." The answer was followed by a prolonged silence.

"I'm sorry the way my mother fawns over you. I think she sees you as someone Caroline could have loved."

"I don't mind at all, Beth. Hell, its weird, but I actually felt something myself when I saw her picture. I don't know what it was, and I can't explain it, but it was enough to draw me more deeply into a case than I've ever been. What about you? Are you staying on for awhile?"

"I'll stay as long as mother does. I'm worried about her, so it works out well that I'm kind of in between things right now. When she goes back to Dad, I may even stay on with Uncle Frank. We talked about it. He could use the help and, for someone looking to start a career in journalism, there's no better city than this."

"I hope you stay then," said Larry, smiling somewhat mischievously this time.

"Larry, the last thing I want to do is offend you, but you have to know that I'm not an image in a photograph and neither is my sister, for that matter. I love her dearly, even if she's gone, but she is, or was, a human being with faults and frailties like everyone else, and we were more different than you could ever know."

"I'd like to know," he said, not in the least offended.

"Well, for one thing she was cerebral and patient, a person of extremely good judgment, but she had a very irritating habit of grinding her teeth," Beth said, smiling almost whimsically. "My judgment, on the other hand, has been called into question in the past and I'm considered to be somewhat impulsive, with a quick temper. I do not grind my teeth, but I hum incessantly."

"Well, I can't see that any of those things requires an apology, so long as you can hum on key.

"Look, I just don't know any other way to say this, Beth. You're in town and I'm in town, and I'd like very much to get to know you while I have the opportunity. Life doesn't have to stop because of this investigation. So what do you say?"

"I say okay," she said, flashing a smile radiant enough to illuminate the darkened street.

Chapter Ten

The drive to downstate Philbin Correctional Center was at least four hours each way, so Hartman was on the road at six Tuesday morning.

Tracking down Willie Boyd had been a piece of cake, just a simple phone call to the Department of Corrections.

Although he hadn't been assigned to the case, Hartman had followed the newspaper coverage of Willie Boyd's trial and knew that Boyd would be a guest of the taxpayers for several years to come.

Boyd was something of a celebrity in the city. He was perhaps the only street gang leader to have ever gained significant name recognition beyond the West Side neighborhoods that had supported his drug operations for years. Liberace would have called him flamboyant. Boyd had been despised and quietly vilified by Jack Lowry almost since the beginning of the administration.

In public, Lowry refused to acknowledge the existence of the man, although there was no political risk in hating drug dealers. What Lowry really objected to, however, was the embarrassment he had suffered as a result of Boyd's high profile antics.

Only a year ago, for example, the Mayor had nearly whipped himself into cardiac arrest when Boyd, scheduled to be released from the county jail on a minor battery charge, arranged to be picked up by a fifty-odd-person entourage, arriving in a procession of white limousines. Two top lieutenants carrying his thirty-thousand-dollar full-length mink coat met Boyd at the jail entrance.

To the Mayor's dismay, the entire scenario had played out live on the six o'clock news because, in addition to being an astute businessman and a brutal taskmaster, Willie Boyd was particularly media savvy.

Those closest to the Mayor would later say that the Willie Boyd jail incident infuriated him more than anything since his Assistant Commissioner of Streets wore a wire for the FBI. It was also Boyd's biggest mistake.

The Mayor had let it be known through the proper channels that the next judge to throw out one of Willie Boyd's cases on a technicality would simply not be slated for re-election.

Although Lowry did not technically control the slating of the few Republican Party judges, they knew full well that Lowry's influence reached far enough into the opposition party to make good the threat.

Lowry then called an informal meeting of his most trusted police officials, including the Superintendent, and effectively suspended the *Writ of Habeas Corpus* for Mr. Willie Boyd, ordering that a case be made, or made up, immediately against Boyd, and that he be arrested forthwith.

Poor Boyd was genuinely baffled when, two hours later, he was arrested and charged with *Possession of Cocaine While Armed With a Deadly Weapon*, an offense mandating a minimum sentence of fifteen years.

As he sat in jail in lieu of one million dollars bail, Boyd told a reporter by phone that the police had hurt his feelings by making up a case based on perjured testimony and planted evidence. He felt they had broken the rules by not catching him fair and square.

Jack Lowry enjoyed the newspaper article so much that he placed a copy in his safe deposit box among his private memoirs.

In any event, the judge who tried Willie Boyd sentenced him to the maximum thirty years after a jury conviction, fearing that anything less would cost him his robe. The State Supreme Court, located downstate and considerably less subject to Lowry influence, found the sentence excessive, however, and reduced it to fifteen years.

Quite coincidentally, Willie Boyd's lawyer, both at trial and on appeal, had been Frank Doherty.

Officially, it was all rumors, of course, but Lowry himself might have authorized the leaks, lest anyone openly defy his authority again. In the end, Boyd had been just a minor annoyance, ill equipped to survive the embarrassment of Jack Lowry.

Even at the time, however, Hartman had marveled at how Lowry's finger rested on every single button. He was reminded of how, periodically, mostly in the midst of the frequent police corruption and brutality scandals, Lowry would be pressured by minority aldermen to appoint a Superintendent from outside the police department to clean up the mess. His response each time was almost verbatim.

"So do we need somebody from Hawaii coming in here to tell us what's right and what's wrong? No. It's an insult to the people of this great city, and I won't do it." Another lackey with credentials would then be appointed to serve the master's will. In the matter of Willie Boyd, the lackey had performed admirably.

Notwithstanding his disastrous encounter with Jack

Lowry, it was common knowledge within law enforcement that Willie Boyd made as much money now from his drug operations as he had as a free man. Within the walls of the county jail, Boyd could make anything happen, including murder, a fact that had occasioned Lonnie Hartman's visit on this cold March day.

There was nothing unusual about a city detective visiting a Department of Corrections inmate. It was regularly required in the course of hundreds of routine murder investigations each year. Witnesses in gang related murder cases were usually gang related themselves, and would frequently be found living as guests of the State on some unrelated charge.

Hartman could see the single story prison clearly from as far as ten miles away. It had been recently built on a slight rise smack in the middle of what looked like the world's biggest cornfield. Although the institution was named for the small town of Philbin, there was no trace of a town in sight, not even a trace of life for that matter.

The detective was fully aware that there was much competition among the downstate areas for these modern *cookie cutter* prisons. The get tough on crime mentality provided much needed economic development and jobs for depressed areas of the state. *Jobs plus money equals votes* was not an equation peculiar to the big city.

After signing in at the guard shack, Hartman waited less than five minutes before being patted down and escorted into the main prison building. He was taken directly to an interview room near the main waiting area. Willie Boyd was already seated on one side of the small metal table.

"Damn! The great Detective Hartman come all the

way down to the corn hole just to see ol' Willie. Man, I already got me a woman up in here. You shoulda called first."

"Looks like prison hasn't got you down, Willie. I'm glad to see it. Been keeping up on what's happening in the old neighborhood?"

Banter was required before serious conversation, much in the same way as mutual head bowing was required in the Far East preceding diplomatic or business conversations.

"My secretary failed to inform me that you was in my schedule today, and I do has a rather pressing lunch engagement. So if this is a sales call, you can git right to it and, if not, then you could git to the motherfuckin point of this visit."

The *sales call* reference related to their prior relationship. Boyd had been around almost as long as Hartman and the detective had known the man long before Boyd had become infamous.

They began bumping heads when Hartman had been a young plainclothes narcotics officer on the West Side. Boyd, at the time, was already a ruthless, yet charismatic young street dealer with ambition and brains. Even at eighteen, Boyd had tons of cash and was constantly throwing out feelers to the susceptible young narcotics officers.

Once, in the course of a routine street stop and patdown, Boyd had let it be known jokingly to young Hartman that he would pay top dollar for any significant confiscated drug caches. Hartman laughed and did not respond.

Two months later, however, in the course of a sham traffic stop, Hartman and his partner found four kilos of cocaine hidden in a door panel. Rather than turn the drugs in, the officers released the suspect and kept the plastic-wrapped packages. It didn't take them long to locate Boyd on the street and, less than two hours later, they were splitting up thirty-two thousand dollars between them.

It wasn't exactly top dollar, but it had been fast and nearly effortless. In the intervening years, several more transactions of a similar nature had transpired between the two men.

"Okay, Willie, here it is. There's a guy in the county jail. I need him to go away, permanent like. In fact, there are two guys. They're cellmates. They gotta go."

"You want me to cap two dudes in the county, and ol' Willie would git exactly what out of this deal?"

"Something very valuable to you, your operation and maybe your ass. Did you think the Mayor would be satisfied with you serving three and a half years on a fifteen-year rap? There's a joint city and Federal task force that's been running an operation on your business for almost a year. It's no secret that the Mayor doesn't like you. They've got a whole fucking room full of videos and two informants who work for you. They think you have three major manufacturing and warehouse operations citywide. When they identify all the locations, they're gonna shut you down and indict you. It's probably the worst kept secret in the department."

"If they got all that, why ain't they done something 'bout it?"

"What they don't have right now are the drugs," Hartman answered.

"So what you got in mind? What you gonna do for me if I decide to cap these motherfuckers?"

"For this favor, you get all the details plus the names

of the two tricks. There's nothing more I can do to get you out of this, but a good heads up should help you limit the damage."

"And what if I don't?" Willie asked defiantly.

"Don't do me this favor, and I'll find a way to tip them that you're onto the plan. They'll move against you soon, and with the witnesses they have, you're pretty well fucked already. Do this job for me by Friday, and I'll give you everything you need. You're smart enough to figure a way to help yourself."

"Just give me the names, the division and the cell number, and I'll talk to you Friday. You one nasty ass motherfucker, fat man."

There was, of course, no joint investigation at the moment, although the extent of Boyd's operation was widely known. Such special investigations were extremely expensive, however, and, with Boyd in jail, the pressure from community groups had abated.

The beauty of Hartman's scheme was that it was both foolproof and risk free. Aside from which, it didn't cost a dime. Boyd would do the job in fear of a long prison sentence and the loss of his empire.

For his part, Hartman would simply give Boyd the names of two particularly annoying drug dealers. They would both be dead within a day and Boyd would move all his operations, thinking he had defeated the investigation. The irony, Hartman thought, was that in arranging the murder-for-hire, he had admirably served, not only his own interests, but those of the Mayor and the general public as well.

On Friday morning, Frank rose before six o'clock and retrieved his morning paper from the driveway. He was relieved that the paper was actually in the driveway and not hidden in the bushes or out in the middle of the street. Digging in the bushes in February clad in a bathrobe could get embarrassing, not to mention damn cold.

There were no paperboys anymore. The phantom grown-ups who delivered the paper these days were almost never seen, even if one was lucky enough to catch a glimpse of the streaking SUV as the newspaper came flying out the driver's window.

Safely back in his kitchen with the kids still asleep, Frank poured the coffee and settled into his chair to read the paper in the lull before the storm.

His quiet time was cut short when he reached the Metro section of the daily paper. There, near the bottom of Page One, he spotted the story entitled, *Two Inmates Found Dead in County Cell.* He immediately scanned the story, but it only confirmed what he had already guessed.

The County Sheriff's Office has confirmed that two men were found dead this morning in the jail's newest wing, apparently by a drug overdose. The source indicated that, although the autopsies have not been completed, the coroner's preliminary report indicates that the men may have mistakenly injected a fatal concentration of cocaine, believing it to be safe. The entire division has been placed on lockdown, pending a thorough search for more lethal drugs. Authorities fear that the drugs injected by the men could be part of a larger shipment smuggled into the jail. The men have been identified as Melvin Lockett, age 20, of 3217 W. Holiday and Sam Walker, age 40, of 28 N. Vermont

Frank read the article again, word for word, dwelling on the names, as if not believing the first reading. He stared blankly at the newspaper, temporarily incapable of meaningful thought. When the shock had subsided, he read the article again, not grieving, but curiously hoping to find something in the article with a ring of truth. Frank desperately needed to believe that Sam had died of an accidental overdose, but the harder he tried the more firmly his mind rejected the conclusion. Both Sam and Mookie had been murdered because of what they knew, just as surely as Denise had been murdered for what she knew.

As he woke the kids for school, Ellen was already emerging from the bathroom fully dressed. Her help had never been more necessary than it was today.

Frank showered and dressed for work, more from habit than any sense of purpose. There would be no work today, not in the usual sense.

Who had been responsible? More importantly, how had they discovered Mookie's identity? Aside from Frank, only three people in the world knew Mookie's relationship to this case.

He never even allowed himself to consider that Ray or Steve could have leaked the information. It didn't take a criminal lawyer to see that Larry Califf had been playing both sides against the middle all along. Frank had accepted his word at face value. That foolish mistake had cost Sam and his friend their lives.

Califf had done exactly what he had been trained to do. He had employed necessary deception for the greater good of solving a serious crime.

In trusting Califf, Frank had dismissed conclusions formed over twenty years of experience. In the end, cops took care of cops, and lying, even under oath, was an acceptable tool for dispensing justice.

Frank arrived at the office at eight-thirty sharp, as

was his custom, but was in no mood for business as usual. He said good morning to Nora and walked through the open door of Ray's office. As he past her, Frank realized that it was Friday and Nora didn't work on Fridays. He decided not to go there and continued into Ray's office. The young lawyer was seated at his desk, apparently paying bills.

"Did you read the paper?" Frank asked matter-of-factly.

"No, but I heard it on the radio on the way in. I'm sorry." Ray decided to leave it at that for the moment.

"I have a couple of cases up this morning, nothing substantive. Could you handle them for me?"

"Sure, Frank."

"I have to talk to Sam's family and make some other calls. We'll all get together and talk about this later." Frank turned and walked out without waiting for a reply.

Ray said nothing, but followed directly into the older man's office. "Frank, where will you be? Oh, I'll need those files too."

"If I'm not here Nora will know. Thanks, Ray," he said, handing Ray two manila folders.

Frank's first thought was to call Sam's family. What would he tell them and which ones would he call anyway? Sam had God knows how many wives and girlfriends. If he called one and not the others, it would just start trouble. He decided to let it go for now.

He couldn't tell them the truth now anyway, so why lie to them? He tried to take his mind off the situation by attending to some long overdo paperwork. It didn't work.

The rage had been building in Frank since breakfast and he didn't want to do anything irrational in this emotional state. Then he remembered that it was nearly time for the eleven o'clock hockey game.

Almost fifteen years ago, he had gotten involved in a weekly hockey game, organized by some guys Frank had played hockey with as a kid. They all grew up and became lawyers, doctors, or salesmen and didn't have the time or the energy to play organized hockey against eighteen-year-olds on weekends.

They reserved an hour of ice time at the local rink every Friday during the lunch hour from October through March. Whoever showed up on Friday would just make up teams and play. The older they got, the more fun it became. It had been a great stress release for Frank, but his back problem had kept him away all season.

Hockey was exactly what he needed today, Frank thought. The gear, all twenty smelly pounds of it, was permanently stored in the trunk of his car.

"Nora, I'm going to play hockey. I'll have the pager if there's an emergency," he said and headed for the door.

"A man of your age, especially one with responsibilities and back problems, should know better than to be playing ice hockey. Why can't you just walk on a treadmill and watch the business channel like everyone else your age?" She seemed genuinely irritated.

"Nora, I told you not to worry about your job security. Our friend Ray has promised to hire you and increase your salary the day they bury me."

"Go play hockey then. Maybe a hockey ball will hit you in the head and knock some sense into you."

He didn't respond, but gave Nora what would turn out to be his only smile of the long day.

A good hard workout was just what Frank needed to get his mind off this nightmare that was his life. He was not disappointed. For a full hour, he pushed, perspired, and was even knocked on his can a few times. His back bothered him only a little and his life not at all.

When the Zamboni roared, the small group of middle-aged warriors filed off the ice through the small door along the boards. Frank stepped off the ice to find Larry Califf standing in the large open waiting area, which doubled as the rink's only locker room. Ignoring him, Frank sat, helmet off, and began unlacing his skates.

Califf approached him and spoke with no hesitation. "Frank, I heard what happened. I'm sorry."

"And exactly what is it you're sorry about, Detective? Sorry Sam's dead? Well, that's possible," Frank said, nodding his head. "Sorry you didn't get what you wanted before they murdered him? I think that's more likely. You lied to us Califf. You betrayed us and it cost my friend his life. Trusting you was a big mistake. You're just like every other cop I ever met, and it's not your character flaws that bother me. It's your goddamn self-righteousness."

"Frank it's not like that. I—"

"Once a cop always a cop," said Frank. "You told us everything we wanted to hear and you were playing both sides of the ice all the time. The thing that infuriates me the most is that, in your own self-righteous mind, you think you did the right thing."

"Exactly what did I do?"

"What you did cost two men their lives, and it drives me crazy that some twisted, narrow-minded concept of duty will absolve your conscience. Well, you killed those men, Califf, as sure as if you pulled the trigger, and I hope to God you realize it some day."

"What happened to *Don't judge me by the way I earn my living*? You would have made a bad detective,

Frank. You're drowning in self-pity and closing all the wrong doors. You only think about Frank Doherty. Everything else is a load of shit to you. Everyone else is baggage. I'm not even angry, Frank. I pity you. I'm still gonna solve this case, and you can go to hell." With that Califf turned and was gone.

Hockey had provided only a temporary break from Frank's misery. He went back to the office but couldn't concentrate on work. Nora was gone and Ray wasn't around. He walked down the hall to Steve's office, opened the outer door and entered the waiting area.

"Hi, Diane. Is Steve in? I just need a minute," he said.

"Oh, hi, Frank. I think he's just back there reading. Go right in," answered Mrs. Panos.

Frank found the old man reading some action novel, just as his wife had said. "Steve, did you see the papers this morning?"

"No, but Ray called me. I'm sorry, Frank." Steve purposely made no attempt to direct the conversation. He was observing.

"It was Califf, Steve. Nobody else knew Sam was involved. Nobody else knew who Mookie was, just us and Califf. I didn't want to believe it, but it's a no brainer."

"Well, I'll admit it looks that way, but things aren't always what they seem. Maybe the best thing to do is let this settle for a few days. Then take a good hard look at it."

"They all close ranks and cover each other's asses when the radar goes up," Frank said, "even the ones without the guns and badges."

"I take it you're talking about the forensic

examiner."

Instead of answering, Frank just stared ahead for a moment with a kind of blank look.

"I'll call you tonight, Steve. Thanks." Frank turned and headed for the door with a purposeful stride.

The entire staff of the crime lab finished for the day at four o'clock in the afternoon, the same time as virtually every other department located in the seventeen-story downtown government building.

Frank arrived at three forty-five and took a seat in the waiting area near the bank of elevators. At precisely one minute after four, government workers began pouring from elevators in groups of about twenty.

Well into the mass exodus, Laura Stanic exited the farthest elevator and headed for the revolving door closest to the parking garage. She spotted Doherty closing in from the corner of her eye.

"Ms. Stanic, may I have a moment?"

"I don't think we have anything else to say to each other, Mr. Doherty." She hadn't stopped walking, or even turned her head.

"I don't want anything from you, Ms. Stanic, but if you will give me just thirty seconds of your time, I have some information for you."

"Very well, Mr. Doherty," she said with a sigh, stopping and turning to face him.

"I can give you the name now," he said. "It's Melvin Lockett. They called him Mookie. He was twenty years old."

"And I suppose that's supposed to mean something to me," she said.

"I hope it does someday, but I'm not optimistic. He

was my anonymous witness and he's dead now, so his name doesn't matter. Here's the article from the paper. I'd like you to read it."

He handed her a photocopy of the article and she took it, saying nothing.

"The other man, Sam Walker, was my friend. He knowingly risked his life to give me the information. He's dead too. He was a good man. They were murdered because you couldn't wait to report everything I told you in confidence. Have a good night's sleep, Ms. Stanic."

"Who the hell do you think you are, you pompous bastard? What confidence? I work for the State, not for you. I don't even know you, and I don't want to know you."

He was already walking away, but she would have none of it. She walked faster.

"If you bother me again, I'm going to have you arrested," she said, holding out her hand and dropping the photocopied article into the breeze as she turned to block his path.

Frank didn't know her either, but he learned in that moment that she was not someone to trifle with.

On the drive home, Laura couldn't get the whole Frank Doherty business off her mind. Her anger at Doherty had really been a knee-jerk defense to his unexpected accusations. He had literally accused her of causing the deaths of two men.

Laura had no doubt that she had acted appropriately in calling the police. What bothered her was that she had really never considered Frank's plea. She had thought, not in terms of right and wrong, but in terms of job security. She should have known that Doherty wasn't some kind of nut case. He had accurate information that she hadn't even revealed to the police.

During their investigation last year, they had accepted her forensic report without ever asking to see her notes. The fact that Doherty knew about the religious medal proved that he was onto something about his wife's accident. Doherty's whole theory was made more plausible by the fact that his niece had gone missing while in the company of Denise only two days before the hit and run. As she drove, Laura wrestled with the conclusion that maybe Doherty had been right.

When she arrived back at her apartment, Laura was still quite upset. Alex had been home from basketball practice for a half-hour and would be in the kitchen doing his homework. Laura tried consciously to put it behind her as she climbed the stairs and placed her key in the lock. She went directly into the kitchen, without taking off her coat.

"Hello, sweetheart. Did you have a good day?" As she spoke, she leaned over the back of his chair and kissed him playfully on the nose.

"It was okay, but what's wrong with you?" Alex seemed genuinely perplexed, almost sad.

"Nothing, why honey?"

"Well, I made that *Happy Birthday* sign last night in my room and you didn't even mention it. Don't you like it?"

Laura hurried back to the front door and saw the sign. It was an unmistakably hand-made creation in crate paper and colored marker. It read *Happy Birthday Mom*. Back in the kitchen, she knelt at the table beside Alex and gave him a big hug.

"Oh, thank you, sweetheart. It was very thoughtful of you and I love it. I'm sorry I didn't see it when I came in. I think I had kind of a bad day. Forgive me?"

"Sure, mom. So can we go out to eat for your birthday?"

"I guess so. I sort of have a taste for pepperoni pizza. How does that sound?"

"Great! I'll go to the bathroom and get my coat."

As he did, Laura reached for the daily newspaper on the counter and went directly to the Metro section. She opened her purse, removed the composite picture of Caroline's abductor, placed it beside the article on Sam's death and silently considered some very disturbing possibilities.

Chapter Eleven

Early on the morning of Sam's funeral, Matt Corliss and Lonnie Hartman were partnered on a day shift. They were assigned follow-up work on a murder case in which two midnight detectives had arrested and detained a suspect. Corliss and Hartman were out on the street trying to pick up the eyewitness to view a line-up at the station.

The witness was a rival gangbanger, and experience had taught the detectives that early morning was the best time to find these guys. They lived much like vampires, and thus could generally be found sleeping while the sun shone. They had just checked out the first possible address without success and were on their way to the second when Hartman decided it was a good time to change the subject.

"What's going on with that Doherty bullshit? Did you get that arrogant shithead to give you any information?" Hartman reasoned that it was a perfectly logical subject on which to inquire, especially since he had been in the car with Corliss the day he had talked to Doherty. Corliss had openly expressed his anger and frustration to Hartman all the way from the lawyer's office to the station.

"For the moment, it's a dead end. The kid who's working the niece's case, Califf I think, tried to talk to him. The kid thought he might do some good reasoning with the guy, but Doherty wouldn't even talk to him. He told the kid to arrest him or get out of his way. What an arrogant fuck."

"Just when did Califf tell you this?" Hartman asked, not even bothering to hide his excitement and agitation.

"Yesterday, why?" Corliss responded.

"Well, I saw them together in the hallway of the courthouse last Monday and they were looking pretty chummy, so I followed them and watched them go into a bar across the street. They were practically holding hands."

"Are you sure about the day?" Corliss asked.

"Absolutely. It was the Monday after your phone conversation with Califf. I was sitting right next to you. Remember?"

"Well, I'll be damned," said Corliss. "What the fuck is going on here? Could this kid really be in bed with Doherty? Do you think he's doing some kind of secret investigation looking at cops?"

"More like private investigation," Hartman offered. "I think our young friend Califf has become a vigilante."

"This is some serious shit, Hartman. Maybe I better just confront the kid and try to straighten him out before this thing gets out of control."

"I don't think so," said Hartman. "This sounds more like a job for Pitney Jenkins."

"You're probably right," Corliss agreed. "This shit's too deep for me. If I don't kick it upstairs right now, I'll probably fuck myself right out of a job. I hate to fuck over another cop, but that's just what Califf is trying to do."

Rory Jenkins, or *Pitney*, as he was known in the department, was something of a legend within the ranks. He was a lieutenant and currently the Watch Commander for the day shift at Homicide/Violent Crimes. He was old for a police officer. Civil Service mandated retirement at age sixty-nine and Pitney had accumulated nearly every day of it.

In addition to being long in the tooth, the man was cynical, bitter, self-absorbed, and just plain mean. He had acquired every one of those traits over the last twenty years, since his demotion from the rank of Captain. Of the former man, only the nickname had survived.

In the early seventies, during the reign of the former Lowry, young Rory Jenkins had enjoyed a meteoric rise to the top ranks of the police department. By 1979, at the relatively tender age of forty-four, he had risen to the rank of Captain and was assigned as Commander of the city's Twenty-Third Police District. He was even rumored to have been in line for the Superintendent's job. The secrets of just how this remarkable feat had been accomplished had long been forgotten in the shadow of Pitney's personal *Waterloo*.

The year was 1978. The Pitney Cab Company, a legitimate and licensed transportation company, had developed a scheme to exploit weaknesses in the Metropolitan Transit Authority.

In the wake of aging equipment and budget cutbacks, the Authority's public bus system had become functionally inadequate. The cab company, quite simply, began operating as a bus line. Cabs began running up and down dozens of the city's most heavily utilized bus routes picking up passengers at designated bus stops. They charged the same fare as the bus and provided the same service. They even employed a crude transfer system.

The scheme was so popular and profitable that the mob couldn't resist moving in. They took over the company and promptly expanded the illegal operation citywide under the protective eye of Captain Rory Jenkins. The operation soon caught the attention of the United States Attorney's Office and *Operation Pitney Cab* was born.

After monitoring the operation for some months, investigators caught a break in mid-1980 when one of the suspected bagmen, a sergeant from the Twenty-Third District, was arrested while providing private security for a major drug deal in a busy suburban motel. Within four hours, he was on the street again after he and his lawyer had cut a deal for him to roll over on Jenkins.

Every Friday morning, he would take a bag to Jenkins' office, where the Commander would count out the appropriate number of fifties and hand them to the sergeant for distribution among the designated beat officers. For whatever reason, the payments were always made in fifty-dollar bills.

On one particular Friday, with court-ordered audio surveillance having been surreptitiously installed in Jenkins' office, the Sergeant picked up the paper bag on schedule and went directly to Jenkins' office with the bag of fifties in his pocket.

As Jenkins entered the Commander's office, the two greeted each other with some banter and Jenkins was heard to say, "Okay, let's see what you got." Jenkins was then heard counting out loud, "One, two, three…" all the way to twenty-two. The Sergeant said good-bye and left the office.

It took less than ten seconds for the agents to rush the building and enter Jenkins' office. They searched it for two hours without finding any trace of the money, not even a single fifty-dollar bill. They did not even inventory the thirteen dollars that was found in Jenkins' wallet, probably in fear of further humiliation.

The story got out and, in the publicity that followed, Jenkins had been christened *Pitney* by the rank and file, but for lack of evidence, had never been charged. He had been, of course, demoted and permanently sentenced to shift work again and remained under a Federal cloud of suspicion for years.

Speculation over what he had done with the money raged within the department for years, and old timers still remembered the jokes about how Pitney could eat lunch faster than any man alive and then shit fifties.

The entire experience no doubt had contributed to Jenkins' miserable personality and his absolute intolerance of would-be Serpicos.

"Yeah. Let old Pitney deal with it. This shit is right up his alley," Hartman said, pleased and somewhat surprised at how easily he had manipulated the conversation.

Califf reported for work at around seven forty-five in the morning. He had barely shed his coat when Lieutenant Mel Harris, Commanding Officer, Missing Persons, appeared at his office door across the room and called to him.

"Califf, in here now."

It was nothing unusual to be summoned into the boss's office, but the tone of Harris's voice gave Califf a bad feeling. He knew this could be the moment he had been fearing and wondered to himself why he hadn't prepared for it. In a strange way, he felt liberated, almost relieved that the hypocrisy was coming to an end.

Having lived for some five years now within this subculture known as the police, he understood full well what police officers most feared. It wasn't being shot or shot at. It wasn't having to shoot someone. It was the fear of losing the security of the brotherhood.

Cops lived only near other cops. They socialized only with other cops. They trusted only other cops. They tolerated bizarre and extreme views, and even illegal conduct, from other cops. They did it all, not because they approved, but because they knew that other cops would in turn tolerate them. Living in the bubble long enough, they could begin to see the world in terms of *us against them*.

As a result, the tightly segregated world became a shelter for the fatally flawed. Not always, but all too often.

Califf had come to understand that it was this collective isolation that had allowed, even fostered, rationalization and acceptance of large-scale corruption. Without the safety net of the brotherhood, one could be left flailing alone in the world, grappling with one's conscience and left to rediscover lost values or sink into the abyss.

More than anything else, a cop feared the loss of his job, which by definition meant exile from the brotherhood.

As he crossed the room to the command office, Califf realized that he had not prepared himself for this moment because he no longer feared it, but welcomed it.

"Califf, do you know Lt. Jenkins from Homicide?" Harris, who was, as a rule, a jovial and personable character, was uncharacteristically grim.

"No. I haven't had the pleasure," said Califf, extending his hand to the miserable looking old fellow still seated at Harris's desk.

Pitney did not acknowledge the gesture in any way.

"Please sit, Califf," said Harris, pointing to a wooden armchair opposite his desk. Califf did as instructed and held his tongue.

As Califf sat, Pitney rose, walking towards the younger man, holding a pad of paper and a pen. Standing almost directly over Califf, he made a point of looking down at the young detective while he spoke.

"I don't like cops who rat out other cops. Some cops do it to keep their asses out of jail, but the ones I really hate are the ones who do it for career advancement. Now, we know that you're withholding information on the Denise Doherty case. We know you're working for that fucking defense lawyer and we know you've been investigating other cops. On top of that, your lieutenant here tells me that he's gone over your time sheets and supplemental reports, and more than half your time isn't accounted for. You're in a world of shit, young man, and you've got exactly one chance to save your job."

"And what would that be?" Califf asked calmly.

With that, Pitney threw the pad and pencil into Califf's lap and continued. "Write it, all of it. Write everything you know about this case and how you learned it. I want everything, names included. If I'm satisfied that you've come clean, we'll talk about why you did it and I may even go to bat for you. Now write, while you can still save your job."

Califf thought it odd that a lieutenant would come over personally from homicide on a matter of internal discipline, but said nothing. He simply picked up the pad and paper and began to write.

Pitney smiled, exposing a seldom exhibited and not quite complete set of yellowish-green teeth, blackening along the gums and long overdo for removal.

After only a minute, Califf held the pad and pen up for retrieval, head still lowered, in a sign of submission.

Pitney grabbed the pad from the young man's outstretched hand, letting the pen fall to the ground. The decaying contents of his mouth began to disappear behind a rapidly expanding scowl as he read: *If you can make this entire pad of paper disappear in ten seconds without leaving the room, I will tell you everything you want to know— and then blow you.*

Sam's funeral started at ten o'clock. It began with a brief prayer service at a West Side funeral home. To Frank's surprise, he was not the only white face in the small visitation chapel.

Of the fifty or sixty adults present, perhaps twenty percent were noticeably Hispanic or white. Each probably had his own interesting Sam Walker story, Frank thought.

The girlfriends, or wives, had come together harmoniously in celebration of Sam's life. They were all there in the front row, as were all of Sam's children, dressed impeccably in black. There was some joyous singing, hand-clapping and shedding of tears.

After a brief reading, all were invited to participate in the procession to the west suburban cemetery where there would be a graveside service at ten-thirty. The procession avoided the expressway, but the trip nevertheless took only forty minutes in post rush hour traffic.

Upon arrival at the cemetery, the procession crawled over the narrow, winding road until it reached the area of the gravesite.

As Frank pulled in turn to the side of the road, he considered the weather briefly. The day was unusually sunny for March and dead calm, although bitterly cold. He reached for the leather gloves in the console and decided to retain the sunglasses.

As Frank approached the gravesite, he could see a crowd of about twenty people already gathered. They had apparently come directly to the cemetery. From the edge of the group of mostly black mourners, it was not difficult to recognize the figure of Laura Stanic, covered in a long navy blue cloth coat, with her back to Frank and standing noticeably back from the group.

Frank approached the group and stopped directly beside her. They were standing shoulder to shoulder, both facing the empty grave. She never turned and, as far as Frank could tell, didn't even flinch in response to his presence, an indication he had been expected.

After a few moments, Frank spoke quietly. "They say ignorance is truly bliss. Sam thought he was on top of the world. What the hell do I know anyway? Maybe he was."

"Mr. Doherty, I think perhaps I misjudged you," she said, still staring at the empty grave as the casket was being positioned above it.

"It's Frank, and I think you misjudged me more than you know," he offered.

"What do you mean?" she asked.

Frank turned and faced her. As their eyes made contact he spoke. "When I came to see you the other day, I was angry. I was just lashing out at anyone I could, trying to blame someone, anyone except myself. You weren't even the first person I blamed."

"Why?" she asked.

"Because I'm the one who got them killed. I knew you would report my visit to the cops. In fact, I was counting on it. Everything I told you was the truth and I wanted you to tell the police, so that whoever did this to my family would start to panic, maybe surface to cover area. Frank managed to get two cups of vending machine coffee, handed one to Larry and said, "Let's go outside for a minute if you don't mind."

Larry followed him out into the rink area.

As they prepared to step out into the cold, a stubby, balding little man stepped front of Larry, tapping Frank on the shoulder.

"Frank," he said. "It's great to see you."

"Ron, this is a friend of mine, Larry Califf. He's a hockey fan, but he doesn't have any money."

Ron laughed genuinely from his ample belly as Frank completed the introduction.

"Ron is the YMCA Director here and his primary job is getting into everyone's pocket."

"Don't let him fool you, Larry," Ron said. "Frank is our most dedicated fundraiser. If everything goes well, construction on the new rink enclosure should start right after the close of the next hockey season."

"No offense, Ron, but we hear that every year," Frank said, reaching for the door. "I hope it happens this year. Who knows? Maybe your *golden goose* is out there somewhere. Good to see you, Ron. We're going out to catch some of the next game."

"See you at the meeting Thursday, Frank," Ron said. "Good to meet you, Larry."

The two men walked into the cold air and stood along the boards watching as the next kid's game got under way. Frank spoke first.

"Look, I was wrong the other day and I want to apologize."

"Forget it, Frank," Larry said.

"Let me finish. The thing is, it wasn't just a mistake. It was who I am and how I treat people. It's partly because of what I do and partly— I don't know what. I just seem to live life on the attack. I did it to my wife and, if she had lived, I might have lost her anyway.

"You're younger than I am, but only in years. I see a mature wisdom in you, Larry, and I envy it. The only thing I can tell you is that this is my demon and I struggle with it every day."

"Christ, Frank, its no big deal. You go from one extreme to the other. I'm afraid if you come any closer you'll try to kiss me.

"I'm not wise, maybe just too naïve to understand the consequences of my actions. Hell, I know it's not easy for you to say those things and I do appreciate it, but can we just forget about it now?"

"Sure," Frank surrendered.

"Besides, its not like I got fired. I suspect it won't be any worse than seven days for now because they don't want a big investigation that could expose police involvement in murder. I'll be back to work next week. My worry is that I'm pretty much useless to you now in terms of the investigation."

"Well, I'd hardly call you useless. Look, you and Beth go have a nice dinner and I'll give you a call in the morning."

"Okay, Frank. See you tomorrow."

Chapter Twelve

Wednesday was the evening Laura had been dreading all month. It was the Attorney General's fundraiser at the swank Waterfront Sheraton Hotel. The ticket had cost her three hundred dollars, as usual, and writing the check this year had irritated her more than ever.

There was no denying that buying the ticket and attending the fundraiser were both conditions of continued employment, although those words had never been directly spoken by anyone in authority.

As a lab employee, Laura worked in the AG's department and knew firsthand that her direct supervisor kept a list of those who purchased the tickets and those who attended. It was really nothing more than a discreet form of job selling, wherein the jobholder would pay an annual commission of three hundred dollars to the politician who had provided the job.

The ticket was irritating enough, but what galled her most was that these male gorillas never stopped to consider that the event also involved the cost of a babysitter, beautician, and pedicurist. More often than not, it also included the cost of a new dress, shoes, and bag.

By the time she got to the thing, she was usually so angry that she spent the entire two-hour required minimum commiserating with her work mates at the bar and listening to off-color stories about the very man being honored, Attorney General Richard Fahey.

Laura's plan, as always, was to arrive precisely at six-thirty, as the event commenced, and to leave at the stroke of eight-thirty. She disliked the event so, that she had never thought of bringing a date and actually trying to have fun. To Laura, it was like working late in nice clothes.

She looked good by anyone's standard, man or woman. The long, sleeveless black gown she had chosen was simple but elegant and slit on the left side to just above the knee.

The event generally brought her more than enough unsolicited compliments from the married but prowling politicians, young and old.

She couldn't even remember, however, the last time that she had dressed up like that to really impress someone, like a real date. She had even caught herself thinking of the distinguished Mr. Doherty in that way lately, but no doubt, Mr. Doherty had enough problems of his own right now to keep him quite occupied.

When she arrived at the second floor ballroom, Laura was pleased to find that she was not nearly the first to arrive. She estimated that thirty-odd people had already shed their coats in the cloakroom and were waiting to greet the Royals in the obligatory receiving line.

She moved directly towards the cloakroom, stopping once to acknowledge a small group of her co-workers, probably some of the same people she would spend the next two hours with, Laura thought.

By the time she reached the receiving line, it had swelled to perhaps forty people. As the line moved slowly forward, she could see that Richard Fahey was the very first dignitary in the line.

She had done this enough times not to worry about recognizing the dignitaries. These were all people who loved to hear the sound of their own names, even from their own mouths. All you did was smile and offer your hand. You would have no trouble hearing the name. Laura could have scripted the entire scene.

"It's so good to see you, Laura. Richard Fahey."

"Thank you, Mr. Attorney General. Its good to see you."

"Good evening, Laura. I'm Representative Elaine Foxwood. Good to see you here."

"Thank you, Ms. Foxwood. Good to see you."

"Good evening, Laura. Richard Greenberg, County Treasurer."

"Good evening, Mr. Greenberg." As she moved from Mr. Greenberg, Laura held out her hand and looked up. Before her brain could register the significance of the event, Laura saw that she was shaking the hand of the man who had kidnapped Caroline Anderson.

"Hello, Laura. I'm Sean Lowry, here on behalf of my father. It's very nice to meet you. Do you work in Mr. Fahey's department?"

"Yes, in the crime lab." Laura answered, staring directly into the man's eyes, hoping to convince herself otherwise.

She turned and walked straight towards the bar, thinking only about the computer portrait of the abductor.

It couldn't possibly be, she thought. She ordered a glass of white wine and quickly retreated into her thoughts. It would explain everything; Denise's murder, the police involvement, everything. She had to see the picture now, but it was in her purse at home.

Laura bolted for the nearest exit, stopping only to retrieve her coat. Within five minutes, she was driving out of the parking garage, heading for the expressway. It was just after seven and rush hour traffic had thinned out nicely.

Inside of twenty-five minutes, she had retrieved the folded computer portrait from her bedroom and was back on the road, probably heading directly into the worst nightmare of her life, she thought.

Laura tried like hell to summon her scientific mind. She knew that she was not just some casual TV watcher who had seen someone resembling one of these composite drawings. Forensic evidence was her life's work. She was highly skilled in comparing evidence, all kinds of evidence, and she knew that Denise had reconstructed the face of Sean Lowry. It could have been coincidence, she thought. She just had to be sure before she accused the Mayor's son of murder.

She parked her car directly in front of the hotel and quickly gave the bellhop a twenty-dollar-bill to take care of it. By the time she reached the top of the stairs and removed her coat, she could see that perspiration was running down her arms. It had stained her dress down to the waist. Her hair and make-up were a wreck. She decided to stay back near the exit until she spotted Sean Lowry, praying that he hadn't left while she was gone. She held the picture folded in her hand as she scanned the faces in the half-darkened ballroom.

There were well over two hundred people in the room, some dancing, some crowded around the bar and still others seated around tables.

Laura moved around the room, sticking as close to the walls as she could, trying her best to do an organized search of each area. Just as her hopes were fading, the band finished its rendition of *Mack the Knife* and Sean Lowry emerged from the crowded dance floor, mounted the stage and took the microphone from the lead singer.

As he spoke, she was able to move closer and closer, until she could see the drops of sweat on his smooth, wrinkle free brow. She was oblivious to what he was saying, focusing only on the face. She unfolded the picture and noticed the distinct lack of age wrinkles or skin blemishes of any kind. It was a characteristic routinely covered by the police artist preparing the composite. It was an indication that the man Denise had seen was young, with extremely good skin. The square jaw, elongated face, and high cheekbones of Sean Lowry had been recreated in the composite with remarkable accuracy.

While it would probably not be apparent to anyone seeing this composite on the six-o'clock news, Laura Stanic was now convinced that Sean Lowry, first born son of Mayor Jack Lowry, was at least a kidnapper and probably a murderer.

It was eight fifty-five in the evening when she called Frank's pager. The message was accompanied by the code 911.

On this occasion, Frank's small band of warriors included a certain Forensic Examiner from the State Crime Laboratory. The group gathered around Frank's kitchen table early Thursday morning. Ellen poured coffee as Laura recounted her experience of the previous evening. She was careful to emphasize that her conclusion was not a scientific certainty, only an educated opinion. When Laura was finished, it was Ellen who spoke first.

"So that's it then. We can call the FBI and get him arrested. They'll make him tell what he did with Caroline."

"I'm sorry, Ellen," Frank said, " but it's just not that easy. Even if Laura's right, and I believe she is, I doubt that Sean killed Denise. There are important people protecting him, not just cops. We have to think about this carefully."

"See, once we make the call, we can't take it back," Ray offered. "We have to consider all the consequences before we act."

"I'll tell you one thing," Califf piped in. "The FBI will check this information out, but they won't take it very seriously. I mean there's no body, no eyewitness, and no physical evidence. There's nothing, other than Sean's resemblance to a computer sketch. The Feds aren't afraid to go after powerful people, but they're not masochistic."

"Can you imagine the fallout if they grabbed him up and grilled him like a common drug dealer?"

"What if he's innocent? Hell, maybe he is. No, what they'll do is follow the book. They'll talk to Sean, quietly and in a very non-threatening way. If he is our guy, I can't imagine what good tipping him off would do. I think we need a lot more before we call the FBI."

There seemed to be general agreement not to call the FBI and Ray led the group to the next logical question. "Then what do we do now to get the evidence we need?"

"Simple, we work hard," Frank answered. "It won't be as easy with Larry out of the loop, but we have to find out who Sean's talking to and who he's meeting with. Let's dig into his past and see what comes up."

"Well, its no secret that, as a kid, he was a wild man," said Califf. "I'm sure most of you remember that incident from high school when he threw a party on some poor guy's yacht and that local kid was attacked. He almost died, as I recall. I was in high school too at the time. We had just moved here, but I remember it from the TV and the newspapers. I'm sure any cop with twelve or thirteen years can remember some pretty good Sean Lowry stories. I still have friends. I can check it out."

"Steve, you're the freelance guy. Dig up whatever you can, wherever you can, anything that could help us. We're looking for people he's relied on to bail him out in the past." Frank was in the zone now. "Ray, when was the last time you went to the library?"

"Law school," Ray answered. "But I'm ready to seek justice wherever it leads me, even if it's the library."

"Good, Sean Lowry obviously earned his reputation as a wild man. Start with everything that was published about the yacht incident ten or twelve years ago; newspapers, magazines, everything. See what else pops up in his high school or college years. We're looking for names. Maybe this cover-up is a repeat performance."

Steve had been relatively quiet during the session.

"Steve, don't hold back on me," said Frank. "If you've got something to say, say it."

"Okay, Frank, I'm not crazy about the plan. In fact, it's not really a plan at all. I, on the other hand, have developed a specific plan tailored to the objective."

"Let me guess," said Frank. "We snatch Sean off the street and you put a gun to his head. You tell him he can either spill the entire story now or die with the secret. How am I doing?"

"Very well, Frank, very well, " answered the old Greek.

"Well, what if he's not the guy, Steve? Better yet, what if he won't talk? Will you shoot him? Let's try it my way first. My kids don't need a father in jail."

"Your family, your rules, Frank. We'll get it done."

Although Steve was somewhat prone to employing Neanderthal methods in his work, he had never been averse to learning new ways of doing things. He attended industry conferences and conventions religiously. The investigation industry had evolved during Steve's time from a foot-pounding endeavor into a swirl of electronic highways and databases.

There were databases for just about any information you wanted. The trick was knowing where to look. Some were free sites. Most were not. Many private investigators themselves had branched out into specialties and offered high-speed access to information for a fee.

For example, you could get access to things like insurance records, medical and psychiatric records, criminal records, and credit records for the touch of a button and the right price.

A good P.I. was still required, however, to distinguish the legitimate vendors from the charlatans. By the time Steve arrived at his office from Frank's house, he had accumulated a small basket of mental notes for Diane on places to start. He hoped he could remember them all.

Despite all the high-tech gear and gadgets in his van, Steve almost never remembered to carry the now low-tech hand-held micro-recorder. It was frustrating, the way he had been forgetting things in recent years. Today, he would put it in the van and leave it there, he thought.

Steve greeted his wife in a perfunctory, distant way and motioned for her to follow him into the inner office. She would never tolerate such caveman tactics at home, but the two had been perfecting this dual relationship for longer than Frank Doherty had been alive.

"Diane, we need to identify all our reliable resources and find out everything we can about Sean Lowry, the Mayor's son. We need everything we can get, above board and below."

The reference was an instruction to her not to distinguish between legally and illegally obtained information. Some information was not legally available for private purposes, but readily obtainable. Those things included credit reports and criminal background checks.

"Why, Hon? Is he involved in the Doherty thing?" Diane asked.

"I'm sorry, Di. That crime lab woman saw him at a big fundraiser and swears he's the face in the composite. It would all make sense."

"Jesus, Mary and Joseph, you had better be very careful, Stavros Panos. You know full well the kind of power that's involved here. That young man is quite a gadabout, if you believe the newspapers, but there's something else, something I just can't quite remember."

"Well, let me know when you do," he said.

Steve didn't need to give her any further instruction. Diane was a licensed private investigator in her own right and was as effective working from the office as the old man was on the street. Steve had barely gotten to his desk when she came barging into his office.

"After forty-seven years, you still won't acknowledge who's the best P.I. in the family," she said, smiling.

"It's all I have left," he groaned. "Please, leave me to my illusions. Now what do you have?"

"Maybe nothing," Diane said, "but at least you'll get some exercise, dear. Do you remember eight or nine years ago when I told you about George's strange near-encounter with young Sean Lowry?"

"Sweetheart, I have great difficulty remembering

eight or nine minutes ago and I left my jacket in the restaurant this morning."

"I took it. It's in the car. Anyway, I was talking to JoAnne one morning on the phone. George was a new detective and little Anna wasn't born yet. JoAnne was really worried about George. She had never seen him so angry. Apparently, he had been taken off a case in favor of another detective. You know how territorial they are about their silly case assignments. Well, the case involved a complaint by a co-ed against Sean Lowry. I don't know if it was a rape, but it was some kind of sexual assault."

"So what did George have to do with it?"

"George was assigned the case and drove over to St. Francis University, where the complaint was made. Before he even got a chance to interview the victim, he was called back to the station and informed that another detective had been given the case. George took it as a personal insult."

"Wait a minute. How do you know all this? I don't know any of this, " he growled.

"JoAnne told me all about it. Anyway, you know his temper. It came from his Greek side. She said he was furious and threatening to file a union grievance. He wouldn't shut up about it, but when I talked to her a few days later, everything was fine. George was okay with it. I thought he had realized that nothing good could come of a bombshell like that."

"You say that you told me about this?" Steve asked, genuinely skeptical.

"Every word."

"Well, I can't ask George about it. If I do, I'll have to tell him everything and that would put him in a compromising position. He'd either have to report everything up the chain of command or violate department rules by withholding the information."

"So what will you do?" she asked.

"I'm not sure. One good cop has already ruined his career over this, but at least it was his choice. George wouldn't have a choice. He'd help me because I'm his father and that wouldn't be fair. I think I'll just take a ride over to St. Francis and nose around. I can't imagine they'd tell me anything, but it can't hurt. At least we have a place to start."

St. Francis University was located in the downtown area, only six blocks from the building that housed the offices of Steve and Frank.

Steve was under a doctor's order to walk thirty minutes each day, an order he had essentially ignored. He briefly toyed with the idea of walking, but dismissed it almost immediately. At my age, he thought, what good would it do anyway?

It wasn't like he ignored *all* the doctor's orders, however. The order to drink two glasses of wine every night, for example, he followed religiously. He decided to drive the short distance and pay the parking. Maybe tonight he'd have four glasses of wine to make up for it.

The downtown campus of St. Francis was a sprawling complex. Instead of sprawling out, however, it sprawled up. The original circa 1920 twelve-story brick building was still in use, but the university had, over the years, acquired the two modern office towers on either side of it. The result was a fully equipped, full-scale campus rising from the heart of the city and occupying only one-half a city block.

Steve located what seemed to be the main entrance on Hudson St. and made immediately for the huge directory, which seemed to take up the better part of the west lobby wall. After a brief search, he determined that the campus security office was on the third floor of the main building.

As he passed through the old glass-windowed mahogany door, Steve found himself facing a service counter that spanned the nearly thirty foot width of the office. Beyond the open workspace, near the rear, there appeared to be a private office.

Although the open area housed five or six work desks with computer terminals, the only employee in sight was a woman seated at one of the desks and, seemingly, deeply engrossed in her current assignment. Steve judged the smartly dressed black woman to be well past middle age. He waited silently for several minutes, hoping the woman would look up and see him standing there, thus avoiding a potentially embarrassing or rude interruption.

After several more minutes, her hands dropped from the keyboard. She looked up and smiled. "Oh, I'm sorry, sir," she said, genuinely apologetic. "Sometimes I get so caught up in my typing that I seem to tune out my other duties. Have you been waiting long?" As she spoke, she was already up and moving towards the counter.

"I have indeed, my dear," Steve said, just as genuinely offering the woman his broadest Mediterranean smile. "You know, computers, wonderful as they are, would be absolutely useless without the energy of the talented young people such as yourself who operate them. It's very fortunate for the world that the things weren't invented when I was a youth. They would likely have been considered too complicated for the generation that saved the world."

"Well now, if I were to guess, I'd say that you came here to borrow money because you are certainly building credit. I'm just glad this isn't a bank 'cause I'd surely give away all the money to a gentleman like you. Now, as long as it's not money, and it's nothing my husband would object to, I'll help you any way I can."

"Ma'am, my name is Steve Panos," he said, handing her a business card. "I'm a private investigator. I'm looking into a very old case, eight years old to be exact. May I ask how long you've worked here?"

"I've been sixteen years in this very office," the woman said. "What would you like to know?"

"It's a very sensitive matter, to say the least. I'll be frank with you. Eight years ago, I believe a young woman came to this office and made a complaint about anther student. She claimed that the man had sexually assaulted her. I have no idea who the woman was, but the man was Sean Lowry, the Mayor's son. I'd like to learn the girl's name and find out where she is."

"Are you working for the girl or for the Mayor?"

The question made clear to Steve that, not only did the woman know something, but she had an agenda as well. He decided to answer truthfully. "Neither, really. It's more like I'm working against Sean Lowry. If, in doing my job, I could help this girl too, I'd be happy to do that. I think that Sean Lowry may have recently hurt another girl."

"Look, Mr. Panos, I remember that incident. I'd like very much to help you, but my hands are tied. I'm raising my grandson and this job is as much his as it is mine. The only thing I can do is refer you to my boss, Mr. Munoz, but I'm afraid it won't do you much good."

Steve thought the response curious, but couldn't say exactly why. "If that's all you can do, then I'd be happy to talk to him, if you can arrange it."

"He's in his office. I'll let him know you're here. It

should only be a minute," the woman said, as she turned and walked towards her desk.

She picked up the phone and, less than a minute later, Ivan Munoz emerged from his office and approached the counter. The man looked to be decidedly middle-aged and obviously Hispanic.

"Mr. Panos, I'm Ivan Munoz, Director of Security." He pronounced the detective's name as though it were Hispanic, as Pan-yos, instead of Pa-nos. "Ms. Booker tells me that you are a private investigator and would like to speak to me. How may help you?" His tone was very businesslike, but not the least unfriendly.

"How do you do, Mr. Munoz? Ms. Booker is quite correct. I am investigating an incident involving a man named Sean Lowry. In the event you do not recognize the name, he is the Mayor's son. I have developed information that, about eight years ago, while young Mr. Lowry was a student here, he was accused of assaulting a young co-ed. I believe it was a sexual assault. No charges were ever brought, but I am trying to determine the name and whereabouts of the young woman involved. I was hoping you could help me in that regard."

It did not require the instincts of a private detective to conclude that Stavros Panos had suddenly become an unwelcome intruder. Before the man even spoke, Steve understood what Ms. Booker had meant. He would receive no assistance from Ivan Munoz. The security chief had clearly been stunned by the request.

When he finally spoke, the anger and annoyance in his voice sounded contrived, a transparent attempt to conceal the cold terror that had crafted his response.

"I beg your pardon? You want me to reveal confidential information from our security files? Who do you work for? Who do you work for? I think perhaps you should tell me exactly where you got your information before this conversation goes any further."

"Look, Mr. Munoz, I'm just asking questions. If you can't answer them, then you can't answer them. It's nothing personal. Good day." Steve turned to leave, but even as he spoke, was aware that the visit had been anything but a waste of time. Munoz not only knew about the incident, but had probably also been involved in some sinister way.

Steve's car had been parked on the third level of the university parking garage. Less than ten minutes after leaving the security office, Steve pulled his van up to the gated exit. As he handed the attendant his ticket with the eight-dollar daily fee, he saw the on-duty security guard copying his rear license plate and recording a description of the van.

It was an assignment he had received via radio from the Director himself.

It took the old Greek nearly a half-hour to negotiate the lunch hour traffic on the way back to the office. Steve never became frustrated with heavy traffic, however. He viewed riding in his van alone as an opportunity to indulge his greatest passion, opera.

The old detective listened intently to Maria Calas, accompanied by The Boston Symphony Orchestra, performing the main aria from Puccini's Madame Butterfly, when the cell phone in his pocket jolted him back into the moment.

"Hello, Steve here."

"Mr. Panos, it's Louise Booker, the lady in the security office. Would it be possible for you to meet me over at the McDonalds in the Crawford Building right before work tomorrow, say about seven thirty?"

"Why, of course, Ms. Booker. I'll be there."

Although he couldn't know for sure, Steve suspected from Munoz's reaction that Louise Booker hadn't been the only security department employee to drop a dime in response to his visit. His suspicion was well founded.

Munoz had Lonnie Hartman on the phone almost before Steve had cleared the garage. He told Hartman everything that had transpired and gave the detective the girl's last known address, along with a detailed description of Steve's van.

Hartman thanked Munoz for the tip, although the detective knew full well that the call had been motivated by self-preservation and not by any sense of gratitude for the five thousand-dollar payoff that Munoz had long since gambled away.

Hartman wasted no time in calling Brad Parkins. When he reached Brad by phone at the latter's airport office, Hartman feigned interest in obtaining Brad's assessment of this *disturbing development*.

In truth, the detective felt no need whatsoever for Parkins' advice, but simply couldn't pass up an opportunity to watch the commissioner squirm a little. They agreed to meet at the airport at three in the afternoon in the food court of Terminal Two.

For a change, the two men arrived almost simultaneously, spotting each other in the crowd of hurried travelers with little difficulty. They converged on a small table in the corner of the area and settled opposite each other, into the plastic swivel chairs on either side of the table.

"Okay, Hartman, here I am. Let's have the news that's too bad to talk about on the phone."

"All right, Brad and, by the way, I appreciate that you've dropped the smart-ass attitude. Sounds to me like some of the cockiness is gone. Are you starting to respect me, Brad, or is it just your fear coming through?"

"Hartman, if we have something to discuss, let's just discuss it, okay?"

"Sounds good. Well, it looks like Doherty's bunch is snooping around St. Francis University. They got wind of Sean's little escapade with the co-ed eight years ago. Looks like they're trying to track her down. Doherty's investigator, that old Greek, Panos, talked to the Security Director. He's the same guy who got five grand of Lowry's money, so he didn't give up any information. As of now, they don't know who she is, but if they keep at it, they're bound to find her. She knows my name. If she talks, we're fucked."

Hartman liked to deliver bad news with a big smile on his face. He knew it irritated Parkins.

"Hartman, did you ever hear the story of the scorpion and the frog?" Parkins asked.

"Fuck the scorpion and the frog," Hartman retorted.

"Okay, Hartman, but sometimes I think you have a compulsion to destroy us both, so listen carefully. We don't need to kill any more people right now. You're out of control. Just settle down and pay the girl a visit tomorrow morning. Make it clear to her that she'll go to jail for extortion if she says one word about what happened, and that's only if we let her live. She wouldn't dare talk."

At about the time that meeting ended, Steve was briefing Diane on the day's events over their customary early dinner.

"Did you tell Frank?" Diane asked

"Tell him what?" Steve responded. "I don't know anything now that I didn't know this morning." Let's hear what Louise has to say tomorrow."

Chapter Thirteen

Late Thursday afternoon, Laura Stanic was in the lab trying, as usual, to pare the ever-expanding list of pending narcotics analyses. It seemed to Laura that her best efforts these days could only succeed in making the list grow at a slower rate.

An hour before quitting time, most of the other examiners were in their cubicles, dictating forensic reports for the day's activities.

She decided to take advantage of the solitude and take a good look at the Denise Doherty file in light of the new information. She signed into the File Storage Section on the fourth floor and quickly located the right file box, using the lab inventory number.

Laura removed the box from the shelf and brought it over to one of the examining tables scattered throughout the area. When she opened the cardboard box, Laura found her original notes, a copy of her report and some items of physical evidence. Those included some blood samples matching Denise Doherty's blood, recovered from the front windshield. She bypassed the blood samples and went directly to the manila envelope containing the Jewish religious medal.

She opened the envelope and found the item as she had last seen it, charred but still structurally strong. She hadn't seen the need to analyze the material, but had judged it to be some variation of aluminum alloy. It had probably been painted.

Owing to the state of incineration, she noted from her notes, no fiber evidence had been recovered from inside the vehicle. Several latent prints had been recovered from the hood of the vehicle, none of which, however, had been suitable for comparison.

As she made her way carefully through the notes, Laura felt the vibration of her digital pager. She held the pager under the fluorescent light and brought the message onto the small screen. It read: *Please call Sean Lowry*. It included a local phone number.

It was nearly four o'clock and, despite her advanced state of panic, Laura reasoned that if she didn't force herself to make the call within the next few minutes, she probably wouldn't reach the narcissistic swine until Monday.

Early responsibility in life had generally deflected her attention from frivolous courting rituals, but had sharpened her intuition and fostered a healthy skepticism. Laura was under no illusion that Sean Lowry wanted to discuss laboratory techniques for identifying lead-based paint. She knew exactly why he had called and she had no clue whatsoever how she would handle it.

Her decision, however, was quickly embraced and not in the least ill considered. It would no doubt impact her life in ways she could only imagine. Making the call could even endanger her life, thus jeopardizing the future of her beloved Alex, in consideration of whom all major decisions were made.

Damn that Doherty, she thought. *Damn him. Damn his sad blue eyes and damn his righteous cause.* What was it about this pathetic wreck of a man that made people want to stand in front of a speeding train for him?

As she had suspected, the number rang to Sean

Lowry's personal cell phone.

He answered on the second ring. "Hello."

"Mr. Lowry, this is Laura Stanic returning your call."

"Mr. Lowry is my father. Mr. Lowry will always be my father. Mr. Lowry may some day be my younger brother, but he will never, ever be me, Laura. It's Sean. The only reason I didn't call yesterday is that my incompetent spies didn't track you down until today. I'm afraid, my dear, that you have bewitched me."

Laura wanted to throw up, but she remembered her sad-eyed lawyer and stepped directly into the path of the speeding train. "Well, Sean, this is quite a surprise coming from someone I've spoken to only once in my life. If I recall correctly, the encounter took place in a receiving line and lasted ten seconds, at most. I had no idea my spell was so powerful."

Laura no longer felt repulsed by her performance or even by the play itself. She found herself curiously warming to the role and strangely exhilarated by the fact that she was about to place her life in grave danger by making a date with a psychotic killer.

Not once since Alex's birth could she recall ever making a significant decision impulsively, never mind recklessly. She was committed to Frank's quest now, hook, line and sinker. It made her feel alive and vibrant in ways that she had long forgotten.

She didn't even try to deny her attraction to the man. Whether or not it ever amounted to anything, it was much more than a physical attraction. This Frank Doherty had come out of nowhere into her life with his passionate cry for help, like one of the lost boys, and it had awakened her from a deep sleep.

In her mind's eye, she could see the little girl named Laura who had once passionately and fiercely defended her sister, Mila, against their stern and uncompromising father.

At age seventeen, Mila had had become pregnant by her boyfriend, a young musician with whom she had been deeply in love. By all indications, the devotion had been mutual.

When Milan Stanic learned of his daughter's plight, he informed her, in the presence of the entire family, that she was no longer his daughter and was no longer welcome in the family home.

Although only eleven years old, Laura immediately went to her room and packed a suitcase with her most precious belongings. She placed it next to her sister's, near the front door, and announced to her father that he had lost two daughters that evening, not one.

Milan had been shaken to his core by the child's insolence, but did not relent. Mila went to live with their grandmother and the newborn was placed for adoption.

To this day, the family had never openly discussed the incident or its aftermath.

Following the birth of Alex out of wedlock, however, Milan clearly had experienced a change of heart. He had rejoiced in the birth of Alex, as any grandparent would, and had openly embraced the boy.

There were, nevertheless, deep scars within the family and Milan had never forgotten the shame visited upon him from the mouth of a child.

Laura loved her father, but was proud of the terrified girl who had faced him down for the love of her sister.

Sean Lowry's voice brought her back to the phone conversation.

"I am desperately hoping that you will agree to have

dinner with me, only dinner and the pleasure of your irresistible company," he said, oozing with all the charm of a snake oil salesman.

"Well, I don't know. I'm not sure. Do you think I'm safe?" Laura asked coyly, wondering silently if her inquiry qualified as a rhetorical question.

"As safe as you want to be, I suppose, but if it's excitement that pushes your buttons, then I'm sure we could cook something up," he said, laughing a laugh that made her skin crawl. "So what do you say, Laura? Saturday? How about I pick you up about eight o'clock?"

Perfect. Maybe when you come to my apartment, you could meet my son and take him out for ice cream. "I'll tell you what, Sean. I'll take a chance, but I'd be more comfortable on a first date if we picked a place and I just met you there. Does that sound okay?"

"Not my first choice, but if it's a take it or leave it proposition, I'll take it. How about Francine's downtown? I have a reserved table there on weekends. Say, eight o'clock? Just tell the *maître d'* you're with me. He'll be expecting you."

She thought about his suggestion for a moment and, in her growing boldness, considered that if she were going to have dinner with a murderer, it wasn't going to be over French food. "Actually, Sean, I don't much care for French food. At the risk of sounding presumptuous, I much prefer Italian."

"Ah, then Italian it shall be. Gianello's on Fourth Street, *Senorina*, same time."

"Okay, see you then. Bye, Sean."

Frank answered his own phone in the office less than thirty seconds later. The portable had been lying on his chest in the dimly lit room. "Law offices. Frank Doherty speaking."

"Frank, I just wanted to let you know that I can't have dinner with you Saturday. I have a date."

"I, uh, well, I guess I just don't remember that we had a–"

"Relax, Frank. You didn't ask me, but I know you were thinking about it. It's just that Sean Lowry beat you to the punch. He called and asked me out. I'm having dinner with him Saturday night."

"Excuse me? Laura, you know that I'm under considerable stress right now and I just can't find any humor in all of this, so let's just talk straight to one another."

"Okay, Frank. I have a date with Sean Lowry Saturday night. We're going to Gianello's for dinner. It seems he finds me irresistible."

"You didn't actually agree to go. Did you? I mean he probably murdered Caroline. What in the name of God were you thinking about? You could end up the same way. Please, Laura, call him back and cancel. We can do this without you taking a risk like that."

"I'm meeting him at a public restaurant. I won't get in his car and I won't go anywhere else with him. It may not solve this case, but I might find out something that could help you. I'm going, Frank."

"Then the rest of us are going too. It'll be a crowded restaurant."

"I guess that would make me feel better," she conceded.

"More than anything else, I'd like to get my hands on his cell phone for at least a few minutes. If I can get the numbers on his speed dial, we might get the break we need.

"I've got to talk to Steve and Larry about this.

Laura, this could be very dangerous for you. Are you sure you know what you're getting into?"

"Wrong question, Frank. I have no idea whatsoever what I'm getting into or how far I'm getting into it or what will come of it, but I know exactly what I'm doing Saturday night. Talk to your wild bunch and call me back tonight when you have a plan."

The next morning, Louise Booker was already seated in a corner booth when Steve entered through the side door of the busy downtown McDonald's. The main entrance sported a revolving door and, for obvious reasons, Steve avoided them like the plague. He spotted her immediately and walked directly to the booth, not even thinking to order coffee or food.

"Good morning, Miss Booker," Steve said. "Might I impose upon you to move to one of these tables in the middle? I fear that if I can get this tired old body into the booth, it may take the fire department to extricate it."

"Oh, I'm sorry, Mr. Panos. Of course I'll move to a table. I'm probably older than you, Mr. Panos, but my grandson always goes right to the booth, so I guess it's just a habit."

Once they were seated, Steve thought it best to come to the point before Louise became interested in the raspberry Danish that sat untouched on the table. "Nonsense, Miss Booker. I have a daughter older than you, but I thank you for calling me. It took great courage and I am deeply grateful for any information you may be able to provide."

Steve had always been able to say things that would sound contrived coming from the mouth of almost anyone else. Although his age and obvious physical limitations made him less threatening, there was an inherent sincerity about the man that had graced him with this license, even in his youth.

"Well, I remember the incident very well. The girl's name is Julie Wells. She was truly a lovely girl. I didn't know her before the incident, but you could just tell that she had been raised by good parents. You know what I mean?"

"I do, indeed," Steve responded.

"Anyway, she didn't call the police. The morning after it happened, she just came into the security office to report it. She was extremely upset. You could see that she had been crying for hours, probably trying to decide whether to report it, poor thing. I was sitting right where I was when you came in yesterday and she just walked in and said it."

"Said what?" The old detective prompted.

"Before I could even introduce myself, she told me that she had been raped by Sean Lowry the night before. She said Sean had put something in her drink. She had decided to report it and have him arrested. The poor thing told me the whole story while I just stood there with my mouth open."

"So what did you do?" Steve asked.

"I went into Mr. Munoz's office right away and told him. He called the police and took her into his office. I tried to comfort her while she waited for the police. She was too upset to talk much to Mr. Munoz."

"So what happened when the police got there? I mean, who got there first? Was it a detective or a uniformed officer?"

"It was a uniformed officer. He spoke to her right in the office. I was there the whole time. Mr. Munoz seemed very uncomfortable and didn't want me to leave."

"What did she say to him?" Steve asked.

"She told him the exact same story she had told me and was very emphatic about the identity of her attacker. She said Sean Lowry had attacked her in the dormitory after their date."

"Well, at some point did the detectives come?" he inquired.

"It was only one and I remember that he took a long time to arrive. It seemed very inconsiderate at the time. When he finally got there he asked Mr. Munoz and me to leave. He was in the office alone with her for over an hour. I could hear her crying the whole time. I even heard her screaming a couple of times, *He raped me*."

"And what happened then?"

"Well, then the detective came out of the office and went into the hallway with Mr. Munoz. I knew right then something was going on because the detective asked me not to go into the room while he was gone. He came back with Mr. Munoz about fifteen minutes later and they both went into the office. They all stayed in there for another ten or fifteen minutes, and then the detective and the girl left."

"How did Julie seem to you when they left?" He prodded some more.

"She was crying non-stop as they walked out. I went into Mr. Munoz's office and asked him if she had been taken to the hospital."

"What did he tell you?"

"He told me no. He said the girl had decided not to press charges because she couldn't identify her attacker. According to Mr. Munoz, Ms. Wells had been mistaken about the identity of her attacker. He told me that, to respect her privacy, no report or record of the incident would be made. I knew that something very bad had been done to that poor girl and it has eaten away at me ever since. Before yesterday, I just never saw any way I could help her."

"That's quite a story," said Steve. "It's just possible that, by telling me this, you've not only helped her, but a number of other good people as well. You've helped more than you know, Ms. Booker, but what I really need now is a way to find her."

No sooner had Steve finished his sentence, than Louise slid a folded piece of paper across the table. "This is her last known address. I don't think she lives there any more, but her parents might. She lived in the dorm at the time, but she could easily have driven home on weekends. It's a very nice little town. I have a sister there. If you're lucky, they still live there. Good luck, Mr. Panos, and God bless."

"From the bottom of my heart, Ms. Booker, thank you."

In mid-morning, it was usually a ninety-minute drive out to Woodland Hills, a far south suburb. Steve had found no listing in the book for a Julie Wells and had counted nine listings under the name of Wells, none of which matched the address on the folded paper. He decided to make a cold call and hoped for the best as he turned the old white van towards the North-South Expressway.

Traffic was particularly heavy that morning and it was nearly ten-fifteen when he finally found the house on a winding street somewhere in the middle of a 1970's style upper-middle-income housing development. It was a good bet the house had at least once belonged to her parents. Even if they didn't live there now, Steve knew he could track them easily through the current occupants and their realtors.

He parked on the street rather than on the driveway, walked up and rang the doorbell. In short order, a rather tall brown haired woman answered the door. Steve judged her to be of the right age.

"May I help you?" the woman asked politely, but nonetheless, made no effort to unlock or open the storm door between her and Steve.

Steve held his business card up to the glass and introduced himself. He was fully aware that the woman would likely be shocked by the nature of his visit and had concluded on the long drive that, if he did not gain her confidence in the first minute of their meeting, there would be no interview. "If you are the mother of Julie Wells, I would very much like to speak with you," he said matter-of-factly.

"This is about my daughter? Has something happened to her? Should my husband be here?"

"Nothing like that, Mrs. Wells. To be frank, I represent the family of a young girl who we believe was abducted and assaulted by Sean Lowry, the Mayor's son. She's missing and it's possible that he even killed her. You may have read about it in the newspapers. Her name is—or was—Caroline Anderson."

"I heard about it on the news, but it didn't say anything about Sean Lowry."

Steve took the dialogue as a good sign. He figured that if she were going to slam the door in his face, he would already be looking at it.

"It wouldn't, Ma'am. That's information that the family is pursuing privately, a fact that explains the nature of my call. We're hoping that you may have some specific reasons of your own to understand why the police are not investigating Sean Lowry in this assault." Steve knew that whatever the woman said or did next would decide the outcome of the trip.

"Come in, Mr. Panos, please. May I get you some coffee?"

"Cream only, Mrs. Wells. Thank you so much," he said as the woman helped him remove his long overcoat.

"Just have a seat in the living room while I hang up your coat and get us some coffee."

Having sat in the living room for less than one minute, he had already determined from pictures on the wall and the piano that Julie was the youngest of three children and that the elder Wells' were grandparents at least three times over, probably not by way of Julie.

Mrs. Wells reentered the room holding two mugs, placed one on the glass table top, within reach of Steve, and seated herself in the chair opposite him. "Now Mr. Panos, you certainly have my attention, so why exactly is it you're here?"

"We believe that young Sean Lowry has a long history of violent and illegal behavior. We think that there are highly placed people in city government and probably even in the police department who, for years, have protected him from prosecution and shielded him from public scrutiny. We believe they have broken laws to do that and maybe even killed people. It's possible that they may even have threatened your daughter with harm had she persisted in her accusation against Sean Lowry."

"And if those things are true, how is it that I can help?" the woman asked pointedly.

"If we can find out who she dealt with from the police department eight years ago, we might go a long way towards solving this case," he answered.

"Well, first off, I don't have the information you want. My daughter might, but why in God's name would she want to drag this all up again, after so many years? It's been very difficult for her, but she has a new life now and a fiancée. Why would she want to open this horrible can of worms again?"

"Well, that's just it. She won't have to open it up. It might give her some real peace to see Sean Lowry and his protectors get what's coming to them. The only thing we want from her is a name, nothing else."

"You know she never told us the whole story. She called me the morning after it happened. She told me what happened, the date with Sean Lowry, the drugging, everything about that night. I'm not sure how much you know."

"I know what happened," he said sympathetically.

"Well, she was really conflicted over whether or not to report it. We talked for a long time. When we hung up, I don't think she'd decided yet. We only had one car at the time. My husband had it at work. Julie was adamant that I shouldn't tell him. In fact, he doesn't know anything about it to this day. So I took a cab to the train station. I had to wait over an hour for a train and, by the time I got to her dormitory, the whole thing was over. I mean it was over."

"What do you mean by that?" Steve was genuinely confused by the remark.

"All of a sudden, she wasn't sure if it had been Sean Lowry. She didn't want to talk about it any more. It was like she wanted me to believe that maybe she'd fallen asleep and just dreamed it up. When I pushed her, she got angry and just closed the door on me completely."

"I hate to ask this Mrs. Wells, but how was your

relationship with Julie at that time?"

"It was good, Mr. Panos. Good enough to know that wasn't like my daughter. We'd always been able to talk to each other. I knew then that something had happened between the time of our phone call and my arrival. I just never knew what until this moment. I'll give you her address. It's her decision and she should have the right to make it."

"Fair enough," said Steve with resolve. "And it's none of my business, but how is she doing now? I mean in terms of all this?"

"I've never been raped so it's difficult for me to know really. After the incident she lost interest in school and went through several jobs over the years. Two years ago, she got a job as a receptionist in a vet's office in the city. He turned out to be a wonderful young man. They're engaged now and just recently bought a new townhouse. I know that she was emotionally wounded for years. Maybe she still is. This may be a way for her to help herself, but only she can decide that. I'll get you the addresses and her phone numbers."

In less than a minute, the woman returned with Steve's coat. After helping the detective don his heavy coat, she handed him the single notebook page containing the addresses and phone numbers. "Good luck, Mr. Panos," she said.

Chapter Fourteen

It had been pure happenstance and blind luck that Lonnie Hartman had arrived at the Wells home at precisely eleven that same morning, only to find an old white van parked directly in front of the house. The van was windowless on the sides and unmarked, but both its appearance and its license plates told Hartman that the van belonged to Doherty's old private detective, Stavros Panos.

Munoz had emphasized that the address was eight years old and had most likely been the home of the girl's parents, so Hartman knew that he hadn't found the girl yet. He had concocted a deceptive tale for the girl's parents, in order to discover her whereabouts, but this pain in the ass PI was upsetting the apple cart.

Hartman waited down the street in the brown, unmarked police sedan for nearly an hour before the old man came limping down the front walk to his car. The woman at the door waved to him as he entered his van, a decidedly bad sign, Hartman concluded. Talking to the mother was out of the question now. It was apparent that the old man had gotten what he came for. Hartman could only follow him now and hope that the chase led directly to his prey.

Afternoon traffic was building early and the drive back into the city took until nearly four o'clock. Hartman took precautions not to be spotted.

The snarled traffic made even the big white van difficult to follow. Hartman was nearly at his wits end, but still on the trail when the van pulled into a city parking lot in the newly gentrified Roosevelt Park area, less than a mile west of the downtown business district.

His vehicle pulled to the curb not ten feet from a NO PARKING sign and he placed the plastic laminated POLICE sign on the dash. He waited and watched as Steve crossed the street and entered the small veterinary hospital on the corner. After only a few minutes, he watched the old investigator leave the building, accompanied by a smartly dressed young woman. They entered a coffee shop two or three doors down.

There could be no doubt whatsoever, Hartman thought, that the old man was talking to Julie Wells who, he was certain, would remember his name forever. If the coffee break lasted more than five minutes, then this would be an ominous development, indeed.

The unannounced visit from a private investigator regarding this ugly incident from her past had jolted the young woman and instantly rekindled long suppressed fear and emotions. She agreed to talk to the old man, more from a sense of resignation than anything else.

As they covered the short distance to the coffee shop, Julie was almost relieved, having long believed that her new life could never really begin until she had made peace with the old one.

As they settled into a corner table, she concealed these emotions from the private detective.

As the waitress filled their two coffee cups, the girl waited, eyes staring down into the blackness of the cup, for the words she feared.

"Ms. Wells, I want to make it very clear to you from

the beginning that I am not here to disrupt your life in any way. I'm after Sean Lowry for something he did to another girl very recently. She's missing and he probably killed her. I think there are some police officers and maybe even some government officials covering up for him. There is reason to believe you were somehow intimidated into withdrawing your accusation against Sean eight years ago."

Julie fought to retain her composure and nearly failed.

After a slight pause he continued. "If that's true, I only need to know the names of the people who were involved, nothing else. There's a good chance that those same people have committed crimes to protect him in our case too."

"I'm afraid it's much more complicated than that, Mr. Panos, and I really don't care any more if all of this finally comes out. I told Mike, my fiancée, the whole story before we got engaged. It helped, but it's not enough. You see, I live my life every day with a mixture of both rage and guilt; rage over the fact that Sean Lowry did that to me without consequence, and guilt over the fact that I took money to keep quiet." Panos appeared unprepared for the later revelation.

"What do you mean you took money? How much? From whom? Why? Tell me about that, please."

"The detective's name was Lonnie Hartman. He was very cold and frightening. Nothing in my life up to that point had prepared me for dealing with someone like him. I sat in that security office for nearly two hours waiting for him."

"Was there anyone else in the office?"

"Yes. There was that awful supervisor and the lady

who worked in the office. She was very nice."

"So what happened when the detective arrived?"

"I expected, well, I don't know what I expected, but I wanted someone to say 'It's Okay. I'll make it right. I'll make him pay.' What I got was a cold-blooded thug who began by calling me a gold-digging whore. He told me that if I forced the issue, all of the Mayor's resources would be used to destroy me publicly and expose me as a money-grubbing slut. He even told me that would happen only if I was lucky. He said the more likely scenario was that I would end up face down in a dumpster somewhere. I've never known such terror."

"Is that when you agreed to take money?" he asked

"Not right away. He sort of changed his tune. When he could see me falling apart, he started acting nice and said that, just in case Sean had really misbehaved, the Mayor didn't want to see me go uncompensated. He talked about how I had lots of bills to pay and would probably need counseling. He said that the Mayor was a fair person and wanted me to be taken care of. Then he gave me an envelope and said it contained twenty thousand dollars."

"He already had the envelope right there? In his pocket?"

"Yes. I mean—I never even saw the money. He put the envelope in my purse. I didn't say anything. Don't misunderstand. I didn't want the money. I didn't ask for it. I never even said I'd take it. I was just scared to death."

"Julie, you don't have to tell me those things. I already know."

She could sense that his empathy was real and it gave her the courage to continue. "For a few days, I just stared at the money on my desk in the dorm. Then I told myself it was the least I had coming from Sean Lowry. My parents and I were struggling with tuition and living expenses. My brother was still living with them at the time. So I just kept the money and used it. I'm so ashamed." She sobbed openly, a single teardrop falling into the untouched coffee.

"Julie, surely you understand that you had no choice. You didn't accept the money at all. It was forced on you to ensure your silence. They had to be sure that you wouldn't change your mind later and come after Sean. They had to dirty you somehow to keep you quiet. You must see that. If you had refused the money, you might even have been killed."

"No offense, but I've been paying a psychologist to talk to me like that for years and it hasn't helped a bit. Knowing it and believing it are two different things. I think you would have to be a woman to understand how it really feels to be powerless, but I believe that you want to help. I feel better for telling you this and if it all has to come out, then I guess I can live with it. Maybe I can pick up a newspaper some day and read about how that bastard Sean Lowry got his medicine."

"Thank you, Julie. I think I can promise you that Sean Lowry will get his medicine, and don't worry about it coming out. The old Greek will never tell. I promise."

Hartman had been parked in the same no-parking zone for nearly an hour and darkness had begun to settle on the early winter evening. Only minutes ago, he had calmly rendered a silent death sentence upon Stavros Panos.

By now, the investigator surely knew every detail of the sordid cover-up, Hartman realized. He could deal with the girl later, but this persistent old fool had stumbled upon the connection that could no doubt lead to the demise of Lonnie Hartman.

Hartman found no satisfaction in knowing that the esteemed Commissioner of Aviation would be going right down the same drain. If he had to save Parkins' ass in the process, then so be it. When this was all over, he might even make the obnoxious little prick disappear permanently.

Hartman decided that, whatever the risk might be for lack of planning, he had to kill the old man now, before he had a chance to get the information back to Doherty. He considered hiding in the old man's van, but couldn't be sure what kind of alarms and electronic gismos might be protecting it. Some of these guys were paranoid and others were just infatuated by all the James Bond electronics. Best not to tamper with the van, he thought. Hartman quickly opted to once again lean on his most dependable crutch, the detective shield.

As the old man left Julie Wells, he walked north, towards the parking lot. He had to cross an alley about a hundred feet beyond the animal hospital.

Hartman sat in the police car, engine running, across the street and facing the unsuspecting old Greek. He was never more alive than in these moments. The adrenaline rush was nothing short of intoxicating. He was no psycho, but he didn't know a single living person more qualified and competent to kill when murder was absolutely called for. As he waited to strike, Hartman thought briefly that he would have made a world-class secret agent in the cold war days.

When the old man was ten feet from the alley, Hartman gunned the engine of the black sedan and the car lurched forward. Violently, he wheeled the car left into the mouth of the alley, blocking the path of a startled Stavros Panos.

Hartman was out of the car with his gun pointed at Steve's head almost before the old man could stop walking. "Police officer, sir. Put your hands in the air. Come around the corner and put your hands up on the building."

Steve did exactly as he was told and did not speak.

"Is your name Stavros Panos?"

"Why, yes and I take it you would be Detective Lonnie Hartman."

Steve would be damned before he gave Hartman the satisfaction of sensing fear or panic, although the old man was feeling an abundance of both. His first thought was that Hartman would never reveal himself in such an obvious way if he thought Steve would ever tell the story.

The Greek's mind was as clear as it had ever been, alert and temporarily free from its arch enemy, old age. Steve concluded almost immediately that, whatever happened on the street, he must not get into the car, even if he died trying to escape. This car was his intended coffin and he would not meet the devil quietly, at least not while he could fight.

Hartman moved around the car, gun in one hand and handcuffs in the other. He could not see in the dark alley that Steve's left hand was holding the bamboo walking stick flush against the building.

As Hartman got to within three feet, Steve summoned all his strength and whirled to the right, giving his left arm room to gain speed and leverage. The bamboo cane struck the stunned Hartman flush on the right cheek and drove him back onto the trunk of the car.

Blood rushed from the gash in his cheek as Steve was on him in a second.

The old man tried desperately to wrestle the gun from Hartman's hand, but his momentary strength had abandoned him. He was old again and no match for the younger Hartman, who subdued and handcuffed him in short order.

By this time, several passers-by had gathered and Hartman flashed his shield and advised them that the situation was under control. He quickly patted the old man down and removed an old snub-nosed .38 cal. revolver and key ring from Steve's coat pocket. Hartman then placed the panting and utterly exhausted private detective into the back seat of the sedan and drove away from the scene without further delay.

In the back seat, Steve had partially recovered from his ordeal, although every bone in his tired body ached. The car seemed to be driving around aimlessly through the city streets. It was difficult to judge time between the pain and the fear, but Steve reckoned that Hartman had driven the car nowhere in particular for over half an hour.

For a brief moment, still alive, he seized upon a glimmer of hope that he might still see his Diane in the next sunlight. Hope turned to sad resignation, however, as he began to recognize the general neighborhood of the animal hospital. Hartman was going back for his van.

As he glanced at his driver through the rear view mirror, the old man could see the clear result of what might prove to have been his last stand.

The cut was long, but not as deep as the unsightly volume of dried blood indicated. Without the attention of a plastic surgeon, Steve thought, this homicidal maniac would wear his mark forever. The thought gave him little consolation, considering the scar's lack of proportion to cold-blooded murder.

Hartman gloated. "You fucks think you're so smart," he said, smiling in the smudged mirror. "I might do the whole fucking bunch of you before I'm through. The difference between me and that faggot you work for is that he doesn't have the balls to finish what he starts. By the way, in case you hadn't figured it out yet, I'm the one who killed his wife. Its just too bad I couldn't have fucked her first."

Steve reached deep into his soul and summoned every trace of discipline, in an effort to deny Hartman the desired reaction. His stoic façade seemed to irritate Hartman more than the bloody slice on his face.

"Just tell me. Do you fools actually think you can bring down Sean Lowry, or even me?" There was a wild look in his eyes now. "You have no idea. Do you? Nobody could win the game you're playing, you fucking moron."

Looking in the rear view mirror, Steve saw disappointment in Hartman's cold, angry eyes when he refused to reply.

"Hey, asshole, did you ever see that old movie with Jack Nicholson, *The Last Detail*? Well, he's an SP and he's taking this young recruit on an overnight train trip to Fort Leavenworth. The kid was convicted of stealing candy or some shit and got like an eight-year sentence.

"You know, I don't hate you at all," Hartman said. "If you want make like a wall, then I'll talk to the wall. After all, I'll be stopping for a beer afterward, and you won't.

"Anyway, Nicholson feels sorry for the kid." The lunatic continued to ramble. "So he takes him into a bar and gets him drunk. The kid has a great time, but he breaks up some furniture and shit. The bartender starts yelling, 'Call the shore patrol.' Well, Nicholson pulls this big old .45 caliber automatic, slams it on the bar and says, 'I am the motherfucking shore patrol.' "

Hartman glanced into the mirror again and Steve saw no trace of anger, only emptiness. This lunatic might murder him, but he would not win this game.

"You know, it kind of reminds me of us. Don't you think? See, you fucking slobs are yelling for help, but nobody hears you. Nobody ever will because I'm an instrument of everything around you."

By that time he could have struck up the band in the front seat and Steve wouldn't have noticed or cared. His anger had begun to subside and he was thinking of other things, important things.

"See, you've always lived under the same rules I do, but you just didn't know it because you never pushed hard enough at the edges. You never threatened the game board until now. It's kind of like you're living in an invisible bubble and you don't know it's there. Most people go their whole lives under the illusion that they're free, but you and your friends had to go and prick the bubble. I admit I didn't really see the big picture myself until recently. I like it though. It makes me feel secure, kind of warm and fuzzy, you know? As long as you know the bubble is there, you can work with it, have a great life and maybe even get rich."

Hartman parked the sedan in a nearby convenience store parking lot and placed the cardboard POLICE sign in the dash. He then leaned over and removed the handcuff from Steve's left wrist and re-secured the old man's wrists around the steering wheel. Key ring in hand, Hartman strolled up the street to the city lot and pointed the remote at Steve's van.

With a momentary beep and flash of headlights, the alarm disengaged and the doors unlocked. Hartman then dutifully paid the drive-thru gate attendant and proceeded on to the convenience store lot, where he transferred his human cargo to the front seat of the van.

As the van moved towards the city limits, the air was extremely heavy and damp. It wasn't snowing or raining, but heavy moisture on the windshield forced him to seek out the wiper switch. After a good while, the detective began to ramble a bit.

"You know, I have no love for this fucking Sean Lowry. Truth is, he's been a thorn in my side for over ten years. He has no balls and I'd say he's probably sucked a few cocks in his day."

Stavros Panos hardly noticed the conciliatory words. He was lost somewhere in the process of assessing the sum total of his life.

Hartman found the closest entrance onto the expressway system and headed west. It seemed the farther they drove from the heart of the city, the darker it became.

For the old man, Lonnie Hartman did not exist. In those minutes, Steve considered whether it was better to die quickly and unexpectedly or to be given thirty or sixty minutes notice of one's impending death.

He never resolved the question, but thought that it was most likely a double-edged sword. Some people might look at the time for reflection as a form of suffering or mental anguish, kind of like what lawyers talk about when an airplane goes down from thirty thousand feet.

Others might consider it comforting; an opportunity to do a no-holds-barred final accounting of one's life, to arrive at the net debit or credit.

Steve wasn't sure which side of the coin he preferred, but he did long for a chance to talk to Diane one last time. He wanted to talk to her about things they had never spoken of openly. He wanted a chance to tear down the barriers that his psyche had erected decades ago and just hold her closely and sob, sob openly together in that way.

As Hartman continued to babble, he may as well have been whispering to a corpse.

Finally, Steve interrupted, rather dispassionately. "Would you mind if I listened to my music until we get where we're going?"

"Not at all," said Hartman, sounding overly accommodating for a man who was about to murder the object of his kind consideration.

"There's CD already in the player. If you just hit the power button, I don't think it will be too loud."

Hartman did as requested without further response.

In another half-hour, Steve was oblivious to the changing landscape. Sprawling suburbs had given way to dark, resting, barren cornfields, and hilly two-lane roads. Less than ninety minutes from its point of departure, the old white van slowed to a stop on a pitch-dark gravel road in the middle of nowhere, amidst a stand of tall wooded scrub.

No words were spoken. Hartman turned and looked at the old man. He was just sitting there, head back, eyes closed, smiling as though he were lying on a beach somewhere, basking the sun. Surely he knew it was coming, Hartman thought.

Steve never moved or even flinched. The old man's body simply did not protest as Hartman brought the pistol barrel to rest barely an inch from his temple and pulled the trigger once.

Had Hartman understood Italian, he might have been unnerved by the powerful irony of the moment. From the van's strategically placed custom speakers, the nearly whispering but angelic voice of Maria Calas, from Act II of *Madame Butterfly*, provided a poetic and fitting accompaniment to the tragic finale:

> *Sleep, my love, sleep on my heart.*
> *You are with God, and I am with my grief.*
> *For you the rays of the golden stars...*
> *my baby, sleep*

CHAPTER FIFTEEN

At nine o'clock Saturday morning, the entire crew was gathered in Frank's office, drinking coffee and considering the very latest and most startling of developments, the disappearance of Stavros Panos.

Diane had waited until the early morning hours to call Frank at home. She had told Frank everything, including George's experience with Sean eight years ago.

Upon learning of Steve's Thursday experience at the college and his early meeting Friday morning with Louise Booker, Frank feared the worst.

At Frank's request, the whole crew was there for the meeting; Ray, Larry, Laura, Beth, Ellen, and even Diane, in her now dual capacities as anxious spouse and proxy for her missing sleuth husband.

Even before the meeting began, Frank and Diane had been resigned to the fact that Louise Booker couldn't be contacted until Monday morning at the earliest. She was not listed in the phone book and the ongoing process of calling every Booker in the white pages would not likely succeed. Diane and Beth had been trying for hours. Some were wrong numbers. Others rang to answering machines and still others went completely unanswered.

Following a brief period of mingling and individual speculation, Frank addressed the group collectively. "Look, nobody here doubts that Steve's disappearance is connected to this case, but for the moment it looks like we're up a tree. Louise Booker is obviously the key, but there's no way we can contact her, at least not in the next forty-eight hours. We just can't wait that long, so the question is where do we start?"

"We have to assume that he found the co-ed from St. Francis, or at least he was on her trail," Laura offered.

"There can't be any doubt about it," Larry Califf added, "and that means Steve's chances are not good. I'm sorry, Diane."

He had only confirmed what the tired, lifeless eyes of the courageous old woman had already revealed to them all.

"It tells us one thing for sure," Ray chimed in. "Whatever cops were involved in that co-ed thing eight years ago are involved in this. They were probably sitting on this girl, watching to see if we tried to contact her. They were determined to keep us from making the connection, but I may be able to shed some light on that."

"Go ahead, Ray. We're all listening," Frank proclaimed.

"Okay, I admit I'm not much for library work, but I did come up with a name in researching the newspaper publicity of that yacht party incident eleven years ago. There was a blizzard of publicity about it, but the thing died out quickly after the civil claim was settled. We know that no charges were ever brought because nobody could identify the attacker."

"I remember," Larry observed. "Supposedly they were all too drunk or something."

"Right, and all media requests for information beyond the press release were handled through the police department public relations people, but the blackout wasn't totally effective."

"How's that?" Frank asked.

"Well, several days after the incident, a Post-Dispatch reporter was hanging around the hallway outside the victim's hospital room. She saw a detective coming out of the room and tried to question him. He just gave her the 'no comment' response and rushed off, but she knew him. I mean she knew his name. There was nothing unusual about it and it wasn't any kind of story, but she noted the encounter in a follow-up article on the investigation. The interesting thing is that she named the detective. His name was Hartman, Lonnie Hartman."

"Good work, Ray," said Larry enthusiastically. "We could start by checking this guy out. If his name pops up anywhere in the St. Francis incident he's got to be our man."

"I think we can do better than that," said Frank, jumping to his feet. "We can connect him to this case. The day I went to the lab to see Laura, Corliss came to see me later at the office. We were expecting it. Well, he wasn't alone. He had a partner that day by the name of Hartman."

"Do you know him, Frank?" Beth asked.

"Kind of. He's been around for years, although I wouldn't have known his name without being told. I didn't attach any significance to his presence at the time. They like to travel in pairs.

"Anyway, Hartman didn't say anything during the entire conversation. He just kind of stood behind me trying to act intimidating. He's got to be our guy. Good work, Ray."

"That would certainly explain his access to information," Larry offered. "He'd want to be in close contact with the investigation to keep tabs on us, but not too close, not close enough to be noticed."

"What about Corliss?" Laura asked. "Is he in on it too?"

"Your guess is as good as mine," said Frank, "but we have to assume he is from this point forward."

"I know one thing for sure." Diane finally had something to say on the subject. "We can't keep George out of it anymore. We'll just have to gamble that he'll play it our way for now and keep it unofficial for a while. He might be able to tie Hartman directly to the St. Francis incident. If he does, then I say we turn this thing over to the FBI. That should be enough to convince them of what's going on here and, if they put some serious pressure on young Mr. Lowry—"

"He'll fold like a bad poker hand," Ray concluded.

"Sounds like a plan, Diane," Frank added. "Can you get George over here right now?"

"Of course I can. He's off today. He's probably home fiddling around in the garage, trying to keep from going crazy. I called him early this morning to tell him his dad didn't come home and it killed me to have to keep all this from him. I'll call him now." She was headed towards the phone in the kitchen, even as she spoke.

"What about the girl, Frank, the girl from the college?" Ray asked. "Do you think she's in danger?"

The question posed a compelling dilemma that Califf addressed directly. "She doesn't really know anything about this case, but let's assume that George can tie Hartman to the St. Francis incident. The statute of limitations has run on anything Hartman did in connection with that cover-up eight years ago. So, it seems to me that the biggest danger she poses to him is that she knows his name. It's hard to say how much of a threat Hartman perceives her to be, but I'd feel a lot better if we could warn her right now."

"Well, nobody could warn her right now because we don't know who she is or where she is," Frank reminded them. "In theory, the FBI has the recourses to find Louise Booker before Monday, but it would take us until then to convince them to even open an investigation. We couldn't do that at all now unless George can make the connection to Hartman. Hell, we don't even know for sure that Steve talked to her."

It hadn't been Frank's intention at this point to offer direction. He had been thinking out loud, hoping someone could fill in some gaps.

"Let's just wait for George," Larry suggested. "Who knows? Maybe he even remembers the girl's name."

When George arrived, around forty-five minutes later, he was confused by both the venue of the meeting and the assembled cast of characters. As his mother introduced him around the room, George suppressed his questions until he came upon the face of Larry Califf. "So, it's true then. You've been working with them all along, giving them access to our case files and confidential information."

It hadn't been intended as a question, although Califf treated it as such. "Anything and everything that would help, yes, George." Califf's demeanor was straightforward and sincere.

"I had no idea my father was mixed up in this, but he was never very discriminating in his associations," George said angrily, glancing in the direction of Frank.

Turning back to Califf, he spoke again. "You know your career is over, Califf."

"George, I mean no disrespect, but if I were you, I'd be listening instead of talking. Oh, and about my career, this isn't it. Oh, I'm a cop all right. That's my job, but it's not my career. See, as you're about to find out, I'm doing my job the best I can, but after this, I think I'll get a new job, maybe even a real career," he said, without any hint of sarcasm.

"Understand one thing, George." Diane felt the need to provide a solid foundation for George's cooperation. "These people are your father's friends, especially Frank Doherty. I'll thank you to show them some respect and to withhold your judgment until you know the facts."

"You're right, mother. I apologize, Mr. Doherty. Now, please tell me what you know about my father's disappearance."

They told him everything. Frank began with Caroline's disappearance and they all helped to brief George on literally every detail of their investigation, including the deaths of Denise, Mookie and Sam, right up to Steve's scheduled encounter with Louise Booker Friday morning.

Frank wrapped up the briefing with the group's suspicions about Lonnie Hartman and its hope that George could link Hartman to the St. Francis University incident eight years ago.

At the conclusion of the briefing, George, still an experienced and street-smart detective, addressed Frank Doherty directly in an even and quiet tone. "Then my father's dead."

"We think that's the likelihood, George. We're all sorry," said Frank.

"Well, the short answer to your question is no," said George. "I can't tie Lonnie Hartman to Sean Lowry's rampage at St. Francis and you won't find any paperwork on it either. As far as I know, there was never even a case file number assigned. I don't think anybody knows which detective did the dirty work, except maybe the girl herself. It was a closely guarded secret."

"Who knew?" Larry asked.

"I don't know, but it had to be someone high up in the department, maybe even higher than that."

"Well, what did you know?" Frank inquired.

"Nothing first hand. I never even met the girl or got her name. I hadn't even left my car when I was called off the case by radio."

"So you don't know anything at all?" Frank asked, not hiding his disappointment.

"I didn't say that," George continued. "Less than two days later it was all over the department, unofficially. They may as well have put it in a department-wide roll call notice for the next day. Lots of good cops were disgusted by it, but officially, it was only rumor, not evidence."

"Okay, tell us about it," Frank said.

"It was right before I got promoted. I was working a day shift in downtown Homicide/Violent Crimes. Anyway, it was my turn and caught this date rape complaint at St. Francis University. Those are easy cases to clear because the victim always knows the offender. The guy may not be easy to convict, but the case gets cleared on the spot. As I was on my way to the campus, I got a radio message directing me off the call."

"So what did you do?" Larry inquired.

"Same thing you would do. I went back to the station. I was really pissed. I found out the Watch Commander had gotten a call from upstairs. He said I'd been reassigned for security reasons. That was all he knew, or at least all he would tell me. He told me to get over it and move on."

"So what did you do?" Frank asked.

"After thinking about it for a few hours, I realized it wasn't worth risking my career for, so I took his advice. I moved on. Then, like I said, within two days, it was common locker room knowledge within the department that Sean Lowry had assaulted a co-ed at the campus and had taken a quiet walk."

"That was it?" Ray asked.

"That's all we heard. No charges were ever filed and no paperwork was done, but they couldn't cover it up completely because a beat cop had answered the original call. He probably had the word out on the street before the detectives even got the call."

"What I don't understand," Ray interrupted, "is why you were so pissed off."

"I can answer that," Larry volunteered. "The numbered assignment system is sacred with detectives. It prevents the ass kissers from catching all the easy cases. And, like he said, date rape is an easy case to clear."

"And the more cases you clear, the faster you get promoted," George added.

"So what do you know about Sean Lowry that could help us?" Frank asked.

"That goddamn Sean Lowry should have been drowned at birth. Since he was a teenager, cops have been protecting him. There's a joke in the department that no cadet can graduate until he can identify a life-size cutout of Sean in a crowd from a hundred yards. It might even be half-true by now."

"So, I guess the next question is what do you know about Hartman?" Frank asked, hoping for at least an insight into the man who may well have murdered his wife.

"Well," George began, "I've known him for years.

Seems like he's been a detective forever. He's definitely old school, kind of a surly type, you know, a loner. The guy's had a few prominent brutality beefs over the years, but, in the past, those were just viewed by the brass as the mark of a job well done. You could get in a lot more trouble staying five extra minutes in the donut shop than whipping a suspect's ass."

"Anything more serious?" Frank asked.

"Hartman's time has come and gone, but I have no reason to think he's out there killing people, if that's what you mean. There's nothing I can really tell you about him that would tend to prove or disprove your suspicions. In the meantime, my father's missing and the police department doesn't officially know anything about any of this. I'd like to know what you propose to do now."

It wasn't the request Frank had been expecting. Pointedly, no one answered the question directly.

While Frank was still puzzling over the comment, Califf picked up the ball. "Well, first George, for reasons that should now be clear to you, we're going to ask you not to report any of this to the department. If you do, more lives will be in jeopardy and we just don't know how high up this goes. It could go right up to the fourth floor of City Hall. We need a couple of days."

"Okay, I agree with you. I'll just make a routine missing persons report. I won't mention any of this. That way, law enforcement will be alerted to watch out for him, but it won't blow the cover off your investigation."

"Thanks, George," said Frank, rising from the table and extending his hand. "We'll keep you posted daily, of course, and we appreciate your confidence."

Nobody had raised the subject before George's arrival, but there now seemed to be a silent conspiracy not to mention Laura's upcoming date in George's presence.

Diane asked George to give her a ride home.

Frank judged that she was knowingly giving them all an opportunity to speak freely in her absence. The evening's plan for Laura's date was high on the meeting's agenda, but nevertheless, the subject was effectively buried until George's car had cleared the driveway.

"Did anybody get the feeling George was a little too quick to submit to our jurisdiction?" Beth asked.

"Well said," answered Ray. "It's almost as if he's protecting his father somehow, but from what?"

"It is puzzling," offered Larry. "His instinct should have been to hijack our whole case. Hell, he's a ranking detective and he walks out of here without so much as asking a question. I thought, for sure, he'd want to take this whole thing over. We might have talked him out of it eventually. It just shouldn't have been so damn easy."

"So what are you getting?" Frank asked, more for the benefit of the others than himself.

"I don't know. He can't possibly be one of the bad guys here, not when it involves the murder of his own father."

"I agree," said Frank. "We could be wrong, but it looks like George has his own agenda and there's no telling what it might be."

The meeting then turned its attention to the evening ahead.

Chapter Sixteen

At eight forty-five, Laura parked a block from the restaurant and waited for the call. At one minute past eight, her cell phone rang and she answered on the first ring.

"Good evening, Frank," she said in a teasing voice.

"Sorry to disappoint you. It's Larry. Frank is probably on his second glass of Chianti by now. Everything is in place. Are you still okay with this, Laura?"

"Ready or not, here I come."

"Remember, Laura. Stick to the plan, no adlibbing."

"Don't worry. I'm famished. I'm in front of the restaurant now. Good-bye."

Laura pulled up directly in front of Gianelli's, surrendered her car to the valet, and was promptly greeted inside the foyer by a broadly grinning Sean Lowry. She had privately concluded on the way over that Sean had likely not assaulted a woman in months, in light of all the trouble, and would be starving for affection.

As she took his outstretched hand, Laura consciously reminded herself that behind those soft, blue, puppy dog eyes, the mind of a psychotic killer was sizing her up, much in the way one would savor the sight and aroma of a prime strip steak on the plate.

It was entirely possible, she thought, that she might enjoy a fine expensive dinner and be home before ten thirty without incident. Enjoy might not be the right word, however, considering the butterflies in her stomach.

This was clearly a dangerous and violent man, capable of doing her great harm in a myriad of ways, without the burden of conscience. She felt, nevertheless, confident and focused; satisfied to her core that Frank Doherty, whatever his flaws, would allow no harm to come to her. As her performance commenced, Laura searched consciously for any trace of fear. Finding none, she took Sean's arm and smiled.

As the handsome couple strolled elegantly into the dinning room behind the *maître d'*, Frank Doherty, seated facing the foyer at a corner table, opposite Ellen, promptly looked up and began choking on a mouthful of antipasto salad.

"I can't believe that someone so obviously responsible and serious minded could be so reckless as to wear a dress like that. It's red! Not only that, but if it were any shorter, she'd have had to powder four cheeks, instead of two. What is she thinking?"

A muted chuckle passed Ellen's lips, notwithstanding the seriousness of the situation.

"The guy is a crazed sex murderer. You don't parade in front of him in a red spandex micro-dress. This isn't supposed to be a sting operation. She's just supposed to get the goddamn cell phone. If she has to get away from the asshole, how is she supposed to run in four-inch heels?"

"Relax," Ellen said, turning back from her own quick glance. "Laura knows what she's doing. She wants to whet his appetite, so he'll be more pliable—and it's not spandex. It looks like maybe a cotton and wool blend. It's gorgeous. Besides, Frank, I have a suspicion it's more for you than for him. I haven't been able to wear anything like that for twenty years. Do you like it, Frank?"

"Enough, Ellen," he said, as the *maître d'* led the couple to a table more or less in the center of the large room.

The lighting was dim and almost entirely radiating from wall-mounted lamps in the Mediterranean style, but nevertheless, Frank had an unobstructed view of the dating diners. From his chair, he had a nearly full frontal view of Laura and could clearly make out the right side of Sean's face. Larry and Beth, seated roughly in the opposite corner, had an equally good view of the couple in reverse.

Before their chairs could even have warmed, the waiter appeared bearing a bottle of what looked to be expensive red wine. As he faded from view, the two raised their glasses. Frank saw Laura laugh and, with her left hand, brush back a long wave of shiny brown hair that had invaded the left side of her face. "Here's to a lovely evening with the loveliest of companions," said the dapper and charming young degenerate, his blue eyes emerging from over the rim of his raised glass. "I can't tell you how delighted I was when I actually found you."

"I can't tell you how surprised I was that you looked," Laura responded, more sincerely than Sean would ever know.

Sean dominated the conversation. He was obviously educated and cultured, but money and exposure to high society had done little to mask the self-indulgent and Hedonistic nature of this boorish young animal.

As the evening progressed, Laura was surprised at her own ability to manage and carry off the deception. She continued to feign interest and infatuation and thought that, even without her knowledge of his evil deeds, she would have seen through this empty ornament of a man long before dessert.

She laughed at yet another unfunny off-color joke and couldn't resist stealing a glance at that pathetic, wonderfully self-deprecating, middle-aged disaster, who had opened her heart after all these years. He didn't notice.

Finally, somewhere in the middle of dessert, when she perceived the time was right, she reached into her purse and removed her pager.

"That was me vibrating," she said with a coy smile. Laura slapped herself mentally for overacting. "Looks like the babysitter," she said, pretending to read the pager. "It's my ex-mother-in-law. My son is staying overnight with her and he gets on her nerves pretty easily. Would you excuse me for a moment?"

"Of course," he said.

"You know, I don't recall seeing a phone. I'm embarrassed to tell you that I don't have any change anyway."

Sean was already reaching into the breast pocket of his sport coat. "No need for that, Laura. You're welcome to use my phone."

Smiling, Laura took the small phone from Sean's extended hand and headed in the direction of the bar and restrooms. Sean and Frank were not the only men watching.

As Laura disappeared into the foyer, she sensed that Sean's loins ached with the craving he could never control. His time of self-imposed celibacy had ended. He probably didn't consider himself a murderer, or even a pervert, for that matter. Most likely, he considered Caroline's murder merely a tragic accident, more the result of a cocaine frenzy than his own perversion.

IMMORAL AUTHORITY

He will be deeply disappointed tonight.

The hallway that provided access to the restrooms was located just beyond the open entrance to the dimly lit bar and not visible from Sean's table.

As Laura passed the opening, she brushed shoulders with a well dressed young man leaving the bar and, by the time she reached the restroom, Larry Califf was busy outside calling up the stored numbers in Sean Lowry's speed dial. There were twelve in all.

Frank had been better positioned to observe the exchange and, although he had been looking for it, hadn't detected it. He turned his eyes back from the foyer just in time to see Sean lean forward across the table and extend his semi-closed hand over the nearly full wine-glass at Laura's place. He was overcome by a wave of fear. "The wine, Ellen. He put something in the wine," he whispered.

No sooner had Frank spoken, than he saw Sean perform a disturbing ritual. He to removed something from his pocket and, right there in the dimly lit restaurant, Frank saw him taking a hit of cocaine up his nose. Although his face was down and sheltered by his right hand, there was no mistaking the backward jerk of Sean's head as he inhaled.

"I'll be right back," said Ellen, already on her feet and lazily headed in the general direction of the restrooms. As she entered the ornately decorated women's restroom, Ellen found Laura stoically facing a wall-sized mirror behind a row of five or six elegant gold-trimmed washbowls. Not engaged in any discernable type of cosmetic repair, Laura was staring intently at herself in the mirror, almost as though she was telepathically communicating with the image.

"Giving ourselves a pep talk, are we?" Ellen asked.

"More like wondering what we're doing here and how we got here, maybe even where we're going from here." As Laura spoke, she was dangerously preoccupied.

"Laura, don't forget that this plan isn't foolproof. No matter how many people are out there to help you, it's still risky, so don't lose your focus and, whatever else you do, don't drink any more wine. He put something in it. It's probably what he did to my poor Caroline. And he's doing coke. Just give it another couple of minutes and close this out. Let's all go home safe and sound, like we planned."

"Okay, Ellen. I'm fine. You go back first. I know the timetable. Larry will be waiting by the bar. I'll get the phone and wrap it up."

Ellen touched her shoulder and kissed her affectionately on the cheek before leaving. "He likes the dress," she said, smiling.

At the pre-arranged eight-minute mark, Laura left the restroom. Larry was standing in the secluded hallway, directly in front of the men's room and watched her emerge. As she passed him, she felt the phone pressed firmly into her right hand and saw Larry wink, a sign she interpreted as one of both the success of his mission and best wishes for hers.

As she re-entered the dining room, Laura could actually feel the heat of Sean's gaze and the strange sensation unnerved her. Gone was the shallow playboy who had worked so diligently to impress her and in his place she found what she guessed to be more the essence of the man. Laura knew instantly that she had gone too far.

He sat forward in his chair with a wry hungry look in his eyes. Laura smiled politely as she handed him the small cell phone across the table. "Thank you," she said.

"Just as I expected, my wild pony was bucking a little too much."

Sean took the phone from her extended palm and, as he did, his fingers engulfed the back of her hand and lingered in an exaggerated and forced gesture. She may as well have been reciting the Ten Commandments. Her escort could no longer feign interest in her life and could barely retain the trappings of civility in his excited state.

As Laura struggled discreetly to take back her hand, the fear that had eluded her earlier now found its mark. She knew for the first time, in a very personal way, that if this man could have his way in the next several hours, she would be grievously harmed or even killed.

"Drink your wine, Laura. The night is young. Let me show you how exciting the city can be at night."

Laura, of course, did not drink the wine but, in her near state of panic, reached for the still untouched water tumbler and drank heartily, partly to relive the sudden parchment in her throat and partly to disguise the fact that she couldn't speak.

As she returned the now half-empty glass to its place, Laura was suddenly struck by the sheer stupidity of her action. To her fear was now added the inconsolable anxiety that one must feel in the moments following unprotected sex with a perfect stranger.

She could not undrink the water and only the next few agonizing minutes could resolve her anxiety. Laura knew that her mission had been accomplished and her only remaining task was to get away from Sean Lowry as quickly as possible.

Although she wasn't a toxicologist, she knew from her understanding of chemistry that the common date rape drugs were generally fast acting compounds and she had no desire to be playing kissy-face with a psychotic killer.

"Sean, I want to thank you for a lovely dinner, but it's time for me to go home now. I always like to keep first dates on an introductory basis."

By the time Sean reacted, Laura was already on her feet extending her hand. She could see by his puzzled look that Sean was unaccustomed to being treated in such a perfunctory way by an intended conquest.

"What the fuck?" he said, his glassy eyes narrowing in anger as he slowly processed her words. "I buy your fucking dinner. You tease me into a fucking frenzy and then you want to shake my hand and go home like we're two fucking salesmen having lunch? Well, not tonight, Sweetheart. In fifteen minutes, you won't be able to keep your hands off my crotch, you bitch. I'll tell you when the date's over. Let's go."

Abruptly, Sean rose and crossed to Laura's chair. He gripped her bare upper right arm and lifted her from the chair. The commotion had been loud enough to attract some attention from the assembled diners, all but four of whom showed little interest in disrupting a domestic squabble.

Frank and Larry barely had time to make eye contact before Sean began to usher her from the room by force. Larry was closest to the action and would have to make the play.

He opted to avoid a confrontation inside the dining room and to confront Sean at the coat check station. Sean was silent, but still held tightly to Laura's arm as he handed the ticket to the girl behind the counter.

As Sean took the coats in his right arm, Laura's open left hand lashed out and caught him flush on the right cheek.

Instinctively, and seemingly oblivious to the

consequences of such a public act of violence, Sean dropped the coats and raised his right fist in preparation for a pummeling of Laura's face.

It never happened.

From behind, Larry simultaneously grabbed the back of Sean's collar and his raised wrist, slamming the young pervert violently into the ornately papered wall, while pulling his arm down and up again, high into the crevice between his shoulder blades. Blood trickled from Sean's nose invisibly onto the red wallpaper as Larry whispered into his ear while holding his detective shield close to Sean's face.

"I know who you are. Every cop knows who you are. I'm going to fight my natural instinct to lock you up and charge you if you pick up your coat and walk out of here now."

Sean dared not speak.

"I don't like worms like you who beat up women and I'll lock you up in a heartbeat if you fuck with me, even if you open your mouth. I don't care who your father is. Now, nod your head if you understand me."

Sean closed his eyes and nodded his head without making a sound. As Califf released him, Sean nearly slumped to the floor before recovering his equilibrium. He turned and picked up his coat, glaring at Laura Stanic in a way that could spawn nightmares. Having clearly made his choice, Sean turned and stormed out of the restaurant without speaking.

Surprisingly few people had witnessed the incident and the group decided to leave quickly, before attracting any more attention. They agreed that Ray and Larry would drop off Beth and Ellen at the house while Frank drove Laura back to her apartment.

Ray had been waiting outside the restaurant in

Frank's minivan, kind of a last line of security for Sean Lowry's dinner companion.

Larry called him on the cell phone and, within a minute, Ray pulled up to the front door, where the unlikely vigilante band piled in. They waited until the valet had retrieved Laura's Ford Escort and Frank was safely in the car with Laura at his side.

At 6'1" and 185 lb., Frank wasn't considered a big man by early 21st Century standards, but he found the compact car cramped and uncomfortable, even with the seat fully extended.

As they pulled away from the restaurant, Frank exhaled dramatically for effect and addressed Laura directly for the first time that evening. "The next time someone asks me if I like Italian food I'll have to think about it for a minute," he said. "In the foreseeable future, I'm opting for Mexican."

"Oh, Frank, you're overreacting. I think it was kind of nice, sort of like a date, a kinky date you could say." As she spoke, her soft brown hair was nuzzling his right shoulder.

The car lurched forward as his brain identified the unmistakable sensation of a single nailed finger tracing the seam of his khaki slacks, along his inner right thigh.

"Don't you think it was kind of like a kinky date, Frank?" Her words were throaty and elongated, serving only to exacerbate the torturing effect of her right index finger.

Until now, such moments had been distant memories to Frank Doherty, but nevertheless, his body silently conveyed its eager submission to her bold advances.

"Laura, I'm not eighteen years old. I haven't driven a car under these conditions in quite some time and if you don't stop now, I can't guarantee your safety." His tone was clearly one of begging, although his clouded mind wasn't sure if he was begging her to stop or to continue.

"You know, Frank, it would be an absolute shame to waste this opportunity."

The more she spoke the slower and more intoxicating was the sound of her voice. "They say that those drugs take away your inhibition and allow you to do things you've only dreamed of."

She was now on the left trouser leg and the seam was running out quickly. "If I'm going to be naughty, Frank, I'd rather be naughty with you than with that pig, Sean Lowry."

The beautiful soft brown hair was beginning to wind its way slowly down his rib cage, as the significance of her confession collided with his libido. Sean had put something in her water without Frank noticing.

"Laura, stop now, please. It's not you talking. He put something in your water. We can't do this. I can't do this. It's wrong. You've got to get to a hospital now."

Frank had his arm around her as he spoke, still talking to the top of her head. When she looked up, her eyes were wanting and penetrating. He nearly lost it.

"Oh, it's very much me, Frank, and by the looks of things, it's very much you too." She returned her eyes to the business at hand and giggled softly.

So much for character. Just when you need it most, you can't find it anywhere. Frank bit his lip and stared, in hypnotic ecstasy, at the broken yellow center line before him, now certain that he was following his own yellow brick road to eternal damnation.

By the time they reached the emergency room, Laura was wobbly and giddy. They walked directly to the registration desk, where Frank reported his suspicion that Laura had been given an unknown drug.

He fumbled through her purse, looking for her insurance card, until the triage nurse appeared and told him to complete the registration later. She and Frank escorted Laura into a small office, where Laura promptly began a rhythmic, if incomprehensible, rendition of some boy-band pop tune.

"What did she take, how much and when?" the young nurse asked in an obviously judgmental tone.

"No, it's not like that," answered Frank. "We were out to dinner and I think someone slipped something into her drink. I'm sure she doesn't use illegal drugs or abuse anything. There were lots of people around. She just started acting very strangely and I thought I should bring her in."

"Exactly when did you notice the change and how was she acting?"

"How was she acting?" Frank gulped, almost audibly. Answering the question with the same question seemed his only alternative to total silence. It was unconsciously calculated to buy time. Time would be needed to formulate a non-embarrassing answer to such an embarrassing question.

By the time Frank thought of a way to respond, his face had already betrayed his predicament. "Well, she suddenly began to get friendly. You know, very friendly and outgoing in a kind of personal way."

"I see," said the nurse scornfully.

As she spoke, Frank felt the need to crawl into one of the packaged syringes lying on the desk.

"Well, I'll get the doctor right away, but I'm sure he'll want to do a toxicology screen and give her something right away to empty the contents of her stomach. In any case, we'll have to keep her here for a few hours."

Within ten minutes after the examination, they had taken Laura's blood sample and, by threat of a stomach pumping, had forced her to drink a big glass of the most disgusting looking thick, black concoction Frank had ever seen. Within seconds, she was heaving violently.

As Laura sobbed and moaned uncontrollably, the nurse injected a sedative into her IV tube and, mercifully, Laura was asleep within a few minutes.

Frank sat near her bed within the oval-shaped privacy curtain and could hear her untroubled breathing. He marveled at how beautiful she looked, even after the strain of the evening's activities.

He so envied that peaceful expression on her face. He would likely never wear one of his own, he thought, not after his despicable conduct on the way to the hospital. No doubt, Laura would never speak to him again. She might even awaken and call the police. He wouldn't blame her if she did.

After nearly three hours of doing penance at Laura's bedside, Frank witnessed her first signs of consciousness. Her lips seemed to reach for moisture and her head moved slightly to the left.

When her eyes opened, the first sight they encountered was the form of Frank Doherty. They locked on his face and, after a moment, closed again, tightly in an exaggerated display. Two hands suddenly appeared from beneath the covers and pulled the sheet forcefully up and over the head that had directed them. There she lay, motionless and absolutely silent.

At first, Frank dared not speak. Then he concluded he no choice but to speak, and before he could reverse course again, he did speak. "Laura, I'm sorry. I don't know what got into me. I can't believe I—"

Laura interrupted but did not lower the sheet. "Not now, Frank, please, not now. I don't want to talk about it.

Just get me out of here and home to my own bed. Did you call my mother? She probably thinks I was out—" She stopped abruptly.

"Yes, of course. I told her they think you ate some bad food. Alex is fine. I'll get the nurse and see about getting you checked out."

As Frank turned to leave, Laura spoke again. "Frank," she began in a kind of controlled and low volume rage, "first, be so kind as to get the make-up bag out of my purse on the nightstand and hand it to me, please. Right this second would be just fine."

He did.

An open palm appeared from under the covers and then retreated with the bag in hand.

On the drive back to Laura's apartment, neither spoke until Frank had actually parked the car at her doorstep. It was Laura who broke the ice. "I could have stopped, Frank," she said, still looking straight ahead.

"What do you mean, Laura?" It had been an inept response to a sincere opening and he knew it.

"Are you stupid, Frank? I said I could have stopped. Tell me you don't remember."

"No, I remember. Of course I remember."

"Well, I was feeling loose all right, but I could have stopped if I had wanted to. I mean, it wasn't against my will or anything. Maybe he didn't give me enough of that stuff. I don't know, but it wasn't your fault."

Thank God. Absolution! Frank wasn't stupid.

As she turned to face him, she detected the hint of a suppressed smile around the corners of his mouth. In that instant they both burst into a fit of laughter.

"That's not to say it will happen again any time soon," Laura said with a coy smile, as she reached for the door handle.

Chapter Seventeen

Brad had always dreaded the bi-weekly, morning cabinet meetings at City Hall. All city department heads, along with the Park District and Municipal Transit Authority Directors, were required to be seated in the fourth floor conference room before eight o'clock. The Mayor was invariably late and no apology had ever been offered.

Real city business, Brad knew, was almost never conducted in the openness of these meetings, but the meetings had always been high on the Mayor's priority list and had apparently served his agenda well enough. In reality, the meetings were little more than locker room pep talks and Mayoral ego massage.

This Lowry, like his esteemed father, had always been a proponent of the carrot and stick approach. In terms of motivational tools, a smile and a hearty pat on the back were just as effective as an angry threat of dismissal.

The entire morning's assembly had experienced both extremes with regularity over the years. They feared the stick, but the carrot had become an ineffective and useless waste of time. The Mayor would still open each meeting by making his way around the large, oval shaped table smiling, shaking hands, touching shoulders and offering some bit of personal praise. They all knew better than to take it to heart.

After the opening prayer, led personally by His Honor, each department head would report. The reports were expected to be general in nature and brief in duration because, after all, these weren't really working meetings.

If anyone unwisely chattered on past two or three minutes, the Mayor would simply thank him and move on to the next report. After all, the unspoken truth at City Hall is that the real business of governing is conducted piecemeal, privately, in one-on-one meetings and phone calls. These reports were simply a concession to formality.

Neither was this practice limited to inter-departmental dealings. City Council votes and, in some cases, even public council debates, had been pre-arranged and even staged with a series of prior phone calls and meetings in which who knows what had been given or promised or done. Government ran more efficiently when anything could be said and anything said could be denied.

Nearly everyone in city government, even many of the Mayor's self-proclaimed *opponents*, ultimately performed according to Jack Lowry's script. The script today called for unanimous praise from the gathered flock as the Mayor rambled on about some bold new idea to transform the city or its government. Despite their collective boredom, they had come together at the trough to feed Jack Lowry's insatiable ego and to indulge his longstanding obsession with trivial issues.

It had all started several years ago with his campaign to beautify the inner city with urban art. The Mayor himself had conceived the idea to run the locally based program from the public schools. The kids would paint free-style murals along the walls of gritty railroad underpasses, bare graffiti-covered walls and even municipal buses.

Within six months, in the wake of some positive feedback, His Honor had gone bonkers and imported expensive "street artists" from around the country. They literally blanketed the inner city with enormous lead-based images of Martin Luther King, colorful slave ships, John F. Kennedy and bizarre multi-colored scenes that defied identification.

Community leaders finally began to rumble when, several million dollars later, the images began appearing on the decaying brick walls of the circa 1920's park district buildings and schools.

The Mayor's *Urban Art Project* had been followed closely by his near-paranoid assault on graffiti. Incensed by the widespread desecration of his inner city art in what he described as a *destructive street gang conspiracy*, the Mayor authorized thousands of overtime hours for police and even hired new officers, in an all-out campaign to arrest and prosecute the responsible criminals.

Night after night, teams of tactical officers conducted time-consuming stakeouts of subway stations, parks, and bus terminals. The Mayor simultaneously lobbied the state legislature for a bill making a second conviction for *Damage to Property by Graffiti* a felony. Widespread newspaper reports, disclosing the escalating cost of the campaign and editorials questioning the Mayor's sanity quickly ended His Honor's self-declared *War on Graffiti*.

As Brad sat in his appointed chair, directly across from the Police Commissioner *de jour*, he tried consciously not to stare at the two young blond haired European types, with skinny ties, engaging each other in conversation at the front of the room. A large flat vinyl case rested against the wall beside them. From the looks of the two young men, Brad figured that the case contained either some kind of artistic sketches for some Mayoral project or graphically explicit gay pornography. He hoped for the former.

Jack Lowry's current flirtation with poor judgment involved flowers. He had recently returned from a trip to Europe, where he had become infatuated over the aesthetic use of flowers by municipal government.

The word was that, since his return, Lowry could talk about nothing but flowers and had reputedly hired two well-respected, Dutch horticulturists as consultants. Rumor had it he was creating a master plan to make the entire city bloom in all the colors of the rainbow from early spring through late summer.

Brad concluded that the two young men were the Mayor's floral decor experts, obviously specializing in *daisy chains*.

It was after eight-fifteen when the Mayor entered, walking directly to his place at the head of the table and flashing a broad smile. Following the obligatory back patting and small talk, he introduced his two flower boys and invited them to retire to his private office until the more mundane portion of the meeting was concluded.

The presentation order never varied. Reports were presented alphabetically and, until the Mayor appointed a Commissioner of Asinine Ideas, Aviation would always be first.

Each of the commissioners knew that the purpose of these reports was simply to put one's best foot forward, thereby instilling in the others a need to excel and succeed. Problems, even publicly aired problems, were simply ignored.

Brad used his two minutes to outline the city's plans

to increase take-offs and landings at the airport by twenty-five percent within the next two years.

The Mayor's plan to increase the number of runways at the airport had been blocked for years by powerful opposition noise pollution forces, representing the interests of the many suburbs surrounding the airport.

The Mayor believed, however, that any opposition to his grand scheme of creating the quintessential international city was temporary, as the billions in revenue generated from increased air traffic was the cornerstone of his plan. He held the suburbs in nearly open contempt, believing that they would still be isolated and remote farming villages, were it not for the vision and fortitude of the Lowry family.

The plans were tweaked and molded a little bit each week, thereby providing Brad with a ready source of briefing material, eagerly anticipated by the Mayor in these twice-monthly meetings. Brad spread portions of the designs on the massive table and began to explain recent additions and modifications.

The Mayor was pleased with Brad's report and commended him openly before moving on to the next report. At the conclusion of the departmental reports, the Mayor motioned to his bodyguard to bring in the flower boys.

Brad feigned interest, along with all the other department heads, as the Mayor outlined his colorful aesthetic vision of the new city. With the help of his flower boys, he explained how each variety of flower would bloom at a slightly different time of the year, making the right combinations absolutely mandatory.

The daffodils would bloom at the first hint of spring. Then came the tulips in early spring and so on, right down to the day lilies, which would provide color right through

August. Annuals would be reserved for use on the lakefront and around government and important public buildings. The city would be more beautiful than ever before.

As a result, people would be happier and more productive in their work. Gangs and crime would recede and wither in the spectral citywide display of color.

The initial seven million dollar annual cost, he explained, was a bargain and would be paid directly through the Street Department's budget, with a careful monitoring of overtime and cutting of fat. There was, of course, unanimous praise from the commissioners.

Moments after adjourning the meeting, the Mayor walked briskly out the door, followed closely by the slightly confused flower boys.

The commissioners milled about making small talk as they gathered their coats and brief cases.

Brad, pre-occupied with more serious matters, elected to forgo the gossip session and head directly back to the office. As he neared the conference room door, however, Brad felt a hand on his shoulder and he turned to see the familiar bifocals of the Mayor's young Chief-of-Staff, Erskin Mandrel.

Erskin, although awkward and nerdy in appearance, was new age and 21st Century all the way. The Yale educated son of an old family friend, he had been with Lowry for three years and was, by reputation, something of a sociopath himself. The man had, on many occasions, proven himself to be utterly without ethics and blindly devoted to the service of Jack Lowry.

It was generally known that Erskin's primary function was to deliver the Mayor's most important communications; the ones that the Mayor dared not utter himself.

On those occasions when the criminal law might collide with the Mayor's objectives, it was Erskin Mandrel who invariably issued the marching orders. A summoned appearance before Mandrel might require the unfortunate commissioner, for example, to tamper with contract bidding regulations in order to placate a Mayoral pal, or maybe even to hang a trusted friend out to dry. Erskin Mandrel was, beyond a doubt, the most discreetly despised individual at City Hall.

"Brad, it's nice to see you looking so well." Mandrel had been trying to emulate the Mayor's *touchy feely* manipulation techniques lately, but the new extrovert façade hadn't won him any new friends in government.

Brad wanted to tell him that somebody with the face of a wanton child molester would be better off keeping his hands to himself.

"Well, Erskin, I'm not sure the feeling is mutual. Did I do something wrong?" It was called kidding on the square.

"Of course not, but as long as you're here, the Mayor would like to speak to you privately for a few moments, if you've got the time."

"I work for the man, Erskin. I'll make the time," Brad said.

"That's great, Brad. Come right along with me. The Mayor is in his office." With that, Erskin headed down the ornate hallway towards the corner office with Brad in tow.

Brad was suspicious, even before he entered the great man's office. Appointments with His Honor were scheduled. They were almost never impromptu. It occurred to Brad that there would be no record of the meeting anywhere, and that fact made him particularly nervous as he followed Erskin past the secretary and directly into the mahogany paneled inner sanctum.

Brad immediately felt the increased plushness of the soft, rose-colored carpeting as he began to cover the forty or so feet to the massive hand-carved solid wood desk. As many times as he had been in the Mayor's office, Brad could never shake the feeling that he was a humble altar boy, delivering the offerings from the rear of the church to the waiting priest.

This time, however, the priest took the unusual step of coming down from the altar to meet his humble servant halfway. It was not a good sign, Brad thought.

"Brad, thanks for seeing me this morning. I apologize for the lack of notice, but with my schedule lately, I'm afraid I've been neglecting some important business. Seeing you at the meeting this morning reminded me that we needed to talk."

"It's always an honor, Mr. Mayor," Brad said, summoning his broadest smile, while extending his hand.

"Brad, you don't mind if Erskin stays around while we talk, do you?"

As he spoke, the Mayor did not so much as look in Erskin's direction, thereby indicating to Brad that the two had carefully planned this *spontaneous* encounter.

"Of course not, Mr. Mayor," Brad responded, already keenly aware that the Mayor wanted a witness to hear what he said, or more precisely, what he did not say.

"Brad, what I wanted to talk to you about was that Paul Branford is retiring from Congress. It's still pretty much of a secret. We'll be looking for someone to slate for his spot next year, someone who knows how to do a job properly and to see it through to the end."

Brad smiled.

"You know, Brad, life is really nothing but a series of choices. The choices we make won't always be the right ones, but the important thing is that, once we make a choice, we do whatever is necessary to make it work. Don't you agree, Brad?"

"Yes, Mr. Mayor, I certainly do," answered Brad, now smelling a rat.

"Good, Brad, good. I'm very happy to hear that and I just wanted to let you know that you're right on top of the list to replace Branford. Just keep up the good work and remember that the team is everything, Brad."

Brad was so good at this game that he had made a running mental translation of the Mayor's little pep talk:

"Don't tell me anything about my son, Brad. Just handle it. I hear that you've fucked up, but it's too late to stop now. Make this go away now and I will see that you are taken care of to the tune of a Congressional seat. Fuck up again and I'll make your life a living hell if you manage to avoid lethal injection."

Brad wasn't stupid enough to believe that it had been a serious promise. It was the standard Lowry appeal to naked ambition and greed. Still, he thought, they would have to slate somebody, and if he could manage to keep a lid on this mess, a seat in U.S. House of Representatives could hardly be considered overpayment.

At times like this, Brad was grateful that he had the ability, not only to identify his weaknesses and character flaws but, when necessary, to embrace them wholeheartedly.

The man was right, he thought. Either way, this would be the defining moment of Brad Parkins' life. As he walked slowly from the great man's chamber, Brad couldn't help but wonder for the first time exactly how much Lowry really knew about this whole business and from whom he had learned it.

It was common knowledge that, despite Sean's proclivity for public embarrassment, the Mayor had never broken with him. Everyone close to the Mayor knew that he still held out hope that Sean would straighten up and fly right.

It was just possible, Brad considered, that Sean himself had been keeping his father abreast of the whole bloody mess. There was even an outside chance that His Holiness had figured it out for himself. After all, for at least six months after the girl's death, Sean had been a hermit, losing twenty or thirty pounds in the process.

Either way, however, it didn't much matter. This thing wasn't about Lowry any more. If he got out of this mess with a Congressional seat, it will have been a well-deserved bonus, but it had now become more a matter of survival.

Chapter Eighteen

Larry's contact at the phone company, a retired city homicide detective, was only too eager to help. Jerry Robbins was now a full-time, phone company employee working in security. His primary duties included review of subpoenas for call printouts and final authorization for their release. The call printouts were known as Message Unit Detail, or MUD, sheets and were a commonly used source of trial evidence and crime solving.

Phone company records are ostensibly private and the company had long maintained a stated policy that records could only be released under the authority of a court subpoena. Policy and practice, however, did not always coincide.

On top of his pension, the generous salary allowed the fifty-two year old Robbins and his family to live a comfortable life, but he found the work boring from the perspective of an old homicide detective. As a result, he was only too eager to assist his old comrades in any way he could without concern for technical requirements such as subpoenas.

Larry had met him through a mutual friend at a retirement party and the two had hit it off immediately. Robbins had become a kind of mentor to Larry and had proven to be a valuable resource in Missing Persons. Robbins' police background meant that Larry could actually brief him on a given investigation and tap into his investigative skills, as well as his access to records.

In tracing phone calls, Califf had discovered, an important call often formed only the first step in a revealing series of related calls. Investigative skills were extremely useful in following these trails and Robbins' assistance had proven so valuable that Larry and several other detectives viewed him as something of a police mole inside the phone company.

Larry called Robbins just after nine in the morning and gave him a general rundown of the relevant facts. He told Robbins that a woman had gone missing in the early morning hours on Sunday, July 20th and gave him the cell phone number of her suspected abductor, along with the list of numbers stored in the speed dial. Robbins' initial response hardly came as a surprise to Larry Califf.

"Is this the case involving the lawyer's niece?"

As he considered a response, Larry wondered why Robbins had decided to retire at all and thought it best to come clean up front. "Yeah, it is, Jerry, and you should also know you'll find that the cell phone number belongs to Sean Lowry. We want to find out who's involved in this with him. This is some serious shit, Jerry. I have no idea where the phone trail might lead, but it could go up pretty high, if you know what I mean."

"Jesus Christ," Robbins exclaimed. "If it involves these people, why aren't the Feds doing this?"

Again, Califf knew that if he tried to deceive or mislead Robbins in any way, he could forget about getting the information. "Look, Jerry, I'll tell you flat out, so all the cards are on the table. We have reason to believe that there are cops, and maybe even some powerful politicians, involved in at least two murders connected to this case. For now, my investigation is on the QT, strictly private.

If you don't want to get involved, I'll understand."

"Larry, I'm sick to death of this office fucking job and if I go on one more relaxing vacation with my wife, I'll be ready for a straight jacket. I'm in. You can count on me. I'll get right to work on it and call you in a couple of days."

While Califf was still on the phone with Jerry Robbins that Monday morning, Frank was in court preparing to litigate a motion to suppress evidence in a run-of-the-mill drug case.

Routine continuances and status calls were one thing, but clients understandably just didn't tolerate substitute lawyers showing up to examine witnesses and argue the case. Despite his near obsessive preoccupation with solving his wife's murder, the business couldn't be neglected. There were still kids to raise and bills to pay.

Before leaving his office, Frank had left a voice-mail message for George Payne at work. He wanted to brief George on the Saturday night caper at the Italian restaurant. When Frank's hearing was ready to begin at around ten o'clock, he still hadn't heard from George and found himself feeling for the pager on his belt, anticipating the vibration that didn't come.

Frank's hearing concluded just before one in the afternoon and he walked directly from the courtroom to his office some three blocks away without even realizing that he had missed lunch.

Once inside the building, he walked directly to the Panos' suite and found the outer door locked. It wasn't a good sign, Frank thought, already sorting through his key chain as he moved swiftly towards his own door. Once inside his office, Frank dialed Diane's home number without so much as removing his overcoat. George answered.

"George, is that you? It's Frank Doherty."

"Yes. It's me, Frank. I just got back to my mother's house from the morgue in DuPree County. A farmer found my father's body on the side of a secluded gravel road out there. My wife stayed with her this morning."

"George, I'm so sorry. I—"

"What have you got, Frank?"

"It can wait George. I know you have arrangements to take care of."

"Thanks, but I'm okay. Now what have you got?"

"Saturday night we got our hands on Sean's cell phone. We've got his phone number, along with all the numbers stored in the speed dial. Larry knows a guy in phone company security, one of your retired detectives. He's a good man. You probably know him. He's running down the MUD sheets to match up the calls made around the time of Caroline's disappearance. We could know as soon as tomorrow afternoon who the main players are."

"Good work, Frank. Will you call me the minute you get the information on those numbers?" George asked, sounding more than a little anxious.

"Of course, George, the minute I get it."

"What's your plan in the meantime?" George asked.

"I figure Larry and I will snoop around the college Tuesday and try to talk to Louise Booker; maybe even throw a scare into that security director. It wouldn't surprise me at all if the security guy was in on your dad's murder with whatever cop did the date rape cover-up. I'd like to play that card a little while we wait for the phone records. Who knows? I might even find the girl from the college."

"Well, be careful, Frank. My mother or I will be in

Louise, it's like an admission of guilt. Don't forget that Louise doesn't have any evidence that Munoz was personally involved in any of this. He can't call attention to himself by retaliating against her in any way, especially not when he might be complicit in a murder. Louise is in the clear because she can't hurt him if he leaves her alone."

"Exactly," Larry confirmed.

As Louise had predicted, Larry entered the security office to find the open office area clear of employees, although the door to the private office in back was half-open. "Anybody home?" Califf called.

In a moment Munoz appeared from inside his office, walking towards the front counter. "Sorry. It's a little early. The secretary isn't here yet. Is there anything I can help you with?" Munoz offered.

"Yes, there is," answered Califf, flashing his detective's shield. "My name is Califf. I'm investigating a homicide and I'd like to ask you a few questions."

Munoz's initial reaction was exactly what Califf had hoped for. The man appeared stunned and completely unprepared for the visit. Califf knew from experience that he had to seize on this element of surprise before Munoz could gain his composure and halt his retreat.

"I don't know anything about a murder. Has there been a murder on the campus or something?"

The more small talk Munoz could make, the greater his chance of recovering his equilibrium. Califf moved directly to the attack. "I'll be very frank with you, Mr. Munoz. You are Mr. Munoz I take it?"

"Yes, I am."

"Well, a man named Stavros Panos came to see you the other day. We believe he was investigating the possible cover-up of an eight-year-old crime. He was shot in the head at close range only hours after leaving your office. I'd like to hear your version of what transpired between the two of you."

"Look, that old man did come in here. He wanted me to give him confidential information about a former student and I categorically refused. You can ask the secretary. She was right here and heard the whole thing."

Larry was relieved by the man's reliance on Louise as a witness. It was her insurance policy. "What about the incident he was investigating? I understand there was an allegation of date rape made by a woman eight years ago. Do you have reports or other information on that incident?"

Califf had maneuvered him carefully into the hot seat. Munoz now had three choices; deny any knowledge of the incident, refuse to cooperate in the police investigation, or capitulate.

Munoz was silent.

"Mr. Munoz, I'm asking for your cooperation in a murder investigation. Are you refusing to cooperate?" Still, the Director did not speak. It was now or never, Califf thought.

"Mr. Munoz, the responses you give now could determine the course of your life for a long time to come. Let me be very clear about one thing. If you set that old man up, then you're guilty of murder and we'll take you down, but you're not the person we're after. We think you were just trying to protect yourself and had no idea they would kill him."

"And for the sake of argument," Munoz asked, "what if you're right?"

"If that's the case, then you need to tell me right now

and there's a good chance you'll walk right out of this, but don't fuck with me. If you lie to me now, I'll use it to bury you later. Make your choice."

The man opted for none of the above and decided to stall for time. "I'll have to think this over carefully, Detective Califf, and call you back later, if you don't mind."

Califf would have none of it. "But I do mind," he answered. "I'm giving you an opportunity here to make this right and to go on record that you're not a murderer. Either you'll do it now, or suffer the consequences."

There were no more cards to play. Still, Munoz maintained his silence, visibly shaken and teetering on the edge of surrender.

Califf remained absolutely motionless, staring relentlessly into the shorter man's frightened eyes in a desperate effort to finish off his wounded prey.

Within the space of those few agonizing seconds, however, Munoz managed to summon his reserve strength and find his resolve.

Even before Munoz spoke, his body language triggered a wave of disappointment and frustration in the young detective.

"I don't think I'll be speaking to you any further without my lawyer," offered the suddenly confident and resolute voice. "When and if you decide to arrest me for something, I'll go quietly, but until that time, I must ask you to leave my office."

"Bad choice," said Califf quietly as he turned to leave. He had cornered the mouse, but had let him escape. Califf returned to the lobby to find Frank waiting anxiously.

"How did it go?" the lawyer asked.

"Don't ask," replied the young detective. "We'll

have to do this the hard way, whatever that might be."

Califf and Frank were still fighting downtown traffic on their way back from the university when Califf's cell phone rang.

"Califf?"

"Hi, Jerry. What's up?"

"Well, I've got some information that might help you out," offered Robbins. "I can't nail it down for you, but I think I can give you a direction."

"Go," said Califf. "I've got my pencil and pad ready."

"At five forty-three that morning, Sean made a call to one of the numbers on the speed dial. Other than that, there wasn't a single call made from that phone between midnight the night before and eleven the next morning. The number was 555-6104. It's one of a block of sixty-five numbers issued to the city's General Administration Department. That's who pays the bills. We can't tell who has the phone. Only the city would maintain those records."

Califf considered the information for a moment. "That helps, Jerry. That helps a lot."

"There's more," said Jerry. "Three minutes after that call, there was a call made from the same city cell phone to the main non-emergency police number."

"Shit," exclaimed Califf. "Then there's no way to find out where that called was transferred to, right?"

"Absolutely right, and I'm sure it was no accident. There are over three hundred individual numbers issued to the police department. Every one of them can be dialed directly. That means if you know who you're looking for, you could just pick up the phone and dial direct to any district, section or office in the whole city. If you know who you're looking for and where he works, there's no reason at all to call the main switchboard. You just look in the phone book. Most of the numbers are right there."

"I see where you're going," said Larry, betraying a sense of resignation. "Our man purposely called the main number, knowing the call couldn't be traced."

"Precisely. He's obviously not a guy prone to panic," said Robbins.

"So, what we know for sure is that Sean called somebody high up in city government for help. Then that guy presumably brought in some cop or cops to clean up the mess."

Califf's business with the phone company had been concluded. He was now talking to Robbins as a peer and seeking his opinion as a detective.

Robbins was flattered and only too eager to help. "No doubt about it," he agreed. "If you want, I could run all the sheets on Sean's phone from that morning all the way through today on the outside chance that Sean called this cop direct at his office. It'll take some work, but I should be able to crosscheck for any police department numbers."

"What would it tell us?"

"It won't tell us who the guy is, but it might narrow it down considerably. While I'm at it, I'll just get a list of everybody he's called in the last couple of weeks. You might see a name that rings a bell."

"Good idea. Thanks, Jerry. If I had to guess right now, I'd say you should watch out for any numbers issued to Homicide/Violent Crimes."

"Okay, I'll see what I can do and be in touch," said the older man.

"I owe you lunch, Jerry, and this time I'll pay up. So long."

Califf briefed Frank on the new information and the men quickly decided that they would need George's help in tracing the city cell phone.

Using Larry's cell phone, Frank tried to reach George at his office without success. Thinking that Diane might have better luck, he tried her at the office but got only the infamous Panos answering machine. He tried Diane at home and George answered.

"George? It's Frank Doherty. I've been trying to get hold of you."

"What have you got, Frank?"

"Larry got some information on the phone check and it looks like we'll need your help," Frank said.

"How so?" George asked.

"Well, it's good information, but it's incomplete. It seems Sean made a single phone call several hours after my niece's disappearance. The phone bill on that number is paid by the city. It's one of a block of sixty-five cell phone numbers issued to the city. That's all we know about it right now. We need you to track it down through the city." Frank gave him the number.

"It'll take some time, but I'll get it. Nice work, Frank," said George.

"There's something else, George," Frank added. "We're absolutely certain there's been at least one cop involved since the very beginning. Less than a minute after termination of the call from Sean, a call was made from that city cell phone to the main non-emergency police number. We think that calling that main number was an intentional precaution taken by the caller"

"To cover up the trail?" George asked.

"Exactly," answered Frank.

"Thanks, Frank. I'll see you at the wake."

IMMORAL AUTHORITY

Frank turned to Larry and handed him the phone. The detective waited patiently for Frank's report, his attention still focused on the road ahead.

"George says he'll check out the city cell phone, but he puzzles me, Larry. He seemed pretty cold on the phone. I can't put my finger on it, but something isn't right with him."

Predictably, the panic-stricken Director of Campus Security had received a return call from Lonnie Hartman within minutes of Califf's departure.

"This is way more than I bargained for, Hartman. There was never any talk about murder. This detective knows the old guy was here and he knows about the thing eight years ago."

"Was the detective's name Larry Califf?" Hartman asked.

"Why, yes, it was," answered Munoz. "Why?"

"Because he's not a homicide detective and he's not even assigned to this case. He's working privately for somebody who's trying to fuck over both of us. As of right now, the police believe that the old man was killed in a carjacking gone bad, but that could change in a split second."

"I had nothing to do with any killing," Munoz whined.

"Now, listen carefully, you spineless fuck. That old man is dead because you fucked up and let him find the girl. This thing goes a lot deeper than just the girl and what we did eight years ago, so I want you to be real clear about one thing. If I go down for murder, you're going with me. You set the old man up. You paid me to kill the old guy so he wouldn't talk to the girl."

"But I didn't tell him about the girl," exclaimed

Munoz in a pathetic tone.

"Well, he found her nonetheless, and the information could only have come from your office," Hartman said.

"It must have been that old busy-body secretary of mine. I've been trying to get rid of her for years, the fucking bitch."

"It doesn't matter. The point is that you're in this up to your ears. You had the perfect motive to want that old guy dead. You need to understand that your only way out of this whole fucking mess is to do exactly as I tell you."

"All right," said Munoz. "What do you want me to do?"

"Absolutely nothing until I tell you to," answered Hartman.

CHAPTER NINETEEN

Pitney Jenkins was more valuable as a bitter old man than he had ever been in his days as a District Commander, Paul thought as he waited patiently late Thursday morning in the second floor *Blue Room* of the South Side Roxbury Heights Branch Public Library.

As a concession to his instinct for self-preservation, Paul generally arrived early for these clandestine meetings and absolutely never used taverns or restaurants.

One could inadvertently establish a pattern of favorite eateries and watering holes, thus increasing the risk of electronic eavesdropping. The bugging of restaurant booths and tables was a practice that had, over the years, caused many a change of address from City Hall to the Federal penitentiary.

In return for his seldom-activated information pipeline, Pitney had never really expected much. His wife had been employed on the general office staff at Emerald Isle for eighteen years and even now earned only a modest forty thousand-dollar salary.

In those six or seven years when Pitney had been particularly helpful, however, Paul had seen to it that Irma Jenkins received a generous bonus. The bonuses were technically gratuitous and had never been spoken of between Paul and Pitney but, as an expert in the economics of *quid pro quo*, Pitney had caught on fast.

He had become a reliable source of confidential

information for the friends of Paul DeBenedetto, even tipping them off several years ago to a joint, undercover investigation of Port Authority operations.

It was one of those perfectly choreographed arrangements that could never be proven. Over the years, Paul had orchestrated dozens of such relationships and liked to boast to trusted associates that he had more spies than the CIA.

As Pitney pulled into the small lot behind the neighborhood library, the only thing on his small and narrowly focused mind was Christmas. Nine months would be a long time to wait for what should be the granddaddy of Christmas bonuses, he thought. He couldn't believe his luck when Matt Corliss had come to him with his concerns about young Larry Califf. Since then, Corliss had dutifully kept Pitney up to date on the case.

There were missing pieces for sure, but he was certain that there were cops out there trying to silence Frank Doherty's little investigation into the disappearance of his niece.

In the beginning, he hadn't even considered that Califf might really be onto something. The only thing that had concerned him in the whole Doherty case was that the details were of interest to Paul and his associates.

The murder of the private investigator, however, had raised the stakes considerably. He had known George's father since the old days and it was common knowledge among everyone who hated defense lawyers that old Panos and that scum-sucking Frank Doherty had been as thick as thieves for years.

Embittered was not synonymous with stupid,

however, and the significance of this wholesale murder was not lost on Pitney.

Somebody really important was in the shit up to his eyeballs and Pitney's information was critical to the solution. He didn't know any more of the details and that's the way he wanted it.

Pitney was off duty when he lumbered into the library *Blue Room* just before the lunch hour.

He was a walking oxymoron, Paul thought, as the obviously over-fed but indigent looking police Lieutenant appeared in the doorway. Glassy eyed, red faced and unshaven, Pitney permeated the room with the stink of tobacco and stale booze, reminding Paul of the old skunk that made his home in the back yard every spring. You couldn't stand to be in the yard with him, but he kept the rabbits from eating the tulip bulbs.

"Good morning, Lieutenant Jenkins," Paul began. There was nothing to be gained by disrespecting the man to his face. "It's good to see you, and how is your lovely wife? I see her in the hallways on occasion, but rarely have time to talk."

I'd rather discuss philosophy with the skunk in my yard, Paul commented silently, his face betraying not so much as a hint of his disdain. Paul wanted to tell Pitney that his wife was so thoroughly disagreeable and uniquely ugly that, if she looked up, she could stop dog shit in mid-air. He only smiled.

"Good morning, Mr. D," Pitney said, settling into the chair across from Paul. "My wife's fine, Mr. D. Thanks for asking. Anyway, I think I have something for you."

"That's why I'm here, Lieutenant Jenkins. Fire away."

"Well, it's about the Doherty case. There's no way you would make the connection, but early Monday morning, some farmer out west in DuPree County found a body on the side of an old gravel road. It was an old private investigator, Stavros Panos, who went missing last Saturday. He'd been shot in the head. We'd found his van the day before, all gutted in a drug neighborhood down on the West Side."

"And?" Paul asked, betraying some impatience.

"I figure it was just made to look like a carjacking or something. I found out the body was identified Monday night. The murder investigation is being handled by the sheriff of that bumfuck county out there."

"And exactly how does this relate to the Doherty investigation?" Paul asked.

"Well, the old guy and Frank Doherty have been closer than a couple of fudge packers for the last fifteen years. According to one of my homicide detectives, old Panos was working with Doherty on his wife's case. It looks to me like somebody's out there trying to clean house in a panic. It seems like the department is buying the carjacking angle, at least for now. It's obvious they have no clue what's really going on."

When Pitney finished speaking Paul showed no reaction. "And what is going on, Lieutenant? Do you have any idea who might be involved?" Paul asked in a non-sarcastic manner. He wanted to know right then and there if, by some miracle, this fool knew more than he should.

"Right now, I don't know any more than I told you. I've got to figure it's at least one cop, and who knows after that?" Pitney answered.

"Well, I certainly do thank you for this information,

Lieutenant Jenkins. You've been very helpful, as usual, and I wish you and your lovely wife a very merry Christmas next year. I suggest you browse the stacks for a few minutes before leaving."

With that Paul rose and left without offering his hand.

Pitney didn't notice the slight. His mind was occupied trying to decipher the meaning of the obviously encoded phrase *browse the stacks*.

On the drive back to Emerald Isle, Paul smiled inwardly at the cunning of this Frank Doherty. The lawyer had obviously concluded that his friend had been murdered by cops and had made a calculated decision not to report his suspicions to the authorities. This was decidedly good news in the sense that it meant Doherty was trying to deal with this whole thing privately. His action and, more precisely, his inaction indicated that Doherty had left the FBI and the cops out in the cold.

If nothing else, it was clear to Paul that Doherty would have to be dealt with directly. Vengeance, Paul knew, was the engine of perseverance. Yes, Doherty would have to be stopped.

Paul, of course, had never killed anyone himself, but in his *de facto* role as liaison between the administration and the underworld, he had never been squeamish or remorseful about a necessary murder or two.

Upon hearing of the latest developments, his friends would no doubt opt to shelve the new policy of subtle manipulation for the moment in favor of a more active and time-honored form of crisis management. Paul reached for his cell phone.

The meeting had been hastily called by Paul and was held that same afternoon in the barn of a Grimsley County dairy farm, owned by a distant cousin.

As the person requesting the meeting, Paul had arrived first and had seen to the arrangements. The next to arrive was Jim O'Keefe, President and Secretary of Local 24 of the International Restaurant and Hotel Workers Association, by far the most powerful and influential union boss in the city. The third and last car into the barn was occupied by Jimmy "Rabbit Ear" Ruffulo, a northwest suburban car dealer reputed to be the top boss of the new, low profile, scaled down, 21st Century version of the mob.

Nobody, of course, called him Rabbit Ear to his face. People who actually knew him never used the nickname, for fear it might get back to him. Jimmy hated the name, notwithstanding the fact that he had earned it honestly.

Some fifty years ago, Jimmy had been in a street fight with an older and much bigger boy. Despite the fact that the boy had bitten off nearly half of his ear, Jimmy continued to fight ferociously for nearly thirty minutes until his superior, but utterly exhausted, opponent collapsed in the street.

Such old-world nicknames were generally frowned upon anyway by the new organization, which had evolved into a loosely connected group of apparently legitimate businessmen with common interests, bearing little resemblance to its drug-running, whore pushing, violent predecessor.

They still made their millions, but now they did it quietly through political access. Control of politicians and bureaucrats assured them invaluable plumbs such as favorable legislation and city contracts. They had become like breeding leeches, nourished by the ample flesh of the political machine.

IMMORAL AUTHORITY

Jimmy himself was somewhere between middle-aged and elderly, nearly ten years Paul's junior.

In private, Paul had only half-jokingly called Jimmy the George Washington of mobsters because Jimmy had been a big part of the old world and now harbored a clear vision of the new. Paul thought Jimmy to be the perfect transitional leader to pave the way for the coming Yuppie mob. The two men had shared a history since childhood and did not conceal their genuine affection for each other.

Jim O'Keefe, on the other hand, had not come from the old neighborhood. Jim was a silver-tongued devil; Jesuit educated and suburban raised.

It was said by politicians, gangsters, and busboys alike, that you couldn't get a man in the city to speak an ill word about Jim O'Keefe. He could sit in a meeting between cops and robbers and have them French kissing in five minutes. The force of his magnetic personality and the influence he wielded over the city's labor unions and their pension funds made him indispensable to every powerful person or group with an agenda, and he used the power unabashedly to make himself obscenely wealthy.

He was known to have glaring weaknesses for large-breasted young women and Cuban cigars. Above all, however, Jim O'Keefe was a life-long, close personal friend of Jack Lowry.

Paul knew that these were not hot-tempered people who would act impulsively or for gratification of ego.

The three men sat around a hastily assembled card table as they spoke, but the table itself was covered with an impeccably ironed white tablecloth. They drank cappuccino from china cups. The two listened patiently as Paul explained the entire situation in as organized and straightforward a way as possible.

Paul was careful not to betray any personal feelings.

Such things were not considered in the decision making process, at least not openly. Neither of the men interrupted him during his thirty-odd minute monologue.

When Paul was finished, the real meeting began. It was interrupted by an early dinner, served in the main house, and resumed on a long walk along the farmer's private road.

After the walk, the meeting was still going strong in the cold barn, heated temporarily by one inadequate space heater. It finally ended at seven in the evening, the participants having agreed on a plan of action.

The summons from Paul DeBenedetto, delivered personally by one of his Neanderthal *employees* had been unnerving, to say the least. But Paul's point in sending the man, rather than picking up a telephone, had been taken.

On the drive to the Port Authority, Brad encountered nothing worse than the normal morning traffic snarl. Uncharacteristically, however, he never thought to turn on the radio or the CD player. In all the years he had dealt with Paul DeBenedetto, Brad had never received such a summons.

His mind raced with speculation and, for the first time, he began to view Paul DeBenedetto as someone to be feared. The fear, he knew, was based on reason and a clear understanding of reality, not on paranoid delusions.

Billions of dollars and powerful fortunes were the Guardian Angels of Jack Lowry; and Brad Parkins, simply because he had answered his phone one morning, had unwittingly become their agent and point man in the field. Extreme caution would be required, he thought.

He arrived at around nine o'clock, about the same

time that the funeral of Stavros Panos was getting under way in a Greek Orthodox Church across town, and found the Port Authority bustling with the early morning business of international commerce.

Indeed, the guard at the main gate was expecting his gold Lexus and waved him through without so much as a close look. It took several minutes for Brad to negotiate the quarter-mile drive down to the waterfront, amidst the lines of tractor-trailers waiting their turn.

Even before he could make out the designation on the front of the building, Brad noticed his blond-haired visitor standing prominently, seemingly oblivious to the icy wind, in front of what could only be Warehouse Number Three.

As Brad pulled up, the man opened his car door and politely directed him to a small entrance, instructing him to climb the stairs inside. He did as instructed.

As Brad entered, he saw Paul DeBenedetto, slowly descending the long metal staircase along the bare brick wall.

"This is my exercise for the month," said Paul, then only three or four steps from the bottom. "How are you, Brad?"

"I'm fine, Mr. D, however, I was somewhat puzzled by my unexpected visitor this morning. I hope there's no problem," said Brad, regretting that he had sounded more like a frightened employee than an equal.

"Let's walk a minute, Brad," Paul suggested, as he turned towards the seemingly endless aisles of crates and containers. "Actually, there is a problem. That's why I asked you to join me here."

Life had been an endless learning session for Brad Parkins and subtleties were almost never lost on him.

As the old man spoke those words, the entire picture

became clear to Brad. Everything that morning had been carefully planned to jolt him off balance; the first buzz at the door, the offer of a ride, the long rush-hour drive, all of it. It was the psychology of terror.

The sophistication of it all inspired admiration in Brad, but did nothing to diminish its inevitable effect.

At the relatively mature age of fifty-three, Brad was forced to concede that there were forces well beyond his powers to manipulate and control. He knew in that moment that, if he crossed these people, they would not hesitate to kill him. He would, nevertheless, survive this and, in so doing, be strengthened by the knowledge he had gained.

"A private investigator was murdered the other day," Paul said matter-of-factly. "He was working with Frank Doherty. What do you know about it?"

"I didn't have anything to do with it," answered Brad, sincerely.

Hartman had obviously murdered the old man, despite Brad's order to the contrary. The detective was now clearly a homicidal maniac on the loose and Brad had to distance himself.

"I didn't ask you what you did, Brad. I asked you what you know about it," said Paul, clearly understanding that he had the younger man on the defensive.

Brad knew it was time to cut bait on Lonnie Hartman. "There's been a cop helping out on this from the beginning," began Parkins. "He's a detective named Lonnie Hartman. He supervised the cleanup when Sean killed the girl and he ran down Doherty's wife because she would have identified Sean. There was no need for any more killing. I told him that. The old private eye was on Hartman's trail and he wanted to make him disappear, but I told him no. The old guy was heading down a dead-end road and I told Hartman to let it go, but it looks like he didn't. He's out of control."

"Okay, Brad. Who else is involved with you on this? Think carefully," Paul cautioned.

"Nobody that I'm aware of," answered Brad truthfully.

"Tell me, Brad, how much does Jack Lowry really know about this business? I need to know that."

Paul's redundancy was not lost on Parkins. "I don't honestly know. I never discussed it with him myself, but he knows something. I'm certain of it. He called me into his office without any record of the appointment and, in his own totally deniable way, threatened me. He told me in a round-about way that, if I didn't make this all go away, I'd be finished."

"Then you misled me from the beginning, Brad. You led me to believe that it was the Mayor who asked for my help directly."

It was an accusation that Brad decided to accept as a question. "Yes, but it's my job. You know that, Mr. D. You understand how it works. I can't ever discuss things like this with him. I'm supposed to take care of it. He learns what he needs to know from people who are much closer to him than me, so I really didn't deceive you at all."

"I understand how it works, Brad. I figured that was it from the beginning. From what you say, I'd bet he knows everything, but just doesn't want to put his finger on the button. He's hoping you and I can clean this up for him while he can still withstand a Federal investigation. Hell, he probably even loves that homicidal, pervert kid of his. I mean, you know what a great family man he is."

"I'm willing to listen to any suggestions, Mr. D."

"Thank you, Brad. Well, it looks to me like you did everything right, but this thing is taking on a life of its own. Hartman is a loose cannon, but Frank Doherty is even more of a danger. He's on a fucking personal crusade and that's a very dangerous thing. He's not going to quit, so he has to be stopped."

"So what should I do?"

"Nothing, Brad. You did what you could, but more experienced people are going to take over now. That little pervert started a real firestorm. But you can still help. Sean has to disappear for a week or so. There's a political junket leaving for Mexico on Saturday morning. You know the kind; a bunch of lobbyists and state lawmakers with a planeload of hookers. Here's the itinerary," Paul said, handing Parkins a plain white envelope. "The limo will pick him up at seven Saturday morning. The driver will have his airline tickets. Make sure he doesn't fuck this up and tell him to keep his fucking mouth shut."

"That won't be a problem," said Brad. "It's exactly the kind of vacation Sean likes."

"I'm so glad," responded Paul, sarcastically. "But there's one more thing. Sean's not the only one who needs to disappear. You need to get away from all of this for a few weeks while we work it out. Take a vacation. Do it tomorrow. Go to the Bahamas. Get a young broad and relax. Let me know where you're staying and, when this all over, I'll call you. When you come back, you can take the credit."

It clearly hadn't been intended as advice and Brad knew it. His good old reliable street smarts told him it was time to declare victory and retreat slowly. "If you think that's best, I'll take your advice, Mr. D. I'll get over to the office and make the arrangements today. I've got six weeks of vacation coming. Good luck."

"Thank you, Brad. Just enjoy yourself and try to forget about this mess for a while. We'll get it straightened out."

On the drive to the airport, Brad tuned in the twenty-four hour jazz station and marveled at his good fortune. He had pitched eight tough innings and kept them in the game. Now, the ace relief pitcher would come in and close out the last inning. Brad couldn't think of a better place to be than the Bahamas when Lonnie Hartman and Frank Doherty got a bullet in the brain.

He stopped near the airport for a scheduled lunch meeting, where he used a public phone to call Sean. Oblivious as always to the complexities of the situation, Sean was pleasantly surprised by the offer of a free vacation and agreed at once.

Brad treated himself to two martinis before finally arriving at his office around two o'clock. What better place, he thought, to arrange a last second vacation than the airport? Within two hours, he had made all the necessary notifications and schedule changes.

He delayed calling Meg because he wasn't in the mood for an argument. A bad scene with her now would surely spoil a very good day. *Fuck Meg*. This was as good a way as any to give her the message.

His real concern was Jack Lowry. What would the Mayor think about his troubleshooting point man suddenly leaving on vacation in the middle of the worst crisis in Lowry family history?

He solved this problem quickly by calling the Mayor's obnoxious Chief of Staff. He told Erskin that, to adequately address certain critical matters on a full-time basis, he was going to use three weeks' vacation.

Erskin offered no editorial comments, but simply

indicated he would pass the information on to the Mayor.

He made the travel arrangements himself and, by five o'clock, had his airline tickets and itinerary in hand. Brad was genuinely excited about the vacation as his Lexus cleared the airport.

On the drive home, he allowed his mind to wander for the first time in weeks, anticipating a much-needed rest. Thoughts of warm weather and young female company made the normally tedious drive home nearly tolerable.

As he neared the underground garage door at the rear of his building, Brad opened it by remote and entered the dimly lit garage, proceeding directly to his designated corner space on the lower of the two levels. Despite the fact that it was the dinner hour, there were no tenants in the garage and fewer than a dozen cars.

As Brad closed the car door, he turned and was horrified to find Lonnie Hartman standing directly in his path to the elevator, not fifteen feet from the car. Hartman was disheveled and unshaven, with the wild, bloodshot eyes of a predatory animal.

Brad didn't stop. He kept walking towards the man, all the while trying to collect what was left of his wits. "Lonnie, it's probably not smart for you to be here," said Parkins, trying to maintain authority without overtly offending this raving lunatic.

"Lonnie? Who the fuck is Lonnie? What's going on here, you sneaky fucking toad? The last time you called me Lonnie you were trying to fuck me."

Despite Hartman's obviously deteriorating mental state, Brad was comforted by the fact that he had not been shot. If Hartman had come here to kill him, he would be dead now. "All right, I'll stick to Hartman, if you prefer.

To what do I owe the honor of your visit?" Brad asked.

"To be honest, I've been getting the feeling lately that you're avoiding me and I kind of miss our quiet little talks." He began to walk slowly towards Parkins in the semi-darkness.

As he came closer, Brad could make out the old sarcastic smile, this time accompanied by a hideous, muted laugh, none of it out of character, but this time betraying a chilling hatred, born of paranoia.

"I'm just lying low until this all blows over. I think if we just keep our wits now and sit tight, Doherty will strike out and this whole thing will blow over. Don't you agree?" No matter how hard he tried, Brad just couldn't summon up the old bravado and the words sounded patronizing, even conciliatory.

Like a big cat on the trail of its wounded prey, Hartman seemed to sense the change and the fear in Brad's voice. He seized upon it, moving ever closer to the shorter man, until he was only inches from Brad's face. He helped himself to a massive fist-full of Brad's shirt collar and reeled him in slowly, until the two faces were virtually touching.

The revulsion of his untreated breath permeated Brad's senses, inducing a semi-hypnotic state of surrender. For the second time in his relationship with Lonnie Hartman, Brad seemed momentarily to accept his inevitable fate, as the gigantic wild man began to whisper.

"Sit tight? You sit tight, you fucking worm. That scumbag lawyer will never drive me underground. If I end it now, they have nothing on me. Once I send Doherty to hell, I'm in the clear."

"What about the Wells girl?" Parkins gasped.

"What about her? Even if she talks, it doesn't prove I murdered Doherty's wife. The worst I can do over it is lose my job. I'll kill anybody I have to, starting with Doherty and then Sean Lowry."

"I can help you," Parkins managed to whisper, now barely able to breathe.

"You'll help me all right, you spineless rat. When this is all over, you're gonna help fund my retirement." This time the laugh came from deep inside his belly and echoed against the walls of the nearly empty garage. "Someday, when you're least expecting it, Parkins, you're gonna get yours, but not today because you owe me money and besides, we're still a team. I know you sold me out to somebody, but believe me, I'll be alive to piss on your grave some day."

"I didn't, Hartman. I really didn't," he finally whispered in return. "Think about it. I'd be rolling over on myself. We're in this together, like it or not."

Brad never saw Hartman's fist as it came from somewhere over his left shoulder and drove violently into the right side of his face, just under the eye. The effect of the powerful blow was aggravated by Hartman's continued vice-grip on Brad's shirt collar.

As Hartman turned to leave, a semi-conscious Brad Parkins slumped slowly down the blood spattered door of the gold Lexus, coming to rest in a sitting position, just ahead of the rear wheel. As he sat broken, motionless and bloody on the cold cement, Brad smiled inwardly, knowing that he had just been beaten to a pulp by a walking corpse.

It was once said of Richard Nixon that 'even the paranoid have enemies.' As Hartman drove aimlessly from Brad's building, his paranoia was acute, but entirely justified. He was convinced that Parkins had already unleashed powerful forces against him and sensed that his life was in imminent danger. He could still weather this in good shape if he could just get that fucking Doherty off his back, he thought. Get rid of Doherty and then Sean. Califf might figure the whole thing out, but nobody would be able to prove it. Even the Wells girl couldn't touch him with Doherty dead. Then he could easily extort some big money out of that chicken shit Parkins. The trick now, he thought, would be to stay alive long enough to execute his plan.

Chapter Twenty

As it turned out, Stavros Panos, in his own unique way, had continued to work the case right through his own funeral on Friday morning. The church service, even on a weekday, had been attended by no fewer than two hundred people, nearly all of whom were well known to Diane.

There were life-long friends from the old middle-class Greek neighborhood where he had been raised.

Near the rear of the church, she spotted Earl and Crusty, two old geezers who had served with Steve in combat during the Korean War. Earl was from New Mexico and Crusty from New York. They had flown in on Thursday for the wake. The annual reunions had stopped years ago due to dwindling numbers, but the survivors had stayed in contact by mail and phone.

Next to Earl, she noticed an attractive young woman whom she had never seen. She would have assumed the woman was the daughter of one of the old boys, but she knew that both of them had traveled alone.

After the service, Diane approached the girl directly to say thank you. The young woman broke into tears and introduced herself as Julie Wells. The news spread quickly among the interested mourners.

Julie accepted Frank's offer of a ride to the cemetery. There was room in the minivan, even with Beth and Larry coming along.

On the drive, no one questioned Julie regarding her attendance at the funeral and Julie herself never broached the subject.

"I don't think there will be this many people at my funeral," she offered, staring blankly out the windshield and speaking to no one in particular as Frank pulled into the long procession.

"He was a remarkable human being," said Frank. "But he always sold himself short. I wish he could have seen this."

"It kind of makes you think about getting a final grade when your life is over," Beth chimed in from the rear seat. "You know, it's almost like school. I mean there are people who came today who knew him for sixty years or more. It just makes you think about all the relationships you have in a lifetime and all the opportunities you have to touch someone, and maybe make a difference."

Sitting beside her, Larry squeezed her hand and smiled warmly as she continued.

"This is when you get your final report card. Sometimes I guess it's a blessing that you never get to see it, but not today. You're right Frank. Steve should have seen this."

"Well, he sure wasn't a saint," Frank responded. "Diane would tell you that he drove her crazy for forty-two years, but he did touch people's lives in positive ways and, despite his faults, he was a good father."

In the Greek tradition, the mourners gathered at the gravesite to offer a final prayer as a light snow fell slowly in the dead still air. When it concluded, Diane invited Julie Wells back to the house for a meal. Julie accepted without hesitation, aware that the remainder of her business awaited her there.

It was nearly dinnertime when the last of the mourners left the house. George remained behind with Julie and Frank's crew, but sent his wife and kids home with his car.

They were all sitting around the kitchen table, Frank nursing a beer and the others a last cup of coffee, when Julie was finally ready to talk.

"I told Steve everything about that whole sorry nightmare. He didn't push me. I told him because he made me want to tell him and now he's dead because of it."

With that, she told them the entire story of the incident eight years ago; about Sean, Lonnie Hartman, even about accepting the twenty thousand dollars.

When she was finished, there seemed to be little doubt in the faces of the small vigilante band.

"Well, there it is," offered Larry. "It's the same pattern we have here. Cover up for Sean and neutralize the witnesses."

"I don't know how this will play out, Julie," Frank began. "The Statute of Limitations has run out on the entire incident at the university. They can't prosecute Sean or Hartman for anything that happened eight years ago, but your testimony might be critical to establish Hartman's pattern of conduct. What Larry is saying is that testimony about your experience might help convict Hartman of Steve's murder, maybe even two others. How do you feel about testifying? I know it would be difficult, even humiliating, to admit that you kept the money."

"I told Steve I was ready," she said, with conviction in her voice. "I don't care about any of that. I'll do whatever I have to put those bastards away."

"What about that security guy from the university?"

Larry asked. "Do you think he might have been involved with Hartman?"

"Up to his ears," Julie answered. "He was only too eager to tear up the paperwork when Hartman finished with me. They did a lot of private talking during my so-called interview. Is he still there?"

"He's still there," said Frank, "at least for the moment."

George then broke his long deliberative silence. "The issue now is whether Hartman is the only cop involved. I'm not sure how we find out."

"We'll find a way. By the way, did you get anything yet on that city cell phone number?" Frank asked anxiously.

"Not yet," answered George. "Nobody seems to know who has the list. I'm still working on it."

"I was really close with Munoz," offered Larry. "He was scared to death and on the verge of giving Hartman up. I get the sense that he didn't know Steve would be murdered. It looks like he was just covering his involvement in Julie's case. My guess would be Hartman spread that money all around. If we could get Munoz to go, we'd have Hartman dead to rights on Steve's murder."

"By now he must have talked to Hartman about your visit, so he knows this isn't an official investigation. There's no point in going at him again," said Frank. "Let's wait and see if George can pin down Mr. Big for us with that phone number. We're close, very close."

They extended their final sympathies to Diane and left together. Only George stayed.

"Would you like me to come back and stay with you tonight, Mother?" George asked. "I could go to the bank with you tomorrow and take you to see the lawyer if you like."

"No, I'll be all right, Georgie. You go home to your family tonight. Take my car. You can pick me up in the morning and we'll take care of your father's business."

"Mother, this is going to be very difficult for you. I could handle all this if you like," he offered.

"I'll be fine, Georgie. But what concerns me more than my own situation is your reaction to all of this. You've always been a hot-tempered boy. Your father was like that when he was young. I just don't understand how you're taking this. I know you must be angry inside."

"I suppose I am," George conceded.

"I'd have thought that your natural instinct would have driven you to take charge of this whole investigation, but you've been staying in the background, letting Frank and the others take the lead. Don't misunderstand me, Georgie."

"Are you disappointed, Mother?" he asked, genuinely baffled.

"Of course not. I mean, I wouldn't want you going off half-cocked. It's just that I wonder if there might be something going on here that I don't know about; more to the point, something that Frank doesn't know about. Talk to me, Georgie. Tell me what's going on."

"It'll work out, mother. Trust me," said George, resting his big hands gently on the tops of her shoulders. "The people who killed my father will pay. I promise you that."

"I'm not concerned about revenge, Georgie. I'm concerned about you. What's going on here?"

George kissed his mother lightly on the forehead and retrieved her car keys from the hook behind the kitchen door. "It'll be okay, Mother. It'll all be okay. I'll be fine. I'll see you in the morning."

As he headed south from his mother's, George removed a small, folded sheet of notebook paper from his shirt pocket and glanced down at the first of two addresses written inside. In his mind, he quickly calculated the most direct route to Lonnie Hartman's apartment and then wondered if the promise he had just made to his mother qualified as a lie.

Hartman lived in a nondescript twenty-odd unit apartment building on the North Side. It was located less that one block from the old, pre-shopping-mall-era Burston Avenue Business District, an area of shops and taverns, complete with an old style, one-screen movie theater, at the busy intersection of Burston and Forty-Seventh Streets.

George arrived just after nine o'clock and parked the car in the small lot behind the sparsely attended old theater. He covered the remaining distance slowly on foot, taking careful notice of detail, such as the alley, street lighting, foot traffic, and gangways.

He walked slowly past Hartman's building without stopping, taking note of the well-lit foyer and the inside security door located near the panel of buzzers. He continued on to the end of the block and turned to re-trace his steps. He knew that, in order not to attract attention, he could only make one more pass safely. After that, he would have to leave and come back in an hour or so.

As he reached the middle of the block, he could make out a short woman pulling a metal grocery carrier. She was much closer to the building, so he picked up his pace in order to time his arrival. Sure enough, she turned up the sidewalk towards the main entrance. He hurried quietly into line behind her.

"Good evening," he said, knowing that his recently

purchased navy blue dress suit and rep tie could hardly be considered the attire of a mugger.

"Thank you very much, Sir," said the woman, already holding the security door key in her free hand.

As he reached to help the woman with the door, George scrolled quickly down the typed and handwritten names, each folded and stuffed into a narrow slot beside the corresponding buzzer. He noted the handwritten name "Hartman" in apartment 304.

George bid the woman "good night" and opted for the staircase just beyond the bank of two elevators. At the third floor, he emerged through he metal fire door into the hallway. Apartment 304 was immediately to his left, one of only four units on the third floor. Aside from the distant sound of a television from somewhere down the hall, the third floor was dead quiet.

He stood motionless for perhaps a minute, ear to the door, hopeful for some clue as to the exact whereabouts of the occupant, Lonnie Hartman. George figured that he couldn't risk knocking at the door. Whatever ruse he decided to employ, Hartman would become immediately suspicious and the element of surprise would be lost. If Hartman should recognize his voice, George thought, the whole thing could end badly in a split second. He would get one free kick and no more. If the door didn't give, then disappear and plan again, he thought.

Out of instinct, George reached for the doorknob and began to turn it clockwise, ever so gently. To his surprise, the knob turned a full forty-five degrees without resistance. It was unlocked. He pushed gingerly on the door and felt it give. The dead bolt was disengaged. Drawing his .9 mm Smith & Wesson from its waist holster, George pushed slowly, trying his best to keep his body out of the likely line of fire, but there was no gunfire.

As he entered, there was no sound at all, save the now even more distant, muffled sound of the television. The entire apartment was a wreck. It had been searched and ransacked in what appeared to be the work of professionals.

In the single bedroom, every bureau drawer had been removed and turned upside down, the contents strewn everywhere. The linen had been stripped from the double bed and the mattress sliced down the middle in a single razor-like cut.

In the small kitchen, the cabinet doors were all open and the cabinets empty, the contents broken and scattered randomly throughout the room. George knew at once that Lonnie Hartman was now a man in great demand.

Whoever had preceded George into the apartment was no amateur. The locks had been picked, no doubt quietly and quickly in the middle of the day.

It was impossible for George to tell whether the burglars had been looking for Hartman himself, or just some specific item that they didn't find. There was one thing for sure, however; this had not been a random burglary.

The television and stereo were still in place, as was the VCR. Most likely, someone was looking for Hartman in connection with this Doherty business—someone decidedly unfriendly. George took considerable comfort in that fact.

When he allowed himself to consider the possible identity of his *allies*, the list he compiled mentally was nothing short of terrifying. Hartman was now on the lamb and would be difficult, if not impossible, to find.

George had one more stop to make before the night

was over. He removed the folded paper from his pocket one last time and memorized the address of Brad Parkins' high rise condominium building.

Frank had just put the twins to bed, no small task at ten o'clock on a Saturday night. He, Laura, Maggie and Alex were just settling in to watch a movie they had rented earlier that evening. Frank was looking forward to an evening of doing absolutely nothing with a glass of wine and an unobstructed view of a warming fire. He couldn't have cared less which of the Disney movies Maggie decided to pop into the VCR.

"Can I make the popcorn now, Dad?" Maggie asked.

"Not yet, Sweetheart. Wait until the butt heads get to sleep. It won't be long now. You know how they are. If they smell that microwave popcorn, they'll be down here in our laps in five seconds."

Halfway into the first glass of wine, Frank began to doze on and off in the plush leather easy chair, intoxicated more by the aroma of the fresh buttered popcorn and the warmth of the fire than by the red wine. He was oblivious to the movie, a fact that seemed to annoy Maggie to no end.

"Dad, aren't you watching the movie?" She would ask, as if the movie would be less entertaining if not enjoyed by her father.

"Yes, Honey. I'm watching it. It's a wonderful movie." Within minutes, he would be gone again, taking care to position himself so that she could not see his drooping eyelids.

The last interruption of his restful slumber, however, was not caused by Maggie, but by his pager buzzing around on the kitchen table. "Mags, could I ask you a favor?"

"Oh, Daddy, this is the best part of the movie," she whined, but already handing the bowl of popcorn to Laura, snuggled between her and Alex on the large sofa.

By the time Maggie handed him the pager, Frank was awake and almost fully alert. He tried to read the digital message but the dim firelight was insufficient. As he walked into the kitchen, the message became as clear as day: *Ivan Munoz ASAP 555-1437*.

Odd, he thought, that Munoz would call him and not Larry Califf. After all, the two men had never even met. He could only have learned of Frank's involvement from Hartman. Certainly Steve would never have mentioned the name. He thought briefly about talking to Larry before he returned the call, but decided against it. Curiosity drove him directly into his small study to return the call.

"Mr. Munoz, this is Frank Doherty returning your call."

"Mr. Doherty," he began, "you know who I am and, believe me, I know who you are. I have nothing to do with any of this and I certainly didn't knowingly participate in any murder. This is way over my head and I need to get out of it. I don't know who I'm more afraid of at this point; the police or the other police, if you get my point. If this all goes badly, I want to be on record as having helped you."

"So talk," said Frank. "I guarantee you have my attention."

"Not over the phone," the man said, "and not without some ground rules in place. We need to meet."

"What do you have in mind?" Frank asked.

"The university is building a new extension campus out in Larson County," Munoz began, "about twenty miles straight west of the city. It's on Route 40, two or three miles west of the town. It's a secure construction site with a ten-foot chain link fence. I'll leave the west gate unlocked. Be there at ten o'clock tomorrow night. I'll wait for you at the main administration building in the center of the site. It's the biggest building, still just a four story steel frame; and please, Mr. Doherty, don't bring any company."

"Why all the cloak-and-dagger?" Frank asked. "You could just tell me what you know right now. If you weren't involved in murder, I'll see that you're protected."

"It's very simple, Mr. Doherty. The fact is that I still have the reports from that incident eight years ago. I also have tapes of recent phone conversations between myself and a detective named Hartman. Besides, you might not exactly come through this with flying colors, if you know what I mean. In that event, I want to have a document in my hand that says I was helping you in your little investigation. Please see that you bring it."

"Okay, I'll be there," said Frank.

When he returned from the study, Laura knew immediately that something was wrong. As the movie played, she waited patiently for Frank to speak. When he didn't, she took the initiative. "Frank, could I speak to you in the study for a minute?" she asked. "Kids, keep watching the movie. We'll be right back, and don't eat all the popcorn."

She closed the study door behind them. "Am I on the outside now, Frank?" she asked.

"Of course not," he answered. "It's just that I don't want to burden you with any more of my troubles than I already have."

"Oh," she exclaimed sarcastically. "You mean, like nearly getting raped and chopped to pieces by that psycho? Don't you think I've earned the right to be included?"

"It's not that, Laura. It's not that at all. You're no longer just some nice person helping out. I mean, you know how I feel. I know how you feel, at least I think I do."

"Stop, Frank. Please, stop right now, before you dig yourself a hole. I suppose even you know that you're emotionally challenged, so just let me give you a little help. You're right, Frank. We care deeply about each other, but that doesn't mean you're supposed to protect me by excluding me from a part of your life. You need to understand that right now, Frank, if you expect this relationship to go anywhere. I won't be some 'dufus' that you come home to for a roll in the hay and a home-cooked meal."

Frank flashed a beaten look. "Touché," he conceded. "I'm sorry, Laura. I'm not exactly famous for considering other perspectives, but this old dog wants to learn new tricks. The call was from Ivan Munoz, the security guy from St. Francis. He wants to meet me and spill the beans on Hartman."

"He wants to meet you where and when?" Laura asked.

"Some remote construction site, late tomorrow night," he answered.

"Well, you're not going. Are you?"

"Laura, this is exactly what I was trying to avoid. I know that it could be dangerous. I have to go, but I'm not stupid. I'll take every precaution. I'll take Larry and Ray with me. The guy just might be on the level."

"It's more likely that he's just setting you up for

Hartman," she said, " just like he did to Steve."

"I'm almost certain of it," Frank agreed, "but that's been our plan all along, Laura; bring these people out in the open where they're exposed. I have no choice now. This thing is coming to a head. I'll be all right. I promise you."

"Frank, call the FBI right now, before this whole thing collapses on you. You've done your part. It won't change a damn thing if you die for her. What's done is done. Even if you don't care about yourself, what about those other two fools? You could get them killed. Goddammit, Frank, your kids could grow up without a parent."

"It's not just Denise, Laura. It's Caroline. It's Steve. It's Sam. I'm fed up with a lifetime of Lowrys and the shit they rain down on people in the names of progress and prosperity. We have a real chance to end it, Laura, once and for all. It would make all their death's mean something."

"Then call George and see what he thinks," she offered. "He can help."

"I can't do that. Something's not right with George, and until I know what it is, we have to keep him at arm's length."

"Frank, even if you win, it won't change anything. You're not the first person to think he could change the world. My God, look what happened to that poor man who blew the whistle on the tobacco companies. He was lucky. They only destroyed him. They're going to kill you, Frank."

"I don't want to change the world," he began. "I just want to find my wife's killers. If that means changing this gleaming cesspool of a city, then so be it. It could happen, Laura. They've never been as vulnerable as they are now."

"Be careful, Frank," she said, resting her palm gently on his cheek.

"I will, Laura. I promise."

Their embrace was a solemn, an unspoken expression of mutual commitment. Frank had already begun to feel a change in the nature of his quest. Gone was the cold bitterness, the kamikaze mentality that had driven him to this point, replaced by a solid sense of mission on the path to what might yet be a real future.

Less than a mile away, Larry and Beth were seated in a secluded booth at Morelli's Ristorante, raising a glass of fine Chianti in celebration of Beth's first real job. She had received the phone call earlier that afternoon and had kept the news a secret, even from her mother. She wanted to share it with Larry first in a private moment.

Larry recognized the significance of the gesture immediately and was genuinely touched. She had been hired to write news copy at a local radio station, an affiliate of a major national network. It was an entry-level job, to be sure, but one with a bright future. This was a milestone in her life and Larry was only too eager to embrace the serious inferences to be drawn from her choice of confidants.

As their wineglasses touched, he could see the change of expression in her eyes. A look of overwhelming sadness overtook her and she began to cry, quietly but unmistakably.

"What's wrong, Beth?" he asked in obvious surprise.

"Well, Larry Califf, you may be sensitive for a man, but you're still a man," she said, almost whispering. "This is the best time of my life. I have the job that I've worked so long to get and, at the same time, I'm in love, truly in love and probably for the first time in my life."

"So?" He didn't get it.

"It's just that all these wonderful things happened to me because my poor sister was murdered. It just isn't right that I should find such happiness while my beautiful, loving Caroline is—" She could no longer speak and cast her eyes down to the table, shielding them with her hand in a determined effort to collect herself.

Larry wanted desperately to say the right thing, but for a moment could find no words. "I love you too, Beth," he finally said, surrendering to his heart. "I know how you must feel. I mean, I understand it, but there's another way of looking at it."

"And what's that, Mr. Sensitive?" she mumbled through the handkerchief, having now come nearly all the way back.

"Do you remember when I told you about seeing Caroline's picture coming off the printer? It was the strangest feeling I've ever had, but it was real. I think I understand it now. It sounds crazy and I can't even believe I'm saying it, but it's true."

"That what's true?"

"Caroline knew that this would happen. She knew that her death would bring us together and she was telling me, telling us, that it's all right. Beth, I'm not religious or crazy, but I'm telling you I felt the power of that message in her eyes. I couldn't understand it then, but I wasn't meant to. Look at me, Beth," he begged.

Her green eyes reappeared to capture his gaze, and at that moment he never wanted to look away.

"Ask me if I believe in destiny, Beth." He continued. "Ask me if I believe in fate. Well, I do and, if you open your mind and your heart, you will too. We can be thankful that we found each other, Beth, because Caroline is. I love you, Beth. I love you more than anything in my miserable, structured existence."

"So what happens now?" she asked, the tears returning in force, not only from sadness, but from her full range of emotions.

"I have no idea," he replied. "I guess you could call me a man in transition."

"What does that mean?" she asked.

"They have me under a microscope at work," Larry replied. "There's this miserable old homicide lieutenant named Jenkins who's keeping the heat on. It's almost a personal thing with him. It wouldn't surprise me if he's involved in it somehow. Anyway, I've been notified that there's an Internal Affairs investigation under way. Eventually, I'll be called in to give a statement, but they're not in any hurry."

"So what will happen to you?"

"Who knows? They don't know how this will play out, so they're hedging their bet. The department can't be seen as persecuting an honest whistle-blowing cop, so I think they'll just wait and see if we sink or swim. I really don't care what they do because my policing days are coming to an end anyway."

"You seem pretty sure about that," she observed, offering him a chance to explain.

"Think about it. If we manage to expose Hartman and his puppeteers, I'll have my fifteen minutes of fame as a media hero, but the rank and file police won't be signing up for my fan club. I just don't need that shit. I mean, the job just isn't that important to me. I'm ready to move on."

"On to where?" she asked playfully.

"I have a degree and I'm only twenty-eight years old. I'll find something. Maybe I'll even go to law school at night." He reflected on his last remark and chuckled. "We'll be okay, Beth, but your Uncle Frank, well, he's another story. Tell me. How well do you really know him?"

"What do you mean?" she asked.

"He's an anomaly to me, a kind of walking paradox. I mean, he's absolutely fearless in his determination to see this through. He has to know that his life is in danger from God knows how many directions, but he just keeps plugging ahead. I sometimes wonder where he gets it, his direction and motivation I mean."

"I'm ashamed to say I've never really thought about it," she answered reflectively.

"I mean, the guy carries around some pretty heavy baggage to be acting like the Lone Ranger. He's a neurotic mess, for God sake. He drinks too much. He's moody. He's ill tempered and has the self-esteem of a panhandler. How in the name of God does he get people to follow him like this?"

"I don't know," she answered. "I never got to spend much time with my Aunt and Uncle since we moved out West. I remember that he was always kind to us as little girls. We loved him very much. Maybe it's nothing more than that. Maybe he just has the ability to connect with people. It seems like flawed characters are always easier to embrace. They're somehow less threatening and allow us to view ourselves in a better light. He's a very kind, but sad man."

As the waiter hurried to fill their nearly empty glasses, they heard the muffled ringing of Larry's cell phone. He removed it from his inside breast pocket.

"Hello. Califf here."

"Larry? It's Frank. Where are you?"

"We're nearby, Frank, having dinner. Why?"

"Would you stop by here tonight? I need to talk to you. There's been a development."

"I have to bring Beth home anyway," Larry answered. "We'll be there in an hour or so. Is that soon enough?"

"See you then. Bye."

"What is it?" she asked, reaching for his arm.

"Whatever it is will wait until after dinner," he answered, reaching for the menu.

Chapter Twenty-one

Sunday night saw near blizzard conditions, with heavy blowing snow and gusting wind. Driving was difficult, but not impossible. Such short-lived storms were not unheard of in March.

Larry was actually scheduled to work, but had taken a personal day at the last minute, a fact that had been discreetly discovered by Lonnie Hartman. Last minute personal time would do nothing to ingratiate Califf with the police hierarchy, but he was beyond caring, wanting only to collect a few more paychecks before tendering his resignation.

Ray arrived at around seven to find Frank and Larry busy in Frank's study with last minute planning. The three men had driven out to the site early Sunday morning and Frank and Califf had spent the better part of the day formulating a plan.

Beth greeted Ray at the door and returned to the family room, where she began the arduous process of getting the kids away from the television and into the tub. Her appointed task was to shield the children from the inevitable tension in the house that Sunday evening.

As the men exchanged greetings with Ray, Larry removed his coat from the back of the chair, reached into the pocket, and produced a blue steel semi-automatic pistol. He placed the pistol on the desk, directly in front of Ray Paxon. "Do you remember how to use one of these?" Larry's tone was serious and business-like.

"It's been a long time since I wore a blue uniform, but I remember how to use it," Ray answered.

"Let's hope you won't have to," offered Frank. "Now, let's go over the plan."

Frank had roughly sketched the site on a sheet of plain white paper. It occupied the equivalent of a one square block area in a primarily residential district of recently constructed homes. It faced the highway on the north side, with the remaining three sides directly opposite rows of private homes. The chain link fence stood six feet high, with no barbed wire or other obstruction. There were two gates; one on the north directly facing the highway and the other on the south end. Both had been locked on Sunday morning. The only parking outside the fence was a wide shoulder off the highway on the north side.

"We'll take Ray's SUV," Frank said. "Nobody will recognize it. We'll drop Ray off here," he continued, pointing to the east side of the site. "Larry, I'll drop you over here on the west end. Once you get over the fence, just keep the best cover you can and make your way to a point where you can observe the main building over here."

He pointed to the spot on the map. "There's heavy equipment parked everywhere around there to provide cover and the weather will help. Just remember, if you see anything remotely threatening, fire a shot in the air and head back for the fence. Cut through the yards and, when I can get the car, I'll cruise the neighborhood and find you. If something goes wrong, try to avoid a confrontation. The last thing we want is to shoot somebody, even Hartman. This Munoz character has every reason to cooperate with us and it's just possible he's on the up-and-up; not likely, but possible."

"And what if he's not?" Larry asked. "What will we have accomplished just by getting out alive?"

"If he's not being straight with us now, I guarantee you he will be tomorrow," Frank answered.

Despite the nasty weather and limited visibility, they found that the major highways remained in relatively good shape. The ever-developing science of meteorology allowed the state and city to assemble huge numbers of plows, salt-spreaders, and personnel in anticipation of an approaching storm. Plowing and spreading began non-stop as the first snowflakes hit the ground.

According to plan, they arrived at the site an hour early. Avoiding the main gate, Ray turned onto the residential street abutting the site on the east. As they drove slowly along the length of the construction site, the three men peered into the darkness for signs of life or recent activity. Visibility was near zero and even Larry's binoculars were useless in the white squall.

As they reached the boundary, Ray stopped the SUV at the side of the road, opened the driver's door, and turned to his two passengers. "It's all yours, boys," he said. "This is my stop."

"Ray, did you set the pager to vibrate?" Frank asked nervously. "We don't need beepers going off."

"Yes, Mother. I did everything I was told."

"Okay, then stay warm and remember; if I roll my flashlight in circles you can come out. Good luck and try not to step on any rusty nails."

Frank took the wheel of the SUV and dropped Larry at the opposite end of the site. There was a major intersection less than a mile away and he figured there might be a convenience store nearby where he could kill a half-hour in the parking lot with a cup of coffee. He was right.

He sat in the lot, nursing a hot cup of bad coffee, engine running. The minutes passed slowly, more slowly, he thought, for his companions hunkered down in the biting wind and snow.

At precisely nine fifty-eight, Frank turned the SUV onto the short service drive and parked less than twenty feet from the front gate. There were no vehicles in sight. He approached the gate on foot, searching in vain for recent footprints in the snow and, as he had feared, found the front gate chained and securely padlocked. He was momentarily overwhelmed by a sense of sheer terror.

Before Frank had even departed the convenience store lot, a nondescript sedan, some twenty miles away, had turned onto a tree-lined suburban lane and pulled to the curb, directly in front of the Doherty residence.

About the time Frank was scrambling clumsily to scale the chain link fence in search Larry and Ray, the driver patiently checked his watch and glanced up at the two lighted bedroom windows on the second floor. Within a few more minutes, the lights in the two upstairs bedrooms dimmed, one after the other.

Inside the house, Beth descended the stairs and settled into Frank's favorite chair to watch the ten o'clock news.

He sat motionless behind the wheel for another few minutes. Then, leaving the car unlocked, he walked briskly to the front door of Frank's home. Pausing briefly on the landing, he pulled a small object from his coat pocket, bent forward from the waist and pulled what appeared to be a stocking completely over his head. Lonnie Hartman rang the doorbell and waited. Beth came to the door almost immediately.

"Who's there?" she asked, having no intention of opening the door until the visitor had been identified.

As she spoke, Hartman was already unscrewing the bulb from the single porch light, rendering the porch pitch dark.

With the quickness of a cat, he swung open his long overcoat, revealing a powerful four foot long sledge hammer, suspended from his inside shoulder by a rope. Saying nothing, he took precisely two steps back from the door as he released the menacing tool from its hiding place.

Beth was still waiting for an answer when Hartman's first blow struck the doorknob and lock with the power of an explosive charge, propelling the inside doorknob past her with the force of a bullet. The second and final blow, aimed at the deadbolt lock, came before she could even fully comprehend the first.

The door swung violently in, sending with it a large portion of the wooden doorframe in dozens of jagged and pointed pieces, a six-inch long portion of which lodged in Beth's left arm. Within eight seconds, he had battered in the door and closed what was left of it behind him.

Beth had finally begun to react by running for the kitchen phone.

Having dropped the hammer, Hartman seized her by the hair with one hand before she even reached the kitchen. With the other hand, he removed a small can of mace from his coat pocket and released a generous spray, most of which settled on the top of her head.

Beth, now free and fighting to keep her feet, was nearly convulsive. Hartman, in a telling and gratuitous act of contempt, coldly measured his helpless victim and launched a powerful backhand, catching Beth directly on the right side of her face. She crashed violently into the glass doors of the built-in double oven, momentarily unconscious.

In a concession to his hatred for Frank Doherty, Hartman took just an extra moment to watch as Beth settled, bleeding, onto the hardwood floor. He couldn't resist crouching near her crumpled form.

Now dazed and battling excruciating pain, but awake, she could make out the smile right through the disfiguring nylon stocking, as the phone began to ring.

Hartman ignored it. "Now I'm going upstairs to get the little girl," he whispered. "We're going to take a drive and have a nice time."

Hartman rubbed her hair, never suspecting that he had spoken his last words on this earth. Still crouched beside her, he heard a noise, turned his head abruptly, and looked up.

In that instant, a look of resignation flashed in Lonnie Hartman's eyes. All this time he had virtually ignored George Payne, whose father he had murdered in cold blood, fatally assuming that George's lifetime of allegiance to the brotherhood would insure his isolation from the hated Frank Doherty.

Like Denise and Steve, Hartman was confronted in that last split second with the fact of his own demise and the knowledge that he was powerless to prevent it.

George did not hold back on the swing. The cold compacted mass of solid steel, designed to drive railroad spikes, caught Hartman flush on the nose and sent him flying into the refrigerator door, dead instantly.

Beth, still half blind and gasping for breath as a result of the mace attack, struggled to stand, as blood flowed freely from her nose.

Dropping the hammer, George rushed to keep her from falling and helped her onto the sofa in the next room.

"The kids, the kids," she mumbled. "Are they okay?"

"They're fine," said George. "They're at the top of the stairs. I'm sure they're scared but they haven't seen a thing. Can't you hear them crying? Here," he said. "Hold this on your nose while I go and talk to them." He wiped the blood from her nose gently with the kitchen towel and placed her hand over it.

"They don't know you," she said. "That was probably Frank calling. Get me the phone. He can talk to the kids and try to calm them down. He can tell Maggie who you are."

As he reached for the nearby telephone, Beth asked the obvious question. "Is he dead?"

"If he's not, then he'll have to live the rest of his life with his nose inside his skull," George answered.

She recited the number and George dialed. Frank answered on the first ring.

"Beth?"

"No, Frank. It's George. The kids are fine and Beth is banged up pretty good, but okay," George offered. "I'll tell you all about it in a minute, but first you have to talk to the kids and tell them I'm a good guy."

Maggie took the extension in Frank's bedroom and he managed to assure her that she and the twins were safe. He explained that George was a good friend and would protect them until Daddy could get home in a little while.

Maggie took the little ones into Frank's bed, where they huddled up to wait for Dad.

Before talking to Frank, George went upstairs briefly to show his face and say good night. Back in the kitchen, he picked up the receiver.

"They're fine, Frank. They're all cuddled up in your bed. How soon can you get back here?"

"Within the hour," Frank answered. "We figured out it was a setup and headed right back a few minutes ago. I called to warn them, but nobody answered. Give me the details."

"Well, the biggest detail is that Hartman is dead on your kitchen floor," George began. "We have no choice now. I'll call the cops and whatever happens, happens."

"Wait, George. I'll be there soon. Just hold up a little while. We don't even know who's involved in this with him."

"That's not quite true, Frank. I'll explain it all to you when you get back. I guess an hour or so won't make any difference to the dead prick."

"What about Beth?" Frank asked.

"She caught an indirect shot of mace and her nose might be broken, but she's alive and well."

"What was he after at the house?" Frank queried.

"The kids, I think," said George. "My guess is he wanted to hurt you before killing you, Frank. It looks like he was going to grab one of the kids and then make you come to him. He was out of his mind."

The three men were back at the house within forty minutes. Frank came through the kitchen from garage, racing towards the foyer staircase with no more than a passing glance at the pulverized corpse on his kitchen floor. Bounding up the stairs, he found all three children sleeping peacefully, legs and arms intertwined and protruding in all directions. He managed a sigh of relief and returned to face the chaos waiting on the first floor.

In the family room, Beth was still resting on the sofa, but the bleeding had stopped and the effects of the gas had pretty much worn off.

"How's the nose, Beth?" he asked.

"I'd say my nose should be the least of your concerns right now," she answered. "Anyway, looking at Hartman's makes mine feel a lot better."

In the kitchen, Frank found his two traveling companions huddled at the kitchen table with George.

"George," Frank began. "If you hadn't been here—I don't even want to think about it. How in God's name did you know to come here?"

"I was following Hartman. It looked to me like he was about to make a move. He didn't show up for work today. I got lucky, I guess; found out where his mother lives and picked him up when he left her house this afternoon. I didn't even know this was your house, but when I saw him pulling a stocking over his head, I figured it out quickly."

"What I can't figure out," asked Frank, "is why Hartman wasn't paying closer attention to you. I mean, he murdered your father. He had to be afraid you'd find out."

In contrast to the prevailing mood, George burst into laughter. "You know, Frank," he began, "even in police circles, I'm considered to be one of the biggest lawyer haters alive. He probably didn't even know Steve was my father. I didn't hide it, but it wasn't exactly common knowledge.

"Even if he did, it would never have occurred to the murdering shit that I might be helping you. He would have just assumed that you and I could never communicate, never mind form an alliance. In that case, it was his faith in the blue brotherhood that killed him.

"But that's not all, Frank," George added, all traces

of humor having vanished. "Hartman knew something about me that you don't; something my mother and father never knew either. It's the Julie Wells thing, eight years ago. I was in it with Hartman, up to my ears."

"What are you saying, George?" Frank demanded. "You were called off the case. You never even spoke to the girl."

"No, but I did speak to Hartman about it," George began. "I was so pissed off about being run off the case that I couldn't keep my mouth shut. Just like now, there were powerful interests threatened by the prospect of Sean's arrest on rape charges."

"So what happened?" Frank asked, anxious to cut to the chase.

"A few days later somebody sent Hartman to see me. He reminded me that, ultimately, we all work for the same guy. He said that by shooting my mouth off I was calling attention to the incident and pissing off some powerful people. He handed me an envelope and told me to relax, enjoy my life, and maybe buy a new car or something."

"You took it?" Beth gasped.

"I took it. He said I could just look at it as an apology. I didn't have to do anything, just stop bitching about it. I did. I knew what they were paying for. It all has to come out now and I'm okay with that"

"Not so fast, George," Frank said. "You probably saved Beth's life, not to mention what he might have done to my kids. You don't have to say anything about eight years ago. Hartman is dead."

"It won't work that way, Frank. I've known about Hartman all along. I've worked with you and given you information. I suppressed evidence in a murder case and I'm a goddamn detective. Don't you think they'll wonder why I did it? Don't you think they'll know I'm hiding something?"

"How will they find out if we don't tell them?" It was more of a suggestion than a question.

"When they get their hands on Munoz, they're going to check and find out that I was originally assigned to that call. There are no reports on the case, but they'll find out I was involved. Contrary to what lawyers might think, cops are not all fools. Besides, there's no reason to try and hide it. They're going to fire me, either way. I violated just about every departmental policy and several felony statutes. I killed this asshole with a sledgehammer, for Christ sake! Hell, my statement might help to fry Sean Lowry and a certain city commissioner who's been directing the cleanup."

"What does that mean?" Frank asked.

"It means I know who's been pulling Hartman's strings. It's Brad Parkins, the Commissioner of Aviation. That's who has the phone. I decided not to tell you and would you like to know why?"

"Yes, I would," answered Frank. "I think we all would."

"Simple. I intended to kill him right after I killed Hartman. That's the real reason I was following Hartman. If I saved some lives along the way, then I'm grateful for that, but you have to know that I meant to kill him in cold blood, just like he killed my father."

"You mean you wanted to kill him. There's a difference," Ray pointed out.

"I meant what I said. I went to his apartment the other night to do it, but he had cleared out. It looks like there were other people after him too because his apartment had gotten the once over in a very professional way. When I left there, I went to Parkins' lake shore condominium building. If I had been able to get past the security guard in the lobby, Parkins would be dead too."

When George had finished, Frank and the others, having been joined in the kitchen by Beth, sat stunned by the confession they had just witnessed.

"So what happens now if we call the police?" Frank asked rhetorically. "George gets fired and maybe worse. Julie Wells has her name and reputation dragged through the mud. Maybe they'll even have an obstruction of justice charge left over for Larry, after they fire him."

"So what the hell are you saying, Frank? Are you saying we shouldn't call the police?" George asked in disbelief.

"That's exactly what I'm saying," Frank replied.

"That's insane, Frank," George began. "Didn't you hear me? I said I murdered him. Maybe I did it to avenge my father and maybe I did it to save my own skin. How do you know? How do I know, for that matter?"

"You didn't murder anybody," said Frank, refusing to accept George's confession. "You killed him to save Beth and my kids and stop trying to deny it. I don't care what you wanted to do. You didn't murder him. I doubt that you're even capable of it; so what are you confessing to then? It's an eight-year-old bribe that nobody gives a fuck about. All it will do is drag that girl's name through the mud and cause your family a lot of unnecessary pain. How much money did you take, anyway?"

"Five grand," answered George.

"Well," Frank said. "Five grand or fifty grand, we have no choice but to play this out ourselves."

"Frank, that's just not an option. Don't misunderstand. I have no moral objection to covering up this shithead's death, but what happens to Parkins if we just get rid of Hartman's body?"

"We'll figure it out," answered Frank pensively.

"Well, you better start figuring it out," George retorted. "Does he just go free for killing my father and your wife? Once we do this, the whole thing is over. There won't be any prosecution of Brad Parkins. Just call the FBI now and turn everything over to them. They can go straight at Sean Lowry with what they have. He'll never hold up."

Beth, still holding a cloth to her nose, suddenly leaned back in her chair, eyes to the ceiling. "Oh, my God," she began. "In all the chaos, I forgot. All I could think about was the kids. Nobody will be going at Sean Lowry. He's dead. Right before Hartman crashed in here, I sat down to watch the news. It's the lead story everywhere. Sean was found dead this morning in a Puerto Villarta hotel room. The Mexican authorities are saying it was an accidental overdose."

The entire group was stunned at the news.

"It was no accident," exclaimed George, finally saying what was on everyone's mind. "It was an execution. The same people who were after Hartman killed Sean to keep his mouth shut."

"Who are we talking about here, George?" Beth asked. "I mean, it can't possibly be Lowry or any of his friends. Can it?"

"I honestly don't know. I can only imagine the fortunes that have been bet on the continuity of Lowry corruption. It could be the mob. It could even be Lowry himself. The only thing I know for sure is that they won't stop with Hartman and Sean. They'll be after you, Frank."

"I'm not worried, George. I've never been much of a tough guy, but I've got some pretty tough guys looking out for me."

"Well, that's it then," said Ray. "There's no way you could call in the cops now, not even the FBI, for that matter. All we have now is a great story and a dead cop in Frank's house. Sean might have talked, but Parkins is no fool. He'll think he's home free and he might be right. Think about it."

There was a general nodding of heads in agreement with Ray's assessment.

"The only real evidence we have is a phone call from Sean to Parkins. What does that prove? On the other hand, George just killed a man in Frank's house, the same man who we allege killed George's father and Frank's wife. Won't they think it's a little too convenient for self-defense?"

"You've got a point. Hell, even the FBI probably won't buy it," Frank suggested, continuing Ray's train of thought. "Not officially anyway. The likely result is that we'll all be left to the mercy of the city cops and prosecutor's office, the Jack Lowry cops and prosecutors. I'd say it wouldn't look good for any of us. I mean, no offense, but even George himself isn't convinced it was self-defense."

"Well, we'd better do something soon," Beth interjected. "Rigor mortis is starting to set in."

Frank rose from the table with a look of resignation. "Okay, let's get to it then. Ray, how about you take Beth over to the hospital for x-rays while we arrange a fitting memorial service for our fallen police officer? We won't leave the house until you get back."

With Beth and Ray on the way to the hospital, a discussion ensued regarding the appropriate depository for the remains of the late Lonnie Hartman. There seemed to be general agreement that making the body disappear would be both a difficult and dangerous endeavor.

Hiding a body permanently, they figured, would entail a serious risk of exposure. Whether it be by burying or sinking, there was a significant chance of being spotted in some random encounter with a passer-by.

By unspoken consensus, more gruesome methods were not even discussed. The group had no desire to deepen its level of revulsion by desecrating the corpse or preventing its discovery.

"Let's leave him just like he left my father," George suggested grimly.

"Nobody would believe that he was a robbery victim," Larry offered.

"I'm not suggesting that," responded George. "He didn't show up for work today, but we could still make it look like he was killed on a surveillance or something."

"An honorable death?" Frank exclaimed. "That's one thing I couldn't live with. You'll have to do better than that."

George walked over to the corpse, lying flat on the vinyl sheet flooring, a relatively small pool of drying blood around the head. He knelt and, using a handkerchief, reached carefully into Hartman's left overcoat pocket, removing a set of keys and a .25 cal. semi-automatic pistol. He searched the right pocket in a similar manner and walked back to the kitchen table carrying a crumpled, brown paper lunch bag.

Using the handkerchief, he carefully opened the bag and turned it upside down. A thick, banded wad of folded cash thumped onto the table, followed quickly by a transparent plastic baggie. Inside the baggie were five or six smaller plastic bags, each containing what appeared to be a small amount of white powder.

"From the small amounts, I'd say it's cocaine,

although it could be heroin," George announced, thumbing through the folded cash. "I think we have our answer."

"So was he using it or selling it?" Beth asked.

"Good question," he answered. "It could be both if his reputation was justified, but it's more likely he just kept a small amount for planting on uncooperative suspects. Let's take a look."

George and Larry walked over to the corpse, maneuvering the long, bloodstained overcoat over the arms and out from under the body. Larry pushed the right sleeve of Hartman's pullover shirt up the forearm towards the elbow. The others were all watching from the table.

"I'll be damned," said George as he saw the countless track marks up the length of the forearm. "He was a junkie."

"What about the money?" Frank asked. "How much do you think is there?"

"Seven, maybe eight thousand," George answered.

"Well, it looks like the kids at the "Y" will be getting a nice donation towards their ice rink enclosure, that is unless someone has a better idea," Frank said.

"You couldn't put it to better use as far as I'm concerned," answered George, flipping the small bundle to a faintly smiling Frank Doherty. "Larry, take his keys and pull his car into the garage. I'll keep the gun and get rid of it."

Accustomed to taking orders from superiors, Larry had the keys and was gone in a moment.

"I'm sure the gun is clean and unregistered. No doubt it's the gun he used to kill my Pop. We'll get his coat on and throw him in the trunk. The bag of drugs goes right back where we found it."

George reached for a dishtowel on the kitchen counter and offered it to Ray. "Here, wipe the hammer and throw it right in the trunk with him. I'll drive his car and you follow me in yours," he said. "We'll drop him somewhere in no man's land, where even the beat cars don't go without an escort. Between the drugs with his fingerprints and the track marks, Internal Affairs won't be looking to start a high profile investigation. They'll have to conclude he was either buying or selling and got into a beef with the wrong businessman."

It was after two in the morning when they put Lonnie Hartman to rest in the violent, drug sodden streets that he had worked so diligently to create. On the drive back to Frank's, they stopped at an all night donut shop to organize their thoughts and keep pace as best they could with this onslaught of events.

George quickly directed the conversation back to his greatest fear. "Frank, what I said back at the house about you being in danger; you have to know it's true."

"I've made no secret of the fact that I won't let this die, but what can I do? I've got three kids. I can't just pack up and go into hiding indefinitely. We all have lives here."

"Except for Hartman, these guys aren't after your kids, Frank," George said. "From now on this is a surgical operation, not a psychotic killing spree. They're after you. I'm going to take a couple of weeks vacation, Frank. Between myself and Larry, we should be able to cover you twenty-four hours a day, at least for a while."

"I'd be a fool not to accept," Frank responded. "Just as long as there's an understanding that you sleep in the guest room."

Chapter Twenty-Two

On Monday morning, a press conference was scheduled for eleven o'clock by the Office of the Mayor. Jack Lowry himself did not appear, but was represented by his Press Secretary and *de facto* political advisor, a cunning and genuinely likable boyhood crony named Martin O'Bannion.

Frank had eagerly awaited the event and tuned in early on the office television with Ray Paxon and his bodyguard *de jour*, George Payne.

All the local stations, feasting on the news of Sean's scandalous demise, interrupted the regular programming at precisely eleven to carry the news conference live.

City Hall news conferences rarely started on time and experience had taught the media to be ready with up to thirty minutes of fill-in material if programming interruption was warranted. On this occasion there was no shortage of fill-in.

While details of the investigation by Mexican police remained sketchy, Sean's infamous and colorful past provided a wealth of material with which to titillate the viewers. Although an army of workers in various city departments had struggled for years to suppress evidence of Sean's wrongdoing, his anti-social behavior was amply documented in the public record.

They reviewed details of the yacht party incident, even running clips of news coverage and mayoral interviews on the subject. There were two Florida arrests for cocaine possession that Ray hadn't even discovered in his library research. One station went so far as to carry a taped interview with an old college girlfriend who recounted Sean's insatiable appetite for drugs and rough sex.

As O'Bannion took the podium to open the conference with a prepared statement, Frank guessed that the stations could easily have done another half-hour of nefarious background material. All of this information, he reminded himself, they had accumulated in less than twenty-four hours.

The camera loved O'Bannion and the feeling was mutual. As he removed the statement from his breast pocket in an exaggerated gesture, the mobile cameras focused in a close-up of the handsome, graying mayoral aide.

"Ladies and Gentlemen," he began. "First, His Honor has asked me to thank each and every one of you for being here today on this sad and painful occasion. Many of you, in fact nearly all of you, have extended your own very personal sympathies to the Mayor and his family in this time of grief, and I assure you that I will convey each and every one of those personal messages to the family..."

"They're geniuses, George," Frank interjected, lowering the sound momentarily. "He's letting them all know that he'll be watching and reading all the coverage carefully and taking names. Crossing the line on this coverage could cost the unfortunate news anchor an exclusive interview or something down the road. Most of the reporters are too altruistic or self absorbed to give a fuck, but not all. It's amazing how skilled they are at conveying these threats subliminally."

"Let me begin," O'Bannion continued, removing his reading glasses from his front breast pocket and donning them in a well-practiced, one handed motion, "by confirming what is obvious to all of you. The Mayor and his entire family are in seclusion and will be attending to the funeral arrangements for the better part of today and tomorrow.

"The service will be private, family and close friends only, but we will provide you with all the details as soon as the arrangements have been finalized. The family thanks you all for your consideration and understanding in this time of unimaginable grief."

As the folded paper disappeared smartly back into his pocket, O'Bannion paused briefly, head lowered, silently announcing the fact that he was about to speak unscripted, from the heart.

"The Mayor understands, full well, that his son, Sean, was a young man who struggled with demons every day of his life. His indiscretions, both public and private, have been well documented. His longstanding addiction to drugs was well known to all of you. During the long course of his addiction, Sean repeatedly sought and received treatment. He was rewarded by long periods of sobriety during this struggle, but each time he eventually succumbed to the disease which has now taken his life.

"The Mayor also understands," he continued, "that, despite the contentious nature of politics in this great city, you ladies and gentlemen of the press have, for the most part, respected the privacy of his family by maintaining a distinction between their public and personal lives. He has asked me to tell you that never has that distinction been more important or necessary than it is today."

Twenty-five hands shot into air, waving frantically,

joined by a plethora of incomprehensible questions. O'Bannion smiled and settled his anxious audience with a simple gesture.

"All in good time folks. The Mayor believes in the public benefits of a free press, but he asks that you allow him and his family as much privacy as possible in their grief. He had planned on speaking to you himself this morning, but, as you can imagine, he is totally grief-stricken today. In my conversation with him this morning, he told me that nothing in life prepares us for the loss of a child. He is confident that you will allow him his space. That's all I have for you today. If you do have questions, I'll take them now."

This time at least fifty hungry reporters all raised their hands and began to speak at once.

"Okay, Jennifer," he said, pointing to the attractive young black woman, Jennifer Billings, co-anchor of the Channel Eight Evening News.

"Mr. O'Bannion, do you have any more details on the investigation by Mexican authorities? Were there witnesses? Has anyone been arrested?"

"Right now we don't know anything more than you do. We're getting our information from the same press releases you are."

As the hands went up again Frank aimed the remote and changed the channel. "Next they'll start announcing that his approval rating has skyrocketed to ninety-four percent," he said sarcastically. "Still, losing a child, even one as sick and worthless as Sean Lowry, has to be more difficult than I care to contemplate right now."

"He's got other things on his mind too," offered Ray, "like the tail wagging the dog. I wonder if he knows that Sean was murdered to insure his silence. If he knows anything about what Sean did, then he has to suspect what's going on. I imagine it's not comforting for him to accept that some group of political allies or another essentially assassinated his son for the good of the body politic, so to speak."

"I suppose you're right," Frank conceded. "But what's worse than that is not knowing exactly which one of his groups of loyal supporters killed his son. It could have been the mob. It could have been his clique of rich real estate developers or the big money bankers. It might even have been the cops, watching out for their little piece of the pie."

"There's really no way he will ever know for sure," Ray added. "I mean, whoever had his son killed is not going to walk up and apologize. They're going to keep on working for his reelection, raising money, burying bodies or whatever it was they did before. It'll drive him crazy not knowing. I think a part of him will want to believe that it really was an accidental overdose, but he knows better."

"The real irony here is that he'll come out of this more popular and powerful than ever," Frank suggested, shaking his head.

"Popular, yes," George commented. "But powerful? Maybe not."

The group's attention returned to the television when one of them noticed Alderman Ralph Nichols involved in a small, round table-type, post-news conference analysis on the local public television affiliate.

Nichols, a highly respected and intellectual former alderman from an upscale African-American ward, was, pure and simple, a sworn enemy of all things Lowry. His railings against corruption had been a legendary thorn in the side of Jack's' father for years. It was Jack who had finally managed to wrest the aldermanic seat from the popular black leader some six years earlier. The successful power play had done nothing, however, to silence the crusading reformer.

"What I'm saying is that people cannot let a tragedy like this deflect them from the important issues. For example, just last week the Post reported that the Deputy Commissioner of Parks and Recreation, Reed Sampson, had accepted over thirty thousand dollars in interest free loans from a wealthy, politically connected developer named Jordan Lundquist. Mayor Lowry responded with a press conference announcing a series of new initiatives in the war on street gangs. Now, at a time when the scandals are piling up and he's running out of tricks, the Mayor has lost his son. Will anyone dare pursue these investigations further? The answer is no.

"I have experienced a lifetime of frustration at the hands of these people. Nothing surprises me anymore. They got rid of me by buying off my own people with jobs, contracts, influence and money. For the most part, the black leaders in this city are bought and paid for Lowry lackeys. You don't hear the voice of black opposition any more. It's gone silent."

Frank switched off the television and turned to his companions. "There's work to do. We need to call Julie Wells and Ms. Booker, and then there's the question of what to do about our friend, Brad Parkins."

"He can't possibly know about Hartman yet, even if they found the body," offered George. "Why don't I take a ride over to his place tonight about dinner time and rattle his cage a little? You never know."

"There's one thing for sure," Ray said. "Once he finds out Hartman's dead, he'll shut down tighter than a clam."

"Good idea," Frank added, nodding his head in agreement. "Let him know he's not anonymous anymore. It can't hurt us to turn the table on him a little bit. Maybe you can shake him up and he'll make a mistake."

The discovery of Hartman's body early Tuesday morning set off a frenzy of closed-door meetings and conference calls at downtown police headquarters. The news media had gotten wind of the story from one of their own police sources and had been clamoring for information all day Tuesday. Finally, near the end of the business day, the Office of the Police Commissioner issued a one-page press release regarding Hartman's death:

> *At approximately seven o'clock Tuesday morning, the body of Lonnie Hartman, a detective on active duty in the service of this department, was found in the trunk of his personal vehicle at 3816 W. Masters, a vacant lot. Uniformed officers assigned to investigate an anonymous tip discovered the body. The preliminary cause of death is homicide by blunt force trauma to the head and face. The officer was not on duty at the time of death and the investigation continues.*

The violent death of a police officer was, regrettably, all too common in a city of a million plus people.

In the course of such tragic investigations, however, press releases often came hourly and on-camera interviews with ranking police officials were routine. All releases of information were transmitted with a sense of urgency and frenzied indignation.

Such was not the case with the death investigation of victim Lonnie Hartman, and that fact was recognized by the media as an unspoken indication of possible police misconduct, although no mention had been made of the narcotics found in Hartman's pocket.

The story headlined the six o'clock news, but was predictably open-ended and lacked the sensational impact of a *fallen hero* story. One of the stations even wrapped the brief coverage of the story by inviting speculation: *"When asked whether the detective's own off duty conduct is under investigation, police sources declined comment."*

Frank and Ray were working late at the office, having been joined by Larry Califf just before the dinner hour. To the chagrin of Frank Doherty, the three had dined on cheese pizza, delivered from a small place down the street. They were sitting around the half-dark office finishing the pizza when the phone rang.

"Law offices, Frank Doherty speaking."

"Frank, it's George. Brad Parkins wasn't home, but that's not the interesting part. I made some calls and found out he's on vacation. He left yesterday on short notice. It looks like he's out of the country for at least two weeks."

"Hold on, George. I'm going to put you on the speaker.

"It's George," he said to the two men in his office. "Parkins is out of the country on vacation. What the hell does that mean?" Frank asked, thinking out loud.

"It's hard to say," answered Larry. "Maybe he was involved in the hit on Sean Lowry and he's gone for good."

"He's too ambitious and he's not that stupid," Ray

piped in. "It's more likely he just lost control of the situation and wanted to be out of town when it played out."

"Whatever the case," came George's voice through the speaker, "that slippery fuck will have a plausible story for Jack Lowry when he gets back."

"Thanks, George, good work," said Frank. "Go home and get a good night's sleep."

"Okay, goodnight guys. I'll be over at your house by nine in the morning. Where are you going tomorrow?"

"Just the office. I've got some good detective novels here for you."

Beth started her new job on Monday. The first week was devoted entirely to training and orientation and the station's newest apprentice journalist was expected to report at precisely seven every morning. Her new responsibilities meant that the job of getting the kids off to school once again rested with Frank.

He hadn't realized how much he had come to depend on Beth. The kids were becoming attached to her in a way that he thought might be unhealthy. Her sudden absence now seemed to annoy them in a way that made them more difficult than ever.

On Wednesday morning, nobody wanted to cooperate. Even Maggie seemed insolent, almost depressed. Despite moments of chaos and lost patience, Frank managed to push all three of them out the door, backpacks and lunches included, at exactly seven fifteen. Standing in the doorway, he could see the old bus driver, Mrs. May, sitting at the wheel waving for the kids to run. Frank waved back, knowing that the old girl would have left the bus and rang the bell before leaving them behind. He watched as the three little bodies disappeared into their seats and the bus pulled away.

Temporarily distracted and captive to the old routine, Frank stepped from the doorway and strolled down the walk and along the driveway to where his *Daily Post* lay half-buried in a corner bush. He was still bent over retrieving the newspaper, not five feet from the street, when a plain white minivan screeched to a halt beside him.

As the cargo door flew open, two powerful hands seized him from behind and literally threw him into the van. He had no time to fight or even scream

Frank lay face down on the floor, a large foot pressing mercilessly between his shoulder blades. Although he had never subscribed to a defeatist point of view, Frank sensed that the end was near. He had pushed these people, whoever they were, to their limits and now they were pushing back, ruthlessly, as he knew they would.

Oddly, he felt almost grateful that these men had scrupulously avoided harming the children, even waiting until the kids had left for school before carrying out their little assassination. He thought of what would happen to the children. He should have made arrangements months ago. They loved Beth, but she was only twenty-two. Besides, Larry and Beth probably weren't even considering marriage.

Why wasn't I more careful? With Hartman and Sean already dead, an attempt on his life had been inevitable, Frank thought.

Even as Frank struggled to accept his fate, however, a cold rage began to build within. He could never surrender to these murdering bastards. He would choose his moment carefully and fight for life, fight as he had never fought, with all the effort he could bring to bear. The kids deserved a real father and not "Eddie the Whale." The thought of Brad Parkins outliving him would increase his strength tenfold. All these things rushed his mind as two of his captors, unmasked, raised him from the floor and placed him on the bench seat between them.

Both men were big, but the one on his left bigger. He looked older too, Frank thought, maybe forty-five. The short brown leather jacket over a black turtleneck sweater made him look tougher than he probably was. The younger one, Frank guessed, was the muscle, probably the one who would pull the trigger.

"You have an appointment," said the bigger of the two matter-of-factly, without so much as turning his head. "We'll be there in about twenty minutes."

"And let me guess," said Frank sarcastically. "You're from my dentist's office. I missed my appointment and he's upset. Well, I've had a lot on my mind lately, so if he could just bill me there won't be a problem." Neither of the men responded to Frank's overture.

The minivan, traveling at or just below the speed limit, winded its way to the nearest entrance ramp and headed east on the expressway, in the direction of downtown and the lake.

Having refused to accept his fate meekly, Frank pushed aside all thoughts of the kids and focused only on the moment, determined to have a plan of action in place when the moment arrived. He was confused by both the daylight abduction and this morning trip in the very direction of traffic and human congestion, all the things a good killer should avoid.

Why was he not dead already? Struggle or not, these

two goons could easily have wrapped his head in a plastic bag five times over by now. What was happening? Did they need information from him first? That was it, he thought. They needed to know something, but what? It had to be Brad Parkins. They needed to know if he had found out about Parkins and, more importantly, if there was evidence linking him to any of these deaths. That had to be it, Frank concluded. They had to know what he knew.

His mind raced over the details of the whole sordid and tragic affair. What was the evidence? Who was implicated by it? What false evidence could he concoct that would prolong his life?

The process consumed him to the exclusion of everything else until he felt the van slow and turn. He suddenly realized that they were no longer on the expressway, but were in the downtown area and headed directly for the waterfront. Nobody would dump a body in the water, right downtown at eight o'clock on a weekday morning, he thought.

The van headed south along the shore and in moments it became clear to Frank that they were headed for Veteran's Park, directly adjacent to the massive and incredibly expensive Waterfront Reclamation Project, now in full swing. For whatever reason, he was not going to die.

Chapter Twenty-three

Paul DeBenedetto sat peacefully on the forwardmost park bench, closest to the water, and imagined himself the captain of a great seagoing vessel. He had always loved the water, much as other men love flight but, sadly, never learn to fly.

The early spring sun hovered unobstructed over the glistening blue water, its rays penetrating the cold morning wind to warm his face. It was a place that Paul had sat often, not only to watch the progress on the largest and most lucrative construction contract of his life, but also to reflect and reenergize in the glow of nature's gem.

In contrast to most men, Paul thought that education had robbed him of his chance to live out his passions as a young man. A Michigan educated lawyer, he had never practiced law a day in his life, other than a brief stint as Assistant Corporation Counsel. The seven years of academic agony, he had endured largely to please his immigrant parents.

Growing up during the war, he had loved reading about far off exotic places like the Solomon Islands and Borneo. He had dreamed since early childhood of a life at sea and his vicarious adventures in World War II only fueled the dream. When he had finished high school several years after the war ended, he nearly mustered the courage to apply for a seaman's card and seek his adventure firsthand. His parents had other ideas, however, and constantly reminded the conscientious young man of their self-sacrifice in the name of his college education, placing squarely on his shoulders the burden of their own unfulfilled dreams.

In all likelihood, he thought, the path would eventually have been the same for him, education or not. He had always been a personal magnet to both men and women; confident but not imposing or offensive, and blessed with a disarmingly self-effacing sense of humor. He had made friends easily and in large numbers from the time he could talk.

The force and ease of his personality could bridge cultures and political differences almost effortlessly. Paul DeBenedetto was, above all else, a fixer, and not in the least ashamed. In his life, he had earned the respect and trust of countless friends and business associates and the undying devotion of his family. On balance, he was a happy man.

At the entrance to Veteran's Park, the white minivan came to a stop. The younger of the captors opened the side cargo door and stepped out. The older man did the talking.

"Mr. DeBenedetto would like to speak with you. He's sitting straight out there towards the water," said the man, pointing.

There were cyclists and rollerbladers everywhere. An old couple was strolling along the blacktop path, not fifteen feet from the minivan.

He was free, well alive anyway. He knew the name Paul DeBenedetto well. Like everyone, he knew that DeBenedetto had been a powerful but shadowy figure around City Hall for more than a generation. He was said to be a trusted advisor and confidant of some of the most influential politicians and notorious gangsters since the mid 1950's.

As a confused but relieved Frank Doherty approached from behind, Paul sat lost in thought, Frank judged, soaking in the warming sunlight with his bare head back and eyes closed.

Frank, not looking to startle the old man, announced his presence when still a good distance away. "Mr. DeBenedetto?" he called loudly.

The old man, obviously expecting him, nevertheless appeared momentarily annoyed that his meditation had been interrupted. "Mr. Doherty, I presume," answered Paul, turning with an extended hand, but making no attempt to rise from the bench.

Frank did not take his hand.

"I trust that my two young assistants were polite in extending this invitation."

"Your trust is misplaced, Mr. DeBenedetto. I would describe it more as a kidnapping than an invitation."

"I sincerely apologize for that. It was not my instruction. They don't really work for me. You might say there're kind of on loan. Please, sit down. I'd very much like to talk to you. You're free to go, of course, but if you stay you may get some of the answers you've been seeking."

Frank moved around to the front of the bench and sat.

"I do hate to be rude," Paul continued. "I would have sought this meeting in a more conventional way, had that been possible, but what I'm about to tell you is for your ears only, as they say. Giving you time to prepare could have been very risky for me and others in a criminal liability sense."

"You mean like wearing a wire?" Frank asked.

"Actually, technology has allowed the government to become much more creative than that. I'm told that now they can even use satellites and mobile equipment without the need for body microphones, but then you probably know more about that than I."

"No, I don't. They generally don't expend those resources on gangbangers and street level dealers. That's more my area."

"Mr. Doherty, I don't wish to sound self-effusive, but do you know who I am?"

"I know that you have connections and influence, probably a good deal of power as well. Does that answer you question?"

"Yes, and I'd say it's accurate. I like to think I have the ability to bring people together, and not just for sinister purposes. I've even prevented violence a time or two."

"How's that?" Frank asked, not hiding his skepticism.

The old man seemed to ignore the question. "I walk in two worlds, Mr. Doherty, equally corrupt and, I believe, equally necessary. I don't expect that you and I have the same perspective on morality, but I assure you that I do prescribe to a code of conduct and my limits are generally acknowledged and accepted among my friends."

"Well, thank God for that," Frank retorted.

"Respect is what gives me access, Mr. Doherty. Don't misunderstand. I have no burning need to earn your respect. I could care less what you think. I tell you these things so that you can leave here knowing that you have the truth; maybe not the whole truth, but enough to give you some peace. Would you like to hear some truth, Mr.

Doherty?"

"Yes, I'd like to hear some truth for once."

"Very well then. Sean Lowry murdered your niece in one of his well-documented sexual frenzies. I think he strangled her to death. After he killed her, he called his father's cover-up expert, Brad Parkins. I suspect that your wife could have identified Sean. The newspapers said that the girl had been with her aunt that night. There was a cop who was doing the dirty work. He killed your wife and then he killed the investigator, but then you already know all about that."

"What makes you think I know so much?" Frank asked.

"Come now, Mr. Doherty. You killed him. You, or one of your little posse, did. Believe me, I'm not a fool. I wouldn't be talking to you like this if I thought you still had the option of bringing the Feds in. I took precautions, just in case, but too many of your friends would be hurt now if it all came out. No, I think what you want, Mr. Doherty, is to know that some justice has been done."

"Well, Mr. De, you may not be a fool, but it wouldn't take a genius to figure that out."

"I also know that you won't quit until you either get it or die trying, and when you'd finally threatened the fortunes of enough highly placed people, you would die, Mr. Doherty, believe me. See, I don't want you to die. There's no reason for your kids to grow up without a parent. It's over."

"You're probably right about me never going to the authorities, but you and I both know that in end it wouldn't have changed a thing. Federal investigations of the Lowrys serve only to increase the government payroll. Someday I may find another way to fight back, one that works. In the meantime, I'll find a way to make Parkins pay, something short of killing him. You see, Mr. DeBenedetto, it's not over while Brad Parkins is alive and free, and you can take the veil off your threats if you like. It won't stop me from seeing this through."

"That's just why I'm here, Frank. You've probably already learned that Parkins is in the Bahamas on vacation. The fact is he's not coming back. In a few weeks you'll hear and read a blizzard of media reports that he absconded with a large chunk of Department of Aviation cash, liquidated as many of his own assets as he could and transferred it all to Bahamian accounts. You'll read a lot of speculation about his shady dealing, but none of it will involve your wife or niece."

"Am I here to get the truth or just fortune telling?" Frank asked sarcastically.

"You want some truth, Frank? The truth is that Parkins never made it to the Bahamas. Some ugly fuck who looked like him made it there on his passport, but it wasn't Parkins. I can assure you of that because Parkins is dead and I'm told he died a very slow and painful death."

"With Hartman and Sean both dead, why would anyone need to kill Parkins?" Frank asked. "There'd be no reason to kill him, that is, unless it was Jack Lowry himself behind this and he was trying to clean the slate. My God, even Jack Lowry wouldn't kill his own son to save his ass, would he?"

"Would he? I don't know," the old man shot back. "But he didn't. Brad Parkins died because of who he was and the way he treated people. It had nothing to do with your wife and niece."

"I sincerely doubt that Parkins was murdered over a point of honor, if he's dead at all. You're the one who said I wouldn't get the whole truth. Remember? If your friends killed him, they did it to save their own asses."

"And how do you figure all that?" the old man asked, impressed with Frank's intuitive ability.

"Even if Lowry didn't orchestrate all this, there was too great a chance that he knew about Parkins' involvement with you, whether Lowry had figured it out himself or learned it from Sean. Whatever forces were involved weren't prepared to have Lowry link the killing of his son to them through you."

"Go on, please," Paul invited.

"There was no way to predict how Lowry would have reacted. He could have declared a *Holy Jihad* and taken all of you down along with him. With Parkins dead, however, Lowry would never know for sure who killed his son and the insecurity would keep him on his toes and under control. Hell, how do I really know he's even dead?" Frank asked.

"Well, I had hoped you'd believe me, but I'm not naïve," the old man answered, seemingly prepared for the question. "I've arranged for you to receive proof, in sufficient quantity to satisfy you. Oh, the authorities will look for him for years and never find him, but I know that's not good enough for you. I ask only that you be patient for a little while longer."

"What are you going to do?" Frank asked. "Send me his ear?"

What tension was left dissipated in the old man's sudden and genuine burst of laughter. "Nothing so gruesome, I assure you. Just be patient, Frank, please. "Brad Parkins was a Hedonistic piece of shit," the old man pronounced, now beginning to slip into his closely held unguarded mode. He smiled, leaned his head back toward the sun and allowed himself to drift.

A part of him had secretly rooted for Doherty since the beginning of this mess. It had taken all of Paul's reserve to conceal his loathing of Brad Parkins. The man had taken him for an idiot. Did he really think Paul was stupid enough to take him at his word?

Paul had suspected from the beginning that Parkins wasn't talking to the Mayor about this. Jack may have known all the details from the beginning, but that wasn't the point. The point was that Parkins had the balls to lie to his face about acting at the direction of the Mayor. That wouldn't have been Jack Lowry's style and Paul knew it.

It hadn't been easy for Paul to suppress his outrage when Parkins tried to rationalize his lie by implying that deceiving Paul DeBenedetto was a part of his job. But Brad's use of the mob's fifty grand to finance his contract murder of Frank's wife was the last straw.

In the end, Parkins had simply been too self-absorbed to appreciate the seriousness of embezzling from the mob, Paul thought.

He had alerted his associates to his suspicions right after giving Brad the fifty, but they had all agreed that fifty grand would be a wise investment in political harmony, just in case Parkins was telling it straight.

It was ironic, the old man thought. If Brad had just come to him in the beginning, there would have been no need for killing. All this trouble could have been avoided by people with the right experience. A bad choice had killed Brad Parkins and relying on that lunatic detective was a mistake that had sealed his fate.

Morons like that, Paul considered, never used to live long enough to do any real damage. There was something to be said for the old ways, but better late than never.

"Then your friends killed Sean Lowry?" Frank asked matter-of-factly.

"Sean Lowry has been killing himself for years," Paul said, still relaxed and motionless. "Let's just say his bad habits finally caught up with him and leave it at that."

"How do I know you and your friends weren't involved in my wife's murder, or in Steve's for that matter?"

The old man raised his head and turned toward the lawyer. "Because, Mr. Doherty, you are alive. You are a very troublesome person to many of my associates, but you are alive. Whether you believe it or not, I would never be a part of killing off an innocent family, leaving kids orphans."

"And what exactly is it we're dealing with here? A more loving and caring mob?"

"I see that you are a man who likes to push limits," Paul observed, with no trace of amusement. "My friends rarely kill people these days and they never do it for sport. Certainly there are compelling interests that would be better served by your death, but as you say, where do the investigations of the Lowrys ever go?"

"Mobsters, as people like to call them, are real people these days," he continued, seeming to find his rhythm again. "Some of them might even earn your respect, given a chance. For the most part, they go to extremes to avoid hurting innocent people. They belong to country clubs and yacht clubs. They own thriving, legitimate businesses. They run unions. Some of them are even practicing lawyers. Most of them wouldn't recognize the old *Cosa Nostra* if it bit them in the ass. Let's walk a while, Frank."

They moved onto the narrow path and began to walk slowly. It was clear to Frank that the old man liked this place and he could see why. The sound of the waves and the offerings of countless songbirds were a treasured contrast to the crowded, noisy streets nearby.

"Those are the people who really run things, Frank. What they want is simply to maintain a prosperous and stable business climate with access and influence at the local level. They want to serve the general welfare and line their own pockets at the same time."

Frank laughed, although he didn't know why. The morning wind chilled his hands and he buried them deep in his pants pockets. "How noble," he observed.

"They want to be left alone, Frank. Jack Lowry gives them all those things, but don't kid yourself. He's nothing but a stooge caretaker. He keeps the *muulenjohns* herded up in the ghetto and out of their hair with a few jobs and city contracts. He keeps the labor peace and hauls the trash. He's so dumb that he probably doesn't even see the truth, but they could make him see it any time they want. They keep him in office."

"So much for generalities," Frank quipped. "What about specifics?"

"As for your wife, Frank, even the most violent mobsters of the past didn't kill innocent women and children. They had no reason to kill your wife. If Parkins had been straight with me from the beginning, your wife would still be alive and, unfortunately, so would Parkins. I'm not a monster and, for the most part, neither are the people I deal with."

They reached an old wooden pavilion, the kind you might expect to see in an old beach movie. Although it was early, a young man was behind the counter, preparing the concession stand for a busy day ahead.

"Come on," Frank beckoned. I'll buy you a cup of

coffee for not killing me."

The old man chuckled.

On the walk back, they found another bench, indistinguishable from the last. The steaming coffee made Frank feel as though he would actually have chosen to be there.

"I live on the South Side, Frank, not two blocks from where I was born. When I was a little kid, just before WWII, my father was a precinct captain. He had been a bookkeeper in the old country and came here with my mother at the age of eighteen. Within six months, he had learned to read and write English and had established a little business doing the books for nearly all the Italian merchants in the neighborhood. There were no Lowrys back then, but there was a political organization. It was more personal then, before television and CBN, but it was our lifeline."

"I can't even remember a time before Lowrys," Frank said.

"In the evenings, my father would go door-to-door throughout the precinct selling tickets for this or that fundraiser or getting out the vote. For Italians in those days, if you wanted a decent job; hell, even if you wanted your garbage picked up, you had to work and be noticed by the local alderman. Ours was one of the most powerful ever. His name was Paddy Crowley. He was like a fucking king in the ward. It was about half-Italian and half-Irish. I used to go with my father on those walks sometimes, when he did his precinct work. He knew everyone in the ward and they all liked him. 'I ring-a-da-bell-for-Paddy C,' he would say. Then he would do his little business and be on his way."

"What did he do, your father, for a living I mean?"

"At first he worked in a factory like everyone else.

Then, one day, during the war, when I was in seventh or eighth grade, they gave him a job in the City Health Department as a food inspector. His job was to inspect restaurants and hotels for health code violations. It was a job coveted by nearly everyone in the neighborhood. He made barely enough to pay the bills, but the perks were royal. We ate like kings and were the only family in the neighborhood renting space in the butcher's cooler. During the holidays he would give finest cuts of meat and steaks to the neighbors as Christmas."

"Did you know where it came from?" Frank asked.

"Sure, it was all graft, of course, but nobody saw it like that in those days. Everyone knew that was the way things worked and my father had earned that position by playing within their rules. In his mind, he had never abused the privilege. He shared everything. We could have eaten free every night at any restaurant in town, but we only went out three or four times a year."

"I get the feeling he didn't live happily ever after."

"You might say that. In 1963 or 1964, during the infancy of investigative journalism, one of the papers started running an expose on corruption in the Inspection Service of the Health Department. Allegations of payoffs were made against my father and six other inspectors. It was front-page stuff. I don't think Pop was even worried about it, but I knew that the world was changing. City Hall dropped him like a rock; fired him eighteen months short of a pension. Six weeks later, Pop was indicted by a Federal grand jury."

"Did he go to jail?"

"No, but he died less than two years later. The shame killed him."

"I can see how that incident went a long way to

shape your career path," Frank consoled.

"I never thought of it that way," Paul smiled. "I was a young lawyer at the time, working for the city. After that I saw politics for what it was; what it still is, a mindless grab for power. I decided to twist it to serve my own interests. It wasn't a difficult thing to do, really. See, I had strong connections to another world as well. I grew up in the neighborhood, like a brother to some of the most infamous people you've ever heard of. Most of them are dead now, but I still enjoy a certain status."

"Why are you telling me all this?" Frank asked.

"I'm not sure," Paul answered. "Maybe I just wanted you to understand that I wouldn't have murdered your wife."

"Maybe what really bothers you is that you're asking yourself that same question and you don't know the answer, not for sure." Frank pressed him. "The stakes here were probably higher than I could imagine."

"You're a very bright guy, Frank," Paul said, as he laughed in obvious amusement. "That's the real question, isn't it? Am I bad or good? Who the hell knows? Well, what about you, Frank? Who killed Hartman? Was he holding those drugs or were they planted on him? Don't tell me because I don't want to know, but you caught me off guard with that one. So we're really not that different, you and I. Who the fuck cares anyway? The one thing we can agree on is that Sean and Parkins were a couple of no good fucks."

"Yes, they were," said Frank, seeing no point in denying complicity in the killing of Hartman. He noticed that they were back where they had started. They sat on the same bench.

"Look out there, Frank," the old man said. "What do you see?"

"I see water with a bunch of huge barges and heavy equipment on it."

"Look harder. There are already thousands of tons of concrete under the water. Try to imagine the place in five years. You will never see a more beautiful place in your life. There will be over three hundred varieties of trees and plant life. Over there," said Paul, pointing, "will be a man-made wetland, virtually indistinguishable from one found in nature. It will become home to countless species of rare birds and small animals."

"You really like this place, don't you?" Frank asked.

"Guilty. I often come here to watch the sunrise and I can see it all so clearly in my mind. I view it as my legacy, Frank. True, I played only a small part in it, but nevertheless, it's the purest form of beauty I can imagine and it will bring so much joy to so many when it's finished.

"I'm an old man, Frank," he continued, "and old men think about death. When I imagine this place in my mind I think what a wonderful and joyous burial place it would make, with this beautiful, living park as a gravestone. Can you imagine a better way to rest in peace?"

"I guess it's something I don't enjoy thinking about, not yet anyway," Frank answered.

"Maybe you should think about it, Frank," said Paul reflectively. "Tell me, the girl's mother is alive, isn't she?"

"You mean my niece, Caroline's mother? Yes, she's out West. Why?"

Paul leaned over and took Frank's right arm. Raising it, he gently pried open the fingers. Holding Frank's open palm, he removed something from his overcoat pocket, placed it in Frank's extended hand, and wrapped the fingers back into a fist around it. "Give it to her and bring her here someday when this park is finished," whispered the old man. "She needs to know. It's a sad thing that such a beautiful young life should be snuffed out for no reason by a fuck like Sean Lowry."

Frank opened his hand, held up the simple gold medallion by the chain, and read the inscription: *The best way to have a friend is to be a friend.* He turned his gaze towards the blue horizon, in the direction of the soon-to-be waterfront nature preserve. His eyes lingered on the water and in his mind he could see the park, just as the old man had described it.

Clutching the medallion, he turned back towards Paul and spoke, nearly in a whisper. "I have to know. Parkins, is he—" Frank hesitated, not wanting to say the words.

"No, Frank. Parkins isn't out there. He didn't deserve it."

Chapter Twenty-Four

Two Months Later

The Farmington Zoo was a crowded and cheerful place on the first day of summer vacation. The trip had been eagerly anticipated by Alex and the three Doherty kids for weeks. Laura had uncharacteristically phoned in sick early that Friday morning, without so much as a trace of apprehension.

The newly promoted Assistant to the Director of Security, Louise Booker, and her grandson, Calvin, accompanied the group on that fine late spring morning. Louise's promotion had not altered her job description in any way, but the extra money that came with the title would come in handy. Besides, every extra dollar she earned now would mean more money in retirement.

For nearly an hour and a half, the three adults kept a quickened pace at the rear, as the youngsters ran from exhibit to exhibit, determined to expend nine months of pent up energy in a single day.

Finally, the exhausted trio was relieved to arrive at the fully enclosed children's petting zoo, where they staked out an inviting bench with a cold drink.

"This damn sciatic nerve problem will be the death of me," Frank whined, easing himself painfully onto the bench.

"Why is it that your back never bothers you when

it's time to play hockey?" Laura asked playfully.

"Frank, I've never really had a chance to say a proper 'thank you' for all you've done, I mean for Calvin and me," said Louise.

"I had nothing to do with it, Louise," he responded. "I just sent you to a good lawyer. That's all. The truth is, if Julie hadn't come forward with her story, it would never have happened. Munoz would still be there, looking forward to retirement."

"Come to think of it, Frank, you've never really said how Ray managed to get Munoz fired and Louise promoted at the same time," Laura pointed out, inviting an explanation.

"It would never have happened without Julie Wells," he began. "That's who you need to thank, Louise. She came forward with Ray and told her story to the university. The threat of a lawsuit like that that was more than enough motivation for them to settle, especially when they learned that Julie didn't want any money."

"Was it a bluff or did Julie have a good case?" Laura asked.

"Depends on how it would have played out. But Ray had collected enough evidence to make a good case if Julie had wanted to push it. It turned out all she wanted was to get Munoz fired without his pension and get Louise taken care of. Ray did a good job."

"But would a jury have believed Julie, I mean after eight years?" Louise inquired.

"It's not just that," Laura added. "Don't forget, she did take the money, whatever her reasons."

"Who can say?" Frank speculated. "He had your testimony, Louise, to back up Julie's story. It would have been hard for the university to call both you and Julie liars.

"Besides, there was physical evidence too. George still had a copy of the original log-in notation he had received from the detective who answered Munoz's original call to the police. Ray volunteered a copy to the university lawyer. When the university checked their own records, of course, they found no trace that the complaint had ever been made. That, in itself, was sufficient evidence of Munoz's complicity. A trial would have been a crapshoot, but the University would have lost either way. So they just hung Munoz out to dry and gave Julie a quiet apology within a week. It was Ray's idea to throw in Louise's promotion as a condition of settlement."

"What about Munoz?" Laura asked. "What if he files a grievance or something to get his job back?"

"You're kidding, right?" Frank asked with a sarcastic smile. "He's ready to live with it. He won't take any chance on stirring up a murder indictment. No, he'll most likely just go off and drown his sorrows in a bottle. What a shame."

"Do you actually think he was involved in killing Mr. Panos?" Louise asked.

"No," Frank answered. "I'm sure he wasn't. He didn't know anything about Caroline or Denise at that point. He just thought he was helping Hartman to throw Steve off their trail on the Julie Wells thing. He had no reason to think Hartman would kill Steve over an eight-year-old bribe. That's not to say he's incapable of murder though. Munoz knew damn well what he was setting me up for at the construction site."

The rest of the outing was more to the liking of the three tired adults. After a picnic lunch, the group lined up for the one-thirty aquatic show, featuring "Eloise" the dolphin and her two newborns. The three-month-old dolphin pups had made their public debut only the week before.

The group thoroughly enjoyed the antics of the entertaining mammals and, by three-thirty, the entire entourage, reenergized and hungry again, piled into the minivan for the trip home. By a roll call vote of five to three, it was decided that the trip home would be postponed in favor of a visit to the kids' favorite pizzeria, followed by a trip to the local ice cream shop.

As Frank headed the loaded minivan back towards the neighborhood, he powered up the radio to catch a few minutes of the all news station. Within a few moments, he could tell that the regular format had been abandoned and there was an impromptu discussion in progress regarding some major news development.

"And so what will it mean in terms of the day to day operation of the city, Alderman Bates?" The announcer was asking of his telephone guest.

"Well," the alderman paused momentarily, "immediately, I suppose very little."

Frank raised the volume and leaned quickly towards his little passengers in the back. "Kids," he said, holding his index finger to his lips. "Quiet for just a minute. I need to hear this."

The announcer continued. "For those of you just tuning in, we are joined from City Hall by Alderman Harold Bates, one of Mayor Lowry's staunchest allies, to discuss the Mayor's resignation from office, which he tendered personally to the City Clerk less than thirty minutes ago. The news was transmitted in a press release from the Mayor's office, perhaps fifteen minutes ago. We are told that the Mayor will schedule a news conference for tomorrow morning, but that his resignation is final and will take effect on the first of next month.

"The sudden and unexpected resignation of the nation's most powerful and popular chief executive will leave Alderman Bates, President of the City Council, to serve out the remaining fifteen months of the mayoral term."

The three adults had all heard the announcement and sat stunned and speechless. Frank spoke first. "Kids, I'm sorry, but we'll have to go for pizza later. Some important business has come up. We'll go out when I get back. I promise."

The kids, being kids, promptly launched into a chorus of boos, jeers and various other expressions of displeasure.

Turning to Laura, he asked, "Can we leave the kids with Maggie for a while and go over to the office? I'm sure Ray and Larry will be there."

"It's okay with me," answered Laura.

"Frank," Louise interjected. "Since my car is at your house anyway, I could take all the kids for pizza. In fact, I would really enjoy it."

"I don't know," answered Frank. "They're not easy."

"Well," said Louise, "I'm not bragging, mind you, but I have run this course twice before. It's not like I'm naïve. Besides, Maggie will help me. Won't you, dear?"

"Of course I will, Mrs. Booker," Maggie offered. "Sitting on buttheads is my specialty."

On the drive back to the house, Frank reflected on the possible consequences of Lowry's resignation. The irony of the whole thing, he thought, was that in their ruthless zeal to maintain the status quo, this invisible group of powerful conspirators actually destroyed it.

The Lowry dynasty was over. Frank wanted to

declare victory to himself, but something in him knew better. They may have misjudged Lowry, but in the end it probably wouldn't hurt them if they moved quickly to fill his shoes with the right guy.

After all, Lowry was going out at the height of his popularity and that didn't bode well for a reform candidate, if there really is such a thing. Somebody would get Lowry's backing and try to pick up the pieces of the empire before it had time to crumble. Maybe they'd succeed. *Only time will tell*, he thought.

They dropped Louise and the five kids at the house and headed downtown. It was nearing five o'clock by the time they had parked the van and reached the building. They stepped off the elevator and headed down the hallway, passing Frank's office without a glance. They stopped in front of Steve's office, where Frank looked at the recently painted lettering across the old frosted glass pane. He smiled as he considered the words.

PANOS AND CALIFF
PRIVATE DETECTIVES
POLYGRAPH EXAMINERS

"It looks pretty good," Frank said. "Don't you think?"

"I think it looks great," Laura responded. "It's the next best thing to having Steve here and I'm sure you won't mind having another buddy down the hall."

"It's not exactly the same, but I think it will work out well for everyone in the end. He starts law school in the fall, you know. I guess it's a good thing we get along so well. I have a feeling we're going to be related by marriage before too long."

"Like you say, it'll work out well for everyone, but

God help that young man if he wants to grow up and be like you."

Frank flashed her a hurt puppy-dog look. She caught his gaze, smiled coyly and, for the second time in their relationship, they burst into spontaneous laughter.

Inside they found Larry, Ray, and Diane all gathered around the TV set in Steve's office. Diane had come a long way since Steve's death, but hadn't yet managed to let go of the memorabilia cluttered mess that had been his office. Surely the time would come soon, but it would be on Diane's schedule and that was okay with Larry Califf.

They were watching a live network interview with, of all people, Jack Lowry's archenemy, old Ralph Nichols, the former alderman. The network correspondent had asked Nichols to comment on speculation that the Mayor's resignation had actually been a capitulation to the increasing number of Federal criminal investigations against members of his administration.

The clear suggestion of the questioner was that the Mayor might have exploited the tragic death of his son to bow gracefully out of the political arena, thus saving face and maintaining the viability of the party structure for a successor.

Old Nichols at once shook his head vehemently, back and forth, obviously having none of it. "Not a chance," he began. "He's just not that kind of an animal; never been a quitter. Oh, not that he didn't resort to a little trickery from time to time in the interest of good politics."

"What kind of trickery?" the host prodded.

"Well, I remember a few years ago, early summer, just about this time of year. The scandals were really piling on him; police drug dealing, that hooker making the rounds at fire department headquarters. On top of everything else, the Post ran a story that his wife's sister, for the last four years, had held a thirty-thousand-dollar ghost payroll job with Sloan Freeman, one the Mayor's developer buddies. He's the primary contractor on the airport redevelopment project.

"So what did our glorious Mayor do, when finally painted into a nice tight corner?" Nichols asked rhetorically. "He faked a heart attack and was rushed to University Hospital in an ambulance. I'm not kidding. He faked a heart attack and then just sat back in the hospital bed and watched the sympathy build. For three months, anyone who said a word against him was vilified in public. See, he's a master of tricks, but quit? Never! He'd never quit, not ever, not for any political reason anyway. No, there are other forces at work here and I wouldn't even venture a guess what they are, but it could be as simple as a broken heart."

Nichols had been doing just fine until the last sentence, when Frank cringed. "Oh, Ralph, don't tell me you're going for it too," he said.

"Come on, Frank," Ray chided. "Don't you think it's possible that the guy's just had enough and he's ready for a quiet life, maybe even a little privacy?"

"No, I don't think it's in him," Frank speculated. "He's driven by a legacy and he would never let personal grief destroy it. He's obsessed with political power and control and, in that twisted mind of his, he's on a righteous crusade. I don't doubt for a minute that the guy is motivated by a deep and abiding love of the city, but he doesn't look at the city as an entity thriving in the service of humanity. He sees it as a monument to his late father.

"He was intoxicated by the power and his life's work

was building the monument. Hell, I don't doubt that, in his own mind, he's just making political compromises for the common good, but it's all gotten out of his control now. In the end, the monster that the Lowrys created jumped up and bit Jack in the ass and he just couldn't deal with the reality that he wasn't really in charge."

"He's probably been going half nuts," Diane suggested, "trying to figure out who betrayed him."

"There are rumors," Larry added, "that he's turned against most of his oldest and closest friends and allies. You can almost sympathize with the guy. Imagine going into an important meeting on any given day and wondering whether the guy who's smiling at you and shaking your hand conspired to murder your son."

"All that may be true," Frank concluded. "But he's not leaving out of grief. He's leaving because he's finished and he needs to preserve whatever he can of the legacy. Grief hasn't dulled his sense of political timing in the least. Is he using his son's death for politics? You bet."

"Frank, It's over," Ray exclaimed. "Can't you see? We brought him down. You brought him down, Frank."

"You're off base, Ray," Frank answered. "It was never about bringing him down and it's not over. We had no control over any of it. All we did was survive. We were just actors in someone else's play, for Christ sake. Look at the news coverage, Ray. He walked off the stage like the fucking Duke of Windsor, renouncing the throne for the love of his life."

Frank walked to the small refrigerator and removed a beer can, popping the top. "Besides, do we even know that people would be better off without the likes of the Lowrys? You can't possibly deny that he's accomplished some great things for this city. No, Ray, I'm not arrogant enough to jump to that conclusion."

"Well, we may not have done much," Larry interrupted, "but even you couldn't have hoped for a better outcome when this whole thing started."

Frank considered the comment silently for a moment before offering his final opinion on the subject. "I suppose you're right, but for me it was always about Denise and Caroline. I didn't learn anything about city politics that I didn't know fifteen years ago. If I had been motivated by altruism, I would have started the fight way back then."

EPILOGUE

It was nearly dark when Frank and Laura pulled into the drive. Frank didn't recognize the car parked in front of the house, but was able to make out the stubby, balding form of Ron Butler from the YMCA down the street, sitting on the front step with the twins.

As Frank stepped out of the van, Butler came bounding off the step towards him, clutching a simple cardboard shoebox to his chest.

"Frank," he yelled. "You know about this, right? Can you believe it? I mean, where did it come from?"

"Hold on, Ron," Frank answered, using his hand to keep the excited little man at bay. "What the hell are you talking about?"

"The rink, Frank, the donation. You mean you don't know?"

"Know what, Ron?"

"The box," Ron said, already removing the cardboard cover. "Look. It's enough to cover the rink and build real locker rooms too. For years, we've been trying to raise the money and somebody just walks in this afternoon and leaves this box at the front desk. I'm dreaming, right? It's a mountain of cashier's checks, Frank. They're all made out to the YMCA."

He reached into his pocket and handed Frank a folded piece of paper. "Here's the note that came in the box. Read it, Frank," he said. Frank opened the note and read:

Please accept this anonymous donation in the name of Denise Doherty. The funds are to be used for the construction of a permanent all-season enclosure for the ice rink. The donor requests that, upon completion, the rink be rededicated as The Denise Doherty Family Ice Center.

Frank looked into the box and saw what appeared to be two stacks of checks, bound with rubber bands. "Well, I'll be damned," he muttered, handing the note back to Butler. "He really did his homework."

Frank walked slowly over to the front step and sat, white as a sheet, as Laura, Butler and the twins laughed and high-fived near the car in a joyful frenzy.

"Frank, do you know how much is here?" Laura cried, finally turning her attention to the front porch.

"Let me guess," he answered. "Six hundred thousand dollars?"

"Exactly, but how did you know? Wait! That's the exact amount that Parkins stole from the city accounts. My God, Frank! It's the proof, isn't it? It's the proof that Parkins is really dead."

"It's proof, all right. You can be sure Parkins didn't make the donation, but it's much more than that, Laura. It's a gravestone. It's a magnificent, living gravestone for Denise. He likes gravestones."

"What do you mean a gravestone, Frank? Who likes gravestones?" Laura asked.

"Come on inside." He put his arm around her and called to Ron and the boys in the drive. "Good night, Ron. Drive safely and no stops on the way home."

As they walked towards the house she asked again. "What did you mean about a gravestone, Frank?"

"I'll tell you all about it in a little while, but I need to call Ellen in South Dakota first. I promise you'll understand. I just had to wait until I was sure." He stopped abruptly as they reached the front door and turned to face her. "You know, there's one thing I've been meaning to ask you."

"What's that, Frank?"

"Have you ever been to Montana?"

She only smiled.

IMMORAL AUTHORITY

Robert W. Smith was born in 1950, raised in the Chicago area and graduated from a local Catholic high school in 1968.

During a subsequent four-year enlistment in the Air Force he was assigned to Air Force Security Service, a branch of the National Security Agency. His service included three years in various Asian and European posts as a Russian Linguist. From 1972 through 1979 he worked as a Security Officer for the Chicago Transit Authority.

During this period he attended DePaul University and The John Marshall Law School at night and holds degrees from both. Since 1980 he has been engaged in the private practice of law as an independently employed criminal defense attorney. His practice is limited to the defense of violent crimes and other felonies, primarily in Cook County, Illinois.

He lives in a Chicago suburb with his wife, Patricia, his nine-year-old twin boys and twelve year old daughter. Favorite pastimes include coaching youth hockey and playing hockey in a local men's league. He writes a little bit every day.

www.bobwsmith.com
rwsmith@echelonpress.com

Other Echelon Press Titles
www.echelonpress.com

Lost and Found
Alexis Hart

Second Chance at Forever
Natalie J. Damschroder

Honor Betrayed
Lauren Kelly

Unfinished Dreams
Pamela Johnson

The New West
Cathy McDavid

Music of my Heart
Dana Elian

**Mage of the Nexus Book One
Journey to Malmillard**
K.G. McAbee

Cursed Comes Christmas
A. Hart, P. Johnson, B. Wing

To Tame a Viking
Leslie Burbank

House of Cards
Blair Wing